LIVIN' THE DREAM

A Jake Arnold Adventure

Book 2

By MJ WATSON

Shirley -
Hope you enjoy
Jake's lastest installment.
Thanks for reading.
Jan

COPYRIGHT

This book is a work of fiction. Names, characters, and incidents are a figment of the author's imagination or are used fictitiously. Any resemblance to actual persons, living or dead, is coincidental.

ISBN-10: 1545425582
ISBN-13: 978-1545425589

Front Cover Photo: Coco Beach, Playa del Carmen, Mexico
Back Cover Photo: El Castillo in Mayan Ruins, Tulum, Mexico.

DEDICATION

For My Son

LOUIE

Life will never be the same without you.

CHAPTER 1

Monday, April 17, 2000

Jake Arnold smiled as he looked out the window of the Boeing 727. There was hardly a cloud in the sky as the plane approached the eastern shore of Cancun, Mexico. Looking down at the Caribbean Sea, he watched the color variations of the water as it changed from a deep rich sapphire offshore to lighter blues and then a rich sea green before becoming an almost mint green where the water was very shallow.

He could see rock formations in the water closer to shore. They looked like they were just under the surface but he knew they were much deeper. Compared to the murky waters of the Atlantic Ocean on the coast of Florida where he lived, the beauty and clarity of the Caribbean Sea never ceased to amaze him.

"Hey, Jake," said his best friend Steve Wilson from the next seat.

"Yeah, Steve?" Jake asked, turning away from the window to look at his friend.

"Is there a reason we're staying at Las Palmas again?"

Jake turned to look out the window again. For the past two years he and four of his lifelong friends, jokingly known as the Boys Club back in their hometown of Port Salerno, had been coming to Mexico's Yucatan peninsula to fish and dive on the Mesoamerican Reef.

The first time they came in the spring and stayed in Cancun. They had a good time, but hadn't particularly liked all the construction going on, so the following fall they ventured a little farther south to Playa del Carmen. There they found Las Palmas Resort, a laid-back little establishment on the beach just north of the tourist zone but within walking distance of everything they needed.

The next year they returned to Las Palmas in both the spring and fall. This was their fourth trip to Las Palmas and Jake was excited to be back, but his excitement had little to do with fishing or diving.

"I thought you guys liked Las Palmas," Jake replied innocently, tearing his gaze away from the idyllic scene outside the window.

"We do, but this is the fourth time in a row and the guys and I were wondering if maybe there was another reason you keep choosing the same place."

"Why don't you just come out and ask what you really want to know?" Jake responded, cutting to the chase.

"Okay. Your, uh, fondness, for Las Palmas doesn't have anything to do with the stunning young woman who owns the place, does it? I only ask because the last time we were here, it seemed like you and Teresa were getting, uh, kinda friendly, if you know what I mean."

"It might," Jake replied smiling. "She's something else, isn't she?"

"Yeah, she's smart and beautiful, I'll agree with you on that, but just don't go getting serious about her. Long distance relationships rarely work out, and the two of you don't even own the same color passport," Steve warned. Steve was constantly giving Jake advice about women but Jake rarely followed it.

Jake nodded and turned back to the window, the words 'long-distance relationship' resonating in his mind. He appreciated his friend's advice, but it was a little late. If he was honest, he'd have to admit that he was already carrying on a long-distance relationship with Teresa. They talked on the phone several nights a week and had been for the past several months.

After their plane landed, they made their way through immigration, and retrieved their luggage. After passing through customs, Jake, Steve, and the twins, Petey and Paul Franklin, navigated their way through the gauntlet of timeshare and vacation club salespeople who were soliciting their deals to everyone who passed.

Once outside, Jake looked for a taxi to take them south to Playa del Carmen. Without Hank Smith, the fifth member of the Boys Club who was unable to join them this trip, Jake thought they could forego the expense of a van. He waved to a taxi driver standing outside his car, pointed to his three friends, and when he got the affirmative nod, headed toward the small white taxi.

"Las Palmas, por favor," Jake said to the taxi driver after their luggage was more crammed than stowed in the trunk.

"Playa del Carmen, si?" the driver asked, showing a few gold caps in his smile.

"Si," Jake replied, as he slid into the front passenger seat.

As they left Cancun International Airport and headed south, Jake turned to look over his shoulder at his three friends who, with shoulders touching, had successfully squeezed themselves into the back seat.

"Teresa said we should go to the cantina for lunch and she'd meet us there."

"That sounds good to me, I'm ready for a beer," Petey said.

"You just drank three between Miami and Cancun, and it's not even noon," his brother Paul said.

"You know I hate flying. I drank a few before we ever left the hotel this morning. It's the only way I can get up the nerve to get on a plane."

Petey and Paul weren't identical twins, but most people couldn't tell them apart until they'd known them for a while. Both were tall, blonde, and rather rugged-looking, as you would expect for men who worked in marine construction, but Paul's face was slightly rounder than his brother's, his lips just a tad fuller.

Petey approached life with a glass-half-full attitude, while Paul tended to be more the glass-half-empty type.

The yin and yang of one person, Jake had always thought, separated into two. Neither had ever married.

"When did you talk to Teresa?" Steve asked. Steve owned a small trucking company which hauled fish for the handful of commercial fishermen remaining in Port Salerno after the state passed a net ban several years ago. Divorced from his high school sweetheart, Steve loved women and they seemed to like his aging surfer-blonde charm and athlete's body. He never lacked female companionship when he wanted it and played the field like a pro athlete.

"Uh, last night when I called her from the hotel," Jake said. They'd had an early morning flight to Cancun, so they'd made the two hour drive from Salerno south to Miami the night before and stayed in a hotel near the airport. He and Steve had shared a room and Petey and Paul had shared another.

"I didn't see you use the phone," Steve said.

"Well, I used this," Jake said, pulling out a small cellular flip phone from his pocket.

"When did you get a cell phone?" Steve asked surprised. "I thought you hated them."

"I've had it a few months now. I thought it would be easier to keep in touch with Casey while I'm down here." Jake had left the Salty Dog Saloon, the bar that had been in his family for decades, in the care of his young friend Casey Bradley, the Salty Dog's manager.

Jake had hired the homeless young man and given him a room in his home four years ago. Now twenty-five, Casey was like the younger brother he'd never had and Jake had no worries that Casey could handle the business while he was on vacation.

"You've had a cell phone for a few months and didn't even tell your best friends? What's up with that?" Steve asked incredulously. "Ohhh, so that's it. You didn't get the phone because you're worried about Casey and the bar. You got it so you could call Teresa, didn't you?" Steve asked reproachfully.

"A little of both, actually," Jake said defensively. "Calling Mexico from my land line was getting pretty expensive." He and Teresa had had an instant connection the first time they'd met and, even though the guys liked her, Jake knew Steve was concerned he was getting in over his head. Jake's last relationship, three and a half years ago, had ended in complete disaster, and now Steve acted like a mother hen whenever Jake showed an interest in any woman.

"I see," Steve said, raising an eyebrow.

"What do you see? I don't see nothin'," Petey slurred, leaning his head back against the seat and closing his eyes.

"It's a good thing you're not driving," Paul said, breaking the tension.

"You know what they say, 'Drink. Don't Drive.' I'm just following orders. Besides, who needs to drive when you have, uh, Pablo, here, who can do it so well?" Petey asked with a laugh as he sat up in the seat and read the driver's ID card hanging from the rear view mirror. "I never have to drive here, so I can drink whenever I want."

"Well, you can drink whenever and whatever you want, but I plan to get in some fishing and if you're not ready when I am, I'm not waiting around," Paul warned him.

"I think maybe I'll hang with Steve this time and try to catch something besides fish," Petey said with a laugh.

"I don't think so, Petey, no offense, but I like to fish alone," Steve said, grinning.

"None taken," Petey slurred, "but I'd still like to know what you use for bait. Personally, I don't think you're anywhere near as good looking as I am; how do you manage to always have two or three beautiful women hanging around you?"

"What can I say… women love me," Steve laughed.

"Until they find out about all the other women," Jake reminded him.

"You'd do better getting your advice on women from

Hank," Paul advised his brother. Hank was the only married member of the Boys Club, and he and his wife Dana had two children.

Jake tuned out his friends and turned to look out the window at the passing scenery. It was a beautiful spring day on the Riviera Maya, sunny with not a cloud in the sky and a mild breeze coming off the Caribbean that helped temper the mid-eighty degree day.

Forty minutes and one military checkpoint later, the taxi turned off the highway and headed east into Playa del Carmen. Winding through neighborhood streets a few blocks north the of resort section, the driver slowed before turning onto a gravel drive between two large clumps of bamboo growing next to the street. Passing a small sign that read 'Las Palmas Resort and Teresa's Cantina', they entered a small gravel parking lot surrounded by colorful tropical vegetation.

After freeing their luggage from the trunk and paying the driver, Jake and his friends walked toward an arched opening in the vivid burgundy bougainvillea hedge that separated the parking lot from the rest of the well-maintained property and followed a sidewalk that ran between two buildings and out toward the beach.

After passing between the buildings, they came to an intersection with another sidewalk that ran in front of a pair of two-story thatched-roofed adobe buildings on the left and one on the right. All three of the buildings faced the beach, but only the two northern buildings were used for rentals, housing four small apartments, two on each floor, in each building. The southern building had an office and an apartment on the ground floor for Señor Garcia, Teresa's father, and the upper two apartments had been converted into a single large apartment for Teresa and her young son, Luis.

They stopped in the office to check in and pick up their room keys. Señor Garcia must have been assigned to desk duty because he got up out of the chair in front of his apartment next door and followed them inside, grumbling in Spanish the whole time. Jake noticed the old man seemed to be moving slower since their last visit six months ago.

Jake had never been around Señor Garcia much, but he'd never heard the old man speak anything but Spanish and not even much of that. He assumed Teresa's father didn't speak much English and since he couldn't speak Spanish, Jake didn't bother with the usual pleasantries.

Señor Garcia knew what they were there for and shuffled around the counter that served as the front desk. He began gathering up the proper papers to sign, his movements terse and almost rude as he threw the pen down on the counter and waved at the piece of paper he wanted Jake to fill out and sign.

After Jake finished the paperwork, he slid it back across the counter. With nothing more than a grunt, Señor Garcia tossed the keys to two of the cottages on the counter, turned his back and shuffled out of sight.

Once they were back outside, Steve turned to Jake. "Was that my imagination, or was Teresa's old man less than delighted to see us?"

"I don't think his lack of enthusiasm has anything to do with you guys; he just doesn't seem to like me," Jake replied.

"Here," he said, handing Petey and Steve each a room key. "We've got the two ground floor rooms in the last building."

"Let's drop off our luggage and then meet back out here," Steve said stopping at the first room that he and Jake would share while the twins passed on the way to their room.

"Sounds good," Paul replied.

Jake and Steve went inside and dropped their luggage and Steve immediately turned to Jake. "Is this thing with Teresa serious?"

"Maybe," Jake replied.

"What the hell does that mean?" Steve asked. "Teresa's not the kind of woman you play with, Jake; you know that, don't you?"

"Yes, Steve. I know Teresa's not a one-night stand kind of girl. I have never thought that."

"And you know that having a relationship with her is a huge commitment, despite the distance, right? I know this sounds crass, but Teresa comes with baggage, and by that I mean her son. No matter how you feel about her, she's a mother and her child is going to mean more to her than you ever will."

"How do you know?" Jake retorted, tired of Steve's advice. He knew his friend was right; it had been on his mind constantly for weeks, but he wasn't going to admit it.

"I've dated several single mothers, and believe me, if the kids don't like you; you might as well pack your toys and go home."

"Then I guess Luis and I will have to become best friends," Jake replied as he walked to the door.

"What about her crotchety old man? He already hates you," Steve said, following him.

"I'll just have to find a way to change his mind, won't I?"

"Yeah, good luck with that," Steve muttered as he shut the door behind them.

Meeting Petey and Paul on the sidewalk outside their rooms, the four men went to the cantina in search of Teresa.

CHAPTER 2

They followed the sidewalk to the cantina as it meandered through a grove of coconut palms with colorful hammocks strung up between the trees, encouraging patrons to relax after a day on the beach or take a leisurely nap after a few drinks.

Teresa's Cantina was tucked up under the palms on the south side of the property next to the beach and consisted of two parts. The first was actually an old concrete building with a metal roof that had probably been a maintenance shed in another life. It housed the kitchen, pantry and freezers. Attached to it and running toward the beach was the cantina's seating area, a large wooden deck built about two feet off the sand with a thatched roof and stairs that faced the coconut grove.

The south side of the deck had walls made of narrow bamboo poles tied together that offered privacy from the neighbors and also helped to diminish the heat from the strong Mexican sun, while the east and north sides were open to catch the breeze.

Inside, barstools sat in front of a long bar along the south side and several TVs, thankfully muted, were mounted near the ceiling showing one soccer game after the next. Tables and chairs for diners ordering from the menu or choosing from one of several flavorful specials each day took up the rest of the space.

Between the lively Mexican or reggae music coming from the speakers mounted inside the thatched roof and the colorful fabrics and artwork Teresa had used to decorate, the cantina's shady interior made an inviting scene for tourists walking down the beach. After dark it wasn't unusual to see the sand in front of the cantina crowded with happy patrons dancing to a live band or disc jockey.

Jake and his friends satisfied their hunger with plates of

tacos, burritos, enchiladas and nachos served to them by a cute young waitress named Maria who had a perpetual smile but a very limited English vocabulary.

As Maria cleared the table, Jake looked up and saw a beautiful young Mexican woman heading toward them. Just over five feet tall and weighing no more than a hundred pounds soaking wet, she carried a tray of shot glasses filled with what looked like milk. He watched as she stopped at a nearby table to greet some people and make sure they had everything they needed before coming over to their table.

Jake smiled. Teresa Garcia Santiago was just as beautiful as he remembered. Long black hair flowing loosely down her back framed a delicate heart-shaped face with high cheekbones, a slender nose and eyes the color of creamy milk chocolate spiked with golden flecks. Her short yellow sundress with spaghetti straps set off skin the color of honey all the way down to her bare feet.

"Mi amigos, I am sorry I was not here to meet you when you arrived. I had some errands to run in town, but I have this treat for you," she said with a smile as she slid the tray onto the table.

"Teresa," Jake said standing, "it's so good to see you again."

"What is this?" Petey asked, referring to the tray on the table.

"Tequila crema. You must try it. It goes down so smooth and leaves a very pleasant glow. There is one for each of us," she said picking up a shot and indicating they should do the same.

"Creamy tequila, who knew?" Paul said as he picked up one of the shots.

"To my good friends, Jake, Steve, Petey and Paul. Bienvenidos, welcome," she said, as they clinked their glasses together and threw back the shot.

"You know, after you stay here three times, you are like family. This is your fourth visit, is it not?" she asked.

"Yes it is, Teresa. We couldn't stay away from our beautiful hostess," Jake said, soaking up the warmth of her eyes. "It's good to be back."

"Oh, man, that's good," Petey said, putting his shot glass back on the tray.

"Kinda like a warm milk shake, if that's possible," Paul said.

"Reminds me of Bailey's, just with tequila. It's good," Steve said.

"But where is my friend Hank?" Teresa asked.

"Hank couldn't make it, but he said to tell you that he'll come next time," Petey said. "Hey, does your cousin Benito still work at the dive shop just up the beach?"

"No, he opened his own shack a few months ago. It's just past the cantina," she said pointing south. "I'm sure he would like to see you."

"Great. Let's go see if he can take us out in the morning. We've got two weeks and I want to enjoy this fabulous water as much as possible," Steve said.

"Go ahead, guys. Count me in on the trip in the morning, but for now I'm going to hang out here with Teresa. I'll catch up with you later," Jake told his friends.

Steve gave Jake a questioning look, and then turned to Teresa. "Thanks for lunch, Teresa," he said as he got up from the table and kissed Teresa lightly on the cheek.

"Yes, thanks for the shot, too," Petey and Paul chimed in together.

"It was my pleasure," she said. "Now go, have fun, but make sure you come back later for supper. We are lucky to have some fresh fish tonight."

"Later, guys," Jake said as his friends turned and walked toward the beach.

"So you are here for two weeks this time," Teresa said as she sat down in the vacant chair beside Jake.

"Yes, that's not too long, is it?" he asked. "I don't want you to get tired of having me around." They'd only stayed a week each of the other three times, but this trip he had wanted more time to spend with her so he'd talked the guys into two weeks.

"No, I don't think that will happen," she said as she slipped her hand into his.

"I've missed you," he said.

"It's good to have you back," she said quietly, giving his hand a meaningful squeeze.

"Do you have time for a walk down the beach?"

"I have a little time, but I have to be back when Luis gets up from his nap," she said as she pulled a hair band off her wrist and tied her hair back. They left the cantina and turned up the beach going in the opposite direction from Steve and the twins.

The crescent-shaped beach in front of Teresa's Cantina was fairly wide with soft white sand and clear green water. Small waves lapped rather than crashed on the shore, making it a great beach for young and old alike.

As they walked down the beach in companionable silence, Jake reached out and took Teresa's small delicate hand in his. He needed to touch her to make sure he wasn't dreaming. Ever since their first meeting, he'd felt drawn to the young Mexican woman who owned and operated the tiny resort with her aging father and young son, and with each subsequent trip, his feelings had grown stronger. He'd been pleasantly surprised at how easy it had been each time for them to pick up their growing friendship exactly where they'd left off. Now he was back for the fourth time and he was pretty sure she knew he wasn't coming back just for the nachos.

"Did you see Papa when you checked in?' Teresa asked once they'd walked a good distance down the beach.

"Yes, though he wasn't exactly overjoyed to see me."

"I apologize if he made you feel unwelcome, but I'm not surprised."

On an earlier trip, Teresa had admitted her father had a huge distrust of gringo men, because his wife, Teresa's mother, had run off with an American when Teresa was four. He'd also learned that Teresa's father, José Luis Garcia, had been working hard to get her married to one of the local young men.

"I trust that he hasn't been successful in his bid to marry you off to one of these young studs?"

"No, but he's certainly tried. I told you how he feels, he thinks you have come to steal me away from him just like the gringo that took my mother," she said as they turned around to head back to the cantina.

"You know it's not like that. I would never steal you away unless you wanted to go. He needs to know that."

"He doesn't want to hear anything good about you. He says I should make you stay somewhere else next time."

"That's pretty serious," Jake said, chuckling at the old man's absurdity. Even if Teresa's father did make him stay at a different resort, he'd still come here and spend most of his time with Teresa.

"Don't laugh, it is serious. He's never been fond of gringos but he usually doesn't mind taking their money. I think he's afraid of you."

"So, we just give him some time to get used to the idea that I'm not going to steal you away."

"I don't know, Jake. Maybe this is a good time to end this before someone gets hurt. My papa is a good man, but he is getting old and frail. Whenever you're here, he's mad at me all the time. That can't be good for his heart, and it's not good for Luis to have us arguing all the time."

"Do you want me to leave?" Jake asked, more calmly than he felt.

"No! I've been waiting so long for you to come back. But it's hard. I just don't see how things between us could ever work. You have your business in Florida and mine is here. That is your home and this is mine."

He could tell that she was bothered by her father's health and his fear of losing his only daughter and grandson. Jake admitted there was the possibility that he would one day make the old man's fears a reality, and felt bad about it, but that was something they would have to deal with when and if the time came.

"We've got two weeks to figure this out. Let's just go slow and see what happens."

"All right, but it doesn't sound like much time, does it?"

"That's why we have to make every minute count," he said, pulling her in for a kiss. A few moments later they were back at the cantina.

"Mama, mama," a little boy yelled as he ran across the sand and grabbed Teresa around the legs. Small boned and slender like his mother, Luis also had his mother's honey colored skin and milk chocolate brown eyes. He had a sprinkling of sand in his chin length black hair.

"I see you are up from your nap, my little man," Teresa said as she knelt in the sand to hug her son.

"He's grown a lot in the last six months," Jake said. The first time Jake had seen Luis he'd been two years old, now he was four. Jake wondered if the little boy would remember him. He'd spent a few mornings with Luis and Teresa each time he'd been here, and knew the little boy was smart, but six months was a long time in a young child's life to remember someone who was only around for a week every six months.

"Yes, my little man is growing up fast," she said, giving the little boy an extra squeeze.

"I have a truck, Jake," Luis said, squirming out of his mother's arms and holding up a small toy dump truck for Jake to see.

"I see that," Jake said, surprised and pleased that Luis remembered him. He knelt in the sand before the boy. "That truck will come in handy if you're gonna move all this sand you have around here."

"I'm going to be a dump truck driver when I grow up," Luis announced. "I am making a mountain, Jake, you want to see?"

"Sure, let's go check out your mountain," Jake said

smiling as Luis grabbed his hand and started pulling.

When Jake looked in the direction Luis was leading him, he saw Señor Garcia sitting on the porch outside his apartment. There was a pile of sand next to the sidewalk at his feet, obviously Luis' mountain.

He knew what he'd just told Teresa about taking things slow, but here was an opportunity to try to interact with the old man and he didn't want to pass it up.

Jake let Luis pull him closer to the mountain while Teresa followed. When they got within a few yards of where the old man sat, Señor Garcia pulled himself out of his chair and shuffled into his apartment.

Jake stopped abruptly as the old man slammed the door behind him.

CHAPTER 3

"I told you he was angry," Teresa said, watching Jake's reaction. "Leave him alone for a few days and let him get used to you being here again. Take it slow, isn't that what you said a few minutes ago?" she asked with a smile.

"You're right. OK, Luis," he said looking down at the patient little boy, "show me what that dump truck can do."

"I need to get back to the cantina. I'm tending bar this afternoon."

"Sure, go ahead. Luis and I will just hang out here and work on his mountain," Jake told her as he ruffled her young son's hair.

"Have fun with Jake, Luis. Mama must go to work," she said kissing him.

"Adios, Mama," he said, returning the kiss.

After Teresa had gone back to the cantina, Jake played with Luis in the sand pile and kept an eye on Señor Garcia's apartment. He could see the old man sitting on the other side of the big picture window pretending to watch TV, while he actually watched Jake play with his grandson.

Jake knew the old man was determined to wait him out and wouldn't come out as long as he was there, but he wanted Teresa's father to get used to the idea of him being around, so he stayed.

After almost two hours of moving sand, Luis announced he was thirsty and went inside his grandfather's apartment. When he didn't come out several minutes later, Jake knew the old man had contrived to keep the boy busy inside.

Standing up and looking through the window again, Jake nodded his head and smiled at the old man sitting in the recliner with the little boy on his lap watching cartoons on the TV. Turning, he headed to the cantina.

By the time the guys returned, Jake was sitting at the bar in the cantina, a half empty pitcher of margaritas in front of him, while Teresa fixed drinks for the rapidly growing crowd that had come for dinner.

"What did you guys do today?" Jake asked as his friends took stools on either side of him.

"Talked to Benito, he's taking us out early in the morning, then went down and hung out at Señor Frogs." Paul replied.

"Yeah, Steve went fishing for some cruise ship babes. Hey, Jake, we're gonna need some glasses so we can help you with those margaritas," Petey said, grinning.

"What did you do?" Steve asked.

"He was an assistant dump truck driver," Teresa said as she walked up and set three more margarita glasses on the bar in front of them.

"What?" Petey and Paul asked in unison.

"Oh yes, and quite a good worker, I'm told," she said, smiling at Jake.

"You talked to Luis?" Jake asked.

"Yes, he said you were a hard worker and a good helper."

"What are you two talking about?" Paul asked.

"It would seem that Jake spent his afternoon playing in the sand with Teresa's son," Steve said flatly.

"Seriously?" Petey asked.

"Oh yes, it was so cute, you should have seen them," Teresa said, her eyes dancing. "I would stay and chat but I have to go back to work. You should try the fish tacos, while they last," she said, walking away.

"What are you doing, Jake?" Steve asked quietly.

"What do you mean?"

"You booked us here again because of Teresa, we all know that, and we all like Teresa, but now you're spending your afternoons playing in the sandbox with her son. Jake, where is this going?"

"I'm not exactly sure at the moment, but I have two weeks to figure it out, so I might be a little preoccupied this trip."

"I think you should keep in mind what happened the last time," Paul said, "and there weren't any little kids involved."

"Thank you for reminding me, Paul," Jake said in a cool and serious voice, "but I'm well aware there's a child involved."

"Are you sure you're not rebounding after Vanessa?" Steve asked.

"That was three years ago, Steve. I think I'm past the time frame for rebounding."

"But you haven't really dated anyone since Vanessa. Maybe you just rebound at a slower rate," Steve replied.

"You sure it's not just the Mexican sun and tequila and beautiful woman syndrome?" Petey asked.

"I can see where you guys might think so, but no, I'm not suffering from any syndrome," Jake said. "However," he added, watching Teresa as she worked behind the bar, "she is definitely a beautiful woman, isn't she?"

"Oh yeah," Petey and Paul said in unison.

"And the sun, the sea, and the tequila aren't bad either," Jake added with a nod.

Over fish tacos served where they sat at the bar, Steve, Petey and Paul talked about walking downtown to watch the fire dancers that set up on the street after dark and did shows for tips. When Steve mentioned that small crowds created good opportunities to meet women, the twins readily agreed.

After polishing off another pitcher of margaritas, the three men left Jake sitting at the bar.

* * *

Steve walked down the beach flanked by Petey and Paul.

"You guys need to help me convince Jake to break

things off with Teresa," he said to the twins.

"Why?" Petey asked. "Don't you think Jake is capable of making his own decision about that?"

"I don't think Jake is thinking too straight these days, at least where Teresa is concerned, and my guess is, he's going to get his heart broken again. Hell, I don't want to watch him mope around and act like a zombie for however long it takes him to get over it again."

"Yeah, he *was* acting a little weird back then," Petey recalled.

"I don't think you'll have to worry about it," Paul chimed in. "It probably won't last anyway."

"Well, that's one thing we don't have to worry about losing," Petey remarked.

"What's that?" his brother asked.

"Your pessimism," Petey shot back with a grin.

"Stop it you guys, this is serious. Will you help me?"

"No," Petey replied. "Jake is a big boy and can make his own decisions. He doesn't interfere in your love life, if I were you, I'd stay out of his."

"I agree," Paul said. "The five of us watch each other's backs but we need to stay out of each other's bedrooms. You guys heard him back there when he started talking in his 'serious' voice. I don't think he wants our help and I don't want a pissed-off friend."

"So that's it? You guys won't help?" Steve asked, giving them one last chance to change their minds.

"NO." Petey and Paul said in unison.

"Fat lotta good ya'll are," Steve mumbled as he picked up a stone and tossed it into the sea.

* * *

Shortly after the guys left, Teresa took off her apron and turned the bar over to Juan, her right hand man in the cantina just as Casey was Jake's right hand man at the Salty Dog. The resemblance ended there as Casey was in his early twenties and just over six feet tall and Juan was probably in his late forties and was no taller than Teresa. Jake thought Juan could have been a jockey if he'd wanted to.

"My shift is over and we have a few hours before the cantina closes. What would you like to do?" she asked as she sat down at the bar beside Jake.

"Let's take a walk down the beach," Jake said, reaching over to take Teresa's hand.

"With all those crazy tourists out there, are you loco?" she asked laughing.

"But I wanted some time to talk to you alone."

"Well, my feet are tired. Let's just go under the trees and find a hammock."

"That's a great idea. Do you need to check on Luis first?"

"No, he will be asleep by now and he is with his grandfather tonight. It can be just the two of us for a few hours."

Under an almost full moon, they walked through the shadowy coconut grove. Jake glanced at Señor Garcia's window and noticed all the lights were out, but in the moonlight he was sure he could see the old man standing at the window watching them.

Jake picked one of the hammocks on the northernmost edge of the property he thought was out of Señor Garcia's view and settled into it before pulling Teresa in beside him.

"I've been waiting all day to do this," she said, giving him a long slow kiss.

"I've got to admit, it was worth the wait," he said when she finally pulled away.

"There's more where that came from, you know."

"Teresa, I think your father…"

"I don't want to talk about Papa tonight. I have waited six months for your return and if only for one night, I don't want to think about Papa. I just want to be here with you and kiss you and feel your arms around me again."

Jake pulled her close and kissed her again. He'd been

going to say he thought her father had been watching them, but was more than happy not to talk about him if that was what she wanted. Holding her and kissing her was a lot more fun than talking about her father anyway.

They were quiet as they lay together in the hammock, silently reveling in being back together again while listening to the waves break on the beach and reggae music spilling out of the cantina.

"What do you want out of life, Teresa?" Jake whispered into her ear, breaking the semi-silence.

"What do you mean?"

"You know, your dreams. Everybody has a dream of how they'd like their life to be."

"Then I guess I have my dream. I am happy with my life," she said snuggling a little closer, "and right now I am very happy you are here to share it with me."

"So this is your dream?"

"Yes, for now. It is not such a bad dream, is it? I have my own little hotel and cantina, I have my beautiful son, and I have my home on a beautiful beach. Most people work all their lives to be able to have what I have and I'm still young. What more do I need?"

"How about a father for your son?" Jake asked.

During a previous trip, he'd learned that Teresa had been badly hurt in a relationship that left her with a young son to care for alone. In the interest of full disclosure, but without mentioning any names, he'd told her of the woman he'd been in love with a few years ago who'd been living with one man, and secretly in love with another, neither of whom were Jake.

"Well, yes, I would like Luis to have a father, but if that never happens, we will be fine," she said. "I have enough love for him in my heart for two parents."

"What was he like? Your husband, I mean." Jake asked

"He was not my husband, Jake. I have never been married," she said and began to pull away. "Does that change the way you feel for me?"

"No, not at all," he said, pulling her back and giving her shoulders a reassuring squeeze. "But then why is your last name different than your father's?" he asked with a note of confusion.

"Because here in Mexico when a child is born it takes its mother's last name. My mother's last name is Santiago. A husband also takes his wife's last name but Papa dropped the Santiago from his name when my mother ran away."

Then tell me what Luis' father is like," Jake said. "How did you meet him?"

"It's the same story you always hear. Small town girl gets a job in the big city and falls for the first man she meets. Doesn't find out he's married until it's too late."

"I'm sorry," he said.

"It's okay. It was a mistake. Fortunately it has brought more blessings than problems, but it was still a mistake and one I promised myself never to repeat. The next man I make love with will be one who loves me enough to marry me first," she said firmly.

There was a momentary lull in the conversation as Jake took in the full meaning of her words. He certainly understood her reasoning, and he also understood what she was saying about their relationship. A flash of disappointment shot through him but after a little thought, he realized she was really just telling him she wanted him to respect her. He had no problem with that, he did respect her, and realized he was actually proud of her for standing up for herself.

But was that also a hint that she wanted him to ask her to marry him? The thought had crossed his mind, several times in fact, but he wasn't sure he was ready for that just yet. And even if he did ask her now it would sound like he was just trying to get in her pants, and he didn't want her to think that. Jake searched for something meaningful to say but realized the silence had dragged on so long that anything he might say now would sound stupid. Deciding to keep his foot out of his mouth, he kissed the top of her head and gave her shoulders another squeeze.

"What are your dreams?" she asked, finally breaking the silence.

"I'm still working on them," Jake confessed.

"Well, let me know when you get it worked out," she said, rising up to kiss him. "But for now, I've got to go start cleaning the kitchen so I can get up and do it all again tomorrow."

"Okay, I'll help you if you'll make some sandwiches for us to take on our diving trip tomorrow," he said.

"That sounds like a good deal to me," she said as she tugged on his arm to pull him out of the hammock.

Once he was on his feet, he pulled her over to a coconut palm and leaned her against its trunk. He looked at her delicate face in the moonlight and felt a tightening in the pit of his stomach. Leaning in, he kissed her longingly.

"Would you ever leave Playa del Carmen, Teresa?" he asked a moment later.

"What for?" she asked. "Look around you. Everything you need for a good life is right here."

After the kitchen was cleaned to her satisfaction, Jake walked Teresa to the stairway that led up to her apartment. The curtains were closed in her father's front window, so he kissed her good night.

On the way back to his room, Jake thought about what Teresa had said. Maybe she was right. He didn't know how or when it had happened, but he'd fallen in love with Teresa and her little boy. Maybe everything he needed for a good life *was* right here.

But was he ready to give up the life he had in the States?

CHAPTER 4

Jake's eyes snapped opened at the sound of footsteps crunching in the sand nearby. Lying perfectly still in the hammock he and Teresa had shared earlier, he wondered who was out walking around in the early morning hours before dawn.

When he went back to his room after kissing Teresa good night, he'd found Steve sprawled across the bed, snoring like a freight train. Steve's snoring had never been a problem before but he'd accidentally gotten his nose broken recently and the result was so loud it could be heard in the next room. The futon was piled high with luggage, moving it would have required more energy than he'd felt like expending, so Jake had simply grabbed a pillow, closed the door behind him, and gone back to the hammock.

He listened carefully until he was sure the footsteps had gone past him, and then raised his head. It was still dark but there was enough moonlight for Jake to see a short stocky man wearing only a pair of shorts cutting a diagonal through the coconut grove on his way toward the beach. He couldn't see the man's face, but he was light on his feet and carried himself well. Jake watched as the man walked out into the water before diving in and swimming out into the Caribbean.

He wondered if it was one of the other hotel guests, but was almost sure the man hadn't come from either of the guest buildings or he would've passed much closer to his hammock than he had.

Closing his eyes, Jake drifted back to sleep.

* * *

The reflection of the sun as it peeked over the horizon

and hit the clear blue waters of the Caribbean Sea before bouncing in his face woke him up a couple of hours later. Rolling out of the hammock he went back to his apartment to wake Steve and get ready for their dive trip with Benito.

Thirty minutes later he stopped in the cantina and picked up the sandwiches Teresa had made for them last night and then met his friends on the beach.

Benito, Teresa's cousin, was a short, stocky guy about the same age as Jake and his friends. He'd pulled his boat up to the beach and was telling the guys about some places he knew that were good for diving. Once the four friends were aboard, Benito put the boat in reverse and backed it off the beach.

They spent the day diving on the reef, marveling at the many species of game fish that roamed the crystal clear waters off the Yucatan. Between all the sea life they'd seen and the beer Benito had iced down in the cooler, Jake was hard pressed to come up with a better way or a better place to spend a day.

He had to admit this was a great way of life. Diving and fishing in a tropical paradise during the day and a beautiful young woman on his arm at night; did life really get any better than this?

He loved the quaint little beachside town with its clear blue waters and swaying palm trees on the beach. Except for Playa del Carmen's touristy Avenida Quinta, which was easy enough to avoid if you wanted to, the town's laid back lifestyle reminded him of the way Salerno used to be.

They did some fishing on the way back in and by the time they pulled up to the beach late that afternoon, they had more than a dozen nice fish for Teresa, who promptly whisked them away to the kitchen.

After a shower and a change of clothes, Jake headed back to the cantina. Glancing over at Señor Garcia's place, he saw Teresa's father shuffling from his chair on the porch to the door. He moved so slowly and was so bent over that Jake wondered if the old man was sick.

He found his friends sitting at a table in the cantina, a half-empty pitcher of margaritas in front of them. He'd just sat down when Teresa dropped her apron on the bar and came over to join them carrying another pitcher of margaritas and two more glasses.

"Do you wonderful fishermen mind if I join you?"

"Please do," they all chorused.

Teresa poured the potent tequila concoction into the two empty glasses and handed one to Jake and took the other for herself before taking a seat between Petey and Paul.

"Thank you so much for the fish. It's been hard to keep it on the menu lately."

"With all this beautiful water, you're having trouble getting fish? How does that happen?" Petey asked.

"The fisherman that has always sold his fish to me is not fishing anymore, and until I find another one, it will be like this."

"But how hard can it be to find a fisherman who will sell you his fish? Look at all those boats out there," Petey pointed out.

"It's harder than you think. The big resorts can afford to pay more for fresh fish, so most of the fishermen go there first. Then they work their way down the line. By the time they get to me, there's usually nothing left that I want to serve to my guests."

"So just don't serve fish," Paul said.

"Ah, people expect to find fresh seafood when they come to the beach and you Americans love your fish sandwiches and fish tacos. Also the locals are mostly Catholics who only eat fish during Lent. I will lose a lot of business if I cannot keep fish on the menu," she explained. She looked across the table at Jake. "Perhaps I could make a deal with one of you to stay and fish for me," she said smiling.

The silence only lasted a beat or two and then Petey

piped up with a question for Teresa. While she answered, Steve kicked Jake's foot under the table.

"Don't even think about it, Jake," he said under his breath.

"Shut up," Jake replied in kind.

"So what are you gentlemen doing this evening? Going to one of the clubs for some uh, companionship?' she asked, turning her attention back to the table.

"If by that you mean women, then yeah. Where are they?" Petey asked.

"What kind of women are you looking for?"

"Single women."

"Ah, if you want to find single women, take a walk down the beach. There are quite a few bars that have nightly entertainment between here and Señor Frogs. Lots of American women in those places."

"Uh, it's okay if they don't speak English as long as they treat me right," Petey laughed.

"You know, you just might be onto something. Finding a woman who doesn't understand a word you say might actually increase your chances of having a long term relationship," Paul said in a loud whisper.

Everyone laughed for a moment when Petey elbowed Paul in the ribs.

"So, what do you want for supper?" Teresa asked, still smiling. We have some very nice fish."

"We had fish last night, so you should save that for your other guests. How about a big platter of beef and chicken fajitas and some of your yellow rice?" Jake asked.

"Add some nachos to that for an appetizer and we should be set," Steve added.

"Yeah, that sounds great," Petey and Paul said as one.

"Coming right up," she said as she got up to go to the kitchen.

"I know what you're thinking and I just have one suggestion," Steve said after Teresa was out of earshot.

"Oh yeah, what's that?"

"Don't do it."

"Don't do what?"

"Don't fall in love with her, and don't become a Mexican fisherman."

"Is that what you think I'm doing?"

"I know it is; I can see it in your eyes. Please don't do it."

"I think it's too late for that, Steve, at least the first part," Jake confessed.

"Oh, shit."

"Not again," Petey and Paul said in stereo.

"Look, this isn't the same. Vanessa was living with one guy, in love with a different one, and sleeping with me. Teresa isn't like that. All she has is her father and son and we aren't sleeping together. You can't compare the two."

"Maybe not, but have you considered the consequences if you and Teresa don't work out?"

"Don't worry about me…"

"I'm not, not in this instance." Steve said. "I'm talking about Teresa and Luis."

"What makes you think Teresa and I won't work out? Just because you can't settle down doesn't mean I can't." Jake retorted.

A long moment followed as the two friends glared at one another.

"You haven't slept with her yet?" Paul asked in a whisper.

"Maybe there's still hope for us," Petey said as he looked at his brother and laughed, breaking the tension that threatened to drive a wedge between his friends.

Just then Teresa came back from the kitchen carrying an enormous platter of nachos. Conversation was minimal as they dug into the mountain of tortilla chips covered in queso and chili; all their thoughts centered on what they'd just heard concerning Jake's feelings for Teresa. Each of them had questions about what Jake might do; even Jake, but no one would ask them. Jake couldn't answer them, anyway.

Their dinner was brought by Maria and after filling themselves with the delicious chicken and beef fajitas and another pitcher of margaritas, Steve, Petey, and Paul decided to take Teresa's suggestion and walk south down the beach to the main resort area.

Jake stayed at the cantina for a little while, watching Teresa as she worked. Realizing she was too busy to spend time with him and wanting a few minutes to himself, he walked north up the beach.

The tourists that had lined the beach earlier with their noisy children, colorful towels and beach mats were gone, replaced only by the occasional couple walking arm in arm and enjoying each other's company. He passed several bars and nightclubs in full swing, the music coming from them an invitation to join their revelry, but Jake wasn't interested in a party right now. He was enjoying the feel of the sand under his feet and the soothing sounds of the gentle waves lapping on the beach.

He loved being able to walk out his front door and be at the beach in less than a minute. He'd been around the water all his life, but it was nothing compared to this. Back home, he lived next to the Manatee Pocket, a small bay located near the confluence of two large rivers on Florida's east coast, but there the water was brown and polluted from the constant releases from Lake Okeechobee, the lake in the middle of the state that collected runoff from areas as far north as Orlando.

There was also no beach within walking distance. Sure, the Atlantic Ocean was less than a mile away if you were a bird, but unless you lived on the barrier island that separated the rivers from the ocean, you weren't going to walk to the beach. People who commented about Florida being a paradise had obviously never been to Mexico's Yucatan Peninsula.

After walking close to a mile, Jake turned around and headed back. By the time he returned to the cantina,

Teresa was closing up for the night and ready to start cleaning.

Jake helped her clean once again and after they finished, he took her back to their favorite hammock. As they lay together talking and gently swinging under the moonlit sky, Jake convinced Teresa to take the next day off so he could take her and Luis to play on Cozumel's Paradise Beach.

When Teresa started to drift off to sleep, Jake, against his better judgment, gently woke her and walked her to the bottom of the stairs of her apartment and kissed her goodnight.

When he got back to the apartment he was sharing with Steve, his friend was passed out and sawing logs again, so he grabbed a pillow and went back to the hammock in the coconut grove.

Sometime in the early hours of the morning, he was once again awakened by the sound of sand crunching under someone's feet. Lying still so he wouldn't be noticed, Jake waited until the footsteps passed before raising his head up for a look.

In the moonlight, Jake recognized the form of the same man he'd seen the morning before, short and solid, and from the way he carried himself, Jake guessed him to be no more than forty-five. But where was he coming from and where did he go when he swam? He'd meant to ask Teresa if she was aware that a man was cutting through her property in the wee hours of the morning to take a swim, but he'd forgotten.

Jake watched the man swim until he was out of sight, then shifted in the hammock and went back to sleep.

CHAPTER 5

The next morning Jake met Teresa and Luis for a ferry trip to Cozumel, while the other members of the Boys Club went fishing with Benito again.

Playa del Carmen's cobblestoned Avenida Quinta was quiet this early, most of the businesses weren't yet open, but Jake knew that would soon change. Tourists from the nearby resorts would begin arriving to plunder the shops and on days when cruise ships were in port in Cozumel ferries shuttled their passengers to Playa and back for the day to join in the plunder and sample the local cuisine that lined the pedestrian only street.

As he and Teresa walked toward the ferry dock swinging the laughing little boy between them, Jake felt a sense of peace and happiness he hadn't known for a long time.

Arriving at the ferry dock, Jake purchased tickets for the ferry that was currently loading and the three hurried onboard. They found seats inside next to the window, and Luis insisted on sitting in Jake's lap so he could see the water.

During the twelve mile ferry ride, Jake looked over the group of people headed to Cozumel. It was too early for the tourists to be out so most of them were Mexicans who lived in Playa and worked on Cozumel. All were brown skinned with dark hair. He realized that with his own dark hair and deep tan, other than his blue eyes and perhaps his height, he fit right in. That was assuming he kept his mouth shut. His Spanish was terrible.

After a leisurely breakfast near the town square and a quick stop to buy some sand toys for Luis, they took a fifteen minute taxi ride south to Paradise Beach and Jake was astonished when he walked through the palapa at the entrance.

Straight ahead, the super-size pool with swim-up bar looked incredibly inviting. A glance to the left yielded sparkling clean bathrooms and changing areas with showers, and to the right a path surrounded by perfectly manicured grounds led to the restaurant, bar and beach beyond.

They took the pathway and walked toward the beach. Several rows of lounge chairs with umbrellas lined the white sandy beach, and behind them a coconut grove like the one at Las Palmas provided plenty of shade for those not wanting to bake in the tropical sun.

Anchored out in the clear turquoise water was an assortment of enormous inflatable toys that included a trampoline, a rock climbing pyramid, a jungle gym with an attached slide and several other slides in various sizes, all of which provided plenty of water fun. It was a popular hangout for cruise ship tourists, but luckily there were no ships scheduled to be in port today, so other than a few locals, they had the place pretty much to themselves.

They chose a couple of lounge chairs on the beach and spread their towels across them while Luis dumped out the bucket of sand toys. Before he had a chance to get sandy, Teresa slathered him with sunscreen and then turned him loose to start building sand castles.

It was a beautiful morning to spend at the beach; with the mid-eighty degree temperature and the light breeze off the Caribbean, a dip in the sparkling water from time to time was all you needed to keep cool and refreshed. With the soft music and cool drinks coming from the beach bar behind them, Jake had never seen a more luxurious and quietly entertaining beach club.

Teresa rinsed her hands in the water and then lay down to catch some rays. "This feels so good, Jake," she said. "I'm very glad you brought us."

"Isn't there some kind of entrance fee or chair and umbrella rental?" he asked looking around.

"Not here," Teresa replied. "All they ask is that you buy your food and drinks here."

"Then why don't you order us a couple of mojitos and take a few minutes to relax while Luis and I do some exploring," he said leaning down to give her a kiss.

"I'll be right here," she said with a smile.

"Let's go for a walk down the beach Luis, and see what else they have here," he said to the little boy.

"Okay. Mama, I'm going with Jake," he said giving his mom a sandy kiss.

"Have fun and listen to Jake, okay?"

"Okay, Mama, I will."

Jake took Luis's hand and together they walked south down the beach to another small palapa with a small pier jutting into the water where snorkeling tours departed. When Luis finished playing with a crab he'd found, they walked down to the other end of the beach and checked out the shops between Paradise Beach Club and another beach club adjacent to it.

After returning from their walk and enjoying a drink, Jake looked over at Teresa. "While I take Luis out to play on the water toys I want you to take this ticket down to that booth over there and get a massage."

"Oh, Jake, that sounds wonderful, but I couldn't."

"Why not?" he asked. "As hard as you work, I think you need it, and since it's already paid for, you wouldn't want to waste good money, would you?"

"No... but,"

"No buts. Just go and enjoy a little pampering. You deserve it," he said giving her a kiss and pulling her up.

"Thank you, Jake. I'll be back as soon as I'm finished."

"Take your time and relax. Luis and I will be fine."

Jake and Luis hit the water and Jake was surprised to see that Luis swam like a fish. They jumped on the trampoline, made several unsuccessful attempts to make it to the top of the pyramid and went down the slide more times than he could count.

Shortly before noon, Jake and Luis plopped down in the sand at the foot of Teresa's chair.

"We're hungry," Jake said. "Why don't I go get us some lunch?" he asked.

"I will do it," Teresa said, getting up. "With your Spanish, there's no telling what you would bring back. I will go while you stay and play with Luis."

"Are you sure? They probably have an English menu," he said.

"No, that's all right. I will be back in a few minutes," she said picking up her beach bag.

"Okay, kiddo, it's you and me for a few minutes. Let's see if we can finish this sand castle."

"Here is my shovel," Luis said holding up the small plastic shovel that came with the little plastic bucket.

"You know, Luis, you speak English very well for such a little guy," Jake remarked.

"I know," Luis replied. "Mama says that I must speak English to everyone who speaks English to me. She says that way, I will learn more."

"Well, I think your mama is a pretty smart lady, don't you?"

"Yes, she is very smart and I am smart too, she told me so."

"I couldn't agree more."

Jake watched as Luis's face took on a more serious expression.

"Jake, do you have the beach where you live? I like the beach," Luis said as he filled up the bucket with sand.

"Yes there is a beach where I live. It's not as close as the one you have in front of your house, but it's not too far."

"Do lots of people live there, like I see on TV sometimes?"

"No, it's not like that at all. It's more like it is here. It's seasonal. That means that there are more people around some times than other times."

"Yes, like in the winter and spring here when all the hotels are full and there are lots of people on the beach, but in the summer not so much."

"Exactly. You really are a smart little guy."

"Do you like it when all the people come to your town?" Luis asked.

"Not particularly," Jake admitted, "do you?"

"No, some of them are strange looking and scare me, but mama says we must be happy for everyone that passes through our lives. She says most of them will leave us, but we should enjoy them while they are there."

"That sounds like good advice, I'll try to keep that in mind."

"Are you one of those people, Jake?" Luis looked up at him with eyes just like his mother's.

"What people?"

"The ones that pass through our lives and leave."

Jake was quiet for a moment as he thought about the little boy's question. "I don't know yet, Luis," he said honestly. It killed him to have to say it, but he wasn't going to lie to the boy. Whatever relationship they might have in the future, Jake wanted it to be built on honesty and trust.

"Well, if you are, then I hope you stay around a long time before you have to go. I like you. Abuelo doesn't like you, but I do."

"I like you too, Luis," Jake said pulling him over and giving him a big hug. "But who is this Abuelo guy that doesn't like me. I don't know that name."

"Abuelo means grandfather," Luis explained.

"Oh," Jake said, putting it together. "No, I don't think your grandfather likes me very much, but he really doesn't know me very well."

"He thinks you have come to take mama and me away."

"Luis, I have no intention of taking you or your mother away from your grandfather."

"That's what Mama says, but he still doesn't like you.

He says Mama should stick with her own kind. What does that mean, Jake?"

"I think he means that he wants your mother to have a Mexican husband and you to have a Mexican father."

"But you are brown just like me and Mama."

"Yes, I am, but I'm an American."

"But you are still brown. Mama says that Abuelo just needs to get a grip. She says we all have things in life that we don't like, but we have to be strong and brave and face them with high heads."

"Oh, yeah? What is it that you don't like?" Jake asked with a smile.

"I don't like taking naps, but Mama says I must, so I do. Mama said when I am five I will be able to stay up all day and you know what Jake?"

"What Luis?"

"My birthday is coming soon and I will be five. I will be big enough to stay up all day."

"And I'm sure you will. When is your birthday?"

"June ninth. That's not very long is it Jake?"

"No, not long at all. Less than two months," Jake agreed. "Now, we better go find a place to wash our hands before your mom gets back with lunch."

They took an afternoon ferry back to Playa del Carmen, and while Teresa put Luis down for his dreaded nap, Jake went back to his apartment to shower and change.

His conversation with Luis ran through his mind as he stood under the shower spray. It was obvious the kid was smart and also obvious that Teresa spent a lot of time talking with her son. He was a great little boy and Jake wondered how any man could give up a son like Luis.

He was also aware that the kid had done a very discreet job of interviewing him for the role of prospective father. But that was fair enough, Jake thought. The kid had a right to ask questions.

Jake just didn't know the answers yet.

CHAPTER 6

Jake sat on what he now thought of as his and Teresa's hammock in the coconut grove later that afternoon waiting for her. When he saw her walking through the sand toward him, he smiled. She was wearing a little red dress that hugged the curves on her delicate frame and dipped just low enough in front to be able to see the swell of her breasts. Barefoot as usual, she was so beautiful she almost took his breath away.

"Luis and I had a great time today," she said, sitting down beside him on the hammock. "It was very nice of you to take us to Cozumel."

"It was my pleasure. I enjoy being with you and playing with Luis," he replied taking her small hand in his.

"He likes you too," she said.

"He really is a smart little boy."

"What do you expect? He has a smart mother."

"Yes, he does. Teresa, you've said so little about him, but what kind of man is Luis's father that he could give up the opportunity of having such a great kid in his life?"

"He was a coward."

"Tell me about him, who is he?"

"I can't tell you his name, but I use to work for one of the big resort hotels in Cancun and he was my boss."

"What happened?"

Teresa freed her hand from Jake's and then clasped both her hands together in her lap. "I was stupid, that's what happened. He was handsome and charming and I fell in love with him. He said he loved me and we talked about getting married, but when I told him I was pregnant, he turned his back on me and walked away. The next day his wife came to my office and told me my services were no longer required. She was his boss and part of the rich American family that owned the resort. I didn't even know he was married until then."

"So, what did you do?"

"What was a pregnant young Catholic girl supposed to do? I came home to Playa and Papa."

"And that's when you bought this place?" he asked, curious. Beachfront property wasn't cheap and she had obviously done a lot of work to the place since she'd bought it. Where had the money come from?

"Yes, you see when my boss's wife came to fire me; she also brought a bag of money that she said was mine if I got an abortion. Of course, I refused. I am Catholic, I do not believe in abortion. But she didn't want to be disgraced in front of her fancy rich friends and family, so in exchange for the money, I agreed not to put her husband's name on Luis's birth certificate."

"You took the money?" he asked.

"Of course I took the money, it was the least they could do for us" she said, annoyed that he might think less of her for trying to protect her family. "Sure, it would have been a noble thing to refuse her deal, but I did not ask *her* for money, she offered it. And without a job and unemployment rates rising daily, how was I to take care of my baby?"

She stood up and walked a step away and then turned back to face Jake, her anger firing. "That man lied to me. He took the most precious thing I had to offer and lied to my face the whole time. So yes, I took the money."

"Hey, that sounds fair to me," Jake said, getting out of the hammock and taking her in his arms. "I hope you took the sorry s.o.b. for a bundle. Raising a kid isn't cheap."

He felt her relax as the anger ebbed out of her tiny body. Giving her a peck on the lips he took her hand and led her back to sit beside him on the hammock.

"It wasn't enough to make me independently wealthy," she replied, "but at least she paid me in American dollars rather than pesos.

"Was that important?" Jake asked. "I thought the people of Mexico would want pesos."

"Do you know nothing of the Mexican peso crisis of 1994?" she asked, shaking her head.

"No, I'm afraid I was wrapped up in my own problems back then. That was the year the net ban was passed that put most of the Florida commercial fishermen out of work. What was it about?"

"It's a long story, but simply put, in a few short months starting in December of 1994, the peso lost half of its value, prices rose almost twenty-five percent and unemployment almost doubled. It got even worse the next year as banks began collapsing and thousands of mortgages went into default."

"So you wanted the American dollars because they held their value while the peso was going in the crapper," Jake surmised.

"That's right. As long as the peso continues to lose value, and it is still losing value to this day, I will hold on to as many dollars as I can, converting them to pesos only when I need to pay my suppliers and employees. If the peso ever rebounds against the dollar, then I will convert all my dollars to pesos."

Jake laughed.

"Don't laugh, things were bad."

"I wasn't laughing about that," he said, trying to keep a straight face. "It's just that for a minute there, you sounded like some kind of financial analyst."

"Well, I do have a business degree and several of my courses were on financial analyses. There's more to me than meets the eye, Mr. Arnold," she said elbowing him in the side.

"Beauty *and* brains, two of my favorite attributes in a woman," he said with a grin. He kept the conversation light, but he was more than a little impressed with the depth of her intelligence. He'd known it was there, you didn't keep a business running very long if you were stupid, but it was a side of her that she hadn't shown him before.

"Laugh all you want, but that's how I bought Las Palmas. The man who owned it also owned the place next door," she said pointing to the piece of property on the northern side of Las Palmas. "He had overextended himself and had to sell half the property to keep from defaulting on his mortgage so I bought it and put all of my unemployed family members to work."

Jake looked at the property to the north. "But it's all boarded up. What happened?"

Teresa shrugged. "I guess he couldn't stay on top of his debt."

Jake put his arm around her and pulled her close. "Luis was right. He really does have a smart mother."

"So now that you know the whole story, you don't think less of me?" she asked tentatively.

"Not at all," he said, kissing the top of her head.

"Truly? I don't think I could handle seeing the disappointment in your eyes the way I saw it in Papa's."

"Seriously, I do understand. Three years ago, I got a settlement from the family of the man who murdered my father."

He went on to explain that his father's death had been ruled "accidental" by the authorities after his battered boat and body were found on the inlet jetty rocks after a storm, but he had subsequently learned that his father had actually been murdered over a gold coin by a salvager hunting for the lost treasure of the 1715 Spanish Plate Fleet. He also told her that the murderer had been killed by one of his own men in the Salty Dog.

"They wanted to protect the image of their family business, so they offered me a settlement in exchange for keeping silent about how my dad actually died."

"Did you take it?" she asked.

"Not at first, no. I didn't want their money; I wanted everyone to know that my father hadn't been stupid enough to crash his boat on the jetty, but my mom said she didn't want to relive his death through another investigation. And since the man that killed my father was dead, I agreed. After all, you can't put a dead man in jail. She suggested I take the settlement and if I couldn't find a good use for it to give it to charity. She wanted to believe something good could come from our loss."

"What did you do with it?" she asked.

"Nothing yet. I don't even know how much it is, but I figure one day, I'll know what to do with it."

"Maybe you will use it to make a new life, like I did," she said.

"Maybe," he said with a smile.

"The place next door is for sale," she hinted with a sly grin.

Jake leaned back and pulled her down into the hammock beside him. "That's an idea," he said looking deeply into her eyes before kissing her.

Teresa broke off the kiss. "Not here where papa can see us if he walks out."

"You know, Luis is quite an informed young man and from what he tells me, you think your papa needs to 'get a grip'. So why are you afraid to let him see that we care for each other?"

"Because he will just dig his heels in and argue with me until he wears me down and gets what he wants."

"Why do you listen to him?"

"Because in Mexico, children listen to their parents. We may not always do as they say, but we listen. I care for you Jake, I really do, but you are only here for two weeks and then you will go back to Florida. That is not enough for me to risk hurting my father and making him hate me as he does my mother."

"So, I guess the less he knows for now, the better."

"Yes, please."

"OK, then we better get up. We'll have to save rolling around in the hammock for after dark."

"Maybe later tonight," she said with a wicked grin.

"Speaking of hammocks," Jake said suddenly

remembering the early morning swimmer he'd wanted to ask Teresa about, "Do you know there's a man that comes through your property in the early morning hours to take a swim on your beach?"

"No, I know of no such man. How do you know about him?" Teresa asked as she wriggled out of Jake's arms and stood up.

"I've seen him the last two mornings. Steve snores so loud I've been sleeping in the hammock."

"What does he look like?"

"I don't know, I've never seen his face, but he's short like most of the locals around here and from the way he carries himself, I would guess his age to be about forty to forty-five."

Teresa was silent for a minute. "Jake," she laughed, "That's the description of more than half the men in this town."

"So you don't know who it is?"

"No, and if he's not bothering anyone or trying to steal something, I don't care. People walk up and down the beach all the time; it's the price you pay for living beside the water. At least whoever he is, he's trying to get some exercise."

"Okay, I just thought you should know."

"Come, let's take a walk down the beach before I have to go to work," she said taking his hand and pulling him out of the hammock.

* * *

When Jake and Teresa returned from their walk they met Steve, Petey and Paul in the cantina.

"Hey Teresa, you look nice," Petey said as he took in the red dress she was wearing.

"Thank you, Petey," she said smiling.

"We brought you some more fish today," Paul said.

"Oh, thank you so much. I'm going to have to start paying you if you keep bringing me fish."

"No, you won't. It's the least we can do since you feed us so well," Steve said.

"Well, what would you like for supper tonight?" she asked.

After a short discussion, they ordered an assortment of quesadillas, tamales, and tacos as well as a pitcher of margaritas. While they waited for their food, Jake watched Teresa as she worked her way around the room, smiling as she welcomed everyone. She actually seemed to enjoy meeting all of her guests.

He remembered what Luis said about his mother's philosophy of enjoying the time you spent with people even though they might only be passing through your life. Would Teresa and Luis just pass through his life? He wasn't sure yet, but he knew he had to get Teresa's father to accept him before he and Teresa would have any chance at a life together.

Jake jumped when the cell phone in his pocket started vibrating. Pulling it out, he noticed the caller ID said 'Salty Dog'. Jake told the guys the call was from Casey and walked outside to take it.

Casey called to let him know that Vanessa had called The Salty Dog looking for him, so Casey had given her his new cell number. Jake strolled through the coconut grove as he and Casey caught up on each other's news. When he hung up, he headed back to the cantina.

Walking past Señor Garcia's apartment he noticed the old man had company. Taller and better built than the average Mexican man he'd seen around town, the visitor slouched against one of the porch posts as he talked to the old man sitting in his chair. The visitor had his back to Jake and Jake could see the bulge under his jacket that suggested he was armed. The man didn't seem to notice Jake, but Señor Garcia did.

As Jake walked back toward the cantina, he could feel the old man's eyes boring into his back.

CHAPTER 7

Just as Jake stepped back up onto the deck of the cantina, Teresa met him. "Is everything OK," she asked. "Steve said you had a phone call from home."

"Yeah, everything's fine. That was just Casey, checking in."

"Oh, good. And how is Casey?" she asked.

"He's fine, he says hello."

"I would like to meet him one day," she said.

"I think we might be able to arrange that," he said with a smile and then nodded over his shoulder. "I see your father has company tonight."

"Who is that? Oh, Dios mio, not him," she said with a note of dread in her voice.

"Why, who is he?"

"That's Miguel Ruiz; our families were friends for many years."

"You don't sound too happy about seeing him."

"I'm not. Papa probably told him to come by to see me. He's been doing that a lot lately and I hate it."

"You mean, this is another one of the guys he's trying to marry you off to?"

"Yes. Listen, Jake, go back and enjoy your dinner, but if Miguel comes in here you must promise me that you will let me handle everything, okay?"

"What do you mean? Are you expecting trouble?"

"I hope not, but you never know. Whatever happens, you must promise to stay in your seat and keep your friends with you."

"But..."

"No buts," she said firmly. "This is not your town, Jake. This is my town and my business and I will take care of my business. Whatever happens, I will handle it, do you understand?"

"Yes, ma'am. I will let you handle it, but if you change

your mind, just let me know and I'll be there."

"It's a deal."

Jake went back to the table to join his friends and Teresa disappeared into the kitchen for a few minutes. When she came out she was wearing a pair of black high-heeled dress shoes. Not spikes, which would have gotten caught in the small gaps between the boards of the cantina's wooden deck, but high, stout heels. Jake liked the way she looked barefoot, but he'd always thought heels did something for a woman's legs and it was no different with Teresa. She looked both sweet and sexy as she went back to greeting her guests and tending bar.

A short time later, Miguel entered the cantina and took a seat across the bar from Teresa. Jake couldn't understand a word of the rapid fire Spanish that went back and forth between them, but he could tell from Miguel's body language that he was on the make. He could also tell that Teresa wasn't interested.

"Who's that guy bugging Teresa?" Petey asked.

"Somebody she knows," Jake said, watching Teresa as she walked out from behind the bar to wipe some tables. As she passed behind him, Miguel turned in his seat and grabbed Teresa's hand, pulling her into him.

Petey, sitting next to Jake, started to get up. Jake quickly put his hand on his friend's arm. "No, Petey."

"But that guy's messing with Teresa," Petey protested.

"She doesn't want us involved. She knew he was here and she made me promise not to leave my seat unless she gave me a sign. She meant you guys too."

"So we just sit here and watch that guy maul her?" Steve asked in disbelief.

"Until she gives us a sign, yes," Jake said. "She was very clear about that."

"I can take care of that prick in less than ten seconds, and he'll never even know what hit him," Steve growled.

"I know you can, but she wants to handle it herself," Jake said, never taking his eyes off Teresa. Steve had been taking karate since he was fifteen-years-old and had black belts in three different forms of martial arts. There was no doubt in Jake's mind that his friend could neutralize Miguel, what worried him was that Steve could very easily kill the guy without meaning to. That was the last thing they needed. From what he'd heard, Mexican prisons were worse than just bad.

Jake continued to watch as Teresa broke away from Miguel, wiped down a few tables, and went back behind the bar. She was busy making drinks and seemed in no danger as long as she stayed behind the bar, so Jake and his friends settled back in their seats and ate their supper.

Jake kept an eye on Miguel throughout the meal and noticed when he started to get antsy. Jake pushed his plate away and wiped his mouth on his napkin before setting it back on the table.

He saw Miguel get up and walk down to the open end of the bar. Reaching through the gap, he grabbed Teresa's arm again. Miguel said something to Teresa in Spanish and she said something back, but Jake was clueless and frustrated. He really needed to learn some Spanish if he was ever going to know what the hell was going on around here.

Jake pushed his chair back, ready to get up, his eyes never leaving Teresa's face, waiting for the sign that she wanted his help. When Teresa slapped Miguel across the face with her free hand, Jake clutched the arms of his chair as tight as he could to keep from jumping up. He knew if Miguel hit her back, he would be forced to break his promise. He wasn't about to sit back and let someone hurt her.

But instead of hitting her, Miguel pulled her close and whispered in her ear. Teresa looked startled for a moment. Jake couldn't stand it anymore. Realizing that he'd been holding his breath for some time, he let it out and started to get to his feet just as four short, stout Mexican men walked past him.

He sat back down when he realized one of the four men was Benito, Teresa's cousin. He watched as they surrounded Miguel and began quietly talking to him. A few minutes later, Benito and his friends escorted Miguel out of the cantina. As they walked past Jake's table, he noticed the distinctive tattoo on Miguel's arm.

A moment later, Benito came back in and said something to Teresa before leaving again.

Jake sat back in his chair, relaxing for the first time since Casey's phone call. He was glad that was over, but he was proud of Teresa. She'd known what his reaction would be to someone bothering her, and had insisted on handling things herself. There was strength of character in that tiny body of hers, but he was happy she had back up in the form of Benito and his friends.

"Well, I'm glad that's over," said Steve, voicing Jake's thought. "I don't know how much longer I could have just sat here."

"I know what you mean," Petey and Paul said in tandem.

"You've got to give her credit for standing up for herself," Jake said. "I'm just glad Benito showed up when he did." He knew firsthand what it was like to keep things on an even keel when you owned a bar and she had handled the situation well. If he and the guys had jumped in, there probably would have been a small riot.

"Now that the drama is over, the twins and I are thinking of going into town for a while. I assume you're going to hang out here with Teresa?" Steve asked.

"Yeah, I'm going to wait until she gets off work."

"Do you want us to stay in case that guy comes back?" Petey asked.

"No, go ahead. We'll be fine."

Steve, Petey and Paul got up from the table and waved to Teresa on their way out. A few moments later, Teresa came over with a fresh margarita for Jake.

"Thank you," he said as she slid the drink in front of

him.

"I'm sorry that happened," she said, referring to the incident with Miguel.

"What was that about, anyway?" he asked

"That was my father sticking his nose in my business again."

"How so?" Jake asked.

"I will tell you about it later. Now I have to get back to work. I will meet you at our hammock when I'm finished."

Jake stayed in the cantina for a while longer, just in case Miguel decided to come back. The guy was obviously some kind of threat in Teresa's mind, and it seemed to Jake like it was more than just her father trying to get her settled down with a local guy. Whatever it was, he intended to find out.

The cantina closed at ten so Jake hung out until a quarter till, then took a walk around the grounds and the parking lot to make sure Miguel wasn't hanging around. Seeing no sign of the young Mexican, Jake walked out to the beach to check there and found Benito sitting in the sand in front of his shack.

"Hola, Jake," Benito said as Jake sat down beside him.

"Hey, Benito, you want to tell me what that scene in the cantina was all about?" Jake asked.

"You mean with Miguel?"

"Yeah."

Benito laughed. "That's something you will have to talk to Teresa about. She doesn't like anyone messing around in her life without her permission, and I don't want to be the target for all that Latin fury she has stored up in her little body."

"She does seem to have a bit of a temper," Jake observed with a smile.

"That comes from being half Spaniard. Very temperamental, those Spaniards. If you think Teresa's temper is bad, can you imagine what her mother's must have been like? Teresa told me that her mother's people were very important and very rich back in Spain, It almost makes me feel sorry for my Tio José Luis, but not quite. Maybe if he weren't so lazy I would feel differently."

"So tio means uncle?" Jake asked.

"Si. I love my cousin and want only the best for her, but if you want peace in your life, you should find a nice, sweet Maya girl that will cause you no problems," Benito chuckled.

"But you got Miguel out of there. Isn't that considered messing around in her life?" Jake asked.

"Probably, but she called and asked me to do it."

"So where did Miguel go?" Jake asked.

"See those guys standing down there on the pier?" Benito asked, pointing to the pier in the distance where the cruise ship ferries landed.

"Yes," Jake said. He could see two men standing under one of the lights on the pier.

"One of them is Miguel."

"Do you think he's planning to come back and bother Teresa again?"

"I don't know, but I'm not sitting out here because I like sand in my shorts," Benito replied. "The cantina is getting ready to close. You should go back and make sure Teresa gets home safely. I will stay here until I am sure they are gone."

Jake hesitated.

"Go, my friend. I have everything under control, and unless Teresa asked you to come down here and help me, she will think *you* are messing around in her life, and you don't want that, I promise you."

"Okay, but let me know if you need any help." Jake stood up, dusted off the back of his shorts and headed back to the cantina.

CHAPTER 8

Light spilled out of the cantina under a starry night as Jake waited on the hammock in the dark coconut grove and watched the entrance to the cantina. He saw Teresa the instant she stepped off the deck and onto the sand. She still had the red dress on, but was once again barefoot.

"What happened to your shoes?" he asked as she came over and sat on his lap.

"Shoes are more trouble than they're worth in this sand. I keep that pair in the kitchen and only wear them if I think I might have to kick someone," she told him.

Jake laughed. "You wouldn't want to break a toe or anything."

"Yes, that's right. And I don't put up with people who grab me."

"I thought you handled the situation with Miguel quite well."

"Of course I did. But I saw you start to get up. You were going to get all macho and come to my rescue."

"Would that have been so bad?" he asked.

"Jake, I live in this town; my business is in this town. If I can't stand up for myself, then sooner or later, I won't have a business."

"I understand. I just have a hard time watching anyone bother you."

"You are a good man," she said kissing him, "but I can take care of myself."

"So, tell me about this guy, Miguel."

"I've known him since we came to Playa. My father and his father worked together and were friends before Miguel's father died."

"And now?" Jake asked.

"Papa found out he was in town to visit his mother and invited him over to see me. We went out once after we both moved to Cancun, but I haven't seen him since then."

"Your father's latest attempt to find you a Mexican husband?"

"Yes, and I am afraid he will not stop until he succeeds. But Papa wants a man who will live here and take care of the work and Miguel lives in Veracruz."

"Sounds like your Papa is getting desperate. He doesn't care if your potential husband is local or not, as long as he's Mexican. What did Miguel say to you when he whispered in your ear?"

"He reminded me of the promise we made to each other."

"What promise?"

"Oh, it is nothing. When Miguel was eight and I was six, we promised each other that we would get married someday. But we were only little children; we didn't even know what it meant."

"Is that why you slapped him?"

"No. I slapped him because he kept grabbing me."

"What did Benito say to you when he came back after Miguel left?"

"Only that Miguel said he would be back. But that is probably just boasting," she said with a dismissive wave of her hand. "I told him I didn't want him in my life."

"I noticed the tattoo on his arm. Does it mean anything?" Jake asked.

"It's a symbol of the drug cartel he works for."

"He's part of a drug cartel?" Jake asked with noticeable concern in his voice.

"Yes. That's why I won't have him around Luis. But don't worry. The cartels usually don't bother anyone unless they get in the way of their business. And I have known Miguel since we were small children. He will not hurt me."

"Is he some kind of boss or something?"

Teresa gave a derisive snort. "Miguel is too stupid to be a boss. He is nothing more than a, what do you call it?… a minion."

"Does your father know he's involved with the cartel?" Jake asked, surprised that the old man would subject either Teresa or Luis to that kind of life.

"I doubt it, he just remembers Miguel as the little boy of his best friend."

"You need to talk to your Papa and let him know what kind of man he's throwing at you."

"Yes, I should, shouldn't I? It's not something that will make him happy, though."

"Well, like Luis says, he needs to get a grip. You and your son are more important than an angry old man's feelings."

"I'm glad you think so," she said as she pushed him back and snuggled in the hammock alongside him.

"I don't just think so, I know so," he said and gave her a long lingering kiss.

"Tell me about your life in Florida," she said. "I want to know everything."

"Okay, that will probably take at least five minutes," he laughed.

They lay together in the hammock, holding each other close while Jake told her about his previous life as a commercial fisherman, the net ban, and his current life as a crabber. He told her about Salerno, the town where his family had lived for almost a century, the Salty Dog, and how he had come to own it, and about Casey and his music.

"Tell me about your family. What do they think about all these trips to Mexico you've been making?" she asked.

"I don't know. Most of my relatives are commercial fishermen and after the net ban they moved to Louisiana so they could continue to fish. I don't talk to them a lot, but I talk to my mom on the phone every week."

"It must be hard to live without your family around. I don't know what I would do without my Papa and his sister, Tia Carmen. I must take you to Puerto Morelos to meet her. I think you will like her. She's been like a mother to me since I was a little girl."

"Tia means aunt, right?" Jake asked.

"That's right."

"I'd like to meet her," Jake said.

While Teresa chattered on about her Tia Carmen and all the things she'd done for her since her mother had abandoned her, Jake listened carefully. His heart ached for the motherless little girl Teresa had been, and was glad she'd had someone in her life to take up the slack. He'd never had a moment's doubt about the love his parents felt for him and each other and couldn't imagine what it must have been like to grow up without both of them in his life.

But despite growing up in a broken home, Teresa was a remarkable young woman. She was open and honest and truly loved her son and her life, and worked hard to keep it all together. Setting aside that fiery temper of hers, Jake thought she was as beautiful on the inside as she was on the outside.

"I have the morning off tomorrow and I'd like to take you to one of my favorite places, if you'd like to go," she said, interrupting his thoughts.

"I'd love to see one of your favorite places," Jake said, kissing the top of her head. "Where is it?"

"Tulum. It's about a forty minute drive south of here."

"What's so special about Tulum?" Jake asked.

"It's the site of an old Maya city, the only one on the coast that's still standing. It's beautiful, Jake. Will you let me show it to you?"

"Of course. Are we taking Luis with us?"

"No. Papa said he wanted to spend the day with him," she replied.

"Oh," was all Jake could think of to say. He was disappointed the little boy wouldn't be going with them and wondered if Señor Garcia was trying to keep Teresa's son away from him.

"There is so much history in Tulum, I know you will

love it," she said.

After the cantina closed and the staff had left for the night, Jake and Teresa left their hammock to clean the kitchen. Jake wasn't sure why Teresa insisted on personally cleaning the kitchen each night. Her staff did a good job of cleaning up before they went home, but it seemed like some sort of therapy for her, so he helped her.

After walking her to the foot of the stairs that led to her apartment, Jake kissed her lightly and waited until she was inside before heading back to the apartment he shared with Steve.

Once again, Steve was snoring louder than Jake thought possible without waking himself up, so Jake grabbed a pillow and headed back to the coconut grove. He'd been lucky so far that it hadn't rained, and hoped his streak continued.

As he lay in the gently swaying hammock, Jake tried to turn his mind off and go to sleep, but he couldn't. He knew he was falling in love with Teresa, but as Steve had pointed out, he needed to make sure he wasn't making another mistake like the one he'd made with Vanessa. Last time he'd led with his heart, but this time there was a child involved and he needed to include his head in the equation.

There was no comparison between the two women in looks or temperament. Vanessa was tall and blonde with an air of mystery about her, but the secrets she'd kept from him had almost gotten them both killed. Despite Steve's suggestion that he was rebounding from Vanessa, Jake was pretty sure he'd let that ship sail long ago. Vanessa had found what she wanted and Jake was happy for her. He still regarded her as a friend and felt the same way about her husband Patrick.

Teresa, on the other hand, was petite and dark. She had a backbone of steel with a temper to match, but she'd also been very open and honest, communicating freely and answering all of Jake's questions whether she thought he'd approve or not. It was easy to imagine a life with her, the two of them working and growing old together. The fact that she had a son didn't bother him. Steve may refer to Luis as 'baggage', but Jake liked the little boy and enjoyed being around him. He might even consider a little brother or sister for Luis.

Eventually his brain ran out of gas and Jake fell asleep, only to be awakened a few hours later by the sound of sand crunching under someone's feet as they made their way past him to the beach. Jake looked up and saw the same man as before as he waded out into the dark, Caribbean waters. Getting up from the hammock, Jake followed, but by the time he made it to the beach, the man was already swimming away with a strong stroke.

It was too dark to see the man's face, but as Jake walked back to his hammock, he decided to find out the identity of the man who stalked through Teresa's property in the wee hours of the morning. He'd have to lay off the margaritas one night and try to catch him before he got to the beach.

Mañana, he thought, as he snuggled back into the swaying hammock and drifted off to sleep.

CHAPTER 9

The next morning Steve, Petey and Paul met Jake for breakfast in the cantina.

"So what are you guys up to today?" Jake asked his friends.

"Benito is taking us cenote diving today," Petey said, pronouncing it 'se nó teh'.

"What's a cenote?" Jake asked.

"It's a fresh water sink hole. They're part of an underground river system and Benito said you can find them all over the place around here," Petey explained.

"He also said the ancient Maya believed cenotes were doors to the underworld," Paul added, "so we might be visiting hell today. I just hope Satan doesn't decide to keep us."

"As long as you keep employing Benito as your guide every day, I don't think he'll let anyone, including Satan, mess with you," Jake chuckled.

"He's not charging us much, he says he's having too much fun to get paid, but we'll make sure he gets a nice tip before we leave," said Steve.

"Yeah, we're thinking about taking the Boys Club international and making him an honorary member. Benito is a great guy," Petey said. "He asked us over to his place tonight to play some cards."

"Yeah, he and his friend Henry run a high stakes poker game out of Henry's house a couple times a month, but we're not doing that. This game tonight is at Benito's place and its quarter limit," said Paul.

"Good," Jake replied, "because I don't have the money to bail you guys out if you lose in high stakes."

"We'll be fine," Paul assured him. "I have no intention of losing more than ten dollars. I figure that's a good price for an evening of entertainment."

"No wonder you can't get a date," Steve said with a laugh.

"What are you doing this morning, Jake?" Petey asked.

"Teresa borrowed a car for the day, so we're going to take a picnic lunch and drive down to the Maya ruins in Tulum."

"That sounds like loads of fun," Paul said sarcastically.

"Uh, yeah, I'll definitely go diving," Petey said.

"Well, you two have a great time. We'll be back in time for supper," Paul said as the three of them got up from the table and walked out of the cantina.

Jake noticed that after the subject of Teresa came up, Steve had nothing more to say. Steve meant well, but Jake intended to live his life as he saw fit and hoped, along with Señor Garcia, his best friend would come around.

A few minutes later, Teresa walked into the cantina carrying a beach bag.

"You look fantastic," Jake said, as his eyes took in her snug Capri jeans and the sleeveless red plaid shirt tied in a knot above her belly button that accentuated her slender build.

"Thank you," she said shyly.

"And you're wearing shoes," he laughed, noticing the pair of white Keds on her feet.

He took her hand and together they walked out to the parking lot behind the resort. Jake took one look at the raggedy VW bug and laughed.

"What? You don't like my cousin's car?" she asked with a grin.

Jake took in the rusted out heap. The back end where the engine was located sat no more than a few inches above the gravel parking lot and Jake wondered if the poor old thing was up to the trip. He hoped there weren't any big bumps they'd have to go over or the old car was sure to bottom out.

"You call this a car?" he asked.

"Of course, this is a great little car. It may not look like much on the outside, but it has heart. Wait until you hear her purr."

"It's a girl?" Jake asked.

"Of course it's a girl. It belongs to my cousin Serena, Benito's sister."

"Okay, let's do this," Jake said climbing in the passenger seat.

Teresa started the engine and put it in gear. The little car shuddered and groaned and then backfired as soon as she gave it some gas. As they pulled out of the parking lot, Jake had serious doubts about making it back.

* * *

It was mid-morning when Jake and Teresa arrived at the Maya ruins in Tulum. Leaving the VW in the parking lot, they followed the pavement up to the entrance gate of the ancient walled city that sat on a cliff high above the sapphire blue Caribbean.

They got their tickets and walked up the hazardous rocky path that led to the northern entrance. Jake had to duck to get through the arch in the more than twenty-foot wide wall, but once inside, they wandered around and caught bits and pieces of the ancient city's history from some of the tour guides that stopped to talk to their groups.

Even though he'd heard that it had been built around 1200 AD and was abandoned after the Spanish arrived in the sixteenth century, it was easy to imagine the city as it had once been. There were quite a few buildings inside the walled compound and they were in surprisingly good condition for as long as they had been sitting on the edge of the sea.

Jake was amazed at the knowledge of architecture and agriculture the ancient Maya had possessed, as well as their remarkable grasp of the solar system they based their calendars upon.

"You know, the ancient Maya have been in this area for more than four thousand years and built cities in parts of Central America and all over the Yucatan," Teresa said. "There is another very large ruin just west of here in Coba. It has an observatory and many other old buildings including a pyramid you can climb."

"It must have taken a lot of manpower to build a city like this. How many people lived here?" he asked

"This was just a small but important city on the trade route, but like all the Maya cities, only the rulers lived inside the city. The rest of the people, the workers, lived outside the city in camps. Their numbers ranged from several thousand to more than ten thousand depending on the size of the city."

They headed up to the biggest and most imposing stone edifice in the ruins, El Castillo, meaning 'the castle'. It was about three-stories high in the center with a two-story wing adjoining each side and was located near the edge of what looked to be about a forty-foot cliff. The front of the structure had steep stairs running up two-thirds of its center that ended at a wide terrace. Behind the terrace was a large rectangular room with three doorways. Looking up at it from the walkway at its base, Jake was momentarily awestruck by the stark and imposing contrast it made to the vivid blue skies in the background.

"When I was little, I use to stay with my friend, Elena, after school and on the weekends when Papa was working," Teresa said. "Her mother would watch over us until Papa came to get me. She has a shop here and would bring us almost every day to help her sell her artwork and souvenirs like statutes of the Maya gods and snacks like empanadas and tacos to the visiting tourists."

They got in line with dozens of other tourists to walk down a set of wooden stairs that twisted down the south side of a narrow promontory to a sandy beach at its base. The going was slow until they passed a couple of young women speaking a foreign language who had decided to sit down on the stairs, essentially blocking half the stairway.

"Elena and I had a name for people like that," Teresa said when they finally reached the beach.

"What kind of people?" Jake asked.

"Those who feel they're entitled to do whatever they want despite the effects it may have on the people around them. We called them 'assoletas'," she said with a laugh.

They walked to the base of the promontory. Time and the sea had eroded the rock, leaving a shallow space underneath it that wasn't noticeable from above. The tide was low and there was plenty of space to walk under it, so they did. On the other side, the cliff fell away to a small sandy beach that would have been perfect for the canoes the Maya had used to fish and trade with other tribes throughout the region.

"This is my favorite place," Teresa told Jake as they made their way back under the overhang to sit on the sand.

"It is beautiful," Jake said as he looked down at sparkling clear water lapping up onto the soft white sand just inches from their toes and then out over the clear blue Caribbean beyond. "Why is it your favorite?"

"Sometimes Elena and I would sneak into the ruins and come down here to the beach. One day we overheard one of the guides tell his group that on special occasions the Maya sometimes offered a human sacrifice to the gods by throwing one of their people off the cliff above us. We would come down here and pretend we were Maya princesses being rescued by a handsome man from the ancients who wanted to sacrifice us to the gods. It was all very dramatic," she said with a shy smile.

"Gods, as in plural?" Jake asked.

"Yes, the Maya have over two hundred and fifty deities."

"Why so many?" Jake asked.

"Well, there's the god Chaak, the rain god, and Ixchel, the rainbow goddess, and…"

"Wait," Jake said, holding up his hand with a laugh. "I get the picture. They had a god for everything."

"Pretty much," Teresa admitted.

"And the Maya would sacrifice their people to the gods? You mean like kill them?" Jake asked. He'd always thought the Maya were a peaceful people.

"Yes, and sometimes children. I've always wondered how they could be so civilized and yet kill children to appease their gods. Children are the most precious gifts God gives to us," she reflected.

Jake heard the sadness in her voice and felt it as well. He didn't want to talk about people dying today; he wanted to spend a pleasant day with his girl, so he changed the subject to lighten the mood.

"So tell me more about this handsome fellow that would rescue you," he said giving her shoulders a squeeze.

"Well, I think he looked a lot like you," she replied with the hint of a smile. "Would you have saved me if I had been about to be sacrificed?" she asked, her smile broadening.

"Sweetheart, nothing could have stopped me,' Jake said pulling her close to his side.

After finishing their tour, they wandered through some of the shops outside the ruins. Teresa stopped and talked to several of the vendors she knew while Jake went inside one of the shops and bought a Mexican blanket.

"What's the blanket for?" Teresa asked when he returned.

"It gets chilly out in that hammock every night."

"Oh, I hadn't thought about that. I should have given you a blanket, I'm sorry."

"Don't be. Every time I use this blanket it will bring me happy memories of our day here together," he said taking her arm. "Now, where's the best place to eat. I'm hungry."

They found a table outside a tiny cantina and ordered lunch and a couple of Sol, a Mexican beer that tasted a lot like Corona, but smoother.

"So what happened to the Maya?" Jake asked after taking a sip of his beer.

"What do you mean?" she asked.

"Well, they're all gone now, aren't they?"

"Not at all. The Maya are alive and well. As a matter of fact there are currently more than seven million Maya."

"Where?" Jake asked.

Teresa laughed. "They are all around you, Jake. You see that woman over there?" she asked pointing to a short, round woman working in the shop next door.

"She is Maya, and so is the woman beside her and that man over there," she said nodding to the man Jake bought the blanket from. "And I am Maya."

Jake looked again at the people Teresa had pointed out. They were all broad and built low to the ground with round faces.

"You don't look anything like them," he said.

"That's because I am only half Maya. My father is Maya, but my mother's family came from Spain. Mexicans with a Spanish heritage are usually taller, and their bone structure is not so round."

"Well, you don't have a round face, but you didn't seem to inherit any of the height you're talking about either," he said with a smile.

"I think I must have gotten my height from my father and everything else from my mother," she said, just as their food arrived.

While they were eating, a tall, slender, young woman walked by, looking closely at them.

"Hola, Teresa," she said as she passed slowly by on her way to the shops.

"Hola, Elena," Teresa said with a smile.

"She must have some of that Spanish heritage you were talking about," Jake said after she was out of earshot.

"Yes, her family moved here from Mexico City many years ago," Teresa said with quiet contemplation.

"Who is she?" Jake asked.

"She is the friend I told you about. Her mother still has a shop here and Elena works at the ruin entrance."

"So what's the problem?"

"She is Miguel's sister and I would rather Miguel not know that I am seeing someone. He will just make problems."

"What kind of problems?" Jake asked.

"Who knows?" she asked. "That crazy fool might do anything. Maybe Elena won't tell him that she saw us together."

"Why don't you just ask her not to? You said she was your friend."

"Yes, she was. But we haven't been friends for a long time and it would not be right to ask her to deceive her brother. Maybe it will be nothing," she said hesitantly.

Jake didn't think she sounded very convinced.

CHAPTER 10

They arrived back at the cantina in time for Teresa to spend a little time with Luis before going to work, so Jake went back to the apartment to take a shower. While the water streamed over his head, he thought about Miguel's involvement with the cartel and what Teresa said about people being relatively safe unless they got in the way of the cartel's business.

Jake had nothing to do with the drug trade and was sure Teresa didn't either, so he wasn't too concerned about getting in the cartel's way. He *was* concerned that Miguel's sister would tell her brother about seeing the two of them together and he would show up again to make trouble.

Jake didn't want trouble, but after all the years he'd tended bar, he was usually able to recognize it, and the whole situation with Miguel and Señor Garcia felt like trouble with a capital T. He wouldn't start anything, but he wasn't going to back away if Miguel did. Jake had lost his last girlfriend to an 'old friend', and, cartel member or not, he wasn't planning to let it happen again.

In the cantina, he ordered a pitcher of margaritas without the tequila, and a salted glass, and sat at the bar as he watched Teresa work. Her white dress with its spaghetti straps looked like it was pieced together from gauzy handkerchiefs, and fit her small frame snug around the top while the skirt was loose and stopped just above her knee. The contrast between her black hair and tanned skin against the pristine white fabric was startling and as he watched her, he felt a deep tightening inside his chest.

He ordered a plate of nachos and shared them with Teresa while she worked. It felt right to be here with her and he let his mind wander, imagining what it would be like to actually live here. Would he feel this happy and content every day?

His reverie was broken when the guys came by the cantina for dinner. After devouring a burger and an order of fries each, they hung around talking for an hour or so before leaving for Benito's place to play cards.

Jake stayed at the cantina with Teresa, just in case Miguel decided to make another unwanted appearance. At closing time, there hadn't been any sign of the cartel man, so he and Teresa went to work cleaning the kitchen as usual.

Walking her to the bottom of her stairs after they were finished, he kissed her good night and headed back to his room for a pillow and his new blanket. He preferred sleeping outside in the peaceful and quiet coconut grove to the noise made by his best friend's snoring in their apartment. It reminded him of the nights he'd spent on the boat watching his crab traps.

* * *

Thanks to the non-alcoholic margaritas he'd been drinking the night before; Jake woke up earlier than usual. Looking around, he didn't see any sign of the early morning swimmer, so he rolled out of the hammock and walked toward the beach.

Positioning himself behind one of the coconut palms closest to the water, he moved around it until he was out of the sight line of the visitor's usual path. Leaning against the tree, he waited. Closer to the beach, the sound of the sea was louder than in the hammock and Jake listened carefully for the sound of sand crunching beneath someone's feet. He intended to get a good look at Teresa's early morning visitor.

While he waited, Jake thought about Teresa and smiled. He cared deeply for both Teresa and her son. He'd considered asking Teresa and Luis to come to Salerno and stay with him, but knew she would never agree. She'd made it clear that this was her home and this was her dream.

She worried about the health of her father, a man who was trying his best, Jake knew, to marry his daughter off before Jake and Teresa had a chance to make things work. Somehow, he needed to get Señor Garcia to change his feelings about him, and that was going to be difficult as long as the old man refused to talk to him.

Jake was lost in thought when he finally heard someone coming. Alert now, he waited until the footsteps were almost even with the tree he was leaning against, before he stepped out from behind it. Teresa's early morning visitor stopped in his tracks.

Both their faces registered shock for a brief moment as they stood no more than two feet apart. Jake looked at the swimmer. Wearing only swimming trunks, he stood up as straight and as tall as his short Mexican frame would allow. Jake noticed his well-developed shoulders and legs and smiled.

"Buenos dias, Señor Garcia." Jake said. His Spanish was practically non-existent, but he wanted the old man to know he was trying.

Obviously shocked to see Jake standing in front of him, the old man stared at him for just a moment before lowering his eyes and grunting. A second later he walked around Jake and continued his trek to the beach.

Jake turned and watched Teresa's father walk unwaveringly into the Caribbean for a short distance before diving in and swimming powerfully away.

Jake leaned back against the coconut palm, a ghost of a smile on his face, as he watched the old man swim farther and farther away. Señor Garcia pretended to be old and frail but he was faking. He was actually in better shape than men much younger.

Jake understood now why the old man favored those loose fitting Mexican shirts and baggy khakis he always wore. He could hide his toned muscles from his daughter and act weak so she'd feel guilty about leaving him.

As he walked back to the hammock, Jake wondered

whether he should tell Teresa her old man was faking. He understood Señor Garcia's reluctance to lose Teresa and Luis, but didn't like the way the old man was handling the situation.

He was making Teresa worry needlessly about his health and meddling in her life by inviting shady characters into it. But letting the cat out of the bag for the old man could very well backfire in his face if Teresa thought he was meddling in her life as well.

Adjusting the pillow as he lay back down, Jake closed his eyes. He needed to think about how to handle this new development.

* * *

Later that morning Jake and the Boys Club went fishing with Benito again. While they fished, Jake contemplated what to do with Señor Garcia's secret.

If he told Teresa that her father was scamming her, he didn't know what her response would be. She loved the old man and Jake didn't want to put her in the position of having to choose between her father and him. He wasn't sure he'd win that one.

On the other hand, keeping quiet seemed like hiding the truth from her and if he wanted an open and honest relationship, she needed to know. He decided to wait and see what the old man did the next time he saw him.

They fished all morning and by the time they returned to the cantina, they had a couple of dozen nice sized fish for Teresa. After dropping the fish off in the cantina kitchen, Jake and Steve walked back to their apartment to shower. Señor Garcia was sitting in his chair on his porch, and as they approached, the old man glared at Jake for a moment. Without breaking his stride, Jake nodded to the old man and watched as he slowly got up and, bent over and shuffling his feet, went inside and closed the door.

Nothing had changed.

"I think Teresa's father is going to be a hard nut to

crack," Steve said, observing the scene. "If you ever expect to have much of a relationship with her, you're going to have to get the old man to talk to you."

"Are you finally coming around to the two of us being together?" Jake asked.

"Not really, I'm just making an observation."

"That's encouraging," Jake said sarcastically.

"Hey, I just don't want to see you get hurt again."

"I know that."

"Okay, so what's your plan to get the old man to accept you?" Steve asked.

"Quite honestly, I'm beginning to think that keeping my mouth shut may be the answer to that," Jake replied cryptically.

"Jake, old pal," Steve said, clapping his best friend on the shoulder, "I think you have lost your freaking mind. You can't talk if you keep your mouth shut."

Jake smiled. If the old man wanted to keep his secret, Jake would let him. Maybe if Señor Garcia learned Jake could be trusted, he might learn to accept him. It wasn't much, but it might be a start.

After a shower and some clean clothes, Jake and the guys went to the cantina for a late lunch. The restaurant was doing a brisk business and Teresa was busy. They got a table and enjoyed some fajitas and a couple of pitchers of margaritas before Steve, Petey and Paul left for a walk down the beach to check out women.

Once the cantina quieted down, Teresa joined Jake at the table.

"Thank you for the fish. You really should let me pay you, though."

"There's no need for that."

"Okay, if you say so," she said with a smile.

"I do."

"Jake, can I ask you a question?"

"Of course. What is it?

"I'm curious about Steve. He doesn't seem to like that

you are spending so much of your time with me. I don't want to come between you and your friends."

"Don't worry about Steve, sweetheart. He's got his panties in a wad right now, but he'll get over it. We've been friends since we were toddlers and he's never been able to stay mad at me for long."

"Okay, but I hope he gets over it soon."

"He will."

"Oh, Elena came to see me this morning."

"Miguel's sister?"

"Yes, the girl we saw at Tulum."

"What did she want?"

"She said it was good to see me and thought we might be able to be friends again. She and her mother don't like her brother's involvement with the cartel any more than I do. She said her mother is sick with worry."

"So what are you going to do?" he asked.

"I told her that between Luis, Las Palmas, and the cantina, I really didn't have much free time, but I would be happy to be her friend again. We are the same age and always got along, so why not?"

"You were worried she might tell Miguel about seeing us together. Did she?"

"No, and she said she will not tell him. She said he was angry that I sent him away the other day, but he's gone back to Veracruz now. I gave her my number and asked her to call me if he comes back."

"That's good," Jake replied. He was relieved Miguel had left town, but wondered how long he'd stay gone. He didn't think the arrogant young Mexican would give up and walk away that easily.

"I have another day off on Wednesday. Would you like to go to Puerto Morelos with Luis and me to meet Tia Carmen?" she asked.

"I'd be honored to meet Tia Carmen," Jake said with a smile, "but how are we going to get there? You're not going to borrow your cousin's VW again are you?"

Teresa laughed. "What, you don't like her?"

"I'm just afraid she'll break down and leave us standing on the side of the road," Jake admitted.

"Okay, we'll take the ADO."

"What's the ADO?" Jake asked.

"It's the bus service that connects towns all over Mexico. Like your Greyhound in America."

"Oh," Jake said, a little dismayed. He'd never enjoyed traveling on Greyhound buses. They were hot, dirty and took too long to get where they were going. Maybe he should rethink his position on the VW.

"You know, you really should learn some Spanish, too. It would make your visits here much more enjoyable if you could understand what people were saying."

"Hey," he said trying to sound offended. "I managed to buy the blanket in Tulum, didn't I?"

"Yes, you did. But I happen to know that Raphael, the man you bought it from, speaks excellent English," she said laughing.

"I was hoping you didn't know that," Jake replied with a sheepish grin.

"How much did you pay for it?"

"It was marked twenty dollars, so I paid him twenty dollars. Why?"

Teresa laughed. "You never pay the price marked. In Mexico, we negotiate everything. You will have to learn that and the language also if you want to hang onto your money."

After Teresa went back to work, Jake wandered back to their hammock to take a siesta. As he lay there enjoying the dappled sunlight and the breeze, he could see visions of an old school bus with boxes tied on top and filled with people and chickens. Just like the ones he'd seen on old TV movies.

He took a deep breath and closed his eyes. He would go with Teresa on the bus, but he wasn't looking forward to it.

CHAPTER 11

On Wednesday, Jake met Teresa in the cantina for breakfast before they embarked on their adventure to Puerto Morelos. Even though he'd learned their destination was only a twenty or thirty minute drive, he still wasn't too enthused about taking the ADO, but Teresa had convinced him to give it a chance.

Under a cerulean sky with only a few marshmallow-looking clouds, they walked down Avenida Quinta, swinging Luis between them just like Jake remembered his mom and dad swinging him. He was happy. He liked the sound of the little boy's laughter and the sweet smell of his beautiful mother. Did life get any better than this?

They arrived at the bus station, bought their tickets and found an empty bench until they were called for boarding. Listening to the voice on the loudspeaker that announced the different destinations, Jake realized that Teresa was right about his need to learn the language. Without her, he'd probably end up on the wrong bus.

He listened to the people next to him talking. The Spanish language obviously moved very quickly, because he couldn't discern when one word stopped and another began. Maybe Teresa would be willing to give him some lessons.

"Come on, they're calling our bus," Teresa said, nudging him and breaking his concentration.

They boarded the bus and found their seats, Jake on one side of the aisle and Teresa and Luis on the other. He looked around, noticing the cleanliness of the ADO bus, and feeling the frigid air coming through the overhead vents. Teresa was wrong; this bus was nothing like the Greyhounds back home. Maybe this wouldn't be so bad after all, he thought.

After the bus left the station, Teresa and Luis turned their attention to the movie playing on the TV above the driver. It was a semi-recent American film that had been dubbed into Spanish. Since he'd seen the movie already, Jake let his mind wander, not surprised to find it going back to the idea of living in Mexico. You couldn't drink the water, but hey, bottled water was available everywhere. At least everywhere he'd been. The topography and weather was about the same as Florida's, so no problems there. But his friends, his business, hell, his entire life revolved around his hometown. As much as he liked being here and being with Teresa, could he really give all that up?

Twenty-five minutes later the bus pulled off the highway onto the shoulder of the road and stopped. When Teresa began collecting her things, Jake glanced out the window and back at her with a look of consternation. If this was Puerto Morelos, where the hell was the town?

She and Luis were getting off the bus so Jake followed. Once they were a few feet away from the bus, Jake turned to Teresa. "I thought we were going to Puerto Morelos," he said.

"We are, it's only about a mile down that road," she said pointing to the cross street ahead.

Jake stood there, flabbergasted. It was hotter than blue blazes and now they had to walk a mile?

"Come, it's this way," she said pulling on his arm.

What the hell, Jake thought. If she and the kid could do it, so could he. "Here, let me take your bag," he said, concerned that she was going to have to lug the bulky beach bag the whole mile.

"It's okay, I've got it," she replied.

When they got around the corner, and Jake saw one of the white passenger vans so prevalent in Playa del Carmen sitting on the side of the road, he breathed a sigh of relief. It must have been pretty loud, because Teresa turned to him and laughed.

"Did you think we were going to walk the rest of the

way?" she asked with a grin.

"Well, yeah."

"The ADO only travels the highway. The collectivo will take us the rest of the way into town," she explained.

Teresa pushed Luis and Jake inside and paid the driver. "Luis and I come up here about once a month to see Tia Carmen, but if I had to walk, I'd probably stay home."

Jake looked out the window of the van as they passed acre after acre of mangrove swamp. He wondered if the van driver knew where he was going, but he kept his mouth shut. The van pulled into town a few minutes later and let them off at the town square.

"This is it," Teresa said waving her arm to encompass a row of buildings on either side of the town square.

Directly in front of them was the Caribbean, the water a beautiful sea green color indicative of shallow water. On the left a pier jutted out into the water with all manner and color of boats bobbing in the water beside it. Jake smiled. Puerto Morelos reminded him of the pictures he'd seen of Salerno in its early days.

"It's only a small fishing village because the mangroves are protected and no building is allowed there, but lately more and more resorts are being built along the beaches up here."

Jake looked around. No Wal-Mart, no superstores, just small mom and pop places. "I like it," he said.

"Let's go see Tia Carmen," Teresa said taking Luis's hand.

They crossed the street to the row of buildings on the north side of the square and entered a small store that seemed to sell everything from groceries to boogie boards.

"This is Tia Carmen's store. She and Tio Carlos live upstairs," Teresa explained.

"Hola Marta," she said to the girl behind the counter.

"Hola Teresa."

Jake listened as Teresa and Marta talked for a minute. He didn't understand much but caught 'Tia Carmen' and assumed Teresa was asking if her aunt was home. When Marta nodded her head, he assumed that she was.

"Okay, let's go," Teresa said, taking his hand and dragging him outside and around the side of the building to a staircase leading up to the second floor.

Tia Carmen was happy to see Teresa and Luis and after giving them both hugs and kisses and rattling off some Spanish that Jake didn't understand, Luis immediately ran to another room where, from the sounds of things, he found some other kids to play with.

Tia Carmen turned to Jake, and after looking him up one side and down the other, she gave him a big hug. "I'm so happy to meet you, Jake," she said. "Teresa has told me much about you."

Jake smiled with pleasure at meeting Teresa's aunt and was relieved that she spoke English. He'd been wondering what it was going to be like sitting with two women and not being able to understand a thing they said. "It's good to meet you, too," Jake said.

"Come and sit," she said ushering them into the kitchen. "Would you like something to drink?"

Jake paused. He was thirsty, but he wasn't about to ask for a glass of water. He'd learned that lesson the hard way on his first trip south of the border. "Uh, no, thank you."

"You look thirsty. Let me get you a nice cold Modelo," she said opening the refrigerator. She popped the top on the can and set it on the table in front of him.

"Gracias," he said hesitantly.

"De nada," Tia Carmen replied.

While he drank his beer, Teresa and Tia Carmen talked a little about a lot of things and then Tia Carmen took Teresa's hands in hers and asked, "How is my brother, José Luis?"

"Papa is not well at all," she said sadly. "He seems to be slipping away right before my eyes."

Jake coughed, a dribble of beer escaping his mouth. "Uh, I'm sorry," he said when they both turned to look at him.

"Are you okay?" Teresa asked.

"I'm fine, it just went down the wrong way," he said, wiping his face with the napkin Tia Carmen handed him.

Jake looked at Teresa's aunt. It was hard to see the family resemblance between her and her brother. She was all sweet and smiles while Señor Garcia was a sour pain in the ass.

He didn't mind spending time with Teresa and her aunt, but if they were going to discuss the old man's health, Jake knew he had to go. He had to get out of there before he broke down and told Teresa the truth about her father.

"Uh, Teresa, I'm going to let you two visit while I go down to the pier and check out the fishing boats. I'll be back in a little while," Jake said getting up.

"Oh, okay, Jake," Teresa said.

"It was nice meeting you, Tia Carmen."

"And you too, Jake. I hope to see you again," she said with a wink.

While he let the two women talk, Jake took a walking tour of the small town. With the light breeze coming off the water, it was cooler here than it had been out on the highway. He walked north up the street for a few minutes, passing single family homes and a few small condos until he ran out of town, then cut over to the beach and started walking south. The beach was very flat and wide with volleyball nets strung up here and there in the soft white sand.

He passed a young man who offered to take him snorkeling, but Jake just smiled and shook his head. He looked out over the water and could see the color variations of the water as it went from pale green next to the beach and then turquoise before finally reaching the sapphire blue of deeper water. Small waves were breaking on the reef about a half mile offshore. He knew he was probably missing a great opportunity, but there was always mañana, he thought.

He made it back to the town square with its short fence of purple obelisk posts and white rails. Coconut palms in raised planters sat in front of the fence that separated the beach from Rafael Melgar Avenue and the small square. A nice looking restaurant with outdoor seating and an adjoining beach club sat just south of the small square.

He walked down to the pier, checking out the equipment on the boats. Everything he saw was at least twenty years old, but it didn't take high tech equipment to catch fish if you knew what you were doing.

He saw a fisherman in his boat near the beach south of the pier and walked down to see what he'd caught. Jake smiled as he approached and realized the fisherman was picking fish out of what appeared to be about fifty yards of gill net.

It'd been more than five years since Florida's net ban had gone into effect and as Jake stood on the beach and watched the fisherman overhaul his net, old memories of his own fishing days washed over him. His hands itched to get hold of that net and, had he been able to speak the language, he would have happily offered to help. Instead, he smiled and waved at the fisherman and then walked back up to the town square.

He did a little more exploring and found some artisan's shacks down a side street that led to the Army base south of town. He bought a braided leather bracelet for Casey and a pair of opal earrings the same green as the water on the beach for his mom.

Going north, he walked up the second street from the water, a divided street with rows of coconut palms, the bottom three feet of them painted white, and crepe myrtle in the median. He passed a few tiny mom and pop hotels interspersed with small restaurants and bars with lively Mexican music emanating from each.

Jake stopped in at one of the open air bars and ordered a beer. He liked this little town with its laid back and peaceful atmosphere and it was easy to imagine spending sun drenched lazy days here. Teresa said there were a few new hotels going up on the beach, but with the mile of protected mangrove swamp between the town and the highway, and the army base to the south, it would never be able to develop the way Playa del Carmen had. Jake wondered if the residents of Puerto Morelos knew how lucky they were.

By the time he got back to Tia Carmen's, Teresa was rounding up Luis for the trip home. Jake thanked Teresa's aunt for her hospitality and she responded by giving him a big hug and an open invitation to visit anytime.

They walked back to the town square and caught the next collectivo back to the highway. It dropped them off at the same place it had picked them up and after walking across the highway, Teresa led them into a gas station where she purchased ADO tickets for the trip back to Playa del Carmen.

Once they were onboard, Luis and Teresa settled down for a nap while Jake stared out the window, lost in the thoughts that were swirling around and around in his head.

CHAPTER 12

Jake's next few days were divided between fishing and diving with his friends in the incredibly clear blue Caribbean and spending time with Teresa and Luis. Teresa got along great with the guys, Jake knew she liked them, and he was happy to see that despite whatever reservations his friends may have had about his relationship with Teresa, they shared the feeling.

Jake was still sleeping in the hammock. Steve's snoring was more than he could take and the hammock was comfortable. Its gentle swaying reminded him of the many nights he'd spent watching his crab traps on his boat back in Florida. Luckily it hadn't rained since they'd arrived, and the balmy temperatures at night made for great sleeping weather.

He'd seen Señor Garcia heading out for an early morning swim a few more times, but Jake had ignored him. He thought it was odd that he'd never seen the old man return, but then again, he usually went back to sleep.

Except for his swimming in the pre-dawn hours, Señor Garcia continued faking ill health with his old man shuffle. He still wouldn't let Jake get close enough for a conversation, and Jake had just about given up trying.

* * *

On Friday, Jake and the guys went diving on the reef with Benito. Jake was amazed at the various species of sea life they saw. Fish in every color you could imagine as well as sea cucumbers, rays, turtles, starfish, seahorses and more coral formations than he could count. They spent most of their time checking out the underwater sights, but managed to haul in a few dozen nice sized grouper to take back to the cantina's kitchen.

After cleaning up, they went to the cantina for dinner and had just sat down at a table when Jake noticed Teresa coming out of the kitchen looking like she'd just walked out of the pages of a magazine.

She was wearing a slinky light blue dress with a draped neckline that set off her dark hair and skin and gently caressed her curves before ending just above her knees. She was talking on her cell phone as she made her way back to the bar and Jake was admiring the shape of her legs in the heels she was wearing when Steve handed him a menu and brought his attention back to the table.

They spent a few minutes deciding to order several different dishes to share. While they waited, they drank margaritas and listened to the guitarist that was playing as he wandered around the cantina. After they'd finished off their dinner and two more pitchers of margaritas, they all sat back in their chairs.

"Oh, that was good," Petey said.

"I saw something interesting while Teresa and I were in Puerto Morelos the other day," Jake said leaning forward.

"What was that?" Petey asked.

"A fisherman picking fish out of a gill net," Jake said with a smile.

"They're still using gill nets down here?" Paul asked.

"Yep," Jake said, leaning back in his chair. He glanced over at Steve and saw the scowl on his best friend's face. "What?" he asked.

"I know what you're thinking, Jake," Steve said.

"What's he thinking?" Petey asked.

"He's thinking of staying here after we go home and becoming Teresa's fisherman. The gill net is just an added incentive," Steve replied.

"Is that true, Jake?" Petey asked.

"Hey, look who's coming in, Jake," Paul said as Miguel walked up from the apartments.

"I thought he was gone," Jake said, and then recalled Teresa's shoes. He hadn't made the connection at first but now remembered what she said about only wearing shoes if she thought she was going to have to kick someone. She must have gotten a call from Elena that Miguel was back in town.

"Well, he's back now," Paul said.

"I see that. Let's just sit tight and see if Teresa wants us to do anything."

They watched as Miguel went over to the bar where Teresa was working. Jake couldn't hear what they were saying over the music, he wouldn't have understood any of it anyway, but he saw the startled look in Teresa's eyes as she slowly shook her head from side to side.

When she threw down the towel she'd been holding and stalked down the bar away from Miguel, Jake realized he'd been holding his breath and slowly let it out. She mixed up a pitcher of margaritas and put them on a tray, and then picked up a bottle of wine off the wine rack and added it to the tray.

Picking up the tray, she came out from behind the bar and headed toward the table where Jake and his friends sat. Miguel tried to grab her hand as she went by but she deftly slipped out of his grasp. Sliding the tray onto the table in front of Jake, she picked up the pitcher of margaritas and set it on the table.

"Your margaritas, Señores," she said loudly.

"Thank you," Jake said, playing along. They hadn't ordered more drinks.

"Please, please, whatever happens in the next few minutes, do not interfere," she whispered.

"Will you give me a sign if you get in trouble?" Jake asked.

"If I need you, you will know it."

"Okay, then. Muchas gracias for the margaritas."

Teresa smiled for just a second then put on her no nonsense face before she picked up the tray with the wine bottle still on it and turned around. Stalking past Miguel, she went back to the open end of the bar. Leaving the tray and wine bottle on the end of the bar, she went behind the bar and started washing glasses in the sink that was located on that end.

Jake watched Miguel as Miguel watched Teresa and noticed the cartel man getting impatient. When Miguel got up off his stool and walked farther down the bar to be near Teresa, Jake slid his chair back away from the table.

"Here it comes," Petey said as Miguel reached through the opening to grab Teresa's arm.

"Sit tight," Jake said, as she pulled away again.

"We're sitting tight, but man, this isn't easy. You know the guy is a major asshole, why are we letting him bother Teresa?" Steve asked.

"Because she asked us to," Paul reminded him.

A hush fell over the cantina as the guitarist finished his last song and started packing up. Now Jake could hear Miguel and Teresa arguing, and so could everyone else as all eyes in the cantina turned to watch the scene play out.

"What are they talking about?" Petey asked.

"Your guess is as good as mine, but whatever it is, she doesn't act like she wants anything to do with it," Jake replied quietly, keeping his eyes on Miguel and Teresa. It sounded as though their argument was escalating as they shot rapid fire Spanish at each other.

A collective gasp could be heard throughout the cantina when Miguel grabbed Teresa and pulled her violently through the open end of the bar. Wrapping his arms around her, he held her close to him as he spoke to her quietly.

Jake waited impatiently to see her response. Just as he was about to get to his feet, Teresa spit in Miguel's face and brought her knee up sharply into his groin. Jake heard the breath leave the man's body and saw his arms release Teresa as he folded at the waist, his hands searching out his injured parts.

"Oh, that had to hurt," said Paul with a grin.

They watched in amazement as Teresa reached over

and grabbed the wine bottle she'd left on the end of the bar. Swinging it with a little more gusto than was perhaps necessary, she hit Miguel in the head with it and stepped back as he collapsed on the floor in a heap at her feet.

"Holy shit, Teresa sure has got a vicious streak. Jake, you better not get her mad at you," Petey said.

At that moment, Benito and his three friends walked in. While Benito had a short conversation with Teresa, one of his friends disarmed Miguel and removed the bullets from his gun before placing it back in the cartel man's belt. Then Benito's other two friends picked up the unconscious man and hauled him out of the cantina.

As soon as they were out of sight, the murmur of voices resumed as diners went back to their conversations as if nothing out of the ordinary had happened. Moments later, someone hit the switch on the CD player and lively Mexican music began to play.

Teresa disappeared into the kitchen, and Benito turned around and walked over to the table where Jake and his friends still sat.

"Teresa said to tell you that she's going home. She needs to have a talk with her father. She'll see you in the morning."

"Is she all right?" Jake asked.

"She's okay, just a little upset."

"We would have helped her but she asked us not to," Petey said.

"It's fine. She told me and it's much better that you let us handle Miguel. He is our problem, not yours," he said before following his friends.

"Well, I guess the show's over, so how about we go down the beach and check out the señoritas?" Petey asked as he and Paul got up from the table.

"You guys go ahead. I'm going to stay here in case Teresa needs anything," Jake said. He was surprised at Teresa's violent reaction and wondered what the hell Miguel had said to her to prompt it.

Steve stood up and looked back down at Jake, shaking his head. "Man, you are getting in way too deep," he said and then turned and walked out of the cantina.

CHAPTER 13

Jake met the Boys Club in the cantina for breakfast the next morning. Today was the last full day of their vacation and he was supposed to fly back home with the guys in the morning

"So, Jake, you ready to go fishing one last time before we leave?" Steve asked.

"No, you guys go ahead. I've got some things to take care of."

"Last time," Paul urged.

"He wants to spend his last day with Teresa, he's not fooling anybody," Petey said with a grin.

"All right," Steve said, "we might try to get in some diving too, so we'll meet you back here for dinner."

"Sounds good," Jake said as his friends got up from the table. He watched them walk across the beach to meet Benito who had just pulled up in his boat.

Jake went back to the hammock to wait for Teresa, He kept an eye on her apartment, and noticed that Señor Garcia was sitting outside his place keeping an eye on Jake.

After an hour and a half with no sign of Teresa, Jake got up and walked out to the beach. He still wasn't sure if he really wanted to leave yet, but the time had come to make a decision. Leaving his flip flops in the sand next to the cantina, Jake turned south and started walking; hoping the bright sun and light breeze would clear his head.

He walked down the beach, getting his feet wet and dodging an occasional child who was playing near the water's edge. He walked past the Kool and Mamitas beach clubs, past the wide public beach and kept going. He could smell the salt in the air and see the island of Cozumel twelve miles away and all the glittering water in between.

When he got to the cruise passenger pier at the end of Constituyentes, he crossed to the other side and kept going, walking past luxury hotels and sunbathers on one side and colorful boats bobbing gently in the sparkling Caribbean on the other. While he walked, he pondered.

He didn't make it back to Las Palmas until almost dark.

* * *

After a quick shower and some fresh clothes, Jake met his friends in the cantina for dinner. They were sitting at a table for four at the end of the bar closest to the beach and were working on their second pitcher of margaritas.

"Hey, we wondered where you'd gone. Teresa said she hadn't seen you all day." Petey remarked as Jake took the last seat at the table.

"I had some things on my mind so I took a long walk. This is a great way to live, don't you think?" Jake asked, looking around for Teresa.

"I could sure do it," Paul said. "Fishing, diving, beautiful women…it's a dream come true."

"To livin' the dream," Petey said, raising his glass in a toast.

"Yeah, livin' the dream," Paul agreed, raising his glass.

"It's not a dream, it's a vacation," Steve grumbled. "It's not the same if you actually live here."

"That's probably true," Jake admitted.

They'd just ordered a huge plate of nachos and shrimp tacos when Jake noticed his friends all seemed to be staring over his shoulder.

"What?" he said as he turned to see what they were looking at.

Jake's heart practically stopped at the sight of Teresa in a tiny yellow dress that was cut low in the front and stopped about mid-thigh. She'd piled all that dark silky hair on top of her head and had a yellow flower pinned above her left ear, and, as usual, she was barefoot.

"In honor of your last night here, I thought I'd take you all out to a party my friends are having just up the beach," she said.

"That sounds like a great way to end a wonderful vacation," Steve said with a slight emphasis on 'end'. He looked over at Jake who was gaping at Teresa with his mouth open and gave him an elbow to the ribs. "Isn't that right, Jake?"

Jake tore his eyes from Teresa and looked at Steve. "Uh…Oh, yeah. Sounds like fun," he said, searching for something to say that didn't make him sound like the blithering idiot he probably looked like right now. He heard Petey and Paul trying to stifle their laughter and shot them a dirty look.

"I have a few things to do and then I will meet you back here after you finish your meal," she said with a smile at the twins.

As she began walking away, Jake jumped up from his seat and followed her.

"Teresa, can we talk for a minute?" he asked, taking her hand and leading her across the sand and away from curious ears.

"What would you like to talk about?" she asked when he'd stopped in the middle of the coconut grove.

"Teresa, why did you hit Miguel with the wine bottle?" he asked.

"You can ask me whatever else you'd like but I do not want to talk about Miguel tonight. This is your last night here and I want to share it with you, not Miguel," she replied firmly.

"But…"

"Go eat your food before it gets cold and let me finish my work," she said.

"Can we talk about this later?" he asked.

"I will see you soon," she said as she turned and walked away.

* * *

After dinner, the five of them walked several blocks up the moonlit beach and stopped at an outdoor bar. Tables and chairs were set up around a circle of sand being used as a dance floor while a live band played in the background. After being introduced to their host and Teresa's friend, Victor, they got some drinks and found a table near the dance floor.

"Would you like to dance?" Jake asked Teresa when the band started a slow number.

"I'd like that very much," she said with a smile.

He took her hand and they moved out to the empty patch of sand. Taking her in his arms, they slowly swayed to the music while gentle waves lapped the beach. Holding Teresa felt like the most natural thing in the world and as Jake looked into her chocolate brown eyes in the glow of the tiny twinkling lights from the bar, he knew he'd made the right decision.

The first song ended and another began, but neither Jake nor Teresa noticed the gap in between. Just before the second song ended, an uneasy feeling came over Jake and he looked up to see Miguel and two of his friends watching from the water's edge. His back immediately stiffened, alerting Teresa, who gave him a questioning look.

"Is everything all right?" she asked.

"With you in my arms, Teresa, everything is wonderful," he said, looking down at her and forcing himself to relax. He remembered what she'd said about not wanting to spend the night with Miguel, so he kept her back to the beach and Miguel. He felt the cartel man's eyes on them and lifted his gaze to return the stare.

Without breaking eye contact, Miguel pointed his finger at Jake as though it were a gun and pretended to fire. Then he and his friends turned away and ambled down the beach, their laughter grating in Jake's ears.

Jake looked over at their table. Petey and Paul must have found a diversion, because Steve was sitting alone. As soon as Jake caught Steve's eye, he knew his best friend had seen Miguel and everything that had just happened.

On the way back to the cantina for a nightcap, Petey and Paul prattled on like a couple of drunken magpies, but both Jake and Steve were alert the entire way, expecting Miguel and his friends to ambush them at any moment, but nothing happened.

The cantina was closed, but Teresa turned on a light and served them each a beer. "I'd stay and have a drink with you but I must go check on Luis and get some sleep. I have some early appointments in the morning, so if I don't see you before you leave, have a safe trip and come back to see me soon," she said, turning to leave.

"Thanks for your hospitality, Teresa," Paul said.

"Yeah, we had a great time," Petey added.

After Teresa was gone, Steve turned to Jake. "We should head back to the apartment and pack," he said, setting his half empty beer on the table.

"Finish your beer first. We need to talk," Jake said.

"What do you want to talk about?" Steve asked, picking up his beer.

"I'm not going home with you tomorrow," he told his friends.

"What, you're staying here?" Petey asked.

"At least for a while," Jake replied.

"Why?" Paul asked.

"It's no secret, but in case you guys haven't figured it out yet, I'm in love with Teresa," Jake confessed. "I have to stay and see if this thing between us will work out."

"If you ask me, Teresa's old man is trying to marry her off and Miguel is a prospective husband," Steve said flatly. "You're afraid that her old man will succeed, aren't you, Jake?"

"That's some of it," he admitted. He hadn't told the guys about Señor Garcia's plan to marry Teresa to a Mexican and was a little surprised that Steve had figured it out.

"Are you sure there's nothing still between Teresa and Miguel?" Steve asked.

"Who is this Miguel guy, anyway?" Petey interrupted.

"He's an old boyfriend of Teresa's that her father invited over to see her," Jake answered with a glance at Petey before turning back to Steve. "But to answer your question, Steve, Teresa said Miguel works for the cartel somewhere in another town and she doesn't want him anywhere near her or Luis."

"What, you mean a drug cartel?" Steve asked, incredulously. "Are you crazy?"

"Maybe, but…"

"What *is* this thing you seem to have about smugglers and their women?" Petey asked jokingly.

"Just lucky, I guess," Jake said with a grimace. "Look, this is not like Vanessa. Teresa is not living with a smuggler."

"I know, I was just kidding. We all love Teresa, you know that."

"Jake, Latin men aren't known for their cool tempers. Especially when it comes to their women. They'd just as soon put a knife in your back as look at you. And now you tell us that Miguel is a member of a drug cartel. Do you know what *they* do to people that piss them off?" Steve asked.

"No, do you?"

"They cut their heads off." Steve said harshly.

"I know you think my staying is a bad idea, Steve, but don't you think you're exaggerating a bit?" Jake asked.

"Not at all. Did you see the newspaper today?" Steve asked.

"What, now you can read Spanish?" Jake asked derisively.

"No, damn it," Steve said reaching over to grab a newspaper someone had left on the table behind them and throwing it down in front of Jake, "but it doesn't take a rocket scientist to understand the similarities between the English word 'decapitation' and the Spanish word 'decapitatacion'," he said angrily.

"Hey, not so loud," Petey said. "You'll wake everybody up."

Jake looked down at the newspaper. Steve was right, but he wasn't going to change his mind. He was in love with Teresa and she and Luis were worth fighting for.

"I'm staying," Jake said calmly as he looked his angry friend in the face.

"Fine," Steve snarled. "I've got to go pack." Without another word he got up from the table and stalked out of the cantina.

CHAPTER 14

After sleeping in the hammock, Jake met the guys in the cantina for breakfast.

"Listen, Jake, I'm sorry about losing my temper last night. I still think you're getting in over your head with Miguel being a cartel member and all, but I think what bothers me the most is that I won't be around to watch your back. Hell, I feel like I'm about to lose my best friend." Steve admitted.

"Hey, what are we, chopped liver?" Petey asked with facetious disdain.

Steve looked over at Petey, saw his big grin, and turned back to Jake.

"I appreciate that, Steve, but this is something I have to do," Jake replied.

"So, you're going to stay and see if the old man will come around. "Then what?" Steve asked. "You know she doesn't want to leave her father, so are you planning on moving down here and becoming an expat?"

"What's an expat?" Petey asked.

"It's short for expatriate, someone who's a citizen of one country and living in another," Paul replied.

"To answer your question, Steve, I don't know yet. But Casey has everything under control at home. Hell, since I made him manager three years ago; he's more than tripled our revenue."

"Yeah, we know all about the old people he has coming in there right after opening. Bingo, bridge and poker players. Your bar looks like an old folk's home between noon and three," Paul said.

"Casey told me those were usually the slowest hours for the bar, but not anymore. He said he got some menus from the nearby restaurants and even has food delivered for them," Petey added.

"What about your crab traps?" Steve asked. "Are you just going to leave them in the water until you decide to come home?"

"Uh, actually I made a deal with Josh to work them in exchange for whatever they bring in. I didn't want to disrupt the fish market's supply." Josh was a friend who owned the dive shop around the corner from Jake's house. "Really Steve, there's no compelling reason for me to be in Salerno right now, so at least for a few months, I'm going to stay here."

"You could use that settlement from the salvage company and live like a fat cat down here for years, couldn't you, Jake?" Petey asked.

"I guess I could, but I hadn't thought about it." Jake had told his friends the real circumstances of his father's death and about receiving the settlement from the Walsh's, but hadn't given up the secret of finding Uncle Willy's treasure. He'd never told anyone about finding it, they'd just assumed he'd given up trying, and he had. He gave up trying as soon as he found it. But that money didn't belong to him. It belonged to the people of Salerno; he was just its caretaker and the less said about that the better.

"How much was it, Jake? Have you looked yet?" Petey asked.

"No, and it doesn't matter. I just want to be with Teresa and Luis, enjoy the clean air and beautiful water, and go net fishing when I want to," Jake replied.

You're going to be Teresa's fisherman, aren't you?" Steve asked.

"Yes. While I was walking yesterday I ran across a boat for rent. I think I can make enough money fishing to pay for my room and board and stay here with Teresa."

"Does she know your plans?"

"Not yet, I haven't had the chance to tell her."

"What if she doesn't agree?"

"I think she'll agree, but if not, I'll find somewhere else to stay and go fishing anyway. Don't worry, it will all work out."

"What about Miguel?"

"After she knocked him out in the cantina the other night, Benito said Teresa went to talk to her father. Evidently Señor Garcia didn't know Miguel was involved with the cartel, so now that he does I'm hoping he'll tell Miguel to back off."

"You want us to stay, in case Miguel doesn't get the message?"

"No, but thanks. I know you guys need to get back to your jobs. Just check on Casey for me every now and then and call me if there are any problems."

"Will do," Paul said.

"Is there anything I can say to change your mind?" Steve asked.

"Steve, if I don't do this, I will kick myself in the butt for the rest of my life. For the last ten years I've dreamed about settling down and having a family. I've thought about it a lot and I want that dream to come true with Teresa."

"I guessed that's what you'd say, but just remember what happened with Vanessa. That almost got you killed."

"Speaking of Vanessa, she called. She and Patrick are coming down to Cozumel on a wedding charter in a couple of months and said they wanted to get together if I was still here." Patrick and Vanessa owned a sixty-eight foot yacht and ran charters out of Savannah, Georgia.

"You gonna do it?" Steve asked.

"Sure, why not? We're still friends. I'd like them to meet Teresa."

"I'm not so sure that's a good idea. You could have a cat fight on your hands. Maybe not physically, but emotionally. Women are jealous and possessive creatures, Jake, the sooner you learn that the better off you'll be," Steve advised.

Jake just nodded. He didn't think Teresa was either jealous or possessive and Vanessa had found what she wanted, but he didn't think arguing with Steve about it was going to change his mind.

* * *

It was almost ten-thirty by the time Teresa walked into the cantina. Wearing a pair of white Capri pants that hugged her slender legs and a little pink tank top that didn't quite cover her smooth tanned stomach, she was barefoot as usual. She looked so fresh and clean, she could have been the poster girl for vacation destinations.

"Good morning, my friends," she said, as she walked up to their table. "Are you all packed up and ready to go?"

Jake looked over at Steve for a moment.

"Uh, we just have a few more things to do, don't we guys?" Steve said, giving Petey and Paul a knowing look.

"No, I'm…" Petey said, before Steve elbowed him in the ribs. "Oh, yeah, I, uh… still need to pack my toothbrush."

"Yeah, me too," Paul added.

"We'll see you back at the apartment, Jake. Thanks for having us, Teresa," Steve said as he and the twins got up from the table.

"That's the best you could come up with; you forgot to pack your toothbrush?" Jake overheard Steve say as they walked out of the cantina.

"What's going on, Jake?" Teresa asked, having also heard Steve.

"The rest of the guys are leaving, but I'm not ready," he said, as she sat down beside him. "I thought maybe we could work out a deal. I'll fish for you...."

"Are you serious?" she interrupted eagerly.

"I am."

"Oh, Jake, that is wonderful," she said with a smile that lit up her face. "How much longer are you planning to stay?" she asked.

"I'm not sure, that depends on how things work out. Do you want me to stay?"

"Of course I do," she replied. Her tone became more serious as she added, "but I can't ask you to. It has to be your decision."

"Do you think we can work things out?"

"That depends, are you a good fisherman?" she asked, coyly.

"I like to think so," he replied.

"Then you may be staying for a long time because I think things will work out."

"I'm going to need a place to live," he hinted.

"Well I was hoping you would decide to stay, so I saved your apartment for you."

"What about your father?" Jake asked.

"He won't like it but I don't care. This is my place and I will decide who fishes for me. But you will need a boat."

"Rented one yesterday," he said. "It will be here later today."

"You rented a boat all by yourself?" she asked surprised. "Your Spanish must be getting pretty good."

"It helped that Señor Hernandez, the man that rented it to me, spoke pretty good English," Jake confessed with a laugh.

"Oh, Jake, I am so happy right now," she said with a sigh.

"Teresa, did you talk to your father about Miguel?" he asked.

"Yes, I talked to him this morning, which is why I was so late getting here."

"Teresa, what did Miguel say to you that made you knock him out with the wine bottle?"

Jake watched as the light faded from her face and the smile dissolved.

"Oh, Jake, this is such a mess. Miguel saw Papa before he came to the cantina the other night and Papa told Miguel that Luis is his son. Miguel was insisting we get married right away."

"I thought you said your old boss was Luis's father."

"I did. He is. I never slept with Miguel and he is not Luis's father… but Papa thinks he is. I never told him what happened with my boss and he knew I had gone out with Miguel. He just assumed Miguel was the father and because I could not bear to see any more disappointment in his eyes when he looked at me, I let him."

"So, if you never slept with Miguel, why does he think he's Luis' father?"

Well… that's probably because Miguel thinks we slept together."

"Why would he think that? How could he not know that?" Jake asked incredulously. He couldn't believe a guy wouldn't remember whether or not he'd made love with Teresa.

"Because I let him think we did. See, when Miguel and I went out, he got really drunk. I got him back to his place and then he started getting… uh, friendly. He wouldn't let me leave so finally I fixed him a really strong drink and told him to get in bed while I went to the bathroom. I just stayed in the bathroom until he passed out and then I went back to my place.

"The next day he called and told me he was moving to Veracruz to work with the cartel. He said he had a great time and wanted to know how it had been for me. I told him the truth. It was great. He thought I meant the sex was great, but I really meant not having sex was great. I let him think what he wanted, because if he was going to be mixed up with the cartel, I wasn't going to see him again anyway."

"Show him Luis's birth certificate. That should prove he's not the father," Jake suggested.

"I am afraid that is not the case. I had a very difficult birth, and was exhausted by the time it was over. The midwife insisted on having the paperwork filled out, so Papa did it himself. Because he didn't know about Luis' real father, he put Miguel's name on the birth certificate as the father. I didn't find out about it until it was too late to change it. I told you it was a big mess," she said, as a tear rolled down her cheek.

Jake wiped away the tear. "Did you tell your father the truth about Luis's father?" he asked softly.

"Yes, I told him everything this morning. Who Luis's father is and about the money I took from his wife to buy Las Palmas."

"What did he say?"

"Nothing. He sat in his chair with his head down and wouldn't even look at me. I could tell he was disappointed in me. He's so frail these days, I worry about him."

"I think your father will be fine," Jake told her. He hated not telling her about her father's morning swims, but he didn't want to meddle in their relationship. Besides, he'd never gain the old man's trust if he ratted him out to his daughter.

"I hope so."

"So what will you do now?" he asked.

"There is nothing to do. Elena called this morning and said Miguel went back to Veracruz. Before I hit him with the wine bottle, I told him that Luis is not his son and that I would never marry him. Hopefully, I embarrassed him so much that he will not come back."

"Will Elena call you if he does?"

"She said she would."

"Then we'll worry about it when it happens. In the meantime, would you care to have supper with me tonight?"

"Yes, I would like that very much."

"Let's find Steve and the twins. Their taxi should be here soon and I want to say goodbye," Jake said as he got up from the table and took Teresa's hand.

Outside his apartment, Steve, Petey and Paul were in the process of hauling their luggage out to the parking lot. The taxi was waiting, so they loaded their bags into the trunk, said their farewells, and kissed Teresa.

"Call me if you need anything," Steve told Jake, giving

his best friend a hug. "I'm only a phone call and a two-hour flight away."

"I'll keep in touch. Take care of Casey for me."

"You got it," Steve replied.

As the taxi pulled away, Jake put his arm around Teresa and held her close while they waved until the taxi rounded the corner. Before they turned to walk back through the gate to the resort, Jake noticed a black SUV sitting next to the curb on the other side of the street. The windows were darkly tinted and he couldn't see anyone inside, but he wondered if its presence was somehow connected with Miguel.

Pulling Teresa into an embrace, Jake kissed her long and hard.

"What was that about?" she asked when he finally released her.

"You looked like you needed a kiss," he responded lightly. And if that SUV was connected to Miguel and someone was watching them, Jake had just declared his intentions in much the same way as a dog pissing on a tree marks his territory.

Crude analogy, he thought, but the result was the same.

CHAPTER 15

After the guys left and Teresa went to work in the cantina, Jake went back to his apartment, glad to finally have the place to himself.

The apartments were simple, yet functional. A small sitting room with a picture window faced the Caribbean and contained a futon, a lamp and end table, and a small round table with two chairs. Beyond the sitting room were the bathroom and a single bedroom. Meals in the cantina were included in the price of each apartment so there were no kitchens. There were no TVs either, but most people didn't come to Mexico to hang out in their rooms and watch TV. Renovated within the last few years, the fixtures had been updated and even though the place would never see a five star rating, the accommodations were clean and inviting.

The maid had already been in to tidy up and had left a bowl of water on the table with about a hundred tiny ixora blooms floating in it. The bright red flowers added a splash of color to the room and made him smile. This was the first day of his new life and he was happy. Taking out his cell phone, he called Casey and told him about his change of plans. Casey assured him that he could handle everything at home and wished him good luck with Teresa.

Then he called his mom. She knew he was in Mexico on vacation, but he hadn't really told her much about Teresa. As the phone rang on her end, Jake knew that it was time to tell his mother he was in love.

And he did. He told her of his decision to stay in Mexico, of his deep feelings for Teresa and also his feelings for Luis, Teresa's son. He told her that he hoped to convince Teresa to marry him.

As expected, his mother wasn't overjoyed with the idea of his living in a foreign country, but she was thrilled to learn of his feelings for Teresa, and Luis as well. Before they finished talking, Jake knew his mom was on board with his plan.

He walked out to the beach to wait for Señor Hernandez, the man he'd rented the boat from. The white sand was soft under his bare feet and the light breeze felt good on his face. He turned to look up the beach then turned to look in the opposite direction before turning his gaze out over the open water.

The beach was about one hundred and fifty feet wide in front of Teresa's cantina and in the center of a crescent shaped beach close to a half mile long. Clear green water rolled gently to shore in small waves that lapped at the sand before sliding quickly back down to the sea. Just offshore the green water turned to a deep sapphire blue that stretched twelve miles to the island of Cozumel that he could see in the distance.

Señor Hernandez pulled up on the beach with the boat a few minutes later and Jake walked down to meet him. They talked for a few minutes, shook hands, and then Señor Hernandez turned and walked down the beach.

Jake turned back to look at the boat. It was a twenty-two foot V-hull with an open bow, painted red with an eight-inch wide blue stripe running down each side. A black Mercury 115 hp outboard motor mounted on the stern was connected to a red five-gallon gas tank nestled in the stern.

It was little more than a shell really, it had no electronics, no fish finder, no depth finder, not even a VHF radio, but it would do. Aft of the open bow, it had two seats mounted behind the divided console and a bench that housed a cooler and storage built a couple of feet behind them. The remaining stern area was divided horizontally by a piece of painted plywood that was cut to fit into grooves on either side of the hull and was removable simply by sliding it up out of the grooves.

The lease included a few tools in a plastic milk crate as

well as fifty yards of gill net that was piled into the stern section closest to the motor. A two-foot tall piece of PVC pipe stuck up above the gunwale in the starboard stern corner that allowed the net to be put in and brought out of the water without getting tangled in the motor's prop.

Jake felt like a kid with a new toy and couldn't wait to get started. This rig was a lot like what he'd started fishing with when he was just a boy and had inherited his great-grandfather's boat. Thoughts of his early fishing days more than twenty years ago washed over him in a wave of nostalgia and Jake smiled. He'd had so much fun back then…and his father and grandfather had been so proud of him.

Jake's thoughts were snatched back into the present when Benito laid a hand on his shoulder.

"Looks like the bottom needs a good scraping if you are going to get decent gas mileage," he remarked.

"I saw that," Jake agreed. He hadn't told Teresa's cousin about his plans to stay in Mexico and wondered if Benito would think it was a bad idea.

Benito nodded his head a few times, seeming to take in the whole situation without having to ask any questions. "I know some good places to fish, it you're interested," he said.

The two men looked into each other's eyes for a moment and then broke into laughter. Then Benito grabbed a stick and started drawing maps in the sand. A half hour later, Benito slapped Jake on the back and headed back to his shack.

Jake spent the next hour taking inventory and reorganizing things and then moved the boat to deeper water before donning his mask and snorkel and going over the side to scrape the grass and barnacles off the boat's bottom with a scraper he'd found in the milk crate.

When he was satisfied that's he'd done all he could to increase his gas mileage, he scrubbed the sides with a stiff bristle brush he'd also found in the milk crate before getting back onboard and overhauling the gill net a couple of times to check for holes. Finding the net in reasonably good shape, he then scrubbed the inside of the boat from top to bottom and rinsed it with several five-gallon buckets full of sea water to test the bilge pump.

Everything seemed to be in good working order so Jake anchored the boat back up on the beach and headed into town to find the fishing supply store Señor Hernandez had told him about.

The store was off the beaten track, meaning Playa's Fifth Avenue, but Señor Hernandez's directions were on the money and the only problem Jake had was navigating the sidewalks. He learned that walking while taking in the sights could be hazardous to your health and spent most of his time dodging tree roots and craters in the sidewalks that seemed to be the rule rather than the exception.

He returned a couple hours later with a pair of fishing boots, a heavy plastic rain suit to protect his clothes while fishing, two cast nets, a couple of rods and reels, several pairs of heavy canvas gloves and a few other odds and ends.

He met Teresa in the cantina shortly after dark. She was finished for the evening, so they found a table and ordered supper.

"I see your boat arrived. Are you ready to go fishing in the morning?" she asked.

"I believe so. I saw Benito while I was on the beach this afternoon and he told me about a few places to try in addition to the spots he's taken us to."

"You will do fine, and I will have fresh fish on my menu," she said smiling at him across the table. "Rosa and Inez are happy; they think you are a good fisherman."

Rosa and Inez were a mother and daughter duo and also the cantina's cooks. Rosa, the mother, did most of the cooking while her daughter, Inez, did the prep work and constantly cleaned up behind her mother. Jake had met them on a previous trip and was amazed at the smooth and efficient way they worked together in the busy kitchen.

"I'll try to live up to their expectations," Jake said.

"Please do," she said with a smile, "good help is hard to come by these days and Rosa and Inez are very good cooks. I would hate to lose them."

"Didn't you tell me Rosa was your aunt and Inez was your cousin?"

"Yes, they are," she laughed. "I was just playing with you. They are not going anywhere."

"Well, tell them I won't come back tomorrow until I have fish for them to cook."

"I hope you really are a good fisherman then, because I don't have to work tomorrow afternoon. It would be too bad if you had to stay out fishing all day."

"What did you have in mind?" he asked.

"It doesn't matter; just spending the afternoon with you is enough for me."

"How many fish do you need?" Jake asked with a smile.

"However many you catch before noon," she said lightly.

"It's a date, then. There's just two little problems I haven't figured out yet," he told her.

"What's that?" she asked.

"Well, the boat has a full tank of gas right now, but how do I get more when I need it? I forgot to ask Señor Hernandez and I haven't seen any marinas around here."

"Let me talk to Paco, the man that delivers propane and bottled water to the cantina. I'm sure he would be glad to deliver gas to you on his cart."

"That would be great," Jake said, remembering the strange delivery rigs he'd seen around town. From the seat back, they looked like a normal bicycle, but a platform about three feet wide and four feet long with wheels on each side had been mounted on the front to carry propane bottles or five-gallon water bottles.

"It will cost a little more than what you would pay at

the Pemex, but the convenience is worth it. You will have to buy another gas tank and leave it for Paco and decide how often you want it delivered and he will bring it down to the beach for you."

"Sign me up," Jake chuckled.

"What is your second little problem?" she asked.

"Ice. I'll need to keep the fish on ice until I get back each day."

"Is forty pounds a day enough?"

"Plenty."

"I will add another bag to the cantina's daily order."

"Sounds great," he said, looking around before giving her a quick kiss.

* * *

Over the course of the next week, Jake's life fell into a calm and peaceful routine. He net fished in the mornings, going out at daybreak to run his shot of net overboard. Even though he hadn't fished this way in years, his muscles hadn't forgotten the familiar rhythm and movements of roping in a net. And watching fish rather than crabs come over the gunnel into the boat gave him a sense of pleasure he hadn't known since the net ban. It felt good to be able to do something you loved without big brother stepping in to declare it illegal.

Occasionally he took one of Teresa's guest's out for some rod fishing in the afternoon if Benito was booked. It gave him enough money to get by on without having to hit his savings.

He spent time with Teresa either in the afternoons or evenings. She still insisted on cleaning the cantina's kitchen five nights a week, so he helped her. He liked working alongside her and even though he missed his friends, for the first time since his father died his world felt complete.

Later that week on Saturday afternoon, Jake came in from fishing. He'd taken a guest out with him and they'd been out longer than usual.

On the way to his apartment to clean up, he looked over at Señor Garcia's place. Since Teresa's father found out he hadn't gone home with his friends, Jake had rarely seen the old man or the little boy outside. He took that to mean the old man still had a burr up his butt over Jake's continued presence. Jake didn't mind that so much, but it didn't seem fair that Luis didn't get to play outside. He missed the little guy.

Jake met Teresa in the cantina a short time later. She had just taken off her apron and was turning the bar over to Juan. They found an empty table and once they had drinks and ordered their supper, Jake leaned across the table.

"I'd like you and Luis to go fishing with me tomorrow. Let Juan take over for the day."

"But Luis is only four. I don't know."

"Ever since he found out I was staying, your father has kept Luis cooped up inside. He needs to get out and fishing is fun. And four is more than old enough. I started fishing with my father as soon as I could walk."

"Papa won't like it," she said.

"It's time for your father to stop acting like a little kid. Luis acts more grown up than he does."

"I know you are right, but he is old and frail. I do not think he will live much longer, and I have disappointed him so much already."

"You can't wait until he's dead to start living your life, and Luis shouldn't have to either."

"Yes, you are right. Okay, we will go fishing with you in the morning."

"Great, tonight we can pack a picnic lunch so we can get out early."

After dinner they took a walk along the beach and wound up in their favorite hammock. Lying beside each other, they talked quietly while they looked up through the palm fronds at the clouds that were rolling in.

They felt the raindrops at the same time.

"It's raining," Jake said.

"I know," Teresa said, lying with her head on his shoulder while looking up at the sky.

"We could go to my apartment," Jake suggested.

"I like it here," she said as the light rain continued.

"Are you afraid to go into the apartment with me?" Jake asked.

"I am not afraid of you," she said, turning to look at him, "I am afraid of me."

"What do you mean?" he asked.

"You are a very good looking man and I like you very much, probably too much, and I don't think it's a good idea to be alone in a room with you and a bed. I made a promise to myself…" she said, turning her face away.

Jake put a finger on her chin and turned her face back to his, then kissed her slowly and tenderly. "You do realize we're getting soaked here," he said into her ear after breaking off the kiss. He hadn't really expected her to agree to go inside with him and wasn't disappointed at her answer. He respected her decision, but he also liked knowing she wanted him.

Teresa laughed. "You should go to bed. I have to go in anyway," she said as she rolled out of the hammock. "I have to make us some lunch for tomorrow."

"Need some help?" he asked.

She bent over to kiss him lightly. "No, I'll meet you first thing in the morning," she said.

The rain stopped as quickly as it started. Jake stayed in the hammock a few minutes longer, Teresa's laugh still ringing in his ears. He loved her laugh. The sound reminded him of the wind chimes his grandmother once had hanging on her porch. Tones that weren't too high and tinny, but sweet and pure. That was the way he thought of her. Sweet and pure.

Sure, she had a son, she wasn't a virgin, but that didn't matter. Her heart was so sweet and tender and the love she felt for her son was undeniably pure.

She also had a temper; Jake had seen it in action. He hoped the day never came when she turned that fiery Latin temper on him.

CHAPTER 16

Jake had filled up the cooler with ice and picked up the lunch Teresa had packed the night before and was waiting at the boat when Teresa and Luis came out the next morning. He smiled at the look of joy in the little boy's face as he and his mother came over the dune.

Dressed in a pair of green board shorts and a yellow tee shirt, Luis ran down the dune in his bare feet to meet Jake next to the water's edge.

"Are you really taking us fishing, Jake?" he asked.

"You bet."

"Mama said I was too little to go fishing before, but now I am big enough."

Jake ruffled his hair. "You certainly look big enough to me. But there are some rules you have to obey."

"What kind of rules?" asked Luis, cocking his head and narrowing his eyes.

"Well, I am the captain of this boat. I might need your help from time to time so whatever I tell you to do; you have to do it, okay?"

"Does Mama have to obey the rules, too?" he asked.

"Yes, she does. Anybody who gets on this boat has to follow my rules."

Luis thought for a moment. "Okay, then. Let's go."

"The first rule is you have to wear this," Jake said holding up the small life jacket he'd borrowed from Benito. "It will keep you afloat if you fall in or something."

"But I can swim, Jake," Luis protested.

"It's one of the rules, Luis. Remember what I said about obeying the rules?"

"Okay, Jake. And then we will go fishing?"

"That's the plan," Jake told the little boy as he helped Luis get the life jacket on and adjusted for a snug fit before picking him up and putting him in the boat.

"Did you bring some shoes for him, Teresa?" he asked.

"Yes, they are in here," she said as she handed him a beach bag.

"Good," he said, taking the bag and setting it in the bottom of the boat.

Turning back to Teresa, he picked her up and put her in the boat beside her son. Settling in the passenger seat with Luis on her lap, she dug around in the bag for a moment, pulled out a little pair of tennis shoes and helped Luis put them on.

Jake pushed the boat off the beach and climbed inside. Starting the motor, he put it in reverse and backed away from the beach.

They went a short distance offshore where Jake took the motor out of gear and picked up one of the cast nets.

"You catch fish with that?" Luis asked, watching carefully.

"Not exactly," Jake told him as he got the net ready to throw. "We need bait to catch big fish, and this is how we catch the bait."

"Oh," Luis said as Jake threw the net, making a perfect circle as it hit the water.

Jake started pulling in the net. "Grab one of those buckets, Luis, and get ready. I think we've got some."

The little boy jumped off his mother's lap and pulled one of the empty buckets over to the side of the boat next to Jake. As Jake pulled the net in the boat, little silver fish started dropping out of it and flopping around the bottom of the boat.

Luis took a step back and laughed as some of them flopped up on his shoes. Jake shook the net up and down, letting the lead line slap the boat floor a couple of times to shake the rest of the bait out.

"OK, let's get them in the bucket, Luis."

"I will help," Teresa said.

Jake smiled as he watched the little boy and his mother scrambling to get the wiggly little fish in the bucket as fast as they could.

Jake picked up the other bucket. Leaning over the side of the boat, he dipped it in the water and then poured the water into the bucket of fish.

"Look, they are swimming," Luis announced.

"They need water to stay alive," Jake explained.

"Can we take them home?" Luis asked.

"No, we're going to use them to catch bigger fish," Jake said.

"And we take the big fish home and eat them, right, Jake?" Luis asked.

"You get the picture, Luis. Sit back up there with your mom while I take us to one of my fishing spots."

After Teresa pulled Luis back up into her lap, Jake put the motor in gear and increased the throttle. When he had the boat up on plane, he glanced over at his passengers. Teresa had plaited her hair into a long braid, but Luis's hair was streaming in the wind. Both mother and son had hair so black that it shone with deep blue highlights under the bright morning sun.

Jake smiled at the expression on Luis's face. His little eyes were bright with curiosity and his smile stretched from ear to ear as he sat up straight in his mother's lap and peered over the bow.

A little over a mile offshore, but still within sight of the beach, Jake cut the motor and threw out the anchor. After Teresa was finished slathering Luis with sunscreen, Jake set up the rods he'd bought, and showed Luis how to bait the hooks and cast his pole.

Luis was a quick learner and by lunchtime, they'd caught a couple of mahi, three small yellow fin tuna and eight mackerel.

"You ready for a swim, Luis?" Jake asked.

"I can swim here?" he asked.

Jake looked over at Teresa and saw her nod. "Sure, why not? I think we have enough fish for today and I'm hot. Leave the life jacket on and just take your shoes off," he said peeling off his shirt and diving overboard.

When he surfaced, Jake swam over and held onto the side of the boat while Luis took his shoes off.

"Stand on that bench right there," Jake said pointing to the center bench in the boat that was level with the gunwale, "and jump on in."

Luis got up on the bench and, with arms and legs flailing, threw himself into the water, coughing and laughing as he surfaced.

"Are you coming in, Teresa?" Jake called.

"Not today," she said. "I will get our lunch ready."

Jake and Luis swam around the boat a few times before Teresa called them for lunch.

* * *

Back at the cantina, Jake tied up to the line that ran from the dune out into the water, and helped Teresa out of the boat. She waded the short distance to the beach and waited while Jake picked up Luis and carried him through the water.

Before he put the boy down next to his mother, Luis gave him a big hug and a kiss on the cheek. "I really liked fishing with you, Jake. Can we go again tomorrow?"

"That's up to your mom," Jake said, still holding the little boy and looking at Teresa.

"Let me think about it," she said. "Right now, little man, you need a bath and a nap."

Jake put Luis down and watched as he ran across the dune and through the coconut grove. He turned to Teresa. "I know you have to work tomorrow, but I really don't mind taking him fishing with me."

"I don't know…he usually stays with Papa, and Papa thinks you take up too much of my time. He's not going to like you taking Luis away from him too."

"Teresa, your father has kept him cooped up inside for days. He's a little boy and he likes being outside. If your father is no longer well enough to keep up with an active little boy, then he should see a doctor," Jake suggested.

Jake knew the old man would never agree to see a doctor; he was as healthy as a horse and didn't want his cover as a feeble old man blown. Jake wouldn't rat him out, but perhaps a little pressure to see a doctor might suddenly make him feel well enough to take Luis outside.

"Let me think about it," she said. "I need to get a shower and get Luis bathed and down for a nap. I will meet you on our hammock in a little while, okay?"

"Okay," Jake said as Teresa turned and walked away.

He went back to the boat and got the rods and cast nets. Using the hose behind the cantina, he washed the salt off them and took them back to his apartment. He took a shower and put on some clean clothes before heading out to the coconut grove.

He'd only been waiting a few minutes when he saw her coming down the stairs from her apartment carrying two Coronas. Her hair was still wet and hung loose down her back and she was wearing a camisole top with thin straps that tied on top of her shoulders and hugged her thin frame. The camisole had a scooped neckline that showed the barest hint of her breasts and ended about two inches above the top of a short denim skirt that showed off her legs. She was barefoot as usual.

She handed him one of the beers and sat down beside him. "I have been thinking about what you said."

"When?" he asked with a smile.

"A little while ago, when we were talking about Luis going fishing with you."

"And what have you decided?" he asked.

"I think you should take him fishing," she said, nodding her head.

"Really? But what about your Papa?" he asked.

"I talked to Luis while I was giving him a bath, and he said he wants to go fishing with you. I told him his grandfather would miss him and Luis said that Papa is grumpy and doesn't want to go outside anymore."

"Like I told you, I really don't mind. He's good company for such a little guy."

Teresa smiled. "After I put Luis down for his nap, I went and talked to Papa. I told him that if he wasn't feeling well I would take him to the doctor."

"What did he say?" asked Jake, holding back the grin that threatened to surface.

"He said there was no need for a doctor. He said he'd been feeling bad, but thought he was over most of it."

"Most of what?" Jake asked.

"He didn't say."

"So, your father is okay with me taking Luis fishing?" Jake asked.

"I didn't ask him. I am Luis's mother and I will decide what is best for Luis. And I have decided that with all this beautiful weather we're having, Luis should be outside. I want him to fish with you until Papa either feels better or goes to the doctor. If he is really sick, I don't want Luis to be around if something should happen to him. Is that okay with you?"

Jake smiled. If Teresa's father felt so badly that he had to stay inside, Jake would be happy to volunteer his services and take care of Luis. He liked the smart little boy, and to be honest, he was looking forward to taking him fishing again. They'd had a good time today, and depending on how stubborn Señor Garcia was, they'd have plenty of time to get to know each other better.

"Of course. Tell your father to take it easy. Luis and I will be fine."

CHAPTER 17

After Teresa had put her foot down with her father and told him that Luis would be fishing with Jake until he either went to the doctor or started feeling better, the old man had retaliated by refusing to talk to her.

For the next four days, Jake took Luis fishing. Teresa's son was smart and learned quickly and Jake enjoyed his company. He sat Luis on his lap and let him steer the boat on their way out and back from the fishing grounds. He'd bought a kid-sized pair of gloves for the boy and shown him how to pick fish from the gill net.

They'd pulled in an assortment of sea life in the net, including a starfish and a few sea horses. Jake had identified and explained each new critter and let Luis touch them before putting them back in the water.

He liked watching the curiosity and enthusiasm on the little boy's face as he made new discoveries and wondered if this was how his father had felt when he and Jake had done the same things so long ago.

Teresa took the day off on Friday to go fishing with Jake and Luis. Jake had gone into town the previous afternoon and picked up some masks and snorkels for the three of them to try after they'd caught enough fish. He'd also bought Luis a shirt that had a SPF rating of fifteen built into the fabric. He didn't want the boy's back to get burnt while they were snorkeling.

After a morning of fishing and a break for lunch, Jake took them to an area where the water was no more than ten feet deep and so clear you could see a dime on the white sandy bottom. He went a little closer to shore until he found a group of rocks on the bottom and then anchored the boat.

Teresa helped Luis change into his new shirt while Jake adjusted the child's mask to fit him. Then the three of them spent the next hour floating on the surface with their faces in the water, admiring the multitude of sea life swimming around the rocks beneath them.

Every so often, Luis would put his hand on Jake's arm and then raise his head out of the water. When Jake raised his head, Luis would ask him the names of the fish they'd just seen or what a particular kind of fish ate, or some other question that only little boys would think to ask. Jake answered his questions as best as he could, impressed with the child's desire to learn.

They returned to the cantina late that afternoon. After dropping the fish in the kitchen, they headed to Teresa's place. Señor Garcia was raking the sand in front of his apartment, leveling the hills and holes that Luis had left the last time he'd played there.

"Abuelo, do you feel better?" Luis called as he took off running toward the old man.

Jake didn't understand what the old man said in response, but he could tell from Señor Garcia's expression and the hug he gave the boy that he was glad to see his grandson.

As Jake and Teresa approached, Señor Garcia released Luis and stood up. With a glare as hot as a laser, he looked Jake straight in the eyes and held his gaze for a long moment. It was obvious to Jake that Teresa's father was none too happy about the current situation.

The silence was broken as Luis started chattering about the many things he'd seen on his snorkeling trip and the old man dropped his eyes to turn his attention back to his grandson. Taking Luis's hand, Señor Garcia led him into his apartment.

Jake noticed the old man seemed to be moving a bit quicker today and smiled. Hopefully Señor Garcia had come to his senses and decided to drop his 'old man' charade.

After cleaning up their gear and putting it away in his apartment, Jake showered before heading back to the cantina to meet Teresa. She wasn't there yet so he found a table in the corner next to the beach and ordered a pitcher of margaritas. He was well into his second drink when he saw her coming.

She moved through the room like a butterfly, stopping here and there to greet guests with a smile. She even resembled a butterfly with the flowing sleeves of her soft silky shirt.

Over a feast of fresh fish tacos, they talked about their day and Luis' first snorkeling trip. They laughed together over some of his questions and antics and Jake couldn't remember a more enjoyable evening…until the subject of Teresa's father came up. She told Jake that she and her father were on speaking terms again and that the old man had asked to keep Luis with him the following day.

Jake was disappointed, he was looking forward to taking the boy with him again, but he was glad that Teresa and her father had resolved their issues. It had never been his intention to come between the old man and his grandson or his daughter, but he wasn't going to let Señor Garcia hold Luis hostage either. The boy didn't deserve to be a pawn in his grandfather's underhanded scheme to guilt Teresa into marrying someone she didn't love.

* * *

The next morning, Jake walked through the palm grove on his way to his boat, but as soon as he hit the dune line he knew something was wrong. His boat had sunk. The bow was sitting on the sand so it was still dry, but the stern was underwater. Luckily, the water was less than three feet deep and hadn't reached the upper unit of the outboard motor.

Stripping down to his board shorts, Jake walked into the water and around the end of the boat, looking for the problem. Finding nothing obvious, he went back to his apartment for snorkel gear and returned a few moments later. Using the mask and snorkel, he swam around the boat, looking for the problem. He found it in the stern. Someone had removed the plug and left it lying on the sand next to the boat.

He picked up the plug and walked out of the water, looking up and down the beach. There were dozens of boats, but none of them was sunk. Was someone trying to tell him something, or was this just a random act of vandalism?

Whatever it was, Jake wasn't going fishing until he replaced the plug and pumped out the boat. After that, he was going to have to change out the gas tank that was currently underwater, clear out the fuel lines and dry out the battery. Providing there was no other damage, Jake was looking at the better part of an entire day to get the boat ready to go again.

He borrowed a battery from Benito and had the boat pumped out and floating by the time Teresa came down to the beach later that morning.

"Good morning," she said. "Are you having problems?"

"You could say that," Jake replied.

"Will you be going fishing?" she asked.

"Not today."

"Why not?"

Jake looked up and down the beach at all the boats bobbing in the water before answering her. "You know, these old boats always need repairs. Today seemed like a good day to get some of them done," he said with a shrug.

Until he learned otherwise, he would assume his boat's sinking was random, but he didn't want to worry Teresa if it wasn't.

* * *

Sunday morning Jake called his mother and wished her a Happy Mother's Day. Mexico's Mother's Day had been the previous Wednesday and hearing everyone wishing Teresa a Happy Mother's Day had reminded him of the opal earrings he'd bought for his mom in Puerto Morelos, so he'd gotten them packaged up and sent to her in Louisiana.

After catching up with his mom, Jake had gotten Teresa's permission to take Luis into town, and now the two of them walked hand in hand down Avenida Quinta's cobblestones.

"What are we going to buy?" Luis asked.

"I was hoping you could help me pick out something for your mom for Mother's Day."

"But Mother's Day is over and Mama is not your mother. Why do you want to get her a present?"

"Well, where I come from today is Mother's Day and a woman doesn't have to be your mother for you to give her a gift on Mother's Day. She just has to be a mother."

"Oh, I didn't know that," Luis said.

They'd walked halfway down to the ferry, stopping here and there to look in the shop windows, when Luis pulled on Jake's hand.

"Mama would like that," he said pointing a finger at a silver filigree bracelet on the other side of the glass. Unpretentious, yet elegant, it reminded Jake of Teresa herself.

"And it would look good on her. You've got pretty good taste for such a small fellow. Let's go in and check it out."

* * *

That evening, Jake and Teresa were lying together in their hammock after a late supper. She had worked the breakfast, lunch and dinner shifts and now had the rest of the night off. Jake knew she didn't usually clean the kitchen on weekends, so they had at least a few hours together.

"What did you go into town for?" she asked.

"Picked up some sunscreen for the boat," he replied. He and Luis *had* stopped at a pharmacy on their way home and bought sunscreen.

"You took Luis to get sunscreen?"

"It was a guy thing," he said and smiled.

"What are you two up to?" she asked laughing.

"We got you something," he said pulling the box out of his shorts and handing it to her.

"What is this?" she asked, obviously surprised.

"In America, today is Mother's Day. Luis asked me why I wanted to get you a gift for Mother's Day when you weren't my mother and I told him that a woman didn't have to be your mother to get a gift on Mother's Day.

"I want you to have this because you are Luis's mother and you are both very special to me," he said, watching her unwrap the package and open the box.

"Oh, Jake it's beautiful," she said as the silver glowed warmly in the moonlight.

"Not as beautiful as you," he said and kissed her.

CHAPTER 18

Jake went fishing early the next morning and had a good catch. After dropping them off in the cantina's kitchen, he took a shower and went back to the cantina for a late breakfast. He'd finished eating and was relaxing over a cup of coffee when he felt a hand on his shoulder.

"Good morning, Señor. Are you practicing your Spanish?" Teresa asked indicating the folded newspaper on the table beside him.

"Not really," he replied.

"I see you had quite a good catch today," she said, taking the chair next to him.

"Yes, I did. You should have fish on the menu for the next couple of days at least," Jake said.

"Luis asked me about going fishing with you again," she said.

"He did?"

"Yes. He wanted me to ask you if it would be okay. He has decided to be a fisherman instead of a dump truck driver when he grows up."

Jake felt a moment of pride that Luis thought he wanted to follow in his footsteps, but knew that it was just a little boy's excitement over a new activity. Whatever the reason, Jake was flattered Luis wanted to spend time with him.

"Of course it's okay. We have fun together."

"How would you feel about taking him with you two or three times a week?" she asked.

"I'd be happy to, Teresa, but won't his grandfather have something to say about that?"

"I don't care. Luis said that Papa is still grumpy and he's not having fun. He would rather have fun and I want that too. He's a little boy now and I want him to remember his childhood as being fun and interesting, not hanging around a grumpy old man and being bored."

"Then I will be happy to take him fishing whenever he wants," Jake said. He may have jumped the gun in his thinking that the old man would come around and drop the animosity toward him that was causing problems for Teresa and Luis.

"How about we start with Tuesdays and Thursdays for now? That will give him something to look forward to each week. I will tell Papa that you will have him back by lunchtime if that is okay with you," she suggested.

"That sounds fine to me," Jake said taking her hand in his. It would be nice to have a couple of mornings a week to fish with Luis. He just wasn't sure how the old man would take it.

"I don't know how to thank you, Jake. Not just for taking Luis fishing and the fish you bring us, but for everything," she said, dropping her eyes to the bracelet on her arm.

"You don't have to thank me, Teresa. I love you," he said lifting her chin gently with his finger and looking into her golden flecked brown eyes.

* * *

Tuesday morning, Jake met Teresa and Luis in the cantina. Luis was excited about going fishing and kept Jake busy answering his many questions. After a quick breakfast, Jake and Luis headed down to the boat. At the water's edge, Jake took the boy's hand and stopped him.

"Wait right here for just a minute, okay Luis. I want to check the boat over before we get going. You may want to back up a little so your shoes don't get wet," Jake said, noticing how close to the water the little boy stood.

"Okay, Jake," Luis replied as he jumped back away from the water.

Jake walked all the way around the boat, checking inside and out for any sign of a disturbance. Seeing nothing, he went back to the beach, picked up Luis and put him in the boat.

Jake smiled as he watched Luis scramble to get into his life jacket and climb up to sit in the passenger seat.

As soon as they left the beach area, Jake accelerated to get the boat on plane and then looked over at Luis. The boy's hair was swept away from his face and the smile he had on his face was at least a thousand watts.

They wiled away the hours fishing and talking, occasionally moving to a different fishing area if the fish weren't biting where they were.

Jake had never spent much time around children except when he was one, and he was amazed at the way Luis picked up on things so quickly. It was almost as though he could see the wheels turning in the boy's head as he learned something new.

They caught a nice variety of fish and then went swimming for a while before heading back to Las Palmas. As soon as Jake beached the boat, Luis jumped down from his seat and grabbed Jake's hand.

"I have been thinking that you and I should be friends, Jake," Luis said. "Mama says it is okay, but Abuelo doesn't like it."

"Did he *say* that you and I shouldn't be friends, Luis?" Jake asked.

"No, but I can tell he doesn't like you."

"Well, we *are* friends, Luis," Jake said taking the small hand in his. "Listen, son, no matter what your grandfather or anyone else says, you should listen to your mother. She knows what is best for the two of you." He didn't like the old man coming between Teresa and her son but he wouldn't stoop to the old man's level and talk trash about him.

"That's what I think, too," Luis said.

Jake got out of the boat, grabbed Luis and set him on the beach. "Let's get these fish to the kitchen and then you can go see your grandfather and have lunch," he said as he handed Luis a small bucket of fish to carry.

After a shower, Jake went to the cantina for lunch. As soon as he walked up the steps, he saw her. She'd put her long black hair up into a loose knot and was wearing a tie-dyed sundress with a smocked halter top that hugged every curve like a glove, and left her honey colored back bare. She looked like a lovely young gypsy as she worked the room to greet everyone and make sure they had everything they needed.

Jake took a seat at the bar and a few moments later, Teresa joined him.

"How was your fishing trip?" she asked.

"We had a good time and brought back some fish, too."

"Has Luis asked you about being captain yet," she asked with a smile.

"Not yet," Jake replied, "but he has decided that we're friends."

"I didn't know there was any doubt of that," she said looking a bit confused.

"Neither did I. You look fantastic, by the way. Sure you don't have some gypsy blood in you?" he asked, deliberately changing the subject.

Teresa and her father had their problems, but he wasn't going to get in the middle of them by telling her that the old man was trying to influence her son against him. That just sounded like too much sour grapes.

Since Teresa's father hadn't actually come out and told Luis not to be his friend, Jake would have to give Señor Garcia the benefit of the doubt and continue to hope the old man would eventually come around.

"If gypsies like hammocks, then I must have," Teresa replied with a seductive smile. "After you have your lunch, why don't you meet me at ours? I will be finished working by then."

They spent the rest of the afternoon and evening together, lying in their hammock and talking, and taking walks on the beach until it was time to clean the kitchen.

By the time Jake kissed her goodnight and headed back to his apartment, he'd all but forgotten about Señor Garcia.

* * *

On Wednesday, Jake left the apartment to go fishing. Since the incident with his boat sinking, he'd started checking things out more carefully before heading out. He got in the boat and looked over the interior to make sure nothing had been disturbed. Nothing jumped out at him, so he put the key in the ignition and walked back to the red gas tank sitting on the floor in the stern.

As he bent down to squeeze the ball on the fuel line to pump gas into the motor's carburetor, Jake noticed a white granular substance around the edge of the cap on the gas tank.

Reaching down to scrape some onto his finger, Jake put it up to his nose and sniffed. Then he touched his finger to his tongue.

"Shit," he said under his breath. Someone had put sugar in his gas tank. He no longer wondered whether his boat sinking was a random act of vandalism. He was sure it wasn't. And this wasn't either. He was being targeted. But why? He was only supplying fish for Teresa; he hadn't cut into the other fishermen's turf. But why else would someone want to keep him from going fishing?

Luckily, he noticed the sugar before he started the motor. Now instead of having to take the motor apart and clean the sticky gunk out of it, all he had to do was change out the gas tank. The only problem was that he didn't have any more gas and Paco wouldn't bring his delivery until Friday morning. Not wanting to worry Teresa, Jake didn't mention the sugar in his gas tank, instead telling her only that he was going to take a couple of days off to work on the boat.

After a trip to the store to buy a new gas tank for the

boat, Jake returned to Las Palmas. As he was walking past Señor Garcia's apartment carrying his purchase, he noticed Teresa's father sitting on his porch. Jake nodded his head in acknowledgment, but the old man just stared back at him.

He saw the old man's gaze drop to the gas tank he was carrying and the brief smile that crossed his features. A second later, when the old man raised his head and looked back into Jake's eyes, the smile had vanished.

With nothing else to do until Paco delivered his gas, Jake hung around Las Palmas the rest of the afternoon and the next day, doing routine maintenance on the boat and mending a few holes in his net. While he worked, he couldn't get Señor Garcia's smile and what it meant out of his head.

The old man had never been anything but blatantly rude to him ever since his second trip to Las Palmas, and after what Luis had told him about his grandfather not liking him, he doubted Señor Garcia had suddenly turned over a new leaf and decided to smile and be nice.

Running it over and over in his head, Jake finally realized that the old man had been looking at the gas tank when he'd smiled, not at him. No, it made more sense that the old fart knew what was going on with the vandalism of his boat and was happy about it. Was this something the old man had cooked up to get him to leave? Was that what this was all about?

Jake couldn't be sure, but he wouldn't put it past him.

CHAPTER 19

After receiving his gas delivery from Paco on Friday, Jake had gone fishing. He'd fished Saturday as well with no additional problems.

On Sunday, Jake, Teresa, and Luis took the ADO to Cancun where they caught the ferry to Isla de Mujeres, a tiny island about five miles east of Cancun measuring approximately five miles long and less than two miles wide.

Literally meaning Island of Women, Isla de Mujeres was an important part of the ancient Maya culture. Each year, thousands of Maya women would make a pilgrimage to the island to pray for fertility at the shrine of the goddess Ixchel.

The ferry dropped them off on the north end of the island where the only town was located. After a short walk into the center of town, they rented a golf cart and drove south to the shrine of Ixchel, where the road ended.

From there they followed the path to the southern tip of the island, a wild and windswept area with rocky cliffs soaring more than forty feet above the sparkling turquoise waters.

The soil there was dry and inhabited by only a few stunted and twisted trees, the most stubborn of scrub bushes and hundreds of iguanas. The area was also the home of a sculpture garden, the pieces of art showing signs of deterioration from the intense sun and salt air.

Heading back toward town, they stopped at Garrafon Natural Reef for some lunch and a short siesta before trying out the snorkeling and the pool. It was a very enjoyable day and Jake had to remind himself at times that Luis was not his son and Teresa was not his wife.

By the time they returned to Cancun to catch the bus back to Playa del Carmen, Luis was barely able to keep his eyes open. Five minutes after boarding the comfortable

ADO bus, he was asleep. It was nearly dark by the time they made it back to Las Palmas, so Teresa took Luis in for some supper and a bath before putting him to bed.

Jake met Teresa at their hammock an hour or so later.

"Do you think Luis will be up for fishing on Tuesday?" he asked as he slid into the hammock beside her and took one of the beers she'd brought with her.

"Oh yes," she replied. "That's all he talked about during his bath."

"Good. I like taking him with me," Jake admitted.

"What about me?" she asked. "Do you like taking me with you?"

"Teresa, darling, I will take you and Luis anywhere you want to go, whenever you want to," Jake replied seriously. "I love you both and think of the two of you as family."

"And Papa? Do you think of him the same way?" she asked.

"Uh, your Papa...honestly, no. Not so much," he said with a laugh.

Teresa laughed with him and then said, "I can't really blame you. He has made it difficult for you to like him. I'm hoping that will change, though."

"No more than I do," Jake replied.

They talked a little more and finished their drinks before Teresa kissed him long and tenderly.

"I have to go in now," she said, getting out of the hammock. "Luis is alone and I am exhausted. I need to go to bed."

"I'll see you in the morning, sweetheart," Jake said as he watched her walk away. Things were good between the two of them and now he felt like Luis was also in his corner. The only hold out was Señor Garcia and Jake was beginning to doubt the old man would ever accept him.

* * *

Jake held Luis's hand as they walked down to the boat Tuesday morning to go fishing. When they reached the water's edge, Jake picked up the little boy and waded out into the water and put him in the boat. He gave the vessel a once-over to make sure everything looked as it should, and finding nothing amiss, told Luis to put on his life jacket while Jake untied the boat.

Jake boarded the boat, checked out the gas tank and throttle cables, and then started the motor.

"Okay, Luis, hang on, here we go," he said as he moved his hand to the gear shifter. As soon as he put the boat into reverse he felt it catch, then nothing. The motor revved up as it should but the boat didn't move.

"Son of a b..," he started, before remembering Luis.

"What's wrong, Jake," Luis asked. "Why aren't we moving?"

"I think we have a problem, Luis," Jake said.

"Do you know what it is?" the boy asked.

"Yes, I'm afraid that I do, son. I believe we've just lost our prop." And unless the cotter pin that held on the nut and the prop broke, this was no accident, he said to himself. He was sure this was the third attempt to prevent him from going fishing, but he still had no idea who was doing it or why.

"You mean that thing that spins around on the back?"

"That's it exactly."

"Can you find it?"

"Probably, it's big and shiny and pretty easy to spot in this clear water. I don't think it went very far, but the problem is the nut and the pin that held it on. They're so small I might not be able to find them and without them we aren't going anywhere."

"We can't go fishing?" Luis asked with a sad face.

"I can't say for sure right now. Why don't you sit there while I tie us back up and then I'll look for the prop and see if I have an extra nut and cotter pin.'

"Okay, Jake."

Jake stripped off his shorts down to his baggies, and swung his legs over the side, dropping down into about three feet of water. He grabbed the bow line and walked the boat back over to the rope it had been tied to and retied it. Then he waded out into the water, moving slowly, and scanning right and left through the clear water to the white sand bottom. He found the prop about ten feet behind the back of the boat, but saw no sign of the cotter pin or nut.

"Well, Luis," Jake said as he waded back to the side of the boat, "I found the prop. Let's see if I have an extra nut and cotter pin in the spare parts Señor Hernandez left in the boat."

Luis waited patiently while Jake got back in the boat and started rummaging around in a box he pulled out from under the bench. He found a nut that looked the right size but no cotter pin. As he was putting the box back into the storage compartment and replacing the top, he looked up to see Teresa coming over the dune.

"Are you having problems?" she asked.

"You could say that," Jake replied. "The prop came off as soon as I put the boat in reverse. I found it and another nut to hold it on, but I need a cotter pin to hold the nut on and there isn't one in the box of spare parts."

"What are you going to do?" she asked.

"I'm going to have to go to town and buy one."

"Oh."

"Come on, Luis, we might as well get out of the boat. There's nothing we can do until we get that cotter pin," Jake said as he got back in the water and held his arms out to the little boy.

Jake put Luis down on the beach next to Teresa and ruffled his hair. "I'm sorry we can't go fishing today."

"Luis, why don't you go see your grandfather. Jake has to go to town."

"Wait just a minute, Luis," Jake said and then turned to Teresa. "He's not supposed to be back at his grandfather's until lunchtime. We may not be able to go fishing but there's no reason why he can't spend the time until then with me. Is there?"

"No. I guess not. I just thought…"

"Fine. Luis, just let me go get some shoes and you and I will go to town. If you're going to be a fisherman, you're gonna have to know how to do all this stuff and today is a good day to start learning, don't you think?"

"You bet, Jake," Luis replied smiling from ear to ear.

Luis walked back up to the cantina with his mother while Jake went back to his apartment and traded his fishing boots for a pair of sneakers.

He returned a few minutes later and he and Luis set off to the boat supply store, only to find that it was closed on Tuesdays. Since the store was open on both Saturday and Sunday, it made sense that they would close at least one day.

"What do we do now, Jake," Luis asked.

"The only other place that might carry cotter pins is a hardware store. Do you have any idea where one is?"

"No, what's hardware?"

"Nuts and bolts and things like that," Jake explained. "I guess we'll just have to look around and see if we can find one."

Heading back to Avenida Quinta, they walked south and Jake kept his eyes peeled for any store that might carry hardware. But almost all of the businesses along the pedestrian street were targeted toward tourists and not too many tourists shopped for hardware.

They finally stopped in at a store where the shopkeeper was very friendly but didn't speak much English. With Luis' help translating, the shopkeeper told them the only hardware store he knew of was several miles away and advised them to go down to the beach just north of the ferry dock and talk to the fishermen. Jake thanked the man in both English and Spanish and then he and Luis headed to the ferry dock.

From there they walked back north, Luis stopping each fisherman he saw and, Jake assumed, asking about spare boat parts. Jake actually had no idea what Luis was saying and what the fishermen were saying in return, but after about the fifth fisherman Luis talked to, the man walked over to his boat, and reaching into an old and dilapidated cardboard box, pulled out a cotter pin and showed it to Jake.

Jake looked at the pin. It looked to be the right size and in fairly decent shape. He nodded at the fisherman. "Ask him how much," Jake told Luis as he reached into his pocket for some pesos.

"No, Señor, no pesos. It is my pleasure to help you. You are Jake, right?" he asked.

"Yes."

"And you are fishing for Teresa's cantina?"

"Ah, yes…how did you know?" Jake asked.

"Benito told us all about you," he said with a sweeping arm to include all the fishermen on the beach. "He said you are one of us and to help you if you needed it. My name is Enrique Salas, but my American friends call me Henry."

"It's good to meet you, Henry," Jake said shaking his hand. He remembered his friends mentioning Benito's friend Henry who ran a poker game out of his house and was sure this was the same man.

"And this must be your partner," Henry said ruffling Luis' hair. "It's good to have a strong and able partner such as this one."

"Yes, he's been very helpful today," Jake agreed. In fact, he didn't know how he would have managed on his own with his woeful lack of Spanish.

"Well, good luck with your fishing," Henry said.

Jake looked at the tall, slender fisherman. "Do you mind if I ask you a question?" he asked after a moment.

"Not at all," Henry said with a smile.

"You… and the rest of these fishermen, ya'll don't mind that I'm fishing for Teresa? I mean, is anyone angry that I'm taking some of their business?"

Henry laughed. "Look around you Señor, we are only a few compared to the thousands of tourists eating in all these restaurants and resorts," he said motioning up the beach where hotels, cantinas and large resorts were lined up as far as you could see. "As a matter of fact, if you wanted to fish for a few other places, I can give you some contact numbers."

"Uh, thanks, but I'm not ready for that yet. I've just been having a few unexpected setbacks recently and wondered if maybe some of the other fishermen were upset."

"No, Señor, nobody here is angry with you or your fishing. Benito says you are one of us, look, you even look like one of us," he said with a big smile as he held his brown arm next to Jake's. The Mexican's skin was browner, but not much.

"Have you or any of your fellow fishermen had any problems lately with boats being vandalized?" Jake asked

"No, not that I am aware of," Henry replied. "Are you having those problems?"

"A few, but nothing really major." Jake said.

"It is probably just some kids pulling a prank," Henry surmised.

"Jake, can we go fishing now?" Luis asked, pulling on Jake's hand.

Jake looked at his watch. "I'm afraid that by the time we make it back to Las Palmas it will be time for you to go to your grandfather's for lunch. We'll go Thursday, okay?"

"Okay, Jake."

Jake turned back to Henry. "Thanks, uh, gracias, Henry."

"De nada, Señor. You're welcome."

"If you ever get up to Las Palmas, stop in. I'll buy you a beer, uh, cerveza," Jake said.

"Muchas gracias, Señor. I will do that."

Jake took Luis's hand and the two walked up the beach. On the way back to Las Palmas Jake thought about what

Henry said. He was relieved that he hadn't angered the local fishermen, but if they weren't the ones sabotaging his boat, who the hell was? And if no one else was having problems, that could only mean one thing. Someone was trying to tell him something.

But who and what?

Could this be Miguel's work? He certainly had a good reason for wanting Jake out of the way. Miguel wanted Teresa and Luis. Jake wasn't sure how far he'd go to make that happen, but sabotaging a boat seemed a little juvenile for a cartel member.

Miguel could have hired someone else to do the job, Jake thought as he began scanning all the people and boats on the beach, looking for something out of place.

Jake felt a moment of what he thought must be paranoia. It was a new and unwelcome feeling for him. Back home in Salerno, he knew the town and the people and tried to steer clear of situations that made him uneasy, but here, in a foreign country and with the language barrier…

Jake ran his free hand through his short dark hair, and told himself to relax. He had no idea what would happen next, but he couldn't let fear cloud his senses. He had to stay alert and figure out what the hell was going on and who was behind it.

CHAPTER 20

After returning from their excursion, Jake dropped the little boy off at his grandfather's apartment. Señor Garcia gave him yet another dirty look, grabbed Luis' hand and all but dragged him inside. It was obvious the old leopard hadn't changed his spots, so Jake went down to the boat and put the prop back on before heading to the cantina for lunch.

Teresa was tending bar, so Jake sat on one of the stools and talked to her while he waited for the enchiladas and nachos he'd ordered.

"Did you find the part you needed for the boat?" she asked.

"Yes, we did. But I have to tell you, I don't think I could have done it without Luis. He was a big help translating for me."

"I keep telling you to learn the language. Things will not be so hard if you do."

"I know. Maybe I'll sign up for some classes."

"They have evening classes at the school, or you can get a private tutor."

"I don't think my wallet will support a private tutor, but the school idea isn't bad."

"Here, eat your food before it gets cold," she said as a waitress set two plates on the bar in front of him.

"What time do you get off," Jake asked and then took a bite of his enchiladas.

"I have to stay until closing tonight. Juan had a family emergency so I told him I would take his shift."

"Okay. Then maybe I'll just hang around until then and help you clean the kitchen, if that's all right with you."

"I would like that very much," she said, stealing one of the nachos off his plate.

* * *

Shortly after midnight Jake walked Teresa to the bottom of the stairs to her apartment and kissed her goodnight before heading to bed. As soon as he opened the door, he knew he had a problem. The air conditioner was still running but the room was about ten degrees warmer than usual.

Walking over to the wall unit, he took the cover off and immediately recognized the problem. The condenser coil was covered in ice. Knowing the easiest way to fix it was to shut it down and let it thaw out, Jake turned it off, grabbed his pillow and the blanket he'd bought in Tulum and headed back outside to the hammock where the sound of the water and the rustling of the palm fronds lulled him to sleep.

Several hours later, he was awakened by the sounds of crunching sand and whispers coming from somewhere behind him. As stealthily as possible, he turned to look over his right shoulder. Two figures were silhouetted in the moonlight and were standing in front of the door to his apartment. Jake watched for a moment and realized one of them was trying to get the door open while the other seemed to be giving directions on how to accomplish the task.

Gently easing out of the hammock, Jake picked up his blanket and crept silently toward them. As soon as he was close enough, he threw the blanket over the first figure's head. They struggled for a moment and finally Jake clasped his hands together and brought them down in a chop across what he hoped was the back of intruder's neck. The man slumped and fell to the ground, letting out a groan as he went. The sound alerted the second intruder who dropped something on the sidewalk with a clatter and took off running like a jackrabbit.

Jake looked at the prone figure on the ground still covered in his blanket, and took off after his partner. He chased him out to the street, only to see him turning the corner a couple of blocks away. He knew he could never catch the guy so Jake took a second to catch his breath and ran back to his apartment, only to find the first intruder gone and a nasty looking knife on the sidewalk beside his blanket.

He didn't think the prowlers had gotten inside his apartment but he went in to be sure. He did a quick inventory of his fishing and snorkeling equipment and nothing seemed to be missing, Finding everything as he'd left it, he walked over to the closet in the bedroom where he'd stashed his backpack. Pulling it out he sat on the bed. Unzipping a small compartment inside it, he checked to see that the item he decided at the last moment to bring with him was still there. He let out the breath he'd been holding when he touched the small velvet box.

He thought about calling the police, but realized that he'd never seen the faces of his assailants. He guessed, but couldn't prove, they were both men, probably very young, considering how fast they could run, but other than the knife, he had no proof.

They hadn't taken anything so he returned his backpack to the closet and, taking the knife and blanket with him, locked the door behind him and went back to his hammock.

* * *

Jake walked into the cantina for breakfast the next morning carrying a folded newspaper that he put on the table beside him.

"Teresa, there's something I need to talk to you about," Jake said when she joined him.

"What is it?" she asked.

Jake looked into her eyes and hesitated. Damn, he hadn't wanted to tell her he thought he was walking around with a target on his back, but last night's incident was the last straw. Whether he wanted to tell her or not, this was her property and she had the right to know.

"Well, there's two things, actually," he said, knowing he was stalling.

"Yes?"

"My, uh, air conditioner quit working yesterday."

"Oh, I will call the repairman right now," she said, starting to get up.

"No, wait," he said, laying a hand on her arm to stop her.

She sat back down, looking at him expectantly.

"Teresa, after you went back to your apartment last night, two guys, at least I think they were guys, tried to break into my apartment. They had this," he said quietly as he moved his hand from her arm and unfolded the newspaper beside him so she could see the knife he'd found.

Her eyes widened. "Madre de Dios," she said in little more than a whisper. "What happened? Are you hurt in any way? I need to call the police," she said, rising again.

"Not yet," Jake said laying his hand back on her arm to stop her. Lowering his voice he said, "there's more. I don't know if they're related to last night's incident but I've also been having a few uh, problems with vandalism to my boat."

"What kind of problems?"

Jake quickly filled her in on the issues he'd had with the boat and his theory that he was being targeted.

"Why didn't you tell me this before?" she asked.

"I didn't want to worry you. You have enough on your plate with the cantina and your father. I don't even know if the vandalism and the attempted break-in are related. It may have been nothing more than some guys trying to rob an unsuspecting tourist. Have you had many break-ins before?"

"No, never," she replied.

"Never?" he asked. It seemed like a stretch for someone to escalate from vandalism to breaking and entering, but if she'd never had a break-in, there was only one other common denominator. Him. The incidents with the boat and the attempted break-in might not be related, but Jake's gut told him they were. Was this more of Miguel's work? He wished he'd been able to catch at least one of the intruders. Maybe then he could have found out who was behind it.

"No. Oh, Jake, I am so sorry, but you're not hurt, are you?"

"No, sweetheart, I'm fine, but I think one of the guys is going to have a hell of a headache this morning."

"Do you know who they were?" she asked and immediately answered her own question. "Of course you don't. How could you? What did they look like?"

"I don't know. I never saw their faces," Jake said and explained exactly what had happened. "Because I never saw their faces, hell, I can't even say for sure they were guys. I don't think the police will be able to do anything."

"I guess it's a good thing your air conditioner was broken or they might have gotten inside," she said with a shiver. "You know, the police may not be able to find out who did this, but I will talk to Benito and have him keep his ears open. Maybe he will be able to find these no-good, dirty rotten scoundrels," she said.

Jake laughed. "Where did you pick up that phrase?" he asked.

"I like the old movies on cable TV," she said, sheepishly. She got up from the table. "I'm going to talk to Benito now. If there's anyone in this town who can find out who did this, it's Benito."

Jake walked back to his apartment and saw Señor Garcia giving him the stink eye again. As the old man turned away, a thought popped into Jake's head. Could the old man have had something to do with all this? Teresa's father didn't like him, that was no secret, and Jake could see the old man having a hand in the boat sabotage, but would he go so far as to hire guys to break into his apartment?

And to do what? Scare him off? Kill him?

Whoa, Jake thought. He was getting ahead of himself. He had no reason to believe Señor Garcia had anything to do with it, it could very well be a plot Miguel cooked up… but he wondered.

For the first time since the Boys Club left, Jake felt vulnerable. He missed having his friends around to watch his back.

* * *

After a few days with no additional excitement, Jake settled back into a comfortable routine. The old man still continued to give him the stink eye whenever he brought Luis back from fishing, but he seemed to accept the compromise. It was obvious Señor Garcia loved his grandson and Luis loved his grandfather and neither Jake nor Teresa wanted that to change.

When Jake and Luis came back from fishing on Tuesday, Teresa was waiting with Benito. As soon as Jake helped Luis out of the boat, Teresa grabbed her son's hand. "Luis, Benito is going to take you for a ride on the jet ski. Would you like that?"

Luis's little face lit up. "Oh, yes, Mama. I have always wanted to ride on a jet ski."

"You already have your life jacket on, that's good, but just remember to do as Benito says, all right?"

"Yes, Mama," Luis replied.

Benito took Luis's hand and they headed down the beach.

"What's going on?" Jake asked as he unloaded the fish to take to the kitchen.

"Take the fish to the cantina and meet me in our hammock and I will tell you," she said curtly.

Jake could tell she was upset but didn't have a clue as to why, so he did as she'd asked. A few minutes later he found her sitting in the hammock, swinging back and forth with a vengeance.

"Teresa, what's wrong, honey?" he asked softly when he got her to slow the hammock down long enough to sit beside her.

She looked at him with fire in her eyes. "If that old man doesn't die soon, I'll kill him myself," she threatened.

"What are you talking about?"

"A little while ago, Benito told me he found those guys that sabotaged your boat and tried to break into your room. He also told me who hired them and why."

"And?" Jake asked, expectantly.

"And it was Papa," she said, bursting into tears.

"Your father hired them?" Jake asked, not really surprised but also relieved that it hadn't been the gun toting cartel member behind it all. "Why?"

"He wanted them to scare you so you'd leave."

"I see." Jake said. "How did Benito find this out?"

"He overheard some kids at a party down the beach last night bragging about what they'd done. Benito asked them what they were talking about, but they didn't want to tell him, so he slapped them around a little bit and finally got the whole story from them."

"What does your father have to say about it?"

"I haven't talked to him yet. Oh, Jake, I am just so very angry, I don't know if I can talk to him right now, but I have to because Benito will be bringing Luis back soon and I don't want him around to hear us fight."

"You want me to talk to him?" Jake asked, even though he didn't think the old man spoke English. Every time he'd heard Teresa and her father talk it had been in Spanish. Nevertheless, he had a few things he'd like to say to the person behind his problems, and even if he wasn't understood, at least he could get it off his chest.

"I will handle him," she said determinedly, wiping her face with her hands.

Jake saw the fire in her eyes and didn't feel much sympathy for Señor Garcia. The old buzzard had brought this all on himself, but he hated to see Teresa so upset.

"He's just trying to protect his family, Teresa," he said with incredibly more understanding than he felt.

"But I can't let him go around treating my guests like that," she said adamantly.

"I don't think your father sees me as a guest anymore, and I hope I'm more to you than just a guest," Jake said with a smile.

Jake saw the fire recede from her eyes, but still felt their warmth as she looked up at him.

"Oh, Jake, you are so much more to me than just a guest. I love you," she said quietly.

"I love you too, sweetheart," he said, kissing the tip of her cute little nose.

She stood up. "Thank you for helping me calm down, but I have to go do this now, before Luis comes back. I'll talk to you later," she said, and with a determined stride headed for her father's apartment.

After taking only a few steps, she turned back to him and smiled. "Oh, by the way, you stink. Go take a shower."

Jake laughed. "Yes ma'am."

He didn't get up right away; instead he watched her march over to her father's door and go inside. He wondered what was going to happen and didn't have to wait long before he heard Teresa's raised voice spewing out a string of Spanish that made him cringe. He didn't understand a single word, but it sure sounded as though Teresa was reading her father the riot act.

Uncomfortable with the feeling he was eavesdropping, even though at this distance it could hardly be considered that, Jake went to take a shower.

CHAPTER 21

For the next two weeks, Jake fished, went diving, and spent his free time with Teresa and Luis. The few times he needed something that Teresa's cantina didn't offer; he'd walked into town for some shopping.

Teresa organized a birthday party for Luis with everything from balloons to burro rides. At least ten piñatas had been strung up in the coconut orchard, blankets laid on the sand under them to catch the treats they held when Luis and his cousins managed to break them open with broomsticks.

Jake had given Luis a new fishing pole and he and the kid had been down at the beach practicing his cast every chance they could.

Jake was happy. Not only happy, but content. He missed Casey and his friends, but not enough to leave Teresa and Luis. They had become a major part of his life.

Señor Garcia was even starting to come around. Jake had never asked Teresa exactly what she'd said to her father the day she'd chewed him out, but whatever it was, it had made a difference. He'd lost more of his old man shuffle and, even though the relationship was strained, father and daughter were speaking to each other again.

Señor Garcia still wouldn't talk to Jake, but he no longer gave Jake the stink eye and went inside when Jake brought Luis home. Now each time they met he acknowledged Jake with a nod of his head. It wasn't old home week, but it was a start. Jake hadn't yet signed up for classes so his Spanish was still fairly non-existent, but he'd learned to read the old man's eyes and gestures.

On their way back from fishing Tuesday morning, Jake and Luis walked across the dune to drop their catch off in the cantina's kitchen. Before they went inside, Jake noticed Teresa, her father, and another man standing outside the old man's apartment. The visitor's back was to him, and from the way Teresa was acting, she wasn't happy to see him. Jake wondered if Miguel had returned.

He sent Luis in the kitchen with one of the fish, and stayed where he was for a minute watching the scene in front of Señor Garcia's apartment. No one was yelling or screaming yet, but he didn't know how long that would last. Still carrying the rest of the fish, Jake hurried to catch up with Luis in the kitchen.

He talked to Rosa and Inez for a minute, and then Jake picked Luis up and put him on his shoulders and carried him out of the cantina.

As they approached Señor Garcia's apartment, Jake watched the visitor until he felt the old man's eyes on him. Turning to look at Teresa's father, he saw the old man cock his head in the direction of Jake's apartment. Jake saw the warning in his eyes and with Luis still on his shoulders, veered through the coconut grove and into his apartment.

"Why did you bring me here, Jake?" Luis asked when they were inside. "Mama and Abuelo are outside, I saw them."

"Yes, I saw them too, and I'm not really sure why I brought you here, but that's what your grandfather wanted, so that's what I did."

"But I didn't hear Abuelo say anything."

"He didn't say it out loud, Luis, but I heard it anyway."

"Who was that man Mama was talking to?"

"I didn't see his face so I don't know. Let's just hang out here until she's finished talking to him."

* * *

A half hour later, Teresa knocked on Jake's door.

"Thank you for keeping an eye on Luis," she said as the boy ran over and caught her around the legs.

"No problem, what's up?" he asked, stepping outside.

"Luis," she said to her son, "Go see Abuelo and have him give you a bath. You stink."

"Okay, Mama," he said before taking off at a run.

"That was Miguel," she said, shaking her head.

"I thought so. Is he gone?"

"Yes, I saw him walking down the beach toward his mother's house."

"What did he want this time?"

"He heard Papa wanted to talk to him, so he came over."

"Did your father tell him he's not Luis's father?"

"Yes, he told him," she said quietly.

"Then what's wrong?" Jake asked as a single tear escaped down her cheek.

"Miguel didn't believe him. He wants to see Luis's birth certificate. He says if the birth certificate says he is Luis's father and I won't marry him, then he will take Luis," she said and burst into tears.

"Oh, shit, sweetheart, don't cry. We'll get this worked out," he said holding her close.

"How?" she asked, pulling away to wipe her face. "If I let him see Luis's birth certificate, it will only make things worse. He can bring in some of the police the cartel have in their pocket and take Luis away from me. There is nothing I can do to stop him."

"Maybe you should get Luis away from here for a while. If he isn't here, then Miguel can't take him. Do you know someone who can keep an eye on him until we get this straightened out?"

"But Luis is my son, he should stay with me," she said with a spark of anger.

"And if Miguel does come back with the police, what will you do then, watch them take Luis away?"

She was silent for a moment as she contemplated that visual. Losing Luis was not an option. "We can take him to Tia Carmen in Puerto Morelos. She will keep him. We will have to use your boat though; I don't want to risk being seen in the bus station."

At that moment, Jake heard a beer bottle shatter as it

hit the sidewalk near the office. He turned to look and a half second later another bottle shattered next to the first one. He could hear someone yelling in Spanish, but couldn't understand what was said.

Out of the corner of his eye, he saw Teresa's head snap around at the sound of breaking glass and immediately take off running toward the parking lot. Jake was hot on her heels.

When he turned the corner of the building, he stopped. Miguel and two other guys were trying to exit the lot in a black SUV while Teresa threw handfuls of gravel at them as fast as she could. Teresa was yelling at Miguel and it sounded to Jake like she was cussing him for the dog that he was.

Before the car left the lot, Miguel stuck his head out the window. Looking directly at Jake, he pointed his finger at him and pulled the trigger on an imaginary gun.

Teresa saw it too. As she turned back to look at Jake, the car spit gravel as it spun out of the lot. She glanced back at the car one more time and then walked over to Jake.

"I will have Papa keep Luis inside today. After it is dark, we will take him to Tia Carmen's."

Jake put a finger under Teresa's chin and tipped her head up so he could look into her eyes. "Sweetheart, considering your father's role in all of this, it's probably better if you don't tell him where we're taking Luis."

"What should I tell him then? I know he's going to ask."

"Tell him anything, tell him nothing, but don't tell him the truth. And make sure you tell Tia Carmen not to tell him either."

"But Jake, I have never lied to my father, I don't know if I can do it."

"Didn't you lie to him about who Luis's father is and about the money that paid for this place?"

"But I did not actually tell him a lie, I just let him think what he wanted."

"Call it a lie of omission or whatever you want, but Luis's safety is on the line now, and as far as I'm concerned, your father being pissed off for a while is a small price to pay for his safety."

"You are right. Luis is more important than anything."

* * *

Shortly after dark, Jake met Teresa at the foot of her apartment stairs. Señor Garcia was sitting in the chair on his porch with Luis on his lap. When the old man looked up, Jake saw the moisture in his eyes.

"Okay Luis, it's time to go," Teresa said.

"Good bye, Abuelo. I will be back soon," Luis said, jumping off his grandfather's lap and waving back at him.

Jake took the bag Teresa had packed for her son and the three of them headed through the coconut grove and over the dune. After helping Teresa and Luis onboard, Jake untied the boat and pushed it off the beach. Jumping in over the side, he started the motor and headed the fishing boat out to sea.

"Okay, Mama," Luis said, looking up at Teresa from his perch on her lap. "We are in the boat now. You said you would tell me where we are going when we were in the boat."

Teresa kissed the top of her son's head. "How would you like to stay with Tia Carmen for a few days?" she asked. "Your cousin, Alejandro, is visiting from Chetumal and would like to play with you."

"Oh, yes, Mama. I would like that very much. Are you sure Tia Carmen will let me stay?"

"Yes, little man. She thinks you will be good company for Alejandro."

"Are you and Jake staying, too?"

"No, Luis. Jake has to go fishing and I have to work at the cantina, but Tia Carmen will take good care of you."

"Okay," Luis said turning to look over the bow.

Teresa didn't say much for the rest of the ride. Jake knew she didn't like giving Luis up, even for just a few days, but a few days was a hell of a lot better than losing her son to Miguel. Luis, on the other hand, was alert with the anticipation of being away from home overnight for the first time.

Jake took the boat out about a mile and then turned north along the coast. After an hour or so, Teresa touched his arm and pointed toward shore. He turned to the west and let off the throttle as they approached, easing the boat across the shallow water above the reef. As soon as they pulled up next to the pier, Teresa jumped out and tied the boat off.

"Luis, stay here with Jake. I will be back in a minute."

Jake watched her walk up the dock and into the town square before he lost sight of her. He and Luis talked while they waited for her return.

"Your first time away from home overnight is a pretty big deal. Are you ready for it?" Jake asked.

"Of course. I am a big boy now, Mama says so. And Tia Carmen has a grandson the same age as me who wants someone to play with for a few days. I think it will be fun to have a friend to play with, don't you Jake?"

"Oh yeah, you're sure to have a great time. Just don't tell your Mama you had too good a time or she might think you didn't miss her," Jake said, with more cheer than he felt. He hoped it was only for a few days, but was afraid it could be longer.

"But I will miss her. I love Mama, but there are some things a man's just got to do, don't you think?"

Jake laughed and wondered where the little boy had picked up that line. Probably TV. He ruffled the little boy's dark hair. "I agree, Luis. There are some things a man's just got to do."

Teresa came back a few minutes later and took Luis and his bag back up to her aunt's house. Five minutes later she was back.

"What's your hurry? You hardly had time to tell Luis goodbye."

"I need to get out of here before I change my mind. Please hurry."

Jake heard the pain in her voice and immediately cast off. While Teresa sat beside him and silently cried, Jake eased back across the reef to the sea. When he was about a half mile offshore, he cut the engine.

"Come here," he said, pulling her into his arms. "You can't go back to the cantina like this."

Teresa pushed a lock of hair aside and sniffed. "I miss him already, Jake. I couldn't bear for Miguel to take him away from me."

"I know and I'll help you do whatever it takes to keep that from happening."

"Thank you, but I don't know what you can do to help me other than kill Miguel."

"Wouldn't it just be easier to have Luis's birth certificate changed?" Jake asked.

"Easier?" she asked pulling away. "It could take years to get Miguel's name off of it. But don't worry, I was just kidding about killing Miguel. I would never ask you to do something like that."

"Okay, other than killing Miguel for you, is there anything else I can do?"

"No. Papa has made such a mess of things with his meddling; it's up to me now to get this worked out," she said, wiping her eyes.

"Did he ask where you were taking Luis?"

"Yes, I knew he would."

"What did you tell him?"

"I didn't tell him the truth, but I couldn't lie to his face either," she said, sniffling.

"So what did you say?"

"Oh, Jake, I was so angry at the thought of losing Luis that I told Papa that this was all his fault and that from now on I will decide what is best for Luis and me," she said, and burst into tears again.

Jake pulled her close again. "How did that go over?"

"He cried," she said so softly Jake could barely hear her. "I've never seen my father cry, Jake, and it made my heart hurt. If it weren't for you and Luis, I would go to Tulum right now and throw myself off the cliff."

Jake's whole body started to tense in alarm, but he forced himself to relax so Teresa wouldn't feel it. It killed him to know she was so distressed and there didn't seem to be any way for him to help. He was, after all, a visitor in a foreign country and he wasn't up to speed on the laws and customs of Mexican society.

"We'll get through this, Teresa, I promise," he said, holding her tightly and rubbing her back.

"Okay, I'm ready to go back now," she said, moving out of his arms to dry her tears.

Jake hesitated a moment to let her get herself together, and then started the motor and headed back to Las Palmas. When he pulled up on the beach, Teresa jumped out of the boat and headed across the dune to the cantina while Jake tied up to the anchor line. He followed her and took a seat at the bar.

She'd managed to pull herself together and he watched as she interacted with staff and customers, greeting each with her usual smile. She was keeping it bottled up inside and Jake knew when she finally blew; it was going to be bad.

She disappeared into the kitchen for a few minutes. When she came back, she set a beer on the bar in front of him.

"Juan is taking over the bar for me. I'm going to stop in the kitchen and then I'll meet you at our hammock. I want to talk to you."

Jake took his beer and headed for the hammock, stopping by his apartment to pick up something first.

A few moments later, Teresa sat beside him on the edge of the hammock.

"I think it is best if you go home now, Jake."

"What? Why?" he asked, sitting up straight and looking at Teresa.

"I just called Tia Carmen to check on Luis and she said that Tio Carlos, her husband, called one of his friends at the Army base in Puerto Morelos and told them they could find Miguel in Playa del Carmen. The Army can't control the cartel in Veracruz and the border towns, but they don't want them expanding to the tourist areas. Things might get ugly and I don't want to involve you."

"Believe me, Teresa, I am already involved. I love you and Luis and I'm not going anywhere. I've been trying to find the right time and the right place for this, and I know this is neither, but," he said as he took the velvet box out of his pocket and held it out to her, "Teresa, will you marry me?"

CHAPTER 22

"Oh, Jake, you can't be serious," she said looking at the small black box, but not taking it.

"Why can't I?" he asked.

"Because it would never work. Your life is in Florida and mine is here. I can't ask you to give that up."

"You aren't the one doing the asking. I am, and my life is wherever I want it to be. I want it to be here with you and Luis. I love you both."

"What about Papa?"

"Well, he's a little harder to love, but I'm trying," Jake said with a smile.

"That's not what I meant," she said, with a ghost of a smile.

"I know. I just wanted to see you smile again."

"What about your business and your home?" she asked.

"Casey can take care of both. I'll need to go back to get my business affairs in order at some point, but I'll come back."

"You would give up your home and life for me and Luis?" she asked quietly.

"You and Luis are my life now, and home is wherever you are," he said holding the box in front of her. "If you and Luis won't come to Florida with me, then you better marry me so I don't get deported. You do love me, don't you?"

"Yes, I do. That's why I don't want you involved in this mess with Miguel. Jake, I don't know what he will do if the Army shows up to arrest him. You saw him pretend to shoot you in the parking lot earlier. If he thinks you had something to do with this, he might send someone to kill you. The cartel has a reputation for horrible violence in dealing with people that cross them."

"I won't leave you here to deal with this alone. Luis told me tonight that a man's gotta do what a man's gotta do, and this is something I gotta do."

"And if you wind up dead, what will I do then?" she asked, tears rolling down her cheeks.

"That won't happen," he said pulling her close. "We'll get through this together."

"I'm sorry, Jake. But I cannot marry you now," she said shaking her head. "I love you, and someday I hope you will ask me again, but until this thing with Miguel is over and I know Luis is safe, I can't think about anything else."

Jake reluctantly put the box back in his pocket. He was disappointed, sure, but at least she hadn't turned him down flat. He knew this was a bad time for her and he probably shouldn't have heaped anymore onto her plate. He just felt like he could protect her and Luis better if he and Teresa were married and living together.

Teresa may have been kidding about killing Miguel, but his death would certainly be the quickest way to resolve their problems. He supposed he could call the man out, Jake was pretty sure he could take the little prick, but expecting Miguel to show up alone was wishful thinking. Every time he'd seen the guy, he'd had reinforcements nearby and Jake was pretty sure they were all armed to the teeth.

Jake had no gun, all he had was the knife he'd picked up after chasing away Señor Garcia's hired thugs, and he knew from past experience that taking a knife to a gun fight was not a brilliant move. But somehow, he had to find a way to neutralize the young Mexican's threats.

"We'll handle this Teresa. Whatever it takes, we will get Luis back home where he belongs," he said, pulling her into the hammock to lie beside him. They lay there quietly for some time, lost in their own thoughts, her head resting on his chest and his hand gently caressing her shoulder as they listened to the music spilling out of the cantina.

They stayed in the hammock together until the cantina

closed and the staff had all gone home. Jake tried to convince Teresa to take the night off from cleaning and relax, but she'd said she wouldn't be able to relax until Luis was home where he belonged.

In the kitchen, Jake watched her attack the floors with a bucket and mop, slinging water as she went as though she were trying to wash Miguel's dirt out of her life. He knew she was worried about Luis, he was too, but he was even more worried about Teresa and felt powerless to help her. After the kitchen was spotless, Teresa said she still had too much nervous energy to sleep, so Jake took her back to their hammock.

Under the canopy of coconut palms, they lay quietly together, each lost in their own thoughts while they watched the stars peeking through the softly rustling fronds and listened to the sounds of the gentle waves lapping at the shore.

After a while, they slept.

* * *

Jake woke up when he heard a shout on the beach. Lifting only his head so as not to wake Teresa, he looked across the coconut grove and saw a group of armed soldiers walking down the beach.

"Teresa," he said gently, "we've got company."

"What," she asked sleepily.

"Be still, the Army is on the beach."

"Right now?" she asked, lifting her head.

"Yes."

"Stay here, please. I want to talk to them. Maybe it is Tio Carlos' friend," she said getting up and running her fingers through her hair to remove the tangles.

She walked across the dune and stopped to talk to the soldiers. A few minutes later, she came back.

"Yes, it was Carlos' friend. He said they are looking for Miguel and that they will be up and down the beach all day. He gave me his cell phone number and said to call if we see Miguel or his friends."

"That's good," Jake said, "Maybe Miguel will get the message and go back to Veracruz to stay."

"Let's hope so. He also said that until they catch Miguel, I should stay away from Tia Carmen's and Luis, in case Miguel is having us watched."

"What did you say?"

"I told him that I would try it for a little while but he had better find Miguel soon, or I would kill him myself. Okay, get up now. You need to go fishing and I need to take a shower and go to work."

"I may be a little late getting back today. I've got some errands I want to take care of," he said as she pulled on his hand to help him up.

"I will be here," she said, giving him a quick kiss before letting go of his hand and walking away.

* * *

After Jake returned from fishing he took a shower and walked down to Benito's shack. Teresa's cousin was sitting in a lawn chair under a wide blue umbrella drinking a beer. As Jake approached, Benito grabbed another chair and pulled it under the umbrella next to his.

"Jake, mi amigo, come and join me."

"Thanks, Benito, don't mind if I do."

Benito pulled another beer out of the cooler next to him and handed it to Jake. "What can I do for you?" he asked. "I know you're not here for a fishing charter, you have probably had enough fishing for today, no?"

"Yeah, I'm done fishing for the day, but there was something else I was hoping you could help me with."

"What's that, my friend?" Benito asked, his eyes following two young women in bikinis walking by in front of them.

Jake lowered his voice. "I was hoping you might be able to help me find a gun."

Benito turned quickly to look at Jake, the bikinis

immediately forgotten. "What kind of gun?"

"Nothing fancy, maybe a .38. Something small so I can carry it on me."

"Is this about Miguel or are you planning to shoot my uncle?" he asked. "Never mind, don't tell me, they both deserve it."

"Sounds like Teresa is keeping you in the loop," Jake observed.

"Si. She also told me that you asked her to marry you," Benito said with a sly grin.

"I guess word travels fast around here. Did she tell you she turned me down?" Jake asked after taking a sip of his beer.

Benito's smile disappeared. "Si, but that is only because she is worried about Luis."

"So am I, that's why I want a gun."

"Jake, my friend, the Mexican government frowns upon private citizens owning guns. I can try to find one for you, but I can't guarantee that I will. But I must tell you, if I do find one, it will be very expensive."

"I don't care about the cost. I care about Teresa and Luis."

"I know you do, you are a good man. Teresa and Luis need a good man like you in their lives."

"I appreciate that, Benito."

"Okay, I will see if I can find you a gun, but you have to promise me something."

"What's that, Benito?"

"If I get one for you, you have to promise me that you will shoot both Miguel and my lazy Tio José Luis," he said laughing.

"I'm not sure Teresa would like that," Jake said with a smile.

"You are right, I am only kidding. I don't want you to shoot my uncle, but you may have to if you want to marry Teresa."

"I hope it doesn't come to that, Benito," Jake said.

"Okay, I will see what I can do."

"Oh, there's one other thing," Jake said.

"Yes?"

"You know that tattoo on Miguel's arm?"

"His cartel badge, yes, I know it."

"Let me know if you see any more of those walking around here." Because Benito was always looking for tourists that would pay him to take them fishing or diving, Jake knew he paid attention to everyone walking past his shack. With his shack being so close to the cantina, he might see a problem before anyone else.

"Jake, men like Miguel are like roaches. They prefer to do their running around after dark, but if I see any of them, I will let you know."

"Thanks, Benito, I appreciate it. Oh and please don't say anything to Teresa about this," Jake said.

"I won't. She has enough on her mind without worrying about her crazy gringo boyfriend going to jail for illegal weapons."

Jake walked back to the cantina with horror stories of Mexican prisons running through his mind.

CHAPTER 23

More than a week passed with no sign of Miguel or his men. The Army patrols had been up and down the beach each day, talking to the locals and trying to find him, but so far had been unsuccessful.

Business in the cantina had been good and Jake went fishing each morning to supply the steadily increasing demand for fish. Teresa had settled into a schedule of working mornings and evenings, so they usually had the afternoons to spend together.

Jake was worried about Teresa. Even though she talked to Luis every day on the phone, her eyes had lost their golden sparkle and she was losing weight that she couldn't afford to lose. She wasn't sleeping well, so most nights they spent together on the hammock, talking until they drifted off to sleep and waking up when the Army patrol came through.

On Friday, at Teresa's request, Jake took one of her guests out fishing in the afternoon. He didn't get back to Las Palmas until almost dark. After a hot shower to get rid of the fishy smell, Jake went to the cantina. Seeing Teresa behind the bar, he took a seat at the end closest to the beach and watched her as she worked.

Being separated from Luis for the past week had been hard on her, but she seemed to possess an inner strength Jake thought was amazing as he watched her smile and talk to people as though nothing was wrong.

Jake noticed a young Mexican woman at the cantina's entrance, looking around like she was lost. She looked familiar but he couldn't place her. She saw Jake looking at her and flashed him a quick smile before turning her attention farther down the bar where Teresa was washing glasses.

She walked over to Teresa and the two women talked

quietly in Spanish for a minute or two before Teresa brought her over to meet Jake.

"Jake, I'd like you to meet my friend, Elena. We saw her when we went to Tulum, remember?"

"Yes, I remember. It's nice to meet you," he said smiling.

"I remember you too," she said, "Teresa has told me so much about you."

"Elena said that Miguel is very angry about the Army looking for him. She overheard him talking about bribing someone to get the Army pulled out of Playa del Carmen."

"That is right. You must be careful, Teresa, my brother is not the nice man he used to be. The cartel has turned him into a vicious, hateful person. You should think about taking Luis away for a while until Miguel finds another target for his anger."

"Sounds like good advice to me," Jake said, looking pointedly at Teresa.

"I must go now," Elena said. "I left my husband with our children and told him I would only be a few minutes. Take care, mi amiga," she said, walking back to the beach.

"What now?" Jake asked Teresa.

"I guess we hope no one will take his bribe."

"Do you think that's possible?" he asked.

"No," she said, and walked away.

* * *

The next morning, Jake looked for the Army patrol, but they were nowhere to be found. It appeared that Miguel had been successful in finding someone high enough in the Army to bribe after all.

He went fishing, but only because Teresa insisted. Without the presence of the Army patrols, it was only a matter of time before Miguel returned and he was worried about leaving her alone. He hoped Benito was right about the roaches only coming out at night.

Jake was back and cleaned up by noon. He had

convinced Teresa to join him for lunch in the cantina and was working his way through a plate of chicken and rice while she pushed her salad around her plate when Benito joined them.

"Hola, Benito," she said with a smile that didn't quite reach her eyes. "Do you want some lunch?" she asked.

"Si," he said pulling up a chair. "Maybe some fish tacos, if you have them," he said grinning at Jake.

"We have the best and freshest fish tacos on the whole Riviera Maya, thanks to Jake," Teresa boasted. "Let me get them," she said, rising out of her chair.

"Make them to go, por favor. I have to get back to my shack."

As soon as she disappeared into the kitchen, Benito turned to Jake. "I am sorry, my friend, but I cannot find a gun for you anywhere. I have asked all over town and if anyone has one, they are not willing to give it up. I told you they were hard to come by," he said.

"What's hard to come by," Teresa asked, walking back up to the table and sitting down.

"Where's my fish tacos?" Benito asked.

"They're coming, you know it takes a few minutes for Rosa to put them together. So, what's hard to come by?" she asked looking at Jake.

"Uh…."Jake began

"Just some, uh, hardware, for his boat," Benito interrupted.

"Oh," she said, picking up her fork and pushing her salad around again.

"Well, thanks for looking for me, Benito. I guess I'll have to get that hardware somewhere else."

"Good luck, my friend," Benito said as Inez walked up with a bag of food and handed it to him. "Adios."

* * *

In the cantina that evening for dinner, Jake noticed a tall Mexican man drinking a beer and smoking a cigarette at one of the tables on the edge of the deck.

Several things about the man struck Jake as odd. Usually people came out in groups or at least pairs, but this guy was alone. And with the temperature in the mid-eighties, he was wearing a long sleeved shirt. He had also positioned himself facing the bar where Teresa was working and seemed to be watching her intently.

Jake watched him as he watched Teresa.

"Do you know that guy?" he asked Teresa when she brought him the food he'd ordered.

"No, I don't think so."

"Has he said anything to you or done anything?"

"No, I feel his eyes on me, but he hasn't bothered me in any way. I must go now, I have drinks to make."

Jake ate his dinner but kept an eye on the stranger. When the man stubbed out his third cigarette and began rolling up his sleeves to beat the heat, Jake recognized the tattoo on his arm. It was the same tattoo Miguel had. The roaches had come out of hiding.

When Teresa came to clear his table, Jake told her about seeing the tattoo. She took another quick glance at the stranger.

"I can't be sure, but he might have been one of the men in the car with Miguel the day they were breaking bottles on the sidewalk," she whispered.

Jake hung out in the cantina the rest of the evening and so did the man with the tattoo. Jake was afraid he might try to make trouble for Teresa and wanted to make sure that didn't happen.

When Teresa called last call, the man got up and turned to face Jake. Jake rose up out of his seat and the two men stared at each other for a moment. Jake slid his hand around to his back while lifting his chin and looking down his nose at the Mexican, the invitation clear in his eyes.

He pretended to be reaching for a gun, but that's all it was, pretending. He knew right then that somehow or another he needed to get hold of a real gun.

Miguel's friend got the message and smiled. He held his hand out like a gun and pulled the imaginary trigger before turning and walking out of the cantina.

Jake followed him out to the beach to make sure he was actually leaving and not just hanging out around the corner. He watched the man amble down the beach until he was out of sight and then pulled out his cell phone and made a call.

"Vanessa, this is Jake," he said when she answered. "Are you and Patrick still coming down to Cozumel?" he asked.

"Yes. We're leaving tomorrow and should be there a week from today, why?'

"Well, I've got a little situation here that I could use some help with," he told her.

"What kind of help?" she asked. "Jake, you're not in some kind of trouble with the Mexican government, are you?"

"No, nothing like that, but I'm a little short on a particular kind of equipment and I was wondering if you and Patrick could bring me what I need."

"Sure, what is it?" she asked.

"Well, I need to borrow a gun," Jake said. Anticipating her response, he moved the phone away from his ear.

"A what?" she screamed.

"A gun," Jake replied, putting the phone back to his ear.

"Jake, what's going on down there? What the hell do you need a gun for?"

"I'll tell you when you get here; you do still have one, don't you?"

"Of course, but it's a pistol. Have you ever used a pistol before?"

"Not really, I'm more of a shotgun man, but they're just point and shoot, right."

"Basically. But if you're planning on hitting anything, you'll need to be pretty close," she advised.

"I'll worry about that when the time comes. Just bring it with you, please.'

"Okay, Jake, but I wish you'd tell me what's going on."

"Thanks, Vanessa, I'll be in touch," Jake said and hung up.

CHAPTER 24

Teresa took the day off on Sunday so Jake took her to Puerto Morelos to visit Luis. It had been two weeks since she'd seen her son and even though she talked to him daily on the phone, she was anxious to be with him.

Once again they went by boat and, just in case someone was watching them, Jake loaded up some fishing poles to make it look like they were just going fishing.

They made the trip with no problems and spent the day with Luis and Tia Carmen, returning to the cantina shortly after dark.

The next evening, Teresa's Cantina was visited by a different tall Mexican who came in alone and watched Teresa. Expecting trouble, Jake had taken up residence on a stool at the end of the bar where he could monitor activities around the room. Once again, all the stranger did was smoke cigarettes and drink a few beers while he watched Teresa. At closing time, the man got up, pointed his imaginary gun at Jake and pulled the trigger. Then he walked out of the cantina and headed down the beach to town.

Tuesday evening, Jake was on his stool at the end of the bar when a third Mexican man came in. His nerves on alert, Jake noticed him immediately and had a feeling he was another of Miguel's henchmen sent to watch Teresa.

Jake expected that this guy would do the same thing as the first two and wondered how many more friends Miguel had. So far, including Miguel, the count was up to four. Teresa had called Carlos' army friend to report their presence on the beach, but so far no one had responded.

Jake kept his eye on the man as he watched Teresa. When Teresa called last call a few hours later, the man stood up and walked to the cantina's steps. He turned and looked at Jake. Just as Miguel and his two other friends had done, he made an imaginary gun with his hand and smiled as he pulled the trigger. Then he turned and began walking down the beach.

After closing Jake and Teresa were cleaning the kitchen. "Have you heard anything more from Carlos about the Army returning?" he asked.

"Not yet, and I'm beginning to wonder if I will. I think Miguel bribed someone above Carlos' friend to send them somewhere else."

"Well, I hope you have Benito and his friends on speed dial. Miguel is giving you a show of force and hoping you'll back down."

"What do you mean, 'show of force'?" she asked.

"He's sent three different men here to watch you. He wants you to know there are more of them than there are of us. They also have guns and we don't."

"What should we do?" she asked.

"I think you should go to Tia Carmen's and stay with Luis."

"But I can't leave, who will run the cantina?"

"Juan can do it."

"I don't know, Jake. I have never left the cantina in anyone's hands for more than a few hours."

"I'm afraid you're in danger, sweetheart, and I don't want anything to happen to you."

"Let's see what happens in the next few days. That will give me time to make sure Juan can handle everything."

"All right, but the sooner the better."

* * *

It rained hard all the next day and into the evening. Jake was hanging out with Teresa in an almost empty cantina, waiting to see if another of Miguel's men would show up. Just after dark, she told him she was turning over the bar to Juan and going home for the night.

Jake dashed through the rain with her and waited until she was inside before returning to the cantina. He was relieved she had decided to go home; he didn't want her around if Miguel decided to put in a personal appearance.

He waited until Juan closed the cantina at ten, but none of the cartel members came in, so he went back to his apartment.

Getting ready for bed, he picked up a book and tried to read but the words blurred while his mind chewed on the problem of Miguel. All he could think of to do was confront the man and tell him to leave Teresa and her son alone, but he was sure that would only serve to piss off both Miguel and Teresa.

He needed to convince Teresa to go stay with Luis at her aunt's house in Puerto Morelos where she'd be safe if things got nasty. And Jake had a feeling things were going to get nasty.

His last coherent thought before falling asleep was to do whatever it took to get Teresa to go to her aunt's tomorrow.

* * *

Jake was awakened in the early hours of the morning by someone pounding on his door. Jumping out of bed, he ran to the door and opened it.

Señor Garcia was standing on the porch dripping with rain and bleeding from a cut on his head.

"What's wrong?" Jake asked.

"Teresa is gone," he said, a note of desperation in his voice.

"You speak English?" Jake asked, astounded, but still groggy.

"Si, not so good, but si," the old man nodded.

"Wait a minute. Teresa's gone?" he asked, as the meaning of Señor Garcia's words sunk in.

"Miguel has her and won't give her back until he gets Luis."

Panic like nothing he'd ever felt before grabbed his heart. Wearing only the boxers he'd been sleeping in, he raced past Teresa's father and into the pouring rain. Running up the stairs to her apartment, he noticed the open door swaying in the breeze while rain soaked the rug just inside it.

Knowing she would have never left her door open, his heart sank. Making a quick check inside, he ran out to the parking lot. Finding nothing out of the ordinary, he ran out to the beach. Seeing no one there either, he stood on the dune and ran his hand through his short dark hair.

"Oh hell, old man, what have you done now?" Jake asked under his breath. Señor Garcia had proven he was devious and manipulative. Had Teresa actually been kidnapped? Or was this something else the old man had cooked up to get rid of him?

CHAPTER 25

"This is my fault," Jake heard the old man say right behind him.

Jake jumped, startled at the sound; he hadn't heard Señor Garcia walk up.

Turning to face him, Jake took in the old man's disheveled appearance. Wearing only a pair of baggy swim trunks, he looked as though he was dressed for his early morning swim. His gray hair was plastered to his head as the rain poured off him, washing the blood from the wound in his forehead in rivulets of pink that ran down his cheek.

"Why?" Jake asked. "Did you have something to do with this?"

"No, no, Señor. I swear to you, I did not want this. Teresa is my daughter, I love her and I would never want to see her hurt," the old man said pointedly. "Please, Señor, help me get my daughter back."

Jake looked down into Señor Garcia's brown eyes and for the first time he didn't see the animosity that usually shot from them. What he did see was fear, and even though the whole situation was the old man's fault, Jake felt his loss. It tempered the anger he felt for Teresa's father for putting his daughter and grandson in this situation in the first place.

"I need some clothes and some coffee and then I want you to tell me everything that happened. Meet me in the cantina in ten minutes," Jake told the old man as he walked through the rain back to his apartment. By the time Jake had dressed and gone back to the cantina to make coffee, it had stopped raining.

Before the coffee was finished, Señor Garcia arrived. He'd cleaned up, put a bandage on the cut on his head and was dressed in khaki pants and one of those loose Mexican shirts that he always wore. Jake noticed that he no longer walked like a feeble old man. His stride was strong and he held himself erect as he walked over and took a seat at the bar.

Jake put a cup of coffee on the bar in front of Señor Garcia and sat down beside him with his own cup.

"Start at the beginning and tell me what happened."

"I was getting ready to go swimming when I heard noises coming from upstairs. When I went to check it out, I saw three men on the stairs, and one of them had Teresa over his shoulder.

"They told me I could have Teresa back when Miguel got Luis. I tried to stop them, but one of them hit me in the head with his gun and knocked me out. When I woke up they were gone.

"Señor, I know this is my fault and I am sorry, but you have to help me get my daughter back," he said. "Teresa told me that you know the situation and why we cannot call the police, we will have to get her back ourselves."

"I have every intention of getting Teresa back, but I want you to promise me something."

"Anything, if it will get Teresa and Luis back home."

"I want you to promise me that when this is over and Teresa and Luis are home, you will give us your blessing and let us get married."

"That's what you've wanted all along, isn't it? You want to take her away from me. I told Teresa that's why you keep coming back," Señor Garcia said, angrily.

"I've told her that I would stay if she married me," Jake told him.

The old man cut his eyes at Jake, and Jake could tell he didn't believe him.

"We will talk about that later. Right now, we must get her back. You should call Benito and have him and his friends see if they can track down Miguel and Teresa," Señor Garcia said as he started to get up from the table.

"He's your nephew .Why don't you call him?"

"Benito despises me. He would do anything for Teresa, but he won't even take a phone call from me."

"Considering the way you treat her, I can't say as I blame him."

Señor Garcia gave Jake one of his stink eye looks, but said nothing. He picked up the phone, found Benito's number, placed the call and handed the phone to Jake.

Jake talked to Benito for a few minutes, and then hung up. "Benito said he'd contact his friends and they would ask around to see if they can find Miguel. He'll call as soon as he knows anything."

"I can't just sit here. I will go find her," the old man said turning to leave.

"No," Jake said, reaching out to stop him. "You need to stay here in case someone tries to contact you. It's important to find out where he's keeping Teresa. Then maybe we can come up with a way to get her back before they know we're coming."

"If Miguel hurts her, I will kill him," the old man said.

Jake had no doubt that Señor Garcia was serious. He felt exactly the same way. "If Miguel hurts Teresa, we will kill him together."

When the staff started arriving, Señor Garcia announced that Teresa was out of town for a few days and while she was gone Juan was in charge.

Jake watched the growing activity in the cantina without actually seeing it. His mind was completely occupied as it ran through scenario after scenario of possible rescue situations, trying to picture what they'd need to free the woman he loved. He knew he was wasting his time; there was no way to know what they'd need until they found out where Miguel was keeping Teresa, but it kept his mind busy.

Knowing there was no way he could even think about fishing, he walked back to the kitchen and told Rosa and Inez not to expect any fish today. Going back to his stool at the bar, Jake waited. His body was still but his mind was going a mile a minute.

Señor Garcia said Miguel wanted to trade Luis for Teresa, but there had been no mention of when or where. He assumed that Miguel would contact them at some point to arrange an exchange, but Jake knew they needed more than that, they needed to find out where he was keeping Teresa and take her away from him, because there was no way he was giving Luis to Miguel.

Later that morning, he called Steve.

"Oh shit," Steve said when Jake told him Miguel had kidnapped Teresa and wouldn't release her until he had Luis. "What are you going to do?"

"Well, I'm damn sure not going to give him Luis," Jake replied.

"Of course not. But how are you going to get Teresa back?"

"I won't know that until I find out where they're keeping her, but I've got Benito scouring the town for information as we speak."

"You want me and the guys to come down there?" Steve asked.

"And what, tell me again how stupid it was for me to stay here?" Jake snapped. "You were against it from the beginning, and now it's my fault this has happened."

"That's not entirely true, Jake. I think most of the fault falls on Señor Garcia for bringing Miguel into the picture in the first place."

"But he wouldn't have done that if I'd just gone home with you guys."

"I tried to warn you, Jake. I ..."

"Look Steve, I don't want to hear 'I told you so' right now. I've got to get her back," Jake said, hanging up at the same time Benito walked up.

Benito had no news then or the several other times he came in during the day. Jake gave him his cell phone number, but by the time the cantina closed for the night, they still had no idea where Miguel was holding Teresa.

* * *

Jake rolled out of the hammock as the sun started its ascent over the horizon. He'd lain there most of the night, still running possible rescue scenarios through his head and hadn't slept a wink.

As he had the day before, Jake cleaned up and went to the cantina. He made a pot of coffee and took a cup with him as he went out to check his boat. He wouldn't be going fishing today either, he wanted to be around in case Benito and his friends came up with something or Miguel contacted Señor Garcia.

Late that afternoon Jake was still waiting when he saw Elena, Miguel's sister, come into the cantina. He knew Teresa and Elena had rekindled their old friendship lately, but he also was well aware that Elena was Miguel's sister.

Had Elena been serious about wanting friendship or had she been involved in Teresa's kidnapping? Maybe Miguel had sent her with information about the exchange. Jake watched her as she stood on the edge of the deck and looked around the cantina.

He saw recognition in her eyes as they came to rest on him for just a second before moving on. Whoever she was looking for, it wasn't him.

She stood there a moment or two longer, her eyes checking out each table and staff member. Turning to look at Jake again, she walked over to the bar and sat down beside him.

"Where is Teresa? I need to talk to her."

"She's not here. I thought you would've known that."

"What are you talking about? Why would I come to see her if I knew she wasn't here? Where is she?" Elena asked, obviously worried.

Jake noticed her concern. It seemed genuine, but was it really?

"Your brother and his friends kidnapped her two nights ago."

"He what?" she said with a look of shock on her face,

then immediately started talking in rapid fire Spanish. Jake wasn't sure, but it sounded like she was chewing her brother a new ass.

"Madre de Dios. Jake, do you know if she is okay?"

"No. Nobody has seen or heard from either of them since it happened. Do you have any idea where he would have taken her?"

"No, I heard he was in town, but I haven't seen him lately. That's why I'm here. I wanted to warn Teresa that he was back. I called many times, but she never answered. I was afraid something like this might happen."

"What do you mean?"

"Miguel was very happy when he came home telling us that he had a son. He said he wanted to raise him to follow in his footsteps as a member of the cartel. But after Teresa said she wouldn't marry him, he was very, very angry and said he was going to take the boy anyway. Miguel is a hot head. He wasn't always like this, but since he became involved with the cartel, he's changed. He likes the power he feels when everyone is afraid of him and his friends."

"If he's not staying at your mom's place, do you have any idea where I might find him or where he might be keeping her?" he asked again.

"No, I'm sorry. Miguel doesn't really have friends in Playa anymore. They don't want to be around him because of his involvement with the cartel. My mother doesn't even want him around but she's afraid of him and won't tell him. But he has a place in Merida, and likes to hang out at a cantina near there. I think it is called El Diablo. I only know that he lives within walking distance of it because he is always talking about staggering home in the early morning hours."

"Well, if you hear anything, anything at all, please call the cantina. Do you have the number?"

"Yes, I have it. If I learn anything I will let you know. I want Teresa back too, she's my friend."

"But Miguel is your brother. Are you willing to betray

your brother?"

"Miguel is not my brother anymore. He is someone else. My brother died a long time ago," she said sadly and walked away.

Jake stared out at the water, Elena's words about Miguel's plans for Luis bouncing around in his head. He knew he could never let that happen. Whatever he had to do, he would make sure that Miguel never got his hands on that little boy.

CHAPTER 26

After placing a call to Benito, Jake went to the old man's apartment. Just before knocking on the door, he looked through the plate glass window in the front and saw the old man sitting in his recliner with a bottle of tequila in one hand and a shot glass in the other.

Señor Garcia noticed Jake and waved him in with the hand that held a now empty shot glass. Motioning for Jake to sit down, the old man poured another shot while Jake looked around. The place was a little over furnished, but neat as a pin, something Jake liked.

"What is it?" the old man asked. "Has Benito found Miguel?"

"No, Benito is still looking but I think you and I need to go to Merida. Miguel's sister, Elena, was just here and told me that Miguel has a home there. He could be keeping Teresa there."

The old man struggled to sit forward in his chair. "I will go to Merida and you will stay here and wait for word from Miguel," he slurred.

Jake looked at the bottle of Don Julio. It was more than half empty and it was obvious the old man had been working on it most of the day. There was no way he was going to let Teresa's father go to Merida by himself and possibly do something to jeopardize Teresa's return. Hell, he wasn't even sure the old man could get there on his own. But he also knew he needed Teresa's father to do any translating that might be needed.

"Lay off the sauce, old man. First thing in the morning, we'll rent a car and go to Merida. Benito will stay here and wait for word from Miguel."

"Do you even know where Merida is?" the old man snarled.

"No, but I'll find it," Jake replied.

"It would be easier and much cheaper to take the ADO," Señor Garcia slurred.

"Fine. We'll take the ADO," Jake conceded impatiently. Having been around a bar all his life, he knew there was nothing worse than trying to talk to a drunk.

"How are we going to find Miguel in Merida?" Señor Garcia asked. "It is a large city, larger than Playa del Carmen."

"Elena told me the name of the bar where he likes to hang out and she said he lives very close to it. We'll stake the place out to see if he shows up. If he does, we'll follow him home when he leaves and see if that's where he's holding Teresa."

"How do you know he will go to the bar tomorrow night?"

"Seriously? Tomorrow's Saturday. I haven't seen a self-respecting Mexican man yet that didn't get drunk on Saturday night."

"And if we find him and follow him home, then what?"

"We wait until he passes out and then we go in and get Teresa."

"How about we just kill Miguel? That would take care of everything."

Like father like daughter, Jake thought wryly. "Do you have a gun?" he asked Señor Garcia.

"Yes."

"Seriously?" Jake asked, sitting forward in his chair. This was the best news he'd heard all week. "Where is it?"

"It's in the bedroom, but I have no bullets."

"An empty gun won't do us much good," Jake said, his spirits sinking. "And it's probably not a good idea to go around shooting people anyway," he admitted.

"The cartel does."

"The cartel is another problem, but killing Miguel is not the answer. How do you know the cartel won't try to get even and take us all out?"

Señor Garcia didn't answer. He was lost in thought and

so was Jake. He didn't know if his plan would work, hell, he didn't even know that Miguel had taken Teresa to Merida, but he couldn't sit here if there was any chance she was there.

Señor Garcia finally came out of his reverie and waved the tequila bottle over the shot glass and poured himself another one. "You know, I haven't been to Merida since Wilma ran away."

"Who's Wilma?"

"Teresa's mother."

"Why did she run away? Teresa said you hated her for it and I can't say I blame you. I can't imagine any mother leaving her child like that. Did you do something to drive her away?" Jake asked bluntly. The old man had opened the door to more of Teresa's history and Jake wanted to know what was behind it.

Señor Garcia shot forward in his chair and snapped his head up to look Jake in the eye. "I don't hate Teresa's mother. I hate that she needed more than I could give her." He slumped back into the recliner. "That's what drove her away," he grumbled.

"What do you mean?"

"What do you want, a history lesson?" the old man asked angrily as he looked back up at Jake.

"Yes, as a matter of fact, I do," Jake replied, staring the old man down.

"Will this help get my daughter back?"

"Maybe, maybe not," Jake said, "but it can't hurt."

"Okay, then I will give you a history lesson." He paused as though to put his thoughts in order, and then began. "You see, I met Wilma back in the sixties when she was very young. I owned a farm in the country south of Merida that produced henequen and chicle. When synthetics were invented and took the place of my crops in the rope and chewing gum industries, I was in danger of losing my farm.

"Then I met Ernesto Cortez Santiago, a man from

Valladolid, Spain who was buying up much of the land bordering my farm to start a cattle ranch. We made a deal and because the ranch was so remote and there was plenty of room in the hacienda, Ernesto and his daughter, Wilma, moved in with me. Wilma was headstrong and independent and her father hoped a life in the country would settle her down.

"She was beautiful with long dark hair and pale blue eyes inherited from her European ancestors, and I fell in love with her, and she with me, or so I thought. Her father didn't like our relationship, but we married anyway. And then Teresa came along. I thought everything was wonderful. I had a beautiful wife, a beautiful daughter and the ranch was doing well.

"The only thing I didn't like was how much time I had to spend away from my family. But Señor Santiago had more money invested in the partnership so he was the boss and I was the foreman. And I can tell you, the foreman spends most of his time on the back of a horse or at auctions.

"And then it all started falling apart," he said wistfully. "I would come home from a week on the range and she wouldn't be there. Her father told me she had gotten into the habit of leaving Teresa with the nanny and spending most of her evenings in Merida enjoying the nightlife. He said Wilma wasn't happy living in the country and missed the excitement the city had to offer.

"Then one day when Teresa was four, I came home from an auction and she was gone. Her father said she had run off to Miami with a rich American."

"And you haven't heard from her since?" Jake asked.

"No. After a month or so, Señor Santiago started talking about sending Teresa to a boarding school in Spain. I had just lost my wife, I wasn't about to lose my daughter too, so I gave him what he wanted most, my hacienda, and he gave me one hundred thousand pesos.

"That's only about eight grand in today's prices.

Sounds like you got robbed."

"Yes, but it was all he would give me and I needed to get away, so I took Teresa and moved to Playa. There I bought two cars and began a taxi service. I hired Miguel's father, Raul, to drive the second taxi and we became friends. His wife, Sophia, would watch the children while Raul and I were working."

"Did you ever tell Teresa where her mother was?" Jake asked. He was sure Teresa would have gone looking for her mother if she knew the woman was only two hours away, but yet she had never mentioned it.

"No, I was afraid that she would want to try to find her and Wilma had already abandoned her once. I wanted to make sure it never happened again."

"Instead you've done everything in your power to keep her here. That whole old and frail act you had going on was a guilt trip you put on her to keep her here," Jake said bluntly.

"Teresa is all I have left of Wilma and I will continue to do everything in my power to keep her and my grandson here," the old man said obstinately.

"Then be ready to catch the first bus to Merida in the morning. I won't wait for you," Jake said as he walked out the door.

CHAPTER 27

Early the next morning Jake found the old man waiting for him in the cantina. They each had a quick cup of coffee and then headed to the bus station. They bought tickets on the eight a.m. bus that would get them into Merida around noon.

After leaving the city the bus took a divided toll road and headed west. As he'd come to appreciate, the bus was cool, clean and comfortable and came with the requisite American movie dubbed into Spanish, but the trip seemed never-ending as Jake stared out the bus's front window at the narrow strip of asphalt running between two walls of green scrub for as far as he could see.

Except for a few cell towers and the occasional dirt road they passed over, there was no visible development out here. No towns, no streetlights, not even a power line for miles and miles. Golden Rain trees with their beautiful array of yellow flowers like the one his grandmother had once had in her yard seemed to grow wild next to the roadway. It looked a lot like inland Florida except for the absence of pine trees.

To pass the time and help curb his anxiety, Jake ran scenario after scenario through his mind of how best to get Teresa back. He asked Señor Garcia questions about Merida and hoped the old man's recollections were still accurate after twenty-six years.

By the time they reached the bus station in Merida, Jake and Señor Garcia had reached an unspoken truce. Both knew the other wanted to get Teresa back and would do whatever was necessary to achieve that goal.

* * *

"Okay, where are we going," Señor Garcia asked as

soon as they were off the bus and headed out the exit

"We have to find a bar called El Diablo. Elena said she didn't know exactly where it was, but Miguel hangs out there and lives within walking distance."

There were several taxis just outside the bus station so they hired one to take them to El Diablo. Jake let Señor Garcia do all the talking with the taxi driver who seemed to be a veritable fountain of information as long as you could understand Spanish. He got the abridged version in English from the old man during short pauses in the conversation.

The taxi driver told them that El Diablo would not open for several hours but he would take them to it so they would know where it was. Then he would take them to his brother's cantina which was only a few blocks away near the Plaza Grande where they could get something to eat and drink.

After driving by El Diablo, Jake paid careful attention to the route the driver took to the Plaza Grande and was pleased that it actually was only a few blocks away. They would have more than enough time to get something to eat and still walk the few blocks back to El Diablo to begin their stakeout when the bar opened.

Traffic travels around all four sides of the main town square called Plaza Grande and shops, restaurants, cantinas and more shoe stores than Jake had ever seen in such a small area lined the sidewalks across the streets along three sides. The fourth side was home to a very large, very old, pink church. The sidewalks were narrow and full of people, but Jake thought they seemed to be in better shape than the ones in Playa.

Despite the ninety-plus degree heat, the Plaza Grande was teeming with people. They were traversing the park on their way to somewhere else, or sitting on benches under the trees that lined its perimeter, hoping to get a break from the unrelenting sun.

The driver took them to a little open-air cantina called

El Parillo which was located just off the square. Jake paid him and included a nice tip and the driver gave him a card that Señor Garcia said was good for two free drinks in El Parillo.

They went inside and were seated at a table near the street. After the waiter took their order and Señor Garcia left to go to the restroom, Jake leaned back in his chair and took in the heart of the old colonial city with its magnificent churches, old world hotels and theaters. Horse drawn carriages vied for space among the many cars that traveled the intricately patterned cobblestone streets. It was a beautiful old city but, man, was it hot.

The waiter came back with drinks and a basket of chips and salsa. Without thinking about it, Jake took a chip from the basket, dipped it into the salsa and took a bite. It tasted good until the burn started. His eyes watered, blurring his vision until he could barely locate a napkin to wipe them. When he could finally see again, he grabbed his beer and took a long swallow.

He didn't notice her until she had already passed by, but she was wearing a backless red sundress with a full skirt, a pair of white heels and a wide-brimmed white hat that shaded her face from the midday sun. She swung a shopping bag in each hand as she walked away from him toward the square.

Jake was momentarily mesmerized by the swinging packages. As he stared at the woman, he realized that she was the same size and build as Teresa. She had the same long black hair and her back and shoulders were the same honey color. And she moved with the same fluid grace as Teresa.

He continued to watch her, noticing the way she nodded and smiled at the people she passed. When she shifted the package in her left hand to her right hand and flicked her long black hair off her shoulder, Jake felt butterflies in his stomach. If he didn't know better, he would swear she was Teresa. Except that Miguel had

Teresa. He was probably just imagining the similarities between the woman in the red dress and Teresa.

She must have felt his eyes boring a hole in her back because she turned around for just a moment and looked in his direction before turning back and crossing into the square. At least that's what he thought. Behind the hat and the oversize sunglasses she wore, he really couldn't see much of her face, let alone tell where she was looking.

Jake started to rise out of his chair to go talk to her when he felt a hand on his shoulder. He turned his gaze away from the woman to see Señor Garcia.

"Here is our food, now," the old man said with the waiter at his side.

"Look at that woman over there, I swear she looks and walks just like Teresa," Jake said as he pointed in the direction he'd last seen the woman in the red dress.

"Where?" Señor Garcia asked as he jerked his head to look where Jake was pointing.

Jake dropped his arm as his gaze scanned the plaza. Between statuary, bushes and trees, there were a lot of obstructions and he didn't see her anywhere. "She's gone. She was right there a second ago."

"Do you really think it could have been my Teresa?" the old man asked.

"No, that's impossible. This woman was walking like she didn't have a care in the world. No, Miguel has Teresa and we have to get her back."

Both men were hungry and the smell of food became more important than an attractive woman who was probably out for a shopping trip. They made short order of the tacos and tamales they'd ordered, washing them down with a couple of cervezas.

When they were finished they headed back to El Diablo. After a quick check to make sure the bar still wasn't open, they wandered the streets near it, looking for any sign of Miguel or the black SUV he was last seen in.

While he kept his eyes peeled for Miguel's black SUV,

Jake noticed the dozens of old VW Beetles still on the road and running well. They sounded much better than they looked as most were in desperate need of body work and paint.

He also noticed that the Mexicans seemed to be big believers in the mixed-use concept of land development. Multi-storied buildings might have business on the ground floor and apartments or offices in the upper floors. Parking was facilitated by the many surface lots scattered around each block.

Jake's stride was long and swift, but the old man stayed on his heels with no trouble at all. As they turned the corner into yet another crowded street, Jake stopped in his tracks when he literally ran into someone walking around the corner from the opposite direction.

He felt the whoosh of breath on his face and saw the woman begin to fall. His hands reached out automatically and grabbed her arms just as Señor Garcia stumbled into his back. He managed to avert the woman's fall but the force of the old man's weight pushed Jake forward until he was chest to chest with her and he was forced to grab her around the waist.

The old man fell on his ass, but Jake managed to keep both he and the woman upright. A fleeting thought that he might help his future father-in-law up off the ground crossed his mind, but he ignored it.

All he could do was stare down into the face of the woman he held in his arms.

CHAPTER 28

"You," Jake said, more to himself than to the woman in the red dress as he dropped his hands and took a step back. "I, uh, saw you walking into the square earlier." He noticed she was no longer carrying any packages.

Taking a step forward, she removed her sunglasses and smiled up at him. Stunned and momentarily speechless, all Jake could do was stare. When he'd seen her walk past the cantina earlier he'd noticed the similarities to Teresa in her appearance and carriage, but looking at her up close, Jake was amazed at the resemblance. Except for her light blue eyes, this woman could easily have been Teresa's older sister if she'd had one.

"Madre de Dios," Señor Garcia said once he'd regained his footing and moved out from behind Jake. He stopped in his tracks and stared at the woman, his mouth dropping open as the color left his face. "No es possible," he muttered, grabbing Jake's arm for support as he shook his head back and forth, his eyes never leaving her face.

Several moments of silence passed as the woman in the red dress and Señor Garcia stared at each other and Jake looked from one to the other.

"Wilma?" Señor Garcia finally asked.

"Jośe Luis?"

A moment of disbelief passed through the three of them as they all looked at each other. Then Wilma's gaze turned back to rest on Señor Garcia's. Jake saw her eyes narrow a moment before she hauled off and slapped him across the face.

Jake was dumbfounded for a moment but even more so a moment later when Señor Garcia slapped her back and she immediately slapped him again.

When Señor Garcia started to draw back to return the second slap, Jake grabbed his arm.

"Hey, what are you doing?" he asked as he pulled the old man back.

"This, this…puta," the old man sputtered, "deserted her family."

"What are you talking about, you old pendejo?" Wilma asked angrily as she rubbed the red spot on her face.

"You left your daughter and your husband and ran off to Miami with a gringo," Señor Garcia shot back.

"I most certainly did not," Wilma said indignantly. "Who told you that?"

"Your father. He was as angry at you as I was."

"That's funny," she said. "He told me you took Teresa and moved to Chetumal with some chica."

"That's a lie," the old man retorted.

Señor Garcia and Wilma looked at each other for a long moment as each other's words sunk in.

"Are you saying he lied to me?" Señor Garcia asked.

"Yes, and he obviously lied to me, too. Do you know how many weeks I spent in Chetumal looking for you?"

"If you didn't go to Miami with a gringo, then where did you go?" the old man asked.

"I did go to Miami, but it was Miami University of Ohio. I went to get a degree in business administration and my father was well aware of that as he paid the tuition. When I came back, you and Teresa were gone."

"But why didn't you tell me you wanted to go back to school?" Señor Garcia asked, plaintively.

"I did tell you, many times. But you just dismissed it as though what I wanted didn't matter. Finally, I just went."

"You should have told me how important it was to you; you should have made me listen."

"And when would that have happened?" she asked with disdain. "You were gone most of the time and when you were home you were so wrapped up in those cows, you never heard a word I said."

"But your father said…"

"My father would have said anything to break us up,"

she said. "All he wanted was your ranch, and you sold out and let him have it."

"He was threatening to send Teresa to a boarding school in Spain. I had already lost you; I wasn't going to lose my daughter."

"She's OUR daughter," Wilma reminded him. "And where is Teresa. I want to see her."

"She's uh…"

"Sorry to break up old home week," Jake interrupted, "but your daughter," he said looking at Señor Garcia. "and your daughter," he said looking at Wilma, "is in trouble and we don't have all day to stand around chatting about the past. Ya'll figure it out on your own time."

Jake turned and started walking back toward El Diablo. He wanted to make sure he got back before the bar opened. He'd only gotten a few steps when Wilma rushed up behind him and grabbed his arm and turned him to face her.

"Who are you and what do you mean about Teresa being in trouble? What has happened?" she asked.

"I'm Jake Arnold and I am in love with your daughter," he said by way of an introduction.

Wilma stuck out her hand and took Jake's. "I am Wilma Santiago," she said holding onto his hand. "Where is my daughter?"

"Teresa has been kidnapped by a member of one of the drug cartels who has a home here, so we came to get her back."

"Madre de Dios, how could you let this happen?" Wilma said as she turned and smacked Señor Garcia with her purse.

"I didn't know he was a cartel member. I was just trying to find Teresa a husband."

"Why would you do that when this handsome young man has professed his love for her? Is there something wrong with him?" she asked with a gleam in her eye, looking Jake up and down like he was a side of beef and it was close to supper time.

"Just that he is a gringo and will take her away," the old man admitted.

"We can worry about that when we get her back. Where is this scumball's house? I will go with you."

"We don't know. We just know that he hangs out at a bar called El Diablo and lives within walking distance of it."

"I know El Diablo. Let's go," she said, turning back to Señor Garcia.

"It's not a place for women," Señor Garcia said.

"It's the twenty-first century, you old fart, women can go anywhere," she retorted.

"I can see you haven't changed," her husband said, shaking his head.

"And you haven't either," she shot back.

"Knock it off and let's go," Jake said. "I want to get back there before it opens."

"Follow me," Wilma said. "I know a shortcut."

They followed Wilma as she wove her way through the narrow streets and back alleys. Jake had just about decided she was lost when she abruptly stopped.

"Okay, if you look around the corner you can see El Diablo. What do we do now?" she asked.

Jake peered around the corner. Wilma was right, but it appeared that they had missed the cantina's opening. El Diablo's front door was propped open to catch the light breeze and as he watched several men walked inside.

"We wait and see if Miguel goes in. If he does, then we wait until he leaves and follow him home to see if that's where he's holding Teresa."

"But that could take the rest of the day and most of the night," Wilma cried with dismay. "We should just go in there. You look like a big strong man. If he's there you can drag him out and make him tell you where Teresa is. If not, we can ask some questions and find out where he is."

"Well, I could probably drag him out if he's there, but

I'd probably get shot in the process. He's armed and so are the three other guys that usually travel with him. And he knows both of us. No, our best bet is to keep the element of surprise and find him before he finds us," Jake said.

"Fine, then I will go in," Wilma replied.

"You can't go in there," Señor Garcia said, appalled. "Madre de Dios, it is the lowest kind of place there is. The cartel's men hang out in there."

"So what?" she retorted.

"But you don't even know what he looks like," the old man argued.

"Maybe not, but I know the bartender," she said lightly. "What is this slimeball's name?"

"Miguel Ruiz," Jake replied. He was desperate to get Teresa back and his patience was running thin, If Teresa's mother could help, he wouldn't stop her.

Wilma turned and walked toward El Diablo, turning back to give them a smile just before she walked through the door.

At the sight of her smile, Jake's stomach began churning with regret. His lunch was making him nauseous and his anxiety level was through the roof as he watched the darkness inside El Diablo swallow Wilma up a few feet inside the door.

He shouldn't have let her go in there alone. He hadn't intended to get her involved, hell, he hadn't even known she was in the country, and now he'd just let her walk into the lion's den. If anything happened to her in there, he'd never be able to face Teresa or her father again.

If he ever saw Teresa again.

CHAPTER 29

When Wilma walked out of El Diablo a few minutes later, Jake let go of the breath he hadn't realized he'd been holding.

"Angela said he hasn't been in town for days and isn't expected for another week," she said when she reached them.

"Who's Angela?" Jake asked.

"She's the bartender and a friend."

"Is she sure?" Señor Garcia asked.

"I wish you could learn to accept that not all women are idiots and need to be controlled by a man," she responded disgustedly. "Of course, she's sure. You don't work in a place like that as long as Angela has and not know what's going on in your patrons lives."

"How do you know her? Is this how you are still spending your evenings?" he asked, remembering her father's words.

"No, you old fool. She is an old friend and my yoga partner. We have a class every Wednesday night and then go out and eat something fattening and talk. And those evenings you're talking about? I was taking night classes at the high school here to get ready for college."

"Okay, you two knock it off. We need to get back to Las Palmas," said Jake.

"Why?" Wilma asked.

"Because if Miguel's not keeping Teresa here, we need to go back to where it all started. Unless you have another suggestion?"

"No, but I am going with you," Wilma said. "Where is your car?"

"We don't have one," Señor Garcia said. "We came on the bus."

"Don't tell me you were planning to use the ADO for

your getaway," she said shaking her head.

"No, I have a reservation for a rental car for the trip back. I'm supposed to pick it up at five o'clock," Jake replied, not sure exactly how he felt about Wilma going back to Las Palmas with them. She was Teresa's mother and had a right to be there but she was also headstrong and impulsive and not at all inconspicuous.

He'd seen the appreciative looks she'd gotten from every man under the age of ninety they passed on the street. He didn't blame them, Wilma was a beautiful woman, but he didn't think that would help get Teresa back. And her bulldozer attitude could only get in the way.

"You won't need it. Come with me. We will take my truck," she said as she grabbed Señor Garcia's arm and took off down the street.

Without pissing off both of Teresa's parents, there was no good way to keep Wilma from going with them, so Jake followed the couple, keeping his mouth shut while the two argued, but urging them along every now and then with a wave of his hand. If Miguel wasn't keeping Teresa in Merida, he had to find out where the hell he *was* keeping her.

"Where is this Las Palmas?" Wilma asked as she led them into one of the surface lots not too far from the plaza and unlocked the doors of a brand new cherry red Chevy pick-up truck with a keyless remote.

"It's in Playa del Carmen, but why don't you let me drive?" Jake asked. He was in a hurry and wasn't familiar with either of the others' driving. "The two of you seem like you have a lot of catching up to do."

She looked him in the eye for a moment as if judging his character. He must have passed muster because when Jake held out his hand, she nodded and dropped the keys into it and then slid into the middle of the seat. Jake got in beside her.

"Is this really your truck?" Senor Garcia asked as he got in on the passenger side.

"Yes, do you like it?"

"Yes. Very much," the old man said as ran his hand over the leather seats.

Jake had paid attention to the route the bus driver had taken, and they were soon on the highway back to Playa del Carmen.

He'd hoped they would do their catching up in Spanish so he could think about Teresa, but Wilma insisted it was rude to have a conversation in front of someone who didn't know the language, so they spoke English. At first he tried to tune Teresa's parents out as they caught up on the last twenty-six years, but soon realized that was impossible. So, as the pavement sped by beneath them, he listened.

During the three and a half hour trip he learned that Wilma's father had been trying to break Señor Garcia and Wilma up all along. It was he who had sent her off to school in the states while Jośe Luis had been on a cattle buying trip. He'd told Wilma that he would take care of explaining everything to Jośe Luis and told her to write often to her husband.

But Señor Garcia never got any letters. Wilma's father had obviously intercepted them. In fact, her father told him that Wilma had been spending more and more time in Merida and had fallen in love with a gringo and moved to Miami to live with him.

Learning what Wilma's father had done to them made Señor Garcia very angry and he told Wilma that as soon as they found Teresa, he was going out to the ranch and talk to her father.

Wilma told him it was too late for that. Her father had had a stroke shortly after her return from school and died a few years later. She'd spent those years caring for him while learning and running the business end of the ranch.

Señor Garcia seemed astounded that Wilma could be able to run a cattle ranch and was immediately chastised with another smack from Wilma's purse.

Jake also learned that neither of them had bothered to get a divorce so were still legally married. When Señor Garcia asked if she had been faithful to him, she quickly threw the same question back at him. He was quiet for a moment and then changed the subject and began asking questions about the ranch.

After her father died, Wilma had inherited the ranch. She said it had always been her dream to raise horses and she hated the cows, she blamed them for keeping her husband away, so she had eaten as many of them as she could before selling the rest and buying horses. She was now in the business of breeding and raising Andalusian horses for dressage and jumping.

Jake wasn't surprised that Teresa's mother could have accomplished so much in such a short time. With or without a wealthy background, it required a lot of determination to live your dream, and just like Teresa; her mother seemed to have it in spades. As he thought about it, he realized Teresa had inherited more from her mother than just her looks.

By the time they reached Playa del Carmen, the conversation had died down. As he pulled into the parking lot at Las Palmas, Jake looked over and noticed that Teresa's parents were holding hands.

"I'm going to check with Benito and see if he has any news," Jake said as he got out of the truck. "Why don't the two of you meet me in the cantina?"

"Yes, we'll get a bottle of tequila and some food," Señor Garcia said, opening his door.

Wilma pulled on her husband's arm and he turned to her. "No bottle," she said firmly, "you are no good to anyone when you are drunk, but maybe a pitcher of margaritas to share."

Jake left them discussing beverages and went through the coconut grove to the cantina. After a quick look around, he headed out to the beach. He found Benito at his shack, sitting in the shade and having a beer.

"Hola, Jake. Did you find Teresa?" Benito said as he pulled up another chair for Jake.

"No, have you heard anything?"

"No. I stayed at the cantina until just a little while ago, but nothing happened. All those people were making me crazy so I came out here for some peace. How was the trip to Merida?"

"Well, it wasn't wasted, that's for sure."

"What do you mean?" Benito asked with a puzzled look on his face.

"We found Teresa's mother."

"You what? Caramba! Is it really her mother? I didn't know you were looking for her, too."

"We weren't. We ran into her on the street. You should have seen your uncle's face when he realized who she was. And she looks and moves so much like Teresa, it's incredible."

"How is my uncle taking the return of his long-lost bride?"

"It's hard to tell, really. The two of them fight like cats and dogs and I don't just mean arguing. Neither seems reluctant to take a swing at the other when they think it's called for."

"Now we know where Teresa gets it from," Benito said with a smile.

* * *

Jake met Wilma and Señor Garcia in the cantina. They were seated at a table with a pitcher of margaritas and three glasses in front of them.

"Any news from my nephew, Benito?" the old man asked as Jake sat down.

"No," Jake replied taking a sip of the margarita in front of him.

"I wish Miguel would contact us. I want my daughter and grandson back."

Jake and Señor Garcia snapped their heads around at

Wilma as she began choking on a sip of her margarita. Señor Garcia slapped her on the back a couple of times and gave her a second to catch her breath. As soon as she did, Jake saw the fire in her eyes as she turned to her husband and slapped his shoulder.

"We have a grandson and you don't tell me?" she said, outraged.

"Madre de Dios. Lo siento. I'm sorry, Wilma. In all the excitement of losing Teresa and finding you, I forgot to tell you. Yes, Teresa has a four-year-old son named Luis. He is a wonderful little boy as you will see as soon as it is safe for him to come home. I have some pictures back at my apartment if you would like to see them."

"Of course I want to see them, you old fool," she shot back, rising.

The old man stood up, grabbed the margarita pitcher and waved it at Jake. "More?" he asked.

"No thanks, take it with you. I'll let you know if anything comes up."

* * *

Jake sat in the cantina for another couple of hours, waiting for word of Teresa or Miguel. It was almost dark when he looked across the beach and saw Elena coming. Jake left his seat and jogged across the sand to meet her.

"Did you find Teresa in Merida?" she asked as they walked back to the cantina together.

"No, we were told that Miguel hadn't been in Merida in days and wasn't expected back for a week," Jake said as he led her to his table and held a chair for her.

"I'm sorry if I sent you on a wild goose chase, but it was the only place I could think of where he might be holding her."

"That's okay, it wasn't a wasted trip." He didn't want Elena to feel bad about sending them to Merida, hell, she was the best source of information they had, but he wasn't going to take the time to explain everything to her now.

Teresa could do that when they got her back.

"I think there is something you should know," she said.

"What? Have you heard something?"

"My mother just told me that yesterday she gave Miguel my spare key to the back room of the ticket booth in Tulum where I work. He told her he wanted to store something there for a few days."

"Do you think Miguel could be keeping her there?"

"They were not there today, but it's possible that he could be keeping her there at night. I saw nothing else he was storing, but I did notice some take-out wrappers in the trash. I know it's not much, but…"

"Thank you, Elena."

"Here," she said, handing him a key. "I had another one made. Please get Teresa back and if you can, try not to tear up the place too much. If my boss finds out I gave you a key I will get fired. I hope you find her. Let me know if there's anything more I can do," she said, getting up.

Jake watched her cross the dune and head back down the beach.

Tulum, he thought, remembering the impressive stone structures, the rocky cliff and the small white beaches. Taking his cell phone out of his pocket, he made a call. While he talked, Jake walked down to the beach and took another look at his boat.

By the time he hung up, he had the makings of a plan.

CHAPTER 30

After a quick stop at his apartment to pick up something, Jake walked back to Señor Garcia's place. If his plan was going to work, he was going to need help.

Through the apartment's front window, he saw Wilma and Señor Garcia sitting on the couch, a photo album covering their laps. Señor Garcia looked up and nodded his head for Jake to come in.

As soon as he walked through the door, Wilma looked up. "I have a grandson, Jake," she said, wiping away a tear.

"Yes, I know. He is a fine young man, and you should be proud to have him."

"Oh, I am. I can't wait to meet him. Where is he?"

"Yes, where is he? He should be here to meet his grandmother," the old man chimed in.

"He's safe," Jake replied to the old man, "and that's all I'm going to tell you. Considering that you started this mess, Teresa didn't trust you to know where she took Luis and I won't betray her confidence."

"I said I was sorry. I never meant for this to happen. I just wanted Teresa to be married and settled here, not in another country."

Wilma gave her husband a look of disgust. "You are so selfish," she said. "Maybe I *should* have run off with a gringo to Miami," she muttered. She looked back at Jake. "You are sure he is safe?" she asked.

"I am sure he is cared for and loved and safer than he would be if he was here."

"Okay," she replied, accepting Jake's confidence. "What do we do now?"

"That's why I'm here," Jake said turning to Teresa's father. "Miguel's sister Elena was here a few minutes ago. She said that her mother gave Miguel a key to a storage room at the ruins in Tulum so he could store something for a few days. She said she didn't see Miguel or Teresa while she was there today, but they might be keeping her there at night."

"Teresa is at Tulum?" the old man said excitedly as he started to rise.

"Let's go get her now," Wilma said as she jumped to her feet.

"Hold on a minute," Jake advised. "We don't know for sure that's where she is, and before we go charging in anywhere, we need a plan."

"What kind of plan?" the old man asked suspiciously as he sank back into the couch cushions.

"A plan you both probably won't like, but if either of you have a better suggestion, let me know and we'll talk about it."

"What is this plan?"

"Let's talk about the long range plan first. I want to make sure the three of us are on the same page about all this," Jake said as he took a seat at the table.

"Okay…" Señor Garcia said doubtfully.

"When we get Teresa back, how are you going to stop Miguel from taking Luis? Teresa said all he had to do was buy off the police and they would give the boy to Miguel, right?"

"Yes, that is right."

"I know you don't want to hear this, but Teresa and Luis are going to have to leave Playa del Carmen and probably even Mexico. At least until Miguel is arrested and out of the picture. Teresa and Luis aren't safe here. Let me take them somewhere safe until a paternity test can prove that Luis is not Miguel's son."

"No. I love Luis as much as Teresa does, but they belong here with me. They are my family and I don't want to lose them as I did my wife," he admitted with a glance at Wilma.

"Perhaps I could bribe someone more powerful than the police," Wilma suggested. "The ranch is doing well and with my father's inheritance, I am quite wealthy."

"And then what? Get in a bidding war with Miguel? Where does it end? No. If they stay in Mexico, Teresa will lose her son and both of you will lose your grandson. And you, Wilma, could wind up losing your ranch. You can't possibly want that to happen."

"Maybe they could stay with you at the ranch?" Señor Garcia said, looking at Wilma.

"No. As much as I would love to have them with me, it won't work. Several of my ranch hands are regulars at El Diablo and once they get a few shots in them, they talk like magpies. Miguel would find them. And if we wait until the police arrest him, we will be waiting a long time. If you want him out of the picture, we will have to kill him."

"Is that the way people do things down here?" Jake asked, raising his voice in exasperation. "Kill anyone that gets in your way?"

"Only if they deserve it," Wilma said calmly, walking over to look him in the eye. "And a drug smuggling kidnapper who wants to steal my grandson just because he can is very deserving, wouldn't you say?"

"He may be deserving," Jake agreed, "but we are not killing Miguel. I have no desire to wind up in a Mexican prison."

Wilma moved closer until her chest almost touched Jake's. "And I have no desire to lose my daughter and grandson," she said in a whisper full of steely determination. They held eye contact for a few moments before Wilma turned back to Señor Garcia.

"I guess he's right, José Luis. We can't just go around killing cartel members," she said. "We wouldn't want to piss them off."

Jake was surprised at her abrupt about-face. He heard a trace of sarcasm in her voice but let it slide. He was relieved the discussion over killing Miguel was finished. He had no problem with people defending themselves or their families, but he wasn't a murderer.

"I had always hoped the two of them would get married. I truly thought Miguel was Luis father," Señor Garcia said, his shoulders slumped. "I didn't know he was a cartel member."

"Well, you know differently now and your plan to marry Teresa to some guy she doesn't love has backfired, old man," Jake said bluntly. "It's time for you to make a choice. You can have Teresa and Luis happy together somewhere else, or, if you can trust Miguel to keep his word, you can have Teresa here alone. Choose."

Jake watched the old man as he struggled with the concept of losing either one of the people he held most dear. He had backed himself into a corner with his meddling and now was in danger of losing the one thing that he'd been so adamant about keeping. His family. As far as Jake was concerned there was no choice, but he needed the old man to make the decision himself.

"You must let Teresa live her own life, José Luis," Wilma said quietly, as she laid her hand on his arm. "But don't worry. In my experience, karma is a bitch and one day Miguel will get what's coming to him, I am sure of that."

"But I don't want to lose either of them. They are my family," the old man argued.

"José Luis, this young man loves her and is willing to risk his life to get her back. And you would not have worked so hard to keep them apart if you didn't know she loved him, too. Let her go with him and be happy." She turned to Jake. "Where do you live in the U.S.?"

"Florida," he replied.

She turned back to Señor Garcia. "See, no problem. Florida is only a two hour flight. We can go and visit, and after this scoundrel Miguel is taken care of, Teresa and Luis can come home."

"You know that could be a while," Jake advised.

"You never know," Wilma said with a gleam in her eyes and the barest hint of a smile. "Miguel has a very dangerous job. He could be arrested or killed at any time."

"That's true," Jake admitted. And it was, but it was the way she'd said it that made him wonder for a split second if it was more than just wishful thinking on her part. But unless she had a hit man on her payroll, that's all it could be. He turned to the old man.

Señor Garcia was quiet for a few moments and then looked Jake straight in the eye. "Will you bring them back when it is safe for them to return?"

"Yes, I promise. But we have to leave tomorrow night. I have friends who own a yacht and are in the area. They will take us to my home in Florida."

The old man got up and poured himself a shot of Don Julio and looked down into the amber liquid briefly before throwing it back. "You know I have no choice. I won't see my grandson taken away from my daughter because of my mistakes. I will let you take them away until Miguel is no longer a threat, but you must promise two more things."

"What's that?"

"You must promise to love and take care of Teresa and Luis, and you must marry Teresa before you take her away from me. I want to see the wedding."

Jake smiled. "The first part is easy, but I'll have to work on that second part, sir."

"If you are going to be my son-in-law you should call me José Luis."

"And you can call me Wilma," she said smiling up at Jake.

"Now, let's talk about how we are going to get my daughter back," José Luis said as he reached for the tequila bottle again.

"Our daughter," Wilma corrected, as she moved the tequila bottle out of his reach.

There was a knock on the door and Jake and Wilma both looked at Jos Luis.

"Expecting someone?" Jake asked.

"No, are you?"

CHAPTER 31

Jake got up and opened the door, surprised to see Steve, Petey, Paul and Benito standing on the other side.

"Hola, Jake," Benito said, "Juan said you were here. Look what I found in the cantina," he said, waving at Jake's friends.

"What are you guys doing here?" Jake asked.

"We decided that you could probably use some help, so we're here," Paul said.

"We're here to watch your back just like you've always watched ours," Petey added.

Jake looked at Steve.

"Well, you did sound like you were pretty upset," he said. "You know, clearer heads, that kind of thing."

"Are your amigos part of your plan?" Señor Garcia asked, walking to the door with the bottle of tequila he had wrestled away from Wilma. "Tell them to come in."

Jake stood aside and let his friends pass. Steve was last and as he walked by he put a hand on Jake's shoulder. "Whatever you need man, I'm in."

Jake just smiled at his friend. They'd had other differences over the years, but Steve never stayed mad at him very long.

As soon as the door closed behind them, all eyes in the place turned to Wilma who had gotten up and was walking into the tiny kitchen that had been added into Señor Garcia's apartment.

"Wilma, these are my friends, Steve, Petey and Paul," he said pointing to each as he said their name. "I don't know if you know Benito, but he's your nephew. Guys, this is Wilma, Teresa's mother."

"Oh….nice meeting you," was said lamely all around. Jake knew the guys were more than a little surprised by her presence, he'd told them what Teresa had told him; that her mother had walked out on her and her father when Teresa was four and they hadn't heard from her since.

Wilma puttered in the kitchen and everyone else found seats. Jake, Benito and Steve were at the kitchen table, Señor Garcia settled into his recliner and Petey and Paul were on the couch.

"About your plan…," Señor Garcia waved his arm at Jake.

"I hope this is where the 'clearer minds' prevail, because all we have right now is a gun with no bullets, a knife, and Señor Garcia's baseball bat over there." Jake indicated the bat leaning in the corner.

"We know there are at least four of them including Miguel, but there may be more. We've got some decent information about Teresa's location, and if she's where I think she is, we'll have the element of surprise," he told his friends as he pulled out the item he'd retrieved from his apartment. It was the brochure he'd gotten with his ticket when he'd visited the ruins with Teresa.

"I talked with Patrick and Vanessa and they'll be coming into Cozumel tomorrow. They're willing to help, too."

"And I will help," Wilma said, coming out of the kitchen.

"I can't let you go with us, Wilma. I'm sorry, I know you want to help, but I can't risk it. If anything should happen to you, Teresa would never forgive me and I would never forgive myself," Jake told her.

"But I want to see her before you take her away."

"I know you do, and I have a plan for that. Do you think you can get to Cozumel alone on the ferry and find my friends' yacht?"

"Of course I can," she responded.

"I'll let you know when they get in and then you can take the next ferry over. When they come for us, they will bring you with them. You can see Teresa then, but I warn you, it will only be for a short time."

"I understand."

"She might not want to leave when she sees you," Jake said, realizing that could be a problem.

"I know she must go, Jake. It will be fine, you will see."

"Back to your plan…" Senor Garcia said, impatiently.

"Right," Jake said noticing the withering look Wilma shot at her husband.

Wilma went back into the kitchen. Listening as she worked, she made a plate of nachos to graze on as they talked late into the night, tossing ideas back and forth, most of which were discarded. By the time they were finished, they had a plan. There were a lot of unknown factors they'd have to deal with on the fly, but it was better than nothing

They'd take tomorrow to round up the equipment they needed and go to Tulum in the early hours of the following morning when, hopefully, Miguel and his men would be sleeping.

Jake just hoped they could pull it off without anyone getting killed.

* * *

The next morning, Señor Garcia stayed at the cantina in case Miguel contacted him about the exchange while Benito and the guys rounded up the equipment they needed and Jake took a walk down the beach. The plan involved taking the boat to Tulum and he needed a quiet trolling motor to get in close to shore without being detected. He also wanted to find Henry.

He kept thinking about Teresa and what she must be going through. She'd held her own with Miguel up until now, but Jake knew she was no match for four men. He just hoped she could keep her cool and not let her fiery temper get her hurt.

He was praying Miguel was keeping Teresa in Elena's store room. It's possible he was storing drugs there; after all, he was a member of a drug cartel, but whatever he was keeping there, they were going to find out tonight.

It was late afternoon by the time he found Henry. The friendly Mexican was more than willing to help with whatever Jake needed and he also had a trolling motor that he let Jake borrow. Jake lugged it back to Las Palmas along with the other supplies he'd picked up while he was out, and then went to the cantina to find Teresa's father.

As soon as he stepped onto the cantina's deck, the old man met him.

"Let's go to my apartment, I have something to tell you."

They walked back to his place and went inside. Jake stood next to the door while Teresa's father poured himself a shot of Don Julio.

"What's wrong?" Jake asked, not sure he wanted to hear.

"One of Miguel's men came here a little while ago and said to bring Luis to the ruins at Tulum at midnight tonight and they would let Teresa go."

"Is she all right?" Jake asked.

"He didn't say, he only said that Miguel wants to trade the boy for Teresa at the ruins tonight," he said and threw back the shot.

"So he is keeping her there. That's good news. I'd hoped to get her back before they were expecting us, but this might still work. We'll just have to push up the timetable a little bit. Call Benito and tell him to be here by seven. I've got to get some things ready and make a call."

Back in his apartment, Jake emptied out his backpack and packed as many of his things that he could fit in the one suitcase he'd brought to Mexico. When that was finished, he packed the backpack with a change of clothes, two rolls of duct tape and some lengths of rope he'd cut from a spool he'd bought earlier, two underwater flashlights, his portable GPS and the knife the intruders had dropped. He topped it off with some bottles of water and a few protein bars.

Opening the backpack's zippered compartment, Jake took out the small velvet box and opened it to reveal its contents. Nestled in a slot in the padding was an emerald and diamond ring. The simple setting held a one-carat square cut emerald flanked by a quarter-carat diamond on each side. Alongside it was a simple gold wedding band. Both the band and the ring's setting were eighteen-carat gold.

Many years ago, his grandfather had found the emerald in the belly of a fish he'd been cleaning and had it cut and mounted as an engagement ring for Jake's grandmother. Jake smiled. If everything went well, he'd put both of them on Teresa's finger tonight.

He closed the box and returned it to the backpack's zippered compartment, then picked up his bags and left the apartment. On his way back from putting everything in the boat, he sat on the hammock he usually shared with Teresa and called Vanessa.

When she answered, she told Jake that she and Patrick were presently docked in Cozumel. They had just dropped off the couple who had chartered the yacht for a last night of partying before returning to Miami in the morning

Jake had her put the phone on speaker so Patrick could be involved in the conversation and then told them about finding Teresa's estranged mother and her desire to see her daughter and grandson before they left the country with Jake.

"We're going to have a load of people on my boat from the ruins to the rendezvous point. Would it be all right if I sent her to Cozumel on the ferry and you could bring her with you tonight?"

"Sure, we'd be happy to give her a ride and after you guys meet us, we'll let Teresa and her parents have the salon for a few minutes of privacy so they can get to know each other again. The rest of us can hang out in the cockpit," said Patrick.

"Thanks for understanding. It's going to be a shock for

Teresa to find her mother and lose her again so soon."

Jake gave them Wilma's name and a brief physical description. He told them he was sending her over on the next ferry and then had Vanessa give him directions to the dock so Wilma could find them. They were okay with moving up the timetable and after consulting his charts, Patrick gave him the coordinates of the rendezvous' location to enter into his GPS.

"Do Teresa and Luis have passports?" Patrick asked. "I'm thinking about how to get them into the U.S."

"I don't know, maybe, but with or without passports, I've got to get them out of Mexico."

"I understand, we'll figure something out," Patrick said. "All we have to do is get them to shore. Then she can apply for refuge or whatever they call it when you're in danger in your own country."

"That's not a sure thing, though," Vanessa said. "If immigration doesn't buy her story, she could still be deported."

"But not if she were married, right?" Jake asked.

"Right. But Jake, are you seriously thinking about marrying Teresa?"

"Her father said one of his conditions to taking her away from here was I had to marry her and he had to see the wedding. Patrick, you've done marriages before haven't you?"

"Sure, Jake, but it won't be legal unless we're in international waters. These are Mexican waters."

"But you could do it anyway, just for her parents?"

"Not unless Teresa knows it won't be legal."

"I suggest you concentrate on getting her back first. I brought the, uh, item you asked for," Vanessa said.

"Thanks, but I'm not going to have time to pick it up. By the time I can get there and back on the ferry, it will be too late. We'll just have to work with what we've got," Jake said. "But plan on having company sometime around eleven."

"Just be careful, Jake. I'm sure Teresa is a wonderful woman, but I don't want you to get hurt."

"Thanks Vanessa, but come hell or high water, I'm getting her back tonight."

"We'll be waiting, Jake," Patrick said.

CHAPTER 32

Jake found Wilma in the cantina's kitchen with Rosa and Inez. She'd found some different clothes somewhere because she'd traded in her red dress for a slim pair of denim capris and a blue and white tank top. Jake watched her for a moment, still amazed at the similarities in looks and mannerisms she and her daughter shared. He was pulled out of his reverie when Rosa tossed a dish rag at him.

"Help," she mouthed silently.

Jake wasn't sure what she meant until he realized that Wilma was standing in the middle of the galley kitchen offering advice on how to handle food preparation more efficiently while Rosa and Inez dodged her. Both women shot him a look of gratitude when he told Wilma he needed to see her outside.

"You need to get down to the ferry dock and take the next one over. Just take a left out of the parking lot and start walking toward town. You won't get far before a taxi will stop for you. My friends are waiting for you in Cozumel on Pier Three. They said you can't miss their yacht, it's got wedding decorations all over it."

"Will we need the decorations?" she asked, referring to her husband's wish to see his daughter's wedding.

"Unless Teresa turns me down."

"Do you think she will?"

"I honestly don't know, but I'm hoping she won't." He had found out the hard way that loving someone didn't guarantee they felt the same. He'd also discovered that his feelings for Teresa ran far deeper than any he'd felt, or thought he'd felt, for Vanessa. But whether Teresa turned him down or not, he was going to get her back.

"And you are planning to get married on your friend's yacht and have the captain perform the ceremony?" Wilma asked. "Because I'm sure you know that unless you are in international waters, the wedding will not be legal."

"I do know that and before there is a wedding Teresa will know it too. But you heard Señor Garcia tell me that he wanted to see the wedding, so I'm going to let him see a wedding. But don't worry, as soon as we're in international waters, we'll do it again to make it legal."

"What do you think Teresa will think of me?"

"As soon as she learns that you and her father were cheated out of a life together, I am sure she'll welcome you with open arms. She is as beautiful on the inside as she is on the surface."

"I can tell that you love her very much. Tell me, will I be able to meet my grandson before you go?"

"Yes, Benito will drive your truck and take you and Señor Garcia to see Luis. Teresa and I will meet you there. You will have a few minutes with your family, but only a few. Then Teresa, Luis and I will have to leave. Even if all goes well, we will have to hurry to get out of Mexico before Miguel and his guys catch up to us."

"I understand. I will just go get my things and then I will go to the ferry dock. Thank goodness I had done some shopping before I ran into you," she said as she turned to go back to Señor Garcia's apartment.

* * *

After mounting the trolling motor on the stern and removing the net to allow for more gas storage and passenger space, Jake took Wilma's truck into town.

He went to the marine supply store where he bought two eighteen-gallon gas tanks and two gallons of oil, then stopped at the Pemex and filled the tanks. When he arrived back at Las Palmas he enlisted Señor Garcia's help to haul the tanks down to the beach and put them in the boat.

He disconnected the five-gallon gas tank he'd been using and connected one of the larger tanks to the motor. Then he went over the boat from stem to stern. He couldn't afford to have any problems. When he was satisfied that everything was in good working order, he walked back up to Señor Garcia's apartment to wait for Benito and the Boys Club.

When Teresa's father opened the door, he had a shot glass of tequila in his hand.

"Señor Garcia," Jake said reproachfully, "don't you think you should lay off that stuff until we get your daughter back?"

"I told you if you are going to be my son-in-law, you should call me José Luis," the old man reminded Jake as he walked back over to his recliner and sat down.

Jake took a seat at the kitchen table. "You can't do your part if you're drunk," Jake reminded him. "You want Teresa safe, don't you?"

"Of course I do, but I want her safe here, with me," the old man said stubbornly.

"Look, we talked about this. You know as well as I do that she and Luis won't be safe here until Miguel is out of the picture. Now lay off the sauce."

Señor Garcia threw back the shot and wiped his mouth with the back of his hand. "Don't worry about me; I will do whatever needs to be done to get my daughter back."

Benito and the guys showed up a few minutes later and Jake told them about Miguel's plans to swap Luis for Teresa at midnight.

"Shit, Jake, that's at least a couple hours before we were planning to be there," Petey pointed out.

"So we'll just have to move our timetable up a few hours," Jake replied.

"But they probably won't be sleeping if they're planning a midnight swap," Paul pointed out.

"No, probably not," Jake agreed, "but they won't be expecting anyone to show up until midnight, so if we're there at, say, nine-thirty, maybe we'll still be able to catch them off guard."

"Okay, Jake," Steve said, "run through the plan one

more time for us. We need to make sure everyone's on the same page."

"Good idea. Okay, Benito and Paul will drive down to Tulum. You were able to get a car, right Benito?" Jake asked.

"Si, Serena's VW is waiting in the parking lot."

Jake paused for a moment. "You realize you're going to have to abandon it, don't you?"

"She needs a new car anyway. The Bug is a piece of shit," Benito said with a grin.

"Okay, change of plans. Paul, you're coming with us. Petey will go with Benito. He's the best mechanic we have and Benito's right about the VW being a piece of shit. If it breaks down before providing us with the diversion we need, we're screwed."

"Don't worry, Jake. I'll make sure it gets there," Petey assured him.

"When you get down there, just sit out by the highway and wait. Steve, Paul, José Luis and I will go down in the boat. We'll have to leave fairly soon, because it will take us longer to get there and I don't want you two to have to sit out by the highway any longer than necessary.

"When we get there, I'll use the trolling motor to take us in close and drop José Luis and Steve off. They're the strongest swimmers and that current running next to the cliff looked pretty stiff. Once you guys make it to shore, you'll have to take out any sentries Miguel may have posted on the beach. As soon as you have the beach secured, give us the signal and Paul and I will bring the boat ashore."

"What's the current going to be doing?" Steve asked.

"The currents generally run north so we'll have to pass our landing zone and then let it pull us back to it," Jake said. "The problem is going to be the moon. We've got a full moon tonight with the chance of a storm later. Until the clouds roll in, everyone is going to have to be careful to stay hidden as much as possible.

"As soon as Paul and I beach the boat, I'll meet up with Steve and José Luis, and once we determine how many men we're up against, I'll call Benito's phone. If I remember correctly, it's about three quarters of a mile from the highway to the ruins. Benito, you and Petey will approach the ruins with the VW's lights off, stopping about a half mile from the main gate. From there you get out and push the car for the next quarter mile so no one will hear you coming. That should be close enough to get their attention and still give you time to get away from the car without being seen.

"Then switch on the car lights, turn the radio on full blast and get into the woods next to the walking path as fast as you can. Head southeast through the woods and you'll come out near the ruin's exit gate that I showed you on the map. Once you get past the gate, and you may have to climb over it, follow the trail on the right. It will take you to the cliff. We'll meet you at the boat. Any questions?"

"No, but I'm sure glad Benito's been there before and knows his way around," Petey admitted.

"We'll be fine," Benito said confidently.

"Once you guys get the diversion going, we'll head down to the storage room. With any luck, Miguel and his men will be out at the road checking out the VW, and we can get Teresa and head back to the boat.

"Paul, you'll stay on the beach and keep an eye on the boat. We may need to leave in a hurry so you'll have to be ready to get us out of there as quickly as possible."

"Did you call Vanessa and Patrick and let them know about the timetable change?" Steve asked.

"Yes, they're up to speed. They'll have Wilma and will be waiting for us about halfway between Tulum and Cozumel. Teresa and I will go with them and the rest of you will head back to Playa. Henry will have a van waiting to take you guys to the airport and Benito will take Wilma and José Luis to Puerto Morelos."

"Luis is in Puerto Morelos?" Señor Garcia asked, surprised.

Jake thought about his answer. It wasn't betraying a confidence if the old man had figured it out for himself, and it was going to be the last time he saw his daughter and grandson for a while.

"Yes, he's at Tia Carmen's. Benito will take you and Wilma there to see him. When we get to Puerto Morelos with the yacht, Benito's father will meet us and take Teresa and I across the reef. You will only have a few minutes to say goodbye and then Benito's father will take Teresa, Luis and I back to the yacht.

"Okay, last chance. If anyone has a better idea, speak now."

Jake looked at Benito and his friends one by one as each of them shook their heads, telling him they hadn't come up with a better plan. When his gaze rested on Paul, Paul shook his head. "You know we'll probably all get killed," he said.

"Gee, Paul, speak for yourself," Petey said and elbowed his brother in the ribs.

"Look Paul, if you're not ready for this, you don't have to go," Jake told him. "I get it."

"No, if you're in, then so am I. That's what we do, watch each other's back. I'm just saying…"

"Just shut up and try being positive for once in your life," Petey interrupted.

"I said I'm in, that should be enough," Paul defended himself.

"It is, Paul. It is," Jake replied. He turned to look at Teresa's father. "What's it going to be, José Luis?"

"What about your promise?" the old man asked.

"That will be taken care of as soon as we get out to the yacht with Teresa," Jake assured him.

Steve and the twins looked at Jake and then at each other. "What promise?" Petey mouthed to Steve. Steve shrugged his shoulders.

"I need to take care of a few things before we leave and you need to pack one bag each for Luis and Teresa. Stick to the essentials, we're going to have seven people on board between the ruins and the yacht and space will be tight."

"I can do this," the old man said as he rose up out of his chair.

"Steve, you and the twins need to change into the darkest clothes you brought with you. I'll meet you down at the boat when you're finished. Bring whatever you managed to scrounge up for weapons." On his way out the door, Jake picked up Señor Garcia's baseball bat and took it with him.

Jake got his backpack out of the boat and sat on the sand in the light coming from the cantina. Opening it, he took out the rolls of duct tape, a couple lengths of rope and the underwater flashlights.

He tied one piece of rope around the hanger on the end of a flashlight, and then threaded the other end through the hole in the roll of duct tape, making a loop to keep the tape secure. Then he tied a slip knot a few inches from the tape and slid the small end of the baseball bat into it and cinched it tight. He tied a loop at the end of the rope big enough to put a belt through. Satisfied with his rigging, he made another one.

Shortly before eight o'clock, Steve, Paul, and Señor Garcia, all wearing dark clothes, met Jake on the beach. Señor Garcia was carrying a small suitcase in each hand, Paul had a short length of metal pipe he'd scavenged from a construction site, and Steve had another baseball bat. Jake also noticed a large knife stuck under Señor Garcia's belt.

Jake helped the old man load the luggage and just before they got in the boat, Señor Garcia turned to him. "I never thought I would have to do this, but here," he said, holding out a brown manila envelope.

"What's this?" Jake asked.

"Teresa's and Luis' passports. I am not supposed to know she has them, but Luis told me."

"Thank you," Jake said. "These will make everything a lot easier."

"Come on," the old man said with a tear in his eye. "Let's go get my daughter."

CHAPTER 33

They went offshore about a half mile and headed south down the coast. Jake was glad to see the clouds covering the full moon, but the threat of rain they carried was nearing and the sea was rougher than he would have liked.

They passed resorts that were all lit up and had partygoers spilling out onto the beach. Jake knew there was music, but he couldn't hear it over the sound of the boat motor.

The constant thrumming of the motor was something he was used to and the familiar sound soothed and relaxed muscles that had been tense for days. He said a silent prayer for Teresa and while he was at it threw in a request for a successful mission.

A shiver ran down his spine as he remembered Paul's prediction, well not exactly a prediction, more like a conclusion, that they would probably all get killed. He didn't want to think about all the things that could go wrong with their plan. He was afraid for his friends, after all this wasn't their mess, but as for him, he knew that Teresa and what he felt for her was worth dying for. He just hoped it wasn't today.

But if it was, he had his affairs in order. He'd had the foresight to have a will drawn up before coming down here this time. He'd left the bar and the house to Casey and the settlement from the Walsh's to his mom. He'd put the will in a safety deposit box along with a letter telling Casey the location of the treasure cache he'd found a few years ago, instructions on how to use it, and the name and phone number of a very discreet collector he'd been lucky enough to find. He trusted Casey implicitly and knew he was the right man to carry on the job.

Jake shook his head to clear the dismal thoughts, said

another short prayer for everyone's safety, and moved his attention to the positive. Now that the Boy's Club had arrived, the odds had changed and it looked like Jake and company outnumbered Miguel and his three thugs. He could only hope Miguel hadn't added any reinforcements to his team. But even if he had, going in earlier than expected would still give them the element of surprise and allow them a few minutes to try to even up the odds.

When they got to within a mile of the ruins, Jake cut the motor and the lights. Switching on the trolling motor, he went the next mile slowly and quietly, staying offshore far enough not to be noticed. He didn't want to alert any guards who might be on the cliffs or beaches.

When they got about a half mile south of the ruins Jake brought the boat closer to the coastline and took the trolling motor out of gear and let the current pull them back to the north. As Señor Garcia and Steve stripped down to their swim trunks, Jake pulled out the rigging he'd made for each of them.

While Jake scanned the shoreline, Steve secured his bat in the rigging and he and Señor Garcia cinched their rigged belts around their waists, Señor Garcia tucking his knife under his belt at his back.

Jake's heart jumped up into his throat when he saw the flash of a cigarette lighter on the beach near the stairs that ran to the top of the cliff. Tapping Teresa's father on the shoulder, Jake pointed to where he'd seen the flash and mimed lighting a cigarette. Señor Garcia turned to look at the beach for a moment, turned back to Jake and nodded, and then slipped quietly over the side.

Señor Garcia had been adamant about going in first, but Jake had been reluctant. Teresa's father was a strong swimmer and could no doubt make it to shore, but Jake wasn't sure if the old man could hold his own in a fight. Until they met back up with Benito, Teresa's father was the only one of them who could understand Spanish and they needed him to translate anything they heard.

Jake continued to let the boat drift north with the current to the second small beach on the north side of the promontory. He scanned the sand and rocks for any telltale sign of another sentry, but saw nothing. Steve nodded at Jake and slipped over the side.

As Jake and Paul waited for the flashlight signals to let them know it was safe to bring the boat in to shore, Jake's thoughts were on Teresa. Memories of lying in the hammock with the tiny Mexican woman who had stolen his heart and soul flooded his mind.

When Paul shifted in his seat, Jake snapped out of the past and into the present, scanning the shore for two quick flashes of light, the signal they had agreed on. It seemed like hours but it was probably no more than a few minutes before Jake spotted Señor Garcia's signal on the south beach. A few minutes later, Steve's signal came from the north.

Putting the trolling motor back in gear, Jake eased quietly toward the cliff. The tide was coming in, but there was still enough room under the cliff to pull the boat in under it. They didn't want it visible from anyone on the cliff.

Just before the bow hit the sand, Steve slipped under the cliff from the north beach and gave Jake a nod and lifted the machine pistol he'd taken from the guard. "Pissing behind big rocks may be hazardous to your health," he whispered with a grin.

As the bow gently hit the sandy beach, Jake cut the motor and reached for his backpack. He got out of the boat just as Señor Garcia joined them dragging the sentry who'd been guarding the stairs by the back of his shirt.

The guard's ankles and wrists were bound with duct tape and another piece covered his mouth. Señor Garcia pulled the man up to the water's edge and dropped him face first into the wet sand. He wasn't moving, so Jake assumed he was out cold.

It was then that he noticed the machine pistol that

Señor Garcia had slung over his shoulder.

"Do you know how to use that thing?" he asked, nodding at the gun as the old man pulled it back into his hands.

"Si. I was in the Army once. I can shoot."

"Two down and two to go," Paul whispered, after retrieving the short pipe he'd brought and getting out of the boat to join them.

"We should move him away from the water," Jake whispered, motioning to the bound guard. "If he's still there when the tide comes up, he'll drown."

"He deserves to drown, the lousy pig. Let's go, we have to find Teresa," Señor Garcia growled, already moving toward the stairs that would take them to the top of the cliff.

Jake hesitated a moment. He didn't want to kill anyone that he didn't have to. Then he thought about what Teresa had been going through because of these men.

"What do you want to do with him, Jake?" Paul asked quietly.

"I'd like to say forget him. It's what he would do to us, but I'm not here to kill anyone. Besides, Miguel will probably kill him for this anyway." Jake said as he pulled the unconscious guard away from the water's edge. "Paul, while we're gone, go ahead and switch to the full gas tank. I don't want to run out of gas if we have to make a high speed escape."

"You got it, Jake."

"And no matter what, as soon as Teresa is onboard, get this sucker cranked and ready to go. If it gets dicey, take her and get the hell out of here. The rest of us will find our way back."

"Jake, man, I can't just leave you guys here," Paul said with a note of exasperation.

"Don't worry, Paul," Steve said. "It'll all be fine. I'll have his back up there and you'll have our backs down here."

"All right, if that's what you guys want, but…

"Thanks, Paul," Jake said, slinging his backpack over his shoulder before hurrying off with Steve to catch up with Señor Garcia. He didn't think it was a good idea for the old man to be running around alone with a gun.

Black clouds blocked the moon as they eased up the stairs in the inky darkness. The wind had picked up or at least Jake noticed it more as they climbed higher. A few steps short of the top, they stopped and hugged the stairs as they listened for signs of Miguel and his men. Hearing nothing more than the wind rustling through the palms, Jake tapped the old man on the shoulder.

Señor Garcia crept up the remaining stairs and stayed low as he made his way behind one of the palms near the top of the stairs. Jake listened for another moment, and then slipped behind a different tree. Steve followed.

They worked their way across the ancient city toward a gate in the west wall. From his previous visit with Teresa, Jake knew it was located at the end of the road approaching the ruins and had an angled view of the buildings at the tourist entrance.

They moved as quickly and silently as possible across exposed areas, hiding behind the stone structures and any other cover they could find. They ran a real risk of spraining an ankle or worse on the uneven and rocky ground, but the use of a light would give their presence away. When they reached the gate, they leaned against the wall next to it and took a minute to catch their breath.

The gate was about six feet high and five feet wide and constructed of one inch diameter metal pipes welded together about four inches apart. Jake leaned over and peeked through the bars toward the two buildings at the entrance to the walled city.

The building closest to the street housed restrooms, and essentially blocked the view of the street from the second building which was approximately thirty feet wide and forty feet long with four ticket booths across the front.

The entrance gates were behind and to the building's right. On the left was a stand of dense woods.

Elena had said the storage area was behind the ticket booths and since Jake couldn't see a door in the side of the building facing him, he assumed it was in the back. As he was trying to figure out the best way to approach, six men walked out from behind the building and stood talking quietly next to it. Jake quickly moved away from the gate.

He'd hoped that only Miguel and the three other men who had come to the cantina were involved in Teresa's kidnapping, but from the looks of things, Miguel had doubled his force. Not counting the two who were tied up down on the beach, Jake, Steve, and Señor Garcia were still outnumbered two to one and Miguel's men had at least five guns to the two Steve and Señor Garcia had taken from the men on the beach. But they'd come this far and, no matter what it took, Jake was not leaving without Teresa.

He checked his watch. Its hands glowed in the dark and he could see that it was almost ten o'clock. He hoped Benito and Petey were in place. He took his phone out to call Benito and have him start down the road for the diversion when suddenly the headlights of an approaching vehicle shone though the bars in the gate.

"I thought Benito and Petey were supposed to wait for your call," Steve whispered. "What the hell are they doing?"

"Listen," Jake whispered, "that doesn't sound like a Volkswagen. Someone else is coming."

"Great," Steve said, under his breath. "I'll bet they've got guns, too."

CHAPTER 34

The headlights got brighter as the car came closer and then suddenly disappeared as the driver reached the end of the road and turned toward the ticket building.

Jake peeked through the gate and saw a big SUV, its motor running and its lights illuminating the group of men alongside the ticket building. Three men broke away from the group and approached the SUV. Jake recognized Miguel and two of the men he'd seen in the cantina. Miguel's hands were empty, but his friends each carried a small machine gun.

Miguel talked to the driver of the SUV for a moment, then turned and said something to the three men still standing next to the building. When he finished, the men turned and went behind the building. Then he opened the back door of the SUV and got inside while the other two men went around and got in on the other side.

"What did he say?" Jake asked Señor Garcia in a whisper.

"He said he would be back soon with food and reinforcements, and when he gets his son; they will kill Teresa and me, and then celebrate. Then he told them to get back to work."

Jake let out an audible breath as the car turned around and began to leave. Miguel, bless his evil black heart, had just evened up the odds, but they wouldn't stay that way for long. As soon as he returned with the promised reinforcements, their chances of rescuing Teresa all but disappeared. If they were going to pull this off, they had to act now.

As the SUV pulled away, Jake quickly dialed Benito's number. "SUV coming your way, don't let them see you, but as soon as they're out of sight, start the diversion," he whispered when Petey answered.

"I'm glad to see the odds reduced," Steve whispered, "but I was hoping to get a chance to take that slimy bastard Miguel out for good."

"Killing him would probably solve the problem, but it will surely bring a set of new ones. Let's just work with what we've got and go get Teresa, before he gets back with those reinforcements."

"Must be Miguel's lucky day. But luck can always change, don't you think?"

"I just hope ours holds out long enough to get Teresa back," Jake replied.

A few minutes later there was a break in the clouds and Jake recognized the shape of the VW Teresa had borrowed from her cousin the day they'd explored the ruins. He peeked through the bars of the gate and watched the little car ease silently down the road stopping about a quarter mile away. He looked back at the ticket building, relieved to see none of the three men guarding Teresa had come back around to the front of the building.

Looking back at the VW, he saw the Bug's lights come on and heard its radio blaring. A moment later he saw Petey and Benito run into the woods next to the walking path.

He moved away from the gate, waited a few moments and then peeked out again. Two armed men were walking toward the road to investigate. They stopped in front of the restrooms and talked for a moment, and then one of the men turned and yelled something in Spanish to the third man who was standing near the back corner of the building.

"What did he say?" Jake whispered to Señor Garcia.

"He said to stay there, they'd be right back. Go now and get Teresa, I will keep them busy if they decide to come back before you get her out of there," he said holding up the gun he'd taken from the beach guard.

"Just hold your fire, old man. We're going to try to do this quietly and we don't need you shooting one of us in the back," Jake said as he felt his pocket to make sure the key Elena had given him was still there. Reassured, he motioned to Steve and the two of them ran across the grounds to the north gate.

Before going through the low stone archway, Jake stopped and turned to Steve. "These Maya guys were only a little over five feet tall. Watch your head going through the wall and be careful on the trail, it's rougher than a cob."

Steve nodded. "What about the old man? You don't really think he'll shoot us, do you?" Jake had told him about his boat's sabotage and who was behind it. "I mean, this isn't another of his stunts to get you out of Teresa's life for good, is it?"

"The thought had crossed my mind, but no, I don't think he'll shoot us. At least not on purpose. I don't believe he had anything to do with Teresa's abduction, he just wants his daughter back."

"Okay, then let's get this show on the road," Steve said with determination.

"Just don't kill anybody unless you absolutely have to. I hear Mexican prisons are nasty places."

"Are you sure?" Steve asked. "Dead men tell no tales."

"And assault charges aren't as bad as murder charges," Jake shot back.

They had to stoop to get through the low passage. Outside the wall, they stayed as close to it as possible as they made their way down the rocky trail to the entrance.

They stumbled a few times and Jake hit his head on a low tree limb, but they made it to the bottom of the trail. Jake peeked around the end of the wall and down the long, straight path to the park entrance. He could see the door in the building where Teresa was being held. He could also see the guard standing next to the building with his back to them. Once they stepped out from behind the wall, all the guard had to do was turn around and he would see them too.

Jake moved back behind the wall so Steve could take a look. As soon as Steve assessed the situation, he handed Jake the gun and the baseball bat he'd used to take out Miguel's man on the beach and pointed to the woods on the other side of the path and then at the guard.

Jake gave him a questioning look, but nodded in agreement. They needed to be discreet as long as possible if they were going to have a chance to get back to the boat without being discovered. Steve's martial arts training had taught him how to take a man out without making a sound. Jake just hoped it had taught him to sneak up on a man the same way.

Jake waited, the gun aimed at the guard's back while Steve slipped across the path and into the woods on the other side, staying in the shadows as much as possible while creeping silently through the brush toward the building.

Keeping his eyes on the guard, Jake waited, hoping the old man wouldn't open fire and give them away. When he saw a flash of movement across the path, he realized that Steve was less than twenty feet from the building. Jake glanced back at the guard who was still in the same place on the side of the building, his back to them as he waited for the other two guards to return.

Jake watched as Steve crept out of the woods and eased across the back of the building. When he got to the corner, he looked back at Jake for the signal that the guard still had his back to them. Jake gave him a thumbs-up gesture and in a flash, Steve was behind the guard, his arms wrapped around the man's head with one hand over his mouth and the other putting pressure on his carotid artery. The man struggled briefly, but in a few seconds he went limp and Steve dropped him on the ground.

With the gun slung over his shoulder and the bat in his hand, Jake came out from behind the wall and ran up to the building, dropping the bat to dig the key out of his pocket.

"Hurry up, Jake. Those other guys will be back any minute," Steve said, as he relieved the guard of his gun and dragged him into the woods on the other side of the building.

Jake unlocked the door, holding his breath and hoping against hope that he'd find Teresa alive and well. Just as he put his hand on the knob, shots rang out from the street on the other side of the restrooms.

"Shit," he whispered under his breath. From the sounds of things, the other two guards were using Serena's car for target practice. He hoped Petey and Benito were well on their way to the beach.

Giving the knob a quick twist, Jake threw open the door and jumped back away from it, just in case there was another guard inside.

He waited a moment, listening for any sounds coming from inside, but didn't hear anything. Sneaking a peek around the door frame, Jake looked inside. The back half of the room was full of stacks and stacks of boxes, and the front half of the room contained nothing more than a couple of chairs and a small table.

He walked through the door, shocked and overcome with confusion and dread as his gaze ran around the nearly empty room. Where was she? Where the hell was Teresa?

"Just get her and let's get out of here," Steve said, picking up the bat and sticking his head in the door. "Hey, where is she?" he asked, looking around the room.

"I don't know," Jake replied with a sinking feeling in his gut. "Nothing makes sense. Miguel hasn't killed her yet or he wouldn't have told his men to kill her and Señor Garcia as soon as he gets Luis."

"Well, she's obviously not in here, so where the hell is she?" Steve asked impatiently. "Listen, the shooting's stopped. If you don't want to wind up with a few dead bodies, ours included, we've got to get out of here, Jake."

Jake fought the panic that threatened to overwhelm him. Where was Teresa?

CHAPTER 35

"Jake, come on," Steve implored. "We're out of time."

Jake ran his eyes over the room again, his gaze stopping on the stacks of boxes that took up half the room. They were stacked from wall to wall and almost as high as the ceiling.

"Jake!" Steve hissed. "Come on, man, snap out of it. She's not here and we gotta go."

"You go ahead, I need to check something out," Jake said.

"I'm not leaving without you," Steve argued.

"And I'm not leaving without Teresa," Jake said walking over to the wall of boxes and pushing one in the top row with the barrel of the gun he held. It wasn't very heavy and moved easily, but most importantly, there didn't seem to be anything behind it. Leaning the gun against the wall, Jake pulled the box off the stack and set it on the floor behind him.

"Steve, give me a hand with these boxes," Jake said, looking back toward the door. But Steve was gone. Jake felt the cold hand of fear beginning to creep into his veins, but quickly tamped it down. He was running out of time.

As he reached to move the next box to the floor, Jake heard a small sound. Could be rats, he thought, or it could be something else. When he pulled the box off the second row from the top and looked through the gap, relief like he'd never felt before filled his whole being.

Behind the wall of boxes, Teresa lay on a cot, barefoot and wearing only the nightgown that she'd had on when she'd been abducted. Her wrists and ankles were secured with black zip ties and her mouth was covered with a piece of duct tape. Her eyes were closed but Jake could see the gentle rise and fall of her chest and knew she was still alive.

Jake quickly cleared a path through the boxes. He knelt

down beside the cot and smoothed the silky black hair away from her face, startling her awake. Jake saw the flash of fear flicker through her eyes until she recognized him.

"Teresa, honey, are you all right?" he asked after pulling the tape off her mouth.

"Ouch. I think so. I knew you would come for me, but what took you so long?" she asked, obviously annoyed. "I've been here four days."

"I told you nothing would stop me from rescuing you, but it took me a little while to find out where you were."

"I hope you will work on your timing for next time," she said flatly, letting her Latin temper show just a little.

"There had better not be a next time," Jake strongly advised.

"Oh, Dios mio, thank you so much," she said as he cut the zip ties binding her wrists and ankles with his knife.

"So are you glad to see me?' he asked with a smile.

"I have never been so happy to see anyone in my life," she said, kissing him and then rubbing her wrists and moving her ankles around to get the blood circulating again.

"I was hoping you'd say that, but I was beginning to wonder," he said with a smile.

Just then, several short bursts of machine gun fire sounded from somewhere outside. Jake wasn't sure who was shooting, but he knew it was time to get the hell away from here.

Come on," he said, grabbing her arm and picking up the gun leaning against the wall, "we don't have much time before the guards come back, unless your father kills them all first."

"Papa is here? But Jake, he is so old and frail, he could get hurt."

"Don't worry about your Papa. He can take care of himself and right now he's armed to the teeth."

Teresa was a little stiff starting out, but loosened up as she followed Jake to the door. He eased out the door and around to the edge of the building so he could see the path down to the street. The shooting had stopped, but he could hear men laughing and speaking in Spanish. He couldn't see them yet, but it sounded like they were getting closer.

"Stay low and run up the path until you get to that clump of trees, then stop and wait for me. The path is very dark and bumpy, so be careful. I'll be right behind you."

"I love you, Jake Arnold," she said as she kissed him. Pushing through the door, she sprinted for the entrance path. When she was across the open stretch and out of sight, Jake exhaled and took another breath.

Going back to the store room door, he pulled the key out of his pocket and took a moment to relock the door. It was probably a waste of time but he didn't want to alert anyone of Teresa's absence before they had a chance to get back to the boat.

Staying low, he sprinted down the path and up the hill, dodging boulders and potholes at every step. When he got to the trees, he stopped. It was pitch black here and he knew better than to try to run through this section.

"Teresa," he whispered, "Where are you?"

"I'm here,' she said, reaching out and touching his leg. "But I think I may have sprained my ankle."

Jake took her hand and realized she was sitting on the path almost at his feet.

"Can you walk?"

"I can try," she said, "just help me up."

"Why don't I carry you? The guards are on their way back to the storage room and we need to hurry."

They both stiffened as another short burst of gunfire broke the silence. Between the wall and the sea, he couldn't tell exactly where it was coming from, but it was definitely closer.

They waited a second or two more, listening intently, and then Jake turned to let Teresa put her arms around his neck and her legs around his waist so he could carry her piggyback up the path.

"Somewhere along here is a low branch. Hold your hand out in front of us, so we'll know where it is before I smack into it," he whispered.

"Stop," Teresa whispered a few feet farther up the path. "Let me down."

Jake was easing her down when a single shot hit the branch beside them. He turned quickly, trying to put himself between Teresa and the shooter, but he stumbled on a loose stone in the path and fell backward toward the wall of the ancient city, dropping his gun in the process.

He heard Teresa's breath leave her body as he fell on top of her. Afraid that he'd hurt her, he moved off her and to the side before trying to get to his feet. He could hear footsteps coming up the path.

Oh, shit, he thought as he reached around in the dark, trying to find the gun. Suddenly a light hit him in the face and Jake froze.

"Don't you two think you should wait until we get out of here before you start with the romantic crap again?" Steve said with a chuckle.

"Steve, what are you doing here?' Teresa asked.

Jake exhaled deeply, relieved that they weren't about to get shot. "Where the hell did you take off to? I turned around and you were gone."

"Watching your back, as usual. You didn't seem like you were ready to leave and I couldn't just stand there and let those two guards discover us."

"Speaking of the guards, where are they now?" Jake asked.

"Taking a siesta," Steve said, holding the baseball bat up to the light. "I volunteered to hold their guns for them while they napped," he added, putting his hand on the gun straps hanging over his shoulder.

"That was very considerate of you," Jake said.

"Yeah, I thought so too. They'll be out for a while, but we should probably get out of here anyway."

"I like that idea," Teresa agreed. "I want to go home."

At that moment, Jake was glad it was dark and Teresa couldn't see his face. He didn't have the heart to tell her she wouldn't be going home anytime in the near future.

After retrieving the gun he'd dropped, Jake helped Teresa through the arched opening of the ancient city and then helped her climb on his back again. With Steve lighting the way, they made it back across the ruins to the pipe gate to collect Teresa's father.

"Hurry up and turn that light off, we have company," Señor Garcia growled. Before Steve switched the flashlight off, Jake saw Benito and Petey standing next to Teresa's father.

"I thought you guys were supposed to meet us at the boat," Jake whispered.

"We thought you might need some help," Benito said, "and since we were in the neighborhood…"

"Oh, shit. We've got trouble," Petey said, looking through the gate to the road in the distance.

Everyone followed his gaze toward the road where two sets of headlights were approaching the ruins. The first one was the SUV Miguel had left in, but the second vehicle was a much larger truck.

"He's brought the fucking Army," Benito said. "We've got to get to the boat and get the hell out of here before they see us."

CHAPTER 36

They ducked down behind the wall as the trucks turned toward the ticket building. As soon as the headlights swung past their location, Steve handed the extra guns he'd been carrying to Benito and Petey.

With Teresa once again riding piggyback, this time on Benito's back, they all took off toward the stairway that led down to the beach and Jake's waiting boat. Using the old Maya structures, big rocks and shrubbery as cover, they leapfrogged their way across the historic city, taking cover in a stand of trees about five yards from the top of the staircase.

Jake motioned to Benito to take Teresa down the stairs first. With her sprained ankle, they would need the most time. When they were below the cliff line and out of sight, Jake sent Petey down next.

Before he sent Señor Garcia down the stairs, Jake looked up at the night sky and knew they were in trouble. Stars were visible through a break in the cloud cover that was quickly heading their way. In just a few seconds the moon would light up the sky in front of them and they would stand out like sore thumbs when they stepped out of their hiding places to cross the open area to the stairs.

Jake turned back and saw men pouring out of the truck and heading toward the ticket building. He looked back at the sky again. More dark clouds were coming in behind the break and would soon blot out the moon again, but not soon enough. He could hear Miguel's men shouting to one another and knew it wouldn't be long before Teresa's absence was discovered.

Jake motioned for Señor Garcia to go next. The old man dashed across the clearing, but before he could take the first step down the stairs the clouds parted and the bright full moon lit up the entire ruins, catching Teresa's father silhouetted in the moonlight.

He heard the shouts of one of Miguel's men as he saw him too. Shots rang out and Jake turned back to see the top of Señor Garcia's head disappearing down the stairs. He turned back again to see armed men spilling out the back of the Army truck. They had less than a minute before Miguel's men made it to the cliff.

"Go!" he said to Steve.

"Not without you," Steve said as he returned fire on the approaching men.

"I'll be right behind you, damn it, just make sure Paul has the boat off the beach and ready to haul ass," Jake said, firing a spray of shots across the open field behind them.

Steve dashed across the clearing and headed down the stairs while Jake covered him. As soon as his friend cleared the top of the cliff, Jake sprayed another burst in the direction of Miguel's men and took off running for the stairs. When he stopped his forward momentum to take the first step down the staircase, he felt a searing heat across his right side.

"Damn it," he muttered. He knew he'd been shot, but he didn't have time to check out the damage. He turned and fired another spray at the approaching men and then jumped down the stairs to the first landing.

Out of the four runs of stairs, it was the longest and he landed hard. Pain shot up from the bottom of his feet all the way up his thighs. It took a second to regain his footing, but as soon as he did, he took off at a run down the next set. The third run was short, only five steps and he briefly thought about vaulting over the railing and skipping the fourth run altogether, but suddenly remembered the big rocks next to the base of the staircase. It was a good thing he'd been here during the day or he might have vaulted to a broken leg or worse. Instead he took the last run two steps at a time.

As soon as he hit the sand at the bottom, he looked up

to see his boat a few yards off the beach and completely illuminated in the moonlight. Paul was at the helm while Señor Garcia and Benito stood in the bow in front of Teresa to protect her from the gunshots. He saw Steve and Petey motioning him to hurry. With his goal in sight, he ran as fast as he could, praying the cloud cover would return.

The next thing he knew, he was sprawled face first in the sand at the edge of the water, his side hurting like hell. He heard Teresa scream and looked up to see Señor Garcia and Benito firing at the top of the cliff.

Dazed and momentarily blinded by the muzzle flash, Jake could have sworn he heard his father's voice telling him the same thing he'd said every time Jake had attempted to overcome a challenge. *"Go for it, son."*

Jake shook his head to clear it and then quickly picked himself up and ran into the surf. His first attempt to crawl over the side of the boat failed. His side was on fire and the gun still clutched in his hand didn't make things any easier.

While Señor Garcia and Benito continued firing on the cliff, Jake dropped the gun and held his arms up. Steve and Petey each grabbed one tightly. "Go," Jake said loudly.

With impeccable timing, Paul hit the gas and Jake jumped as high as the wound in his side would allow. With Steve and Petey still tightly holding his arms, Jake let the water rushing past him push his legs almost horizontal to the gunnel. When he got one foot hooked over the side, Steve and Petey hauled him in the rest of the way. The whole process took only seconds.

"Hit it, Paul," Steve yelled as soon as Jake was in the boat.

With bullets peppering the water all around them, Paul slammed the throttle to the limit. The engine screamed at the onslaught of power and the weight of seven people, but the prop bit into the water and soon the boat was up on plane and moving away from the beach.

As soon as they were out of range of the guns on the cliff, Teresa crawled over to where Jake still lay sprawled in the bottom of the boat.

"Madre de Dios, Jake," she said, kissing him first and then slapping his shoulder, "don't you ever scare me like that again. I thought they'd shot you."

"I'm fine, sweetheart," he lied. "As a matter of fact, I'm better than fine now that I've got you back." He wasn't fine and he knew it, but he didn't want to scare her. The salt water was burning the wound in his side and hurt like hell.

"What the hell, Jake, we all thought you'd been shot," Steve said.

"I just tripped over a rock," Jake said with a grimace he hoped would pass for a grin.

While Jake took a few minutes to pull himself together, Paul headed south, hugging the rugged coast for shelter. The clouds rolled back in to cover the moon and once again plunged them into inky darkness. Jake pulled himself to his feet and with the aid of a flashlight, found his GPS and plotted a course for the rendezvous point with Patrick and Vanessa before taking over the wheel. Turning the boat north, he headed into the night.

The pain in his side had subsided to a dull ache, but he knew they weren't out of the woods yet. If Miguel had the kind of pull to get the Mexican Army involved, it wasn't out of the realm of possibility that he could involve the Mexican Navy, if that's what they called the military boats he'd seen patrolling the coast the last few weeks.

The clouds opened up and the deluge began, soaking everything and everybody on board. Jake had been counting on being able to see the lights of Cozumel to help him find the yacht, but the clouds and the rain had obliterated any possibility of that. He was down to the only navigational aid he had left, his GPS, and as he thought about it, a sinking feeling started in the pit of his stomach. He hadn't replaced the battery since he'd been in Mexico and he wasn't sure how much juice the old one had left.

Jake checked his GPS every few minutes, making course corrections when needed and keeping his fingers crossed that the battery wouldn't give out. The limited visibility and the fear of colliding with another vessel had forced him to reduce their speed to half of what he would have liked, but the need to reach the yacht kept him from stopping until the weather improved.

Jake looked down to check his GPS again, and his heart sank. It was dead. He tapped on it with his finger, shut it off and then turned it back on but nothing happened. Shit. He knew they were close to the rendezvous point, but without the GPS, he couldn't be sure which way to turn to reach it. He reduced the throttle even more, hoping he'd see the yacht before they plowed into it.

A few minutes later, and with still no sign of the yacht, Jake took the motor out of gear. All he was doing was wasting gas. Gas that his friends and Señor Garcia were going to need to make it back to Playa.

"What's up, Jake?" Steve asked.

"My GPS is dead and without it we'll never find the yacht in this soup," he said dejectedly.

"So hook it up to the boat battery," Paul suggested.

"No, the boat battery has way too much juice," Petey said. "It'll fry it as soon as you turn it on."

"Why don't you just call Vanessa and have her turn some lights on? We're close, right?" Steve asked

"I thought so, but now I can't be sure," he admitted, reaching into his pocket for his phone. "Damn, why didn't I think of that?" He opened his phone and his heart sank even lower at the sight of the black screen and he remembered slogging through the surf to get to the boat.

"Uh, that's not going to work. It's dead, too."

"Here," Benito said handing over his phone, "use mine, it's one of those new waterproof ones."

Jake took the phone reluctantly. "There's just one other problem."

"Jesus, Jake, we're all soaking wet. Just call her and let's get out of this shit before someone comes along and puts two and two together," Paul said, annoyed.

"God damn it, Paul, I can't. I had her number saved in my contact list, so I never bothered to memorize it," Jake said losing his temper. He wasn't angry with his friends, he was angry with himself. He should have covered this possibility by bringing a water tight bag for his phone, but he hadn't thought of it.

"Hey, Jake, just relax," Petey said, soothingly. "Look, every time you make a call, the number pops up on the screen. Just close your eyes and concentrate on what you saw each time you called her."

Jake closed his eyes and thought hard. He opened them and dialed a number. After a few rings with no answer, he hung up, looked back at his friends and shook his head. He tried again with the same results.

"Try again, Jake, but put it on speaker this time," Teresa said softly.

Jake closed his eyes again and tried to visualize Vanessa's number as he'd seen it on his phone. After several moments, he opened his eyes and dialed again.

Everyone waited expectantly as they listened to the phone ringing on the other end. His heart skipped a beat when someone answered.

"Vanessa?" he asked hesitantly.

"Jake, where the hell are you?"

CHAPTER 37

A collective sigh went up at the sound of Vanessa's voice and Jake slumped back in his seat, overwhelmed with relief.

"Jake, can you hear me?" Vanessa's voice came over the phone.

Steve took the phone out of Jake's hands. "Hey, Vanessa, this is Steve. I think our friend is speechless at the moment, but you could do us a big favor by turning on some lights so we can find you."

"Is everyone all right?" Vanessa asked.

"We're fine, just need a little light," Steve answered.

"No problem. We should have thought of that. All right, Patrick's turned on the anchor light. Do you see it?"

"There," Petey pointed off to port.

Jake followed his finger and saw a dim glow through the fog in the distance.

"We see it. Be there in five," Steve said and hung up.

By the time they pulled up next to the yacht, Patrick had the engines idling and the anchor pulled and was waiting with Vanessa and Wilma on the covered back deck.

Steve and Paul secured lines from the bow of Jake's boat to cleats on the yacht's stern while Benito picked up Teresa and carried her across to the yacht. Señor Garcia followed with Teresa's baggage and Petey and Paul were right behind him with Jake's suitcase and backpack.

As Steve started to make his way across he stopped and slapped Jake on the shoulder. "Dodged another bullet, Jake. Good job," he said as he stepped across the gunwale to the yacht.

While the Boys Club greeted Vanessa, Patrick escorted Benito, who was still carrying Teresa, and her parents inside. Jake eased up out of his seat, picked up his backpack and gingerly crossed over, the pain in his side making movement difficult. As soon as he made it under the overhang, Vanessa met him, standing on tiptoe to kiss his cheek.

"You all look like a bunch of drowned rats," she said running a hand down his side.

Jake flinched when she touched the sore spot next to his ribs. She pulled back and took her hand away and looked down at it.

"Oh shit, Jake, you're bleeding," she said with alarm.

Steve heard her and whipped his head around. "Maybe you didn't dodge that bullet after all," he said, walking over to lift up Jake's shirt.

"Let's get you inside and see how bad it is," Vanessa said.

"I need to see about Teresa first," Jake argued as he walked toward the salon.

Patrick had thrown a towel across the sofa's upholstery so Benito could put Teresa down, and was passing out additional towels to everyone else when Jake walked into the salon.

"Teresa, I'd like you to meet my friends Patrick and Vanessa," he said. He turned to Patrick and Vanessa. "This is Teresa Santiago, and her father, Señor Garcia, and her cousin, Benito Garcia and you've met Wilma. Patrick, these guys are Petey and Paul, friends of mine and I'm sure you remember Steve."

"My ambulance driver, yes. I've heard a lot about the three of you," Patrick said with a round of handshakes. "And it's good to meet all of you, too," Patrick said nodding at Teresa and shaking hands with her father and cousin.

"It's very nice to meet both of you," Teresa replied. "I'm sorry we are messing up your beautiful boat."

"Don't worry about that," Vanessa said. "Patrick, will you get Teresa an ice pack for her ankle and the first aid kit? Jake's been shot."

All eyes turned to look at Jake.

"What?" Teresa said trying to get to her feet.

"It's just a scratch, sweetheart, I'm fine," Jake said, pushing Teresa back on the couch and shooting Vanessa a dirty look.

"I don't believe you, let me see," Teresa said stubbornly.

Jake hadn't seen it himself, up until now it had been too dark and he hadn't wanted to alarm anyone, and he wasn't about to let Teresa see it if it turned out to be worse than he thought. Patrick came back from the galley with an ice pack and laid it gently on Teresa's ankle and then handed Vanessa the first aid kit.

"I swear there's nothing to worry about. You just keep that ice on your ankle and I'll let Vanessa fix me up with a Band-Aid," he said calmly.

Teresa turned to Vanessa. "You will take good care of him?" she asked.

"Yes, I will," she said, seeing the fear in Teresa's eyes. "Don't worry; I've got two younger brothers who are constantly getting hurt. I've had to patch them up many times.

"Patrick, take the guys up to the cockpit and show them how fast this thing can get us out of here while Señor Garcia talks to the ladies. Come on Jake; let's go to the galley where I can clean you up."

Jake followed her into the galley where she slid the door shut behind them. "Hell, Vanessa, you didn't have to scare the crap out of her like that," he said with a note of annoyance.

"I'm sorry about that, but I wanted to get you away from everyone so we could talk," she admitted.

"What's there to talk about?" he asked as she cut his shirt off and threw it in the trash.

"You told us about this guy Miguel who kidnapped Teresa, and that he's part of one of the drug cartels down here, so pick it up from there. What exactly happened when you went to rescue her?"

"Things started out pretty good. We got there just in time to see Miguel and a couple of his men leave. Señor Garcia said they were going to get reinforcements, so we got it in gear, took out the remaining guards and got Teresa," he said going into as little detail as possible.

"So if you took care of the guards, then who the hell shot you?" she asked, wiping the blood off his side with a piece of moist gauze.

"Benito said it was the, uh, Mexican Army," Jake admitted.

"Oh, Christ. The Army shot you?" she asked. "That's not good, Jake."

"Well, we were shooting at them."

"With what? You said you didn't have a gun, that's why you asked me to bring you one, remember?'

"Yeah, well, we relieved the guards of several."

"Where are those guns now?" she asked, dabbing the wound with peroxide.

"Damn, that stings," Jake said, jerking away from her.

"That's what you get for screwing around with the Mexican Army, you idiot. Answer the question."

"I threw mine overboard trying to get in the boat, but there's four more still in the boat."

"You need to get rid of them," she said, looking him in the eye.

"And then what do we use if they come after us again?" he asked.

"Look, Jake. Patrick and I go in and out of a lot of these banana republics and one thing I can tell you is they don't like their citizens or visitors, especially visitors, having guns. Patrick was against letting me bring you one. He's never been too fond of them in the first place and after getting shot himself you can probably understand his reluctance.

"I think the only reason he agreed was because it was for you and he feels like he owes you something. But places like Mexico, if they catch you with a gun; they put you in jail and let you rot."

"I'm aware of that, but I'm not letting them get their hands on Teresa, even if it kills me," he said adamantly.

"Well, you are not, NOT, going to bring them onboard this yacht, do you hear me? If you've got the Army after you, you may very well have the Navy after you and if we get boarded, and by the way, the chances of that are pretty damn good, I am not about to rot in a Mexican prison for your girlfriend," she said slapping the bandage on his side.

"Jesus, Vanessa, take it easy, will you?"

"I'm serious, Jake, get rid of the guns."

"Okay, I'll get rid of the guns. What the hell is going on with you anyway?"

"What are you talking about?"

"You were never this mean and crabby before. Are things okay with you and Patrick?"

"Things are just fine with me and Patrick. Thanks for asking," she said tossing the tape in a drawer. Gathering up the trash bag she'd put his shirt and bloody gauze in, she went to the cabinet, took out a can of beans and dropped it in the bag before tying it shut. Opening the window behind the galley sink, she threw the bag into the Caribbean.

"You should go to the cockpit and let the guys know you're okay," she said on her way out the door.

Jake watched her retreating back, wondering what was really going on and why she wasn't telling him.

CHAPTER 38

While Señor Garcia introduced Teresa to her mother in the salon, Jake got a clean shirt out of his backpack and joined the others in the cockpit for a drink. He knew they didn't have a lot of time, but he also knew that once Teresa learned what had happened so long ago with her parents, she and her mother would need time to reconnect.

"Looks like you made it out in reasonably good shape," Patrick said after Jake reached into the cooler and popped the top off a cold one. "What's the body count for the other side?"

"We knocked out a few of them, but I don't think anybody died."

"That's better than the last time," Patrick noted as he made a minor course adjustment.

"Won't this tub go any faster, Patrick?" Vanessa asked, joining them. "Jake said this guy Miguel had the Mexican Army shooting at them. It sounds like he's connected pretty well and I don't want to be anywhere near here if they decide to send out a patrol boat."

"I'm going as fast as I dare in these waters, babe. Any faster would look like we're running from something."

"Aren't we?" she asked.

"Well, yes. We just don't want to look like we are," Patrick returned with a smile.

"Jake, don't forget about that thing we talked about," Vanessa reminded him with a pointed look.

"What thing was it that you and Vanessa talked about?" Steve asked after she'd left.

"We need to dump the guns overboard," Jake told Steve.

"But what if we need them?" Steve asked.

"Hopefully you won't. If you guys get stopped on your

way back to Playa, just pretend you're on a fishing charter. Everyone knows Benito takes out charters and there's a couple of fishing poles on board. Fake it. The guns will just cause more problems than they're worth."

"Madre de Dios, I need a drink," said Senor Garcia as he walked into the cockpit. "Do you have any tequila?"

"No, you've had enough tequila for the night, but you can have a beer," Jake said reaching into the cooler.

While Benito and the Boys Club checked out the instruments on the yacht, Señor Garcia turned to Jake. "Thank you for saving my daughter," he said.

"I couldn't have done it without everyone's help."

"And thank you for not telling her about my deception and allowing me to keep my dignity," he added in a whisper.

"No problem," Jake replied.

"Now we must have the marriage. Do you have a priest and a ring?" Señor Garcia asked loudly.

Jake looked into the shocked faces of his friends. This wasn't exactly the way he had intended to tell them he was getting married, but it was too late for that now.

"As captain of this ship, Patrick can perform the ceremony, but I think you should take a few minutes and talk to Teresa first. She needs to know what's going on and I think you should be the one to tell her," Jake calmly replied.

"Yes, you are right. But you should come with me. She is worried about you." he said.

"You're right, I should," Jake agreed. He drained the beer and put the empty in the trash.

"You're getting married?" Petey and Paul said in unison.

"Yes, if Teresa will have me, I'm getting married."

"You're sure you want to do this?" Steve asked.

"I'm sure. Now let's get this show on the road," he said, following Señor Garcia back to the salon.

"You know, Vanessa's right about those guns. Let me

stop this baby for a minute so you guys can get back to Jake's boat and dump them," Patrick said to Steve.

He took the yacht out of gear, and Steve and Petey went out through the side door and around the edge of the yacht to the back deck. Petey pulled Jake's boat as close as he could and Steve jumped on it. It didn't take him but a few seconds to locate the guns and toss them overboard.

Then he was back on the yacht and he and Petey went back to the cockpit the same way they'd left. As soon as they came through the door, Patrick put the engines back into gear and hit the throttle. Then he set the heading and engaged the auto pilot.

* * *

In the salon, Wilma sat with Teresa on the sofa, running her hand down Teresa's back while Vanessa stood a few feet away.

"Don't worry, Teresa. The bullet only creased his side. He'll be fine," Vanessa reassured her.

"He is a fine and strong young man, it will take more than that to stop him," Wilma agreed.

"Thank you for taking care of him for me," Teresa said.

"It's what friends do," Vanessa said.

"What is all this?" Teresa said looking around at the wedding decorations. "Is someone getting married?"

"Our charter is a wedding party. The bride and groom got married a few nights ago in Miami. We have to pick them up in the morning and then we'll head back," Vanessa explained.

"What is going on, Papa?" Teresa asked as soon as her father and Jake entered the salon. "Why are my suitcases here?"

Jake stopped just inside the salon while José Luis walked over and sat on the other side of his daughter. He took her hands in his and said, "You must go with Jake. He will take you and Luis and keep you safe until Miguel is no longer a problem."

"What? Where is he taking us? To America?" she asked, indignant. "I told you Papa, I would not leave you, and I meant it."

"You only said that because you knew it was what I wanted to hear. Now I'm telling you that you must go."

"But papa," she argued.

"Enough. You love him, don't you?"

"Yes, Papa, I do," she admitted.

"Then you will marry Jake and go to America with him and he will bring you back when it's safe."

"But Papa, how will you manage without me? The apartments and the cantina require a lot of work and you have not been well," she said.

José Luis looked over at Wilma and smiled. "I am feeling better than I have in a long time, my daughter. My heart was sick for many years, but no longer. Knowing that you and Luis are safe and happy is the only medicine I need. Please, marry Jake and go with him to America."

"Are you sure this is what you want, Papa?" she asked.

"I am sure," he said with a smile on his face and sadness in his eyes.

Patrick, Benito, Steve and the twins entered the salon in time to catch Teresa hugging her father.

"Now it is up to you," Señor Garcia said to Jake, breaking off the embrace.

Jake looked at his friends and then at Teresa, before looking back at Teresa's parents.

"Can you all give us a minute in private?" Jake asked.

"Okay, but make it quick," Wilma said. "I don't want to risk losing my daughter now that I've finally found her again.

"Patrick, grab their bags and take them below, please," Vanessa asked.

Jake waited until everyone had left and then turned to Teresa. Dropping down on one knee if front of her, he took her slim brown hand into his. "This wasn't how this was supposed to happen, but I love you Teresa. Will you be my wife?"

"Yes, I would love to. When we get to Florida we can have a nice church wedding…"

"I meant right now. In the next five minutes."

"But there is no priest. How do you get married without a priest?"

"Patrick can perform the ceremony."

"Now?" she asked in disbelief. "I have no dress and I can't get married in a dirty nightgown. Look at me, Jake. A girl waits all her life for her wedding. It's not supposed to be like this," she said as tears rolled down her cheeks.

"I know, and it won't be, really. What I'm trying to say is that your father wants to see a wedding before we go. Patrick said it won't really be legal since we're not in international waters, so we won't actually be married. I was thinking that we could give your father the wedding he wants now and then have a real wedding once we're at sea. That is, if you want to marry me."

"What about Luis?"

"As soon as this preliminary wedding is over, we're going to go get him. I'd like to be his father."

"Then yes, I will marry you."

Jake rummaged around in his backpack for a minute and brought out the velvet box. He took out the emerald and diamond ring and slid it onto Teresa's finger.

"Oh, Jake it is so beautiful," she said with tears in her eyes as she looked down at the vivid green stone with its pair of half-carat diamonds, one on each side.

"It was my grandmother's and I know she would be proud to have you wear it," Jake said.

"Are you sure this is what you want, to marry me, I mean?"

"I'm sure, but I have to ask you something and I don't want you to take it the wrong way?"

"What is it?"

"Back there, at the ruins, did Miguel uh, force himself

on you?"

"If he had, would you still want me?" she asked with a note of concern, but holding her head high.

"Of course I would," he assured her. "I'd just have to go back and kill him."

"Then no, he didn't force himself on me. He slapped me a couple of times when I tried to escape, but that was just so he could look important to his friends, I think."

"Then I guess I won't have to kill him. Now that that's out of the way, are you ready to go home with me?"

"Oh yes," she said, throwing her arms around him. She pulled back a second later. "But I can't. Our passports. Jake, we will need them if we are going to America with you."

"Your father gave them to me. They're right here in my backpack."

"Papa gave them to you? But how did he know I even had them?"

"Luis told him."

"Oh."

"Teresa, why did you have the passports? Were you planning a trip?"

"The thought did cross my mind," she admitted before dropping her gaze to study her hands. "I got them so Luis and I could visit a friend who lives in Florida," she said softly.

"Who is this friend?" Jake asked, trying not to sound jealous.

"You," she said smiling up at him. "Only seeing you twice a year is hard. I wanted to see where and how you live. I wanted to meet Casey and see your Salty Dog Saloon. But I knew Papa would not approve, so I didn't tell him."

"He loves you, Teresa. He was afraid of being alone, but I think he realizes now that the safety of his family is more important."

"And the two of you are friends now?" she asked.

"Yes. Your father and I are friends. At least until he's realizes he's going to have to find a new fisherman to supply the cantina with fish," he said with a smile.

"Oh, that won't be a problem. I have had one lined up since you got here. I just wanted to give you an incentive to stay," she said with a sly smile.

"I see. It seems you are as devious and scheming as your father," he said teasing.

"Jake?" she asked with tears in her eyes.

"What, sweetheart?"

"Thank you for finding my mother and bringing her to me."

"You're welcome, but I don't think I could have stopped her if I tried," Jake admitted. "She's as determined as you are."

Teresa was drying her tears when the men came back into the salon and Vanessa and Wilma came up from below.

"I'd like you all to meet Teresa, my soon-to-be wife. She just agreed to marry me," Jake announced proudly.

After a round of back-slapping and hugs, Wilma sat beside her daughter. "I hope you don't mind, but Vanessa and I went through your bag and found a dress that might work for a casual wedding," she said to Teresa.

"Let us help you downstairs so we can get you cleaned up and dressed," added Vanessa. "Excuse us for a few minutes, guys."

"Yes, I need to change, too. Is there a room I could use?" Wilma asked Vanessa.

"Of course."

Jake watched the three women go down the stairs and checked his watch. He hoped they wouldn't be long. Patrick was making good time on their dash up the coast but it had already been over an hour since they'd left Tulum with part of the Mexican Army on their tails.

How long would it take Miguel to bribe someone in the Navy?

CHAPTER 39

While Teresa took a quick shower, and Wilma changed for the wedding in another stateroom, Vanessa rounded up a few supplies and found an ace bandage for Teresa's ankle. After helping her into a fluffy white robe, she wrapped the swollen ankle loosely before looking up at the tiny Mexican woman.

"How do you want to wear your hair?" she asked, standing and plucking the towel off Teresa's head.

As the mass of wet dark hair cascaded down, Teresa grabbed it with both hands. "I can do it," she said picking up the brush Vanessa had dropped on the bed beside her.

"No, let me," Vanessa said, holding out her hand for the brush. "I know how relaxing it feels to have someone brush your hair, and you've had a rough few days."

Teresa was quiet for a moment. "That would be nice, thank you," she said, handing the brush over. "It's still wet so I think I'd like to have it up if that's okay."

"I think I can manage that," Vanessa said.

Vanessa worked quickly to untangle what four days with no brush had made, braided it loosely, and then began pinning it into a coil on the back of Teresa's head. She left a few wispy strands in the front to frame her heart-shaped face.

"How did you meet Jake?" Vanessa asked.

"Jake and his friends came down a few years ago and stayed in my apartments for a week. I talked to him several times during their stay and thought he was a nice man, very good-looking, but nothing more really. But the day he left he stopped in to say goodbye and gave me a hug. Just a simple hug, but that's all it took. From the first moment he touched me, I knew he had changed my life.

"When he wrapped his arms around me and held me tight, I felt an energy flowing through him, a strength that

I hadn't expected to feel, but one that I was immediately attracted to. Jake and his friends went back to their homes in Florida, but for weeks, that hug was all I could think about. My skin still tingles when I think about it," Teresa admitted.

"He must have felt it too," Vanessa said.

"How do you and your husband know Jake?" Teresa asked.

"That's a long story, but I'll make it short. I used to date him and hurt him badly when it ended."

"Oh. He told me about that but I didn't know it was you. But you are all still friends?"

"Yes, I hope we'll always be friends. Jake is one of the best men I've ever known and he deserves to be happy. You're lucky to have a man like him love you."

"Yes, I am. And besides being strong and very good to look at," she said smiling, "he loves Luis, too. He will be a good father, I think."

A couple of seconds passed before Teresa turned to look at Vanessa. "I know Jake was in love with you once and you must have had feelings for him as well. Are you jealous?" she asked.

"Maybe a little, but not the way you think. I'm perfectly happy with Patrick. I love the ground that man walks on, he's my knight in shining armor, but I have to admit I'm a little jealous about the excitement and the thrill of your story-book romance. We've been married three years now and everything is good, but we've settled into a routine. Don't get me wrong, I like it, but sometimes it feels a little short on excitement."

"I could do with a little less excitement, thank you," Teresa said with a smile. "After hearing Miguel tell his men that once he had Luis he was going to kill my father and me, I was filled with fear. Then Jake rescued me just like in the dream I had as a child. When I opened my eyes and saw him standing in that storeroom, a sense of relief like I've never felt came over me."

She thought for a moment and then said. "Yes, I think I would like a more comfortable routine and less excitement."

"Well, if the two of you are lucky, you'll have the next thirty or forty years to work on that."

"Then I hope we will be very lucky, because I do not believe in divorce," Teresa said.

Vanessa finished Teresa's hair and began working on her makeup. Except for the dark circles under her eyes from lack of sleep, her skin was flawless, so all that was required was a little concealer and a dab of lip gloss.

"Teresa, did Jake tell you this wedding won't be legal?" Vanessa asked, getting back to the task at hand.

"Yes, he said that this was just for Papa and we would do it again later."

"Okay, I just want to make sure you know what you're getting into, or not into, as the case may be."

"Thank you for helping us, Vanessa. Jake has good friends."

"He's earned them."

* * *

Jake took a quick shower and changed in the third stateroom, and then met the rest of the guys in the roomy cockpit while they waited for the women.

He popped the top off a beer and walked over to Steve. "How do you feel about being my best man, Steve?"

"I'd be honored, but I think you should ask Benito."

"Don't tell me you're still opposed to the idea of Teresa and I getting married," Jake said.

"No, I'm fine with it. But the twins and I told you we were taking the Boys Club international, and I think this would be a good opportunity to break Benito into our little club," he said with a grin.

"You don't think getting shot at and practically being stranded at sea is initiation enough?" Jake asked.

"Nah, that's the easy stuff. All this touchy feely stuff is

much more of a challenge."

"You sure about this?" Jake asked.

"Jake, there's nothing I would be prouder to do than to stand up for you at your wedding, but I think this would mean a lot to Benito. Besides, in the interest of time and all that, I told Patrick I'd watch the helm while he performed the ceremony," Steve confessed quietly. "This thing will drive itself but it will also run over anything in its way. I don't think we want to risk that tonight, do you?"

Jake turned to Benito. "So, what do you say, Benito. Will you be my best man?"

"I would be proud to help you marry my cousin," Benito said with a smile. "She's been a difficult one to find a husband for."

"I'm glad she waited for me."

"You have seen her temper, are you sure you can deal with it for the rest of your life, because you know, she does not believe in divorce."

"Hush, Benito," Señor Garcia said, "let them get married first, and then you can scare him."

They were all laughing when Vanessa came up the stairs with her camera in her hand and Wilma and Teresa behind her. Jake noticed the nod Vanessa gave Patrick to let him know the wedding was on and then looked at Teresa.

She looked beautiful in the gauzy white summer dress with spaghetti straps and zig zag hem she was wearing, but Jake hardly noticed. He would have married her in her old dirty nightgown.

"Let's get everybody together in the salon and get this show on the road," Patrick said, turning the wheel over to Steve.

In the salon, Vanessa began arranging people for the ceremony when she noticed Teresa's bare feet.

"Hang on a minute, Patrick. Teresa needs some shoes and I think I have a pair of white pumps downstairs that she can wear. Let me go get them."

"No," Jake said sharply and then looked down into Teresa's eyes. "Teresa's never been much for wearing shoes and I like her just the way she is," he said before kissing her lightly.

"She should fit in well back home," Petey whispered to Paul.

"Yep," his brother agreed.

While Vanessa darted around taking pictures, Teresa and Jake stood before Patrick with Benito and Wilma at their sides. Patrick used an abbreviated version of the marriage ceremony hitting the highlights and getting it done in less than two minutes.

"You may kiss the bride," he told Jake after he'd slid the gold band on Teresa's finger.

After congratulations, hugs all around, and a sip or two of champagne that Vanessa had found in the galley, Patrick went back to take over the helm from Steve.

Jake looked out the window. The rain had stopped and unfortunately, the full moon was once again shining brightly. Scanning the shoreline, he recognized some of the landmarks and knew they were about halfway back to Playa.

Pulling his boat behind the yacht had eliminated the worry of having enough gas for his friends to make it back, but he would have preferred the cloud cover. He knew Benito would hug the shoreline to reduce their visibility, but there was no way Patrick could do that in a craft this size. Unless the clouds suddenly moved back in, the yacht would stand out like a sore thumb.

It couldn't be helped. All they could do now was hope Miguel hadn't bought the Navy.

CHAPTER 40

As soon as Jake felt the yacht begin to slow, he took Benito and José Luis aside.

"It's time to go. Benito, drop the guys off to Henry at Las Palmas then use Wilma's truck and take Teresa's parents to your mother's house. Teresa and I will meet you there. José Luis, you and Wilma will have a few minutes with Luis and Teresa to say goodbye."

"And you will have to listen to my mother for a few minutes, too, I am sure. She's not very happy with her brother, Tio José here, over his part in all this," Benito said. clapping his uncle on the back.

"I will never hear the end of this from her," Señor Garcia muttered.

"Here, keep my cell phone," Benito said, handing it to Jake. "It has my father's number in the contact list. Call him in case anything goes wrong. But he will be waiting, don't worry."

"Take care of my daughter and grandson," Señor Garcia said.

"Or I will come and kick your gringo ass," Benito added, laughing and slapping Jake on the back.

"I will, don't worry."

"Is there anything I can do to help?" Wilma asked as she joined them.

"Just keep things moving. I know you've only had a short time with your daughter, I'm sorry about that, but the sooner we leave the country the safer she and Luis will be."

"Don't worry about me, Señor. I have already missed most my daughter's life, and want nothing more than to make up for all those lost years, but I would rather send her away now and visit her later than risk her or my grandson's safety.'

Jake turned to Steve. "As soon as you get home, check in with Casey. I'll call him tomorrow and make sure you got back all right."

Jake helped Teresa out to the back deck to see her parents and the Boys Club off. They all kissed her goodbye and then got in Jake's boat for the trip back to Playa del Carmen.

As soon as they were away, Jake felt Patrick increase the power to the yacht's engines as they continued north to Puerto Morelos and the rendezvous with Benito's father.

* * *

While they cruised up the coast, Teresa and Vanessa relaxed in the salon and talked while Jake sat with Patrick in the cockpit.

As they were passing Playa del Carmen, Patrick noticed a new blip on his radar.

"Looks like we have company coming. Take Teresa downstairs and tell Vanessa to come here please."

"Who is it?" Jake asked.

"I don't know, but this time of night, I'm guessing a Mexican patrol boat."

"Oh shit, now what do we do?"

"Tell Vanessa to come here, please, and then take Teresa downstairs to the master cabin. I have an idea."

Jake rushed back to the salon, sent Vanessa to see Patrick and picked up Teresa and headed down the narrow stairs. Less than a minute later, Vanessa joined them, carrying the empty bottle of champagne, another full one and two glasses.

Setting the wine bottles and glasses on the bedside table, she looked at Teresa.

"Teresa, honey, I'm sorry, but we need to stash you in the head for a few minutes. We're about to be boarded by a Mexican patrol boat and we can't take the chance that they know what you look like. Just climb in the shower and shut the door. Don't make a sound until I come back and get you," Vanessa said as she helped Teresa into the adjoining bathroom.

"While I get her settled, Jake, you need to take your clothes off and get into bed. On second thought, you should leave the shirt on to cover the bandage. Patrick's going to tell the patrol that he's just taking the happy couple out for a honeymoon ride before heading back in the morning."

"And you and I are supposed to be the happy couple?" he asked.

"That's the way it's going to work tonight," she said. "You got a better idea?"

"No," Jake said as he felt the yacht slow. Shucking his pants quickly, he got in bed, taking them with him.

Vanessa ducked out of the bathroom long enough to throw a plush bathrobe across the end of the bed.

"Mess the bed up some more, open the wine and pour some into the glasses," she whispered, before ducking back into the head.

Jake did as he was told and then waited. He could hear voices, but he couldn't understand what they were saying.

A few minutes later, Jake heard footsteps coming down the stairs. There was a tap on the door and Patrick stuck his head in.

"Excuse me, sir, but I have a Mexican official who would like to talk to you for a moment."

"I'm kinda busy right now; can you ask him to come back later?"

"He says he's looking for a woman and her young son and just wants to make sure they aren't onboard. It will only take a minute."

"Oh, all right. Send him in."

The door opened the rest of the way and Jake looked at the soldier standing in the doorway. He was at least forty, dressed in army fatigues and carrying a rifle.

He eyed Jake briefly, taking in the wine bottles and

messy bed.

"Where is your wife," he asked in heavily accented English.

"She's in the bathroom."

"I want to see her."

"I'm sure she'll be right out."

"Now," the man said and started for the bathroom door.

Jake's heart was in his throat as the soldier got closer to the door. As he was reaching for the knob, the door opened and Vanessa stuck her head out.

"Oh, I didn't know we had company," she said.

"You will come out now, please," he said.

"Now?" she asked. "But I have no clothes on."

"Come out now," the soldier insisted.

Vanessa stuck her head back out the door. "Throw me that robe, honey, so I can get this man out of here."

Jake tossed her the robe and she pulled it inside the bathroom. Two seconds later the door opened and Jake, the soldier and Patrick all got a brief look at Vanessa's naked body before she pulled the robe closed and tied it.

Jake remembered her body well, and noticed that she had put on a few pounds since he'd seen her last. Her breasts were larger and she had the beginnings of a slight belly.

"Are you happy, now?" she asked, flipping her long blonde hair outside the robe.

"Yes, thank you. We are looking for a Mexican woman and her young son. I can see now that you are not her," he said with a leer.

"Then you can go, now," she said, sitting on the edge of the bed and dismissing him as if she were the queen of the castle.

The tension was thick for a moment, and then the soldier smiled and turned. Taking one last look, he headed back up the stairs while Patrick followed.

Jake and Vanessa sat, listening and hardly breathing

until they heard the patrol boat leaving. After the sounds of the patrol boat's motor had subsided, Vanessa went back into the bathroom and Jake retrieved his pants and quickly dressed.

Patrick met him at the door.

"They're gone now. You can get Teresa out of the head."

"Vanessa's in there with her. Uh, Patrick," Jake started. What he was about to ask was really none of his business, and he wasn't sure he should.

"You noticed?" Patrick asked.

"How far along is she?"

"Three months, but let's talk about that later, when she isn't around. Dear sweet Vanessa is a little sensitive these days."

CHAPTER 41

Meeting up with Tio Carlos proved to be relatively easy considering everything else they'd been through, but just before boarding her uncle's boat to go across the reef, Teresa turned to Jake.

"If you don't mind, Jake, I'd like to go alone," she said, laying her hand on his arm.

"Are you sure that's what you want?"

"Yes. Telling my family goodbye will be difficult for me, but's it's not something you can help me with. I only hope it will not be too long before I can see them again."

"Then I'll wait for you." He'd rather go with her to make sure she was safe, but he had to respect her wishes. After all, he was the reason she was leaving.

While he waited for Carlos to bring Teresa and Luis back, Jake talked to Patrick.

"I see you renamed the yacht," Jake said.

"Yeah, Vanessa was none too happy about Sean's choice of names. She thought *Naked Lady* was an insult to women everywhere, so I let her rename it. I think the *Lucky Lady* is more appropriate for us," he added.

"So how is everything going for you guys?" Jake asked.

"Very well, actually. Vanessa's sister, Sarah, got her degree in accounting and started her own little business working out of the house and that works out great. If Vanessa and I are out on a charter, she's there to keep an eye on the boys after school."

"Sounds like you two have everything under control."

"I wish I could agree, but…."

"But what?"

"Jake, about Vanessa. I think she's a little scared about the baby."

"What is she afraid of?" Jake asked.

"Almost everything. She's afraid of getting fat, so don't

mention her weight, she's afraid of how her life will change, she's afraid she won't be a good mother, you name it, she's worried about it."

"Hormones?" Jake asked.

"Probably, but knowing what it is doesn't help much when you have to deal with it all the time. We talked about it and decided that maybe it would be a good idea if I stayed home with her for a while."

"Quit taking charters, you mean?" Jake asked.

"At least until the baby is big enough to come with us."

"What will you do for work?" Jake asked.

Patrick laughed. "We don't need the money any more than you do; Jake. Thomas Walsh gave us this yacht and everything on it which included more than a hundred thousand dollars and a pile of emeralds that we sold for college funds for her brothers. He also gave Vanessa a million dollars for all the grief Sean put her through. I'm sure he gave you about the same, didn't he?"

"I don't actually know," Jake said remembering the envelope that Ian Kelly, Thomas Walsh's agent, had left with him three years ago.

"You've never looked?" Patrick asked.

"Not yet," Jake said, thinking for the first time about what he might do with the settlement that Thomas Walsh had given him in return for his silence concerning the real circumstances of Jake's father's death.

"Anyway, we've built up a pretty solid business and we wondered if you would be interested in taking over the yacht and running charters for a couple of years while we have a baby. I would continue to take reservations and do the scheduling and books from home. All you'd have to do is run the boat."

Jake was surprised that Patrick would consider him able to handle this monster of a boat. His old fishing boat was pretty big, but nothing compared to Patrick's yacht.

"I've never handled anything this big before," Jake confessed, "and I've never really been out of the country by boat except for a few trips over to the Bahamas to do some diving."

"You won't have a problem once you get used to the way she handles. She'll plot the chart and take you there all by herself; all you have to do is give her a destination and get her into the dock."

"What about Teresa and Luis?"

"Take them with you. Except for the occasional wedding charter, it's a pretty kid friendly atmosphere. Vanessa's younger brothers usually crew for us during the summer when they're not in school."

"Where are they now?" Jake asked.

"Well, after you called and asked her to bring that, uh, piece of hardware, she made them stay at home with Sarah. She didn't want them at risk if anything went south."

"Listen, I'm sorry to put you both through this, but I couldn't think of any other way to get Teresa and Luis out of the country."

"Trust me, it's not a problem. I don't think wild horses could have kept Vanessa from coming down here to help you. She feels bad about the way things ended between you two."

"That's funny, while she was bandaging me up; she said the same thing about you."

"Ah, the girl gives me too much credit. I don't feel bad about taking her away from you at all. But considering her crazy mood swings the past month, I was thinking about asking if you wanted her back," he said with a laugh. "I guess it's too late for that now, isn't it?"

"I don't think I can handle both of them. Teresa has enough of a temper."

"Seriously though, we'd like you to think about taking on the yacht for a while."

"Let me talk to Teresa and see how she feels about it. This is all new territory for me."

Jake checked his watch and looked out the cockpit

window toward Puerto Morelos. It had been a good hour since Teresa had left with her uncle and even though they'd already been boarded, he still felt uneasy about how much time everything was taking. He wanted to get out of Mexican waters before someone decided to take a second look.

After another half hour had passed with still no sign of Carlos, Teresa and Luis, Jake was beginning to get worried.

Had Miguel found them at Tia Carmen's and Teresa had walked into a trap? Or had her parents talked her into staying in Mexico? Is that why she wanted to go alone? She knew their marriage wasn't real, was she backing out?

He'd give it a few more minutes, and then if he had to, he'd swim over the reef and find out.

CHAPTER 42

Jake paced the yacht's back deck. He was just about to shuck his clothes and go over the side when he spotted Carlos' boat coming.

He let out a sigh of relief when he recognized Teresa and Luis. He helped them onboard the yacht and waved goodbye to Carlos. Luis was happy to see his mother and Teresa couldn't stop hugging him.

Vanessa helped Teresa get settled in the empty crews quarters so she could get Luis settled into bed and then went to straighten the master cabin

Jake sat with Patrick in the cockpit as they headed into the dock at Cozumel. Patrick was supposed to board his passengers at six a.m. and it looked like they were going to make it with a few minutes to spare.

Just before they pulled into the dock at Cozumel, Jake went down to the crew's quarters. Teresa and Luis were lying on one of the two lower bunks, both mother and son asleep.

He wasn't anticipating any more trouble, but you never knew and he wasn't leaving her side again until they were out to sea and legally married. He lay on the other lower bunk and thought about all the changes that were about to take place in his life.

Looking at the two people he loved most, he smiled. They were his family now and whatever came their way, they would handle it together.

They were married again two days later, somewhere between Mexico and Miami, surrounded by the sapphire blue waters of the Caribbean. Teresa wore her gauzy white dress and white tee shirts and khaki shorts were scrounged up for Jake and Luis. All were barefoot.

When he slipped his grandmother's ring on her finger again under the bright summer sun, the emerald glowed and the diamonds sent out sparks.

Jake and Teresa were now legally man and wife.

The newlywed couple who had chartered the yacht, Tom and Nicole, had been more than happy to continue the party and helped them celebrate on the back deck after the ceremony.

They pulled into the Port of Miami before daylight the next morning, cleared customs and immigration, and thanks to the marriage certificate Vanessa had printed out for them, had no trouble at all. Then they re-boarded the yacht.

Vanessa talked to Tom and Nicole about extending their trip an extra day so they could drop Jake, Teresa and Luis off in Port Salerno. They would spend the night there and head north the following day. When she hinted of the probability of a party at a local bar, Nicole agreed immediately, but Tom was a little reluctant until Vanessa added that there would be no extra charge for the additional day on board.

They came through the St. Lucie Inlet just after noon. The *Lucky Lady* drew too much water to moor at the fishing docks, so Jake told Patrick to drop anchor in the middle of the Pocket and called Steve.

His best friend just happened to be at the docks working on his boat, and was happy to run out to the yacht and shuttle its passengers to shore.

Once they were all on dry land and introductions complete, Steve gave Teresa a hug, ruffled Luis' hair, and then turned to Jake. "Let me help you get those bags to your house and then we can walk down to the Salty Dog. Casey can't wait to see you. He's pretty stoked about meeting your new wife, too. That's what he says, 'new wife'. Like you ever had an old one."

They walked across the street and up the wide front steps of a stately little home overlooking the picturesque bay. At the top of the stairs a ten-foot wide screened porch wrapped all the way around the house. Ceiling fans mounted every twelve feet or so kept the air moving while comfortable chairs and side tables as well as a wooden porch swing hanging from the ceiling provided plenty of seating.

"This is where you live?" Teresa asked, laying her hand on Jake's arm.

"This is where *we* live," he corrected, dropping the bags he was carrying and digging in his pocket for his keys. "What do you think?"

"I like it," Teresa said with a smile.

"I was hoping you would," he said as he moved to put his key in the lock.

"Jake, why don't you leave your luggage there for now? You know nobody will mess with it and we're all thirsty," Vanessa asked as everyone but Teresa nodded in agreement.

"Yes, Jake, I am thirsty, too. Vanessa said you have Pepsi at the Salty Dog. Can we go there now and get one?" Luis asked before looking up at Vanessa and smiling.

Jake and Teresa looked at each other. It was obvious they were the only ones who didn't know what was going on. When Teresa nodded her assent, Jake shrugged.

"Okay, let's go."

Less than a five-minute walk from his house, the Salty Dog was located in 'downtown' Port Salerno, a short stretch of A1A that included the Post Office, a small restaurant and one long building that housed several businesses, including the Salty Dog on one side of the street and the Florida East Coast Railroad on the other.

First opened in the 1920s, the Salty Dog held the county's oldest beer license. For years it had been the only drinking establishment in town and a hangout for the local fishermen. Over time the bar had seen its share of fights and even a couple of murders; consequently, it had developed a less than stellar reputation. A reputation Jake had been doggedly trying to change since inheriting the place.

Inside, the long section of the bar was located along the south wall with an opening for the bartender on the end closest to the restrooms and back door. An office walled off in the northeast corner shared space with an ice machine, and a large walk-in cooler. High-top tables with stools, two pool tables and a small stage took up the rest of the space.

Many of Jake's friends had donated old fishing pictures, maps, and artifacts that Jake had framed and hung on the walls along with the collages of baseball and football teams the bar had sponsored ever since his grandfather started the tradition more than forty-five years ago.

He thought he'd succeeded in changing the visual character of the bar, but changing a more than seventy-year-old reputation had proved a challenge until Casey had come up with the idea of marketing the bar as a place for senior citizens to play bridge and poker games.

Casey had turned the weekday hours between twelve and three over to the retirees. It being Thursday about two o'clock, Jake was interested to see what kind of crowd Casey had.

It wasn't that far, but the intense summer sun beat down on them and by the time they got to the Salty Dog they really were thirsty. They walked in the back door, each one stopping just inside to let their eyes adjust to the dim interior. When he could see clearly again, Jake stood looking at a roomful of people who were all staring back at him. They weren't retirees, though; they were all his friends.

A drum roll sounded from the small stage set up in the front corner of the room. "Congratulations!" a multitude of voices yelled as soon as it finished.

Jake pulled Teresa and Luis up to the stage and faced the room. "Everybody, I'd like you to meet my wife, Teresa, and our son, Luis. Teresa, Luis, I won't try to name everybody because you wouldn't remember them all anyway, but it won't take you long to learn who everybody is."

There was a lot of hugging, back-slapping, and hand-shaking all around and then Jake turned to face the band Casey had hired for the occasion.

"Bucky," he said to the tall red haired drummer, "it's good to see you again. I'd like you to meet my wife, Teresa. Teresa, this is Bucky, Casey's friend."

"It's nice meeting you," Teresa replied as she shook the young man's hand.

"You, too," Bucky said taking her hand in both of his. "Casey told me a little of what happened down there in Mexico. I hope you'll be happy here."

"Thank you," Teresa said, as Luis tugged on her arm. "Excuse us, please. Luis wants to check out the games."

"What's up with the new band? You and Bill break up?" Jake asked Bucky after Luis led his mother toward the bowling game. Bill was the other half of the Bill and Bucky Show, a two man reggae band that had often played at the Salty Dog.

"I guess you could say that. Bill went back to Philly for a while. Personal stuff. In the meantime, my friends and I started this new band. We're calling it Smoking Section and we've got a new lead singer that I know you'll like. She's got a voice that'll knock your socks off," Bucky said, grinning from ear to ear.

"I'll let you get to it, then," Jake said, slapping his young friend on the back before stepping down off the stage.

After the initial meet and greet was over, Jake took Casey and Steve aside.

"It's good to have you back, Jake," Casey said after giving him a big hug.

"It's good to be back," Jake admitted. "But I'm not sure how long I'll stay. I promised Teresa's father that I would take them back to Playa as soon as it's safe for them to return."

"The guys told me about that slimeball Miguel and

what happened to Teresa. I wish I could have been there to help."

"I know, but you're helping me enormously by staying here and running the Salty Dog. It's our bread and butter, kid, and I know it's in good hands with you. By the way, I thought you'd have a room full of retirees playing poker and bridge. Where are they?"

"I made an executive decision and closed the place for the day. But don't worry, I called all the players and told them about it. We'll be back to business as usual tomorrow. Uh, I hope you don't mind, but you should also know that I told everyone that drinks are on the house today."

Jake laughed. "I can't think of a better way to celebrate than popping the tops off a few with my friends. Even if I'm buying."

Casey excused himself and Steve turned to Jake. "If you really want to eliminate your, uh, little problem down south, just let me know. I have no problem disposing of pond scum."

"I would have thought you'd be happy knowing that we can't go back," Jake replied.

"I admit I want you around, hell, you're my best friend, but I also want you to be happy," Steve said. "And if living in Mexico with Teresa makes you happy, then I'll do whatever it takes to make that happen. Even if it means wiping Miguel off the face of the earth."

"Thanks for the offer, but I don't want to see my best friend rotting in a Mexican prison. If you really want me to be happy, stay out of it."

Just then Casey came out of the office, wheeling a cart that held several bottles of champagne and a three tiered wedding cake complete with bride and groom on top. He popped the top off the bottles and began pouring, handing out the glasses until everyone had one.

"To Jake and Teresa and Luis," Casey toasted with his glass in the air. "May you have many happy years together and may all your problems be little ones."

"To Jake and Teresa and Luis," everyone repeated.

The party continued throughout the rest of the afternoon and evening. Friends drifted in and out, congratulating Jake and Teresa and taking Casey up on the free drinks.

Luis stayed busy playing electronic darts and a bowling game Casey had added. He was high scorer on the bowling game and defended his championship to any and all of Jake's friends who dared to challenge him.

Jake was pleased with the way everyone had turned out to welcome his new family. More than anything else, he wanted Teresa and Luis to feel at home here and it looked like things were off to a good start.

Casey called last call at ten o'clock, citing the need for Jake and Teresa to get Luis home to bed.

"Thanks for doing this, Steve," Jake said as his friend drained his beer mug.

"You should thank Vanessa. It was her idea and she kept us updated on your arrival time so we could get everybody here. It was no coincidence that I just happened to be down at the docks when you dropped anchor in the Pocket."

"Vanessa did this? Why?"

"I know. It makes no sense, does it? Women are usually absurdly jealous. You'd think she and Teresa would be at each other's throat, but Vanessa said she wanted Teresa to feel welcome here."

"I guess you don't understand women as well as you think you do, Steve," Jake said slapping his friend's shoulder. "Makes me glad I don't listen to you where they're concerned."

On the walk back to Jake's house, Steve carried Luis and walked with Teresa, Tom and Nicole while Jake lagged back a little with Patrick and Vanessa.

"Now that all the drama with Miguel is over, I want to thank you guys again for everything you've done. I don't know what I would have done without your help. And Vanessa, thanks for the party. Steve told me you organized it and I really appreciate everyone making the effort to welcome Teresa and Luis."

"You're welcome, Jake. I hope the two of you will be very happy. After everything you've gone through, you both deserve it, but are you sure it's over?" she asked. "What's stopping Miguel from coming after you here?"

Jake was speechless for a moment. He'd never considered the idea that Miguel might follow them to the States.

"Of course it's over," Patrick said, taking his wife's hand. "You're just tired. Let's get you back on the boat so you can get some sleep."

Jake watched them get onboard Steve's boat for the ride out to the *Lucky Lady* before catching up with Teresa on the porch. As he unlocked the door, he couldn't help but wonder if their problems with Miguel really were over.

CHAPTER 43

While Teresa fixed breakfast and Luis pushed a truck around the living room floor, Jake sat at his drafting table in the kitchen of his home in Salerno, working on a set of blueprints that would enlarge his home by almost forty percent.

Built by his great-grandfather, Wade Arnold, in the mid-1940s, the house was situated in the center of two lots facing the Manatee Pocket. While the front yard was open and sloped toward the street and the bay beyond, the back yard was several feet higher in elevation, relatively level, and surrounded by a six-foot privacy fence covered in some areas with vibrant salmon, burgundy, and purple bougainvillea bushes whose long supple limbs climbed up to cascade a profusion of colorful blooms over the top.

A brick-paver patio took up a large portion of the back yard and held a BBQ on one side and a hot tub, screened on three sides by areca palms for privacy, on the other. Between the BBQ and the hot tub, a tiki hut with a string of small white lights around the overhead edges covered a patio table with six chairs. In the northwest corner, a small shed housed Jake's workshop.

Inside, the house had a main center hallway running from the front door straight through to the back door. Two wide arches trimmed in stained oak were cut into the left side of the main hallway. The first arch opened into a bright and airy living room decorated with comfortable furniture and a few pieces Jake had rescued from the attic and refinished. Old maps, nautical charts, and a brass ship's wheel hung from the walls while colorful rugs partially covered varnished pine floors.

Beyond the living room, an island of oak cabinets with gleaming granite countertops and six barstools served as the dining area and separated the living room from the kitchen. More oak cabinets and granite countertops, along with top-of-the-line appliances, lined the kitchen walls and a long narrow closet on the south wall housed laundry facilities, a freezer and a well-stocked pantry.

The back of the house faced west and had a view of the back porch and yard through several sliding windows above the kitchen sink, and a second arch opened back into the main hallway on the right.

The right side of the main hallway was divided in half by another short hall with a half bath at the end. Two bedrooms, one on either side of the hall and each with a private bath, had large windows to let in the breeze and light.

The bedrooms were generous in size, but since their arrival more than three months ago, Jake and Teresa, with Luis on a cot, had been sharing Jake's room.

Casey had offered to share his room with Luis and even though it would've given him and Teresa the privacy they craved as newlyweds, Jake turned him down. Luis was a light sleeper and there was no way he would be able to sleep through Casey's crazy schedule. His job at the Salty Dog had him coming home in the wee hours of the morning and a wispy blonde waitress had him out early every morning.

Space had never been a problem when it was just Jake and his mom or Jake and Casey, but he'd never realized how small the house was until he let a tiny Mexican woman and five-year old little boy loose in it.

What they needed was another bedroom so he'd begun a design for a new wing that would add a master suite and an office. When it was finished he and Teresa would have their privacy and Luis would have his own room.

He paused in his calculations of beams and supports for a moment and let his thoughts drift. Since coming back to Salerno, his life had settled into a pleasant routine, one he enjoyed more than he'd ever thought possible.

After discussing it with Teresa, he'd declined Patrick's

offer to take over the yacht charters and gone back to crabbing. She hadn't liked the idea of living a vagabond life with Luis, she wanted a stable life on land where he could run and play, and Jake had agreed.

But Steve and the twins had jumped at the chance to take over the *Lucky Lady* for a couple of years. The twins quit their marine construction jobs and Steve's dad had come out of retirement to take over Steve's job at the small trucking company he owned. They stopped in for a beer and a poker game whenever they were in town and both Jake and Teresa welcomed their company.

Teresa and Casey had hit it off immediately and it wasn't unusual to find Teresa helping him tend bar or working on the books at the Salty Dog while Jake and Luis went crabbing or worked on some project around the house.

His mother had come from Louisiana for a visit, excited about her new daughter-in-law and grandson. She'd accepted Casey as the little brother Jake had never had and had fallen in love with Teresa and Luis immediately. Before she left, she'd given Jake her complete approval and invited all of them to come to Louisiana for Thanksgiving.

Teresa called her father every week on Sunday to find out how he and the cantina were doing and to check on any news about Miguel. He'd been around a few times but hadn't caused any more trouble. Benito had put the word out that he wasn't welcome in Playa.

Through Elena, Teresa had learned of Miguel's refusal to participate in a paternity test. He insisted that he didn't need proof to know the boy was his son and had vowed to take Luis if Teresa ever returned to Mexico. Jake knew she missed her father and her life in Playa del Carmen, but she made the best of the situation and seemed happy.

During the short time they'd had together in Mexico, Wilma had given her phone number to her daughter and urged her to call often, so Teresa did. They talked at least twice a week, sometimes for an hour or more with Luis getting on the line to talk to his grandmother. Jake had changed his cell service to allow unlimited calls to Mexico. It had cost a little more but he didn't mind spending a few extra dollars each month to help Teresa and her mother establish a new relationship.

From her mother, Teresa learned that Wilma and her father were still seeing each other. Sometimes Wilma would go to Las Palmas for a day or two and sometimes Señor Garcia would go out to the ranch and spend a couple of days.

When she told him that, Jake had laughed. Remembering the pitiful old man that José Luis had pretended to be, he had trouble thinking of Teresa's parents as a couple. Wilma, who was only ten years Jake's senior, was headstrong and impulsive, but still a very beautiful and vibrant woman. It was even hard, Jake admitted only to himself, to think of Wilma as Teresa's mother and Luis' grandmother. She looked and acted much too young to be anyone's grandmother.

After the last call to her mother, Teresa reported that Elena had been back to the cantina and told Teresa's parents that Miguel would be back in town soon. He'd been called back to Veracruz but would have a month's vacation in November and planned to visit his mother. He'd asked Elena to call him if she ever saw Teresa around, but Elena had assured them that she wouldn't.

Jake was worried that Miguel would take his anger out on Teresa's parents or her property. He hoped the young hot-head wouldn't start any trouble in Playa, but he'd called Benito and given him a heads-up, just in case.

He put down his pencil and brought his mind back to the present when Teresa called him for breakfast.

CHAPTER 44

Wilma showed up on Jake's doorstep the morning before Halloween with a pirate's costume complete with plastic sword for Luis. She'd called Teresa the night before and told her daughter that she was coming for a visit and had taken a room just down the street at the Pirate's Chest Resort.

"If Teresa and Luis cannot come to me, then I will come to them," she said, sweeping past Jake like a gale force wind as soon as he opened the door.

Jake stuck his head outside, half expecting to see Señor Garcia behind her. But Wilma was alone, so he shut the door. "Come in," he said, turning to see her back as she made a beeline to the kitchen where Teresa was making breakfast.

Wilma hugged and kissed her daughter and grandson and then, seemingly as an afterthought, gave Jake a quick hug and air kissed both sides of his face like he'd seen Europeans do on TV. Then she immediately turned back to her daughter.

Knowing he'd been dismissed, Jake sat down at the kitchen island and picked up the stack of yesterday's mail. As he sorted it, putting junk mail in one pile and bills in the other, he listened with half an ear as mother and daughter chatted like old friends. They spoke English most of the time, slipping into Spanish only when a giggle or a furtive glance his way told him he was the current topic of their conversation.

After breakfast, Jake went to get ready to go crabbing. He'd relieved his friend Josh of that particular duty upon his return and had given up his routine of spending four nights each week sleeping on his boat in favor of sleeping with his lovely new wife. Now he usually went after breakfast and more often than not Luis went too. He liked taking the boy with him.

"You ready to go to work, Luis?" Jake asked, sitting on the couch to put on a pair of socks.

Luis ran over to sit beside Jake. In little more than a whisper, he said, "I think I should stay here today with Mama and Abuela, don't you?"

"If you want to, sure. You think they might run into some problems that require a man to handle?" Jake asked with a smile. Since the moment Luis had seen the pirate costume, he'd been fascinated and Jake knew the boy couldn't wait to try it on.

"You never know," Luis said evasively.

Remembering his own childhood of swashbuckling pirates and buried treasure, Jake ruffled Luis' hair. "I guess I can handle those crabs by myself today. You better stay and keep an eye on your mom and grandmother."

He walked into the kitchen where Teresa and her mother were cleaning up after breakfast. Watching the two of them work, Teresa washing dishes at the sink and Wilma scrubbing the stove, he understood where Teresa got her compulsion to clean.

Moving up to stand behind his wife, he put his hands on her shoulders and bent to give her a kiss on the cheek. "I'm going crabbing but Luis is staying here today," he whispered in her ear. "He thinks you might need a man around today."

Teresa returned the kiss and smiled. "And he is right. Mama wants to get to know her grandson," she said quietly.

"Luis may have a different reason," Jake chuckled.

When Jake let himself out the front door a few minutes later, Luis was in the process of trying to convince his grandmother to let him try on the pirate suit.

Upon his return a few hours later, Jake wasn't surprised to see Luis running around in the back yard in his pirate's costume, vanquishing imaginary foes while Teresa and

Wilma sat talking on the porch swing with a glass of wine.

He knew Teresa and her mother needed time to reconnect after their twenty-six year estrangement, so after saying hello, he went inside to shower and then went back to work on his house plans, wondering if he should add a guest room.

He made himself scarce after dinner and then again after returning from crabbing the next afternoon, allowing the two women and little boy as much time together as possible while he made progress on his house design.

He'd given up the idea of a guest room; Wilma's use of the Pirate's Chest Resort just down the street was working out just fine and he kind of liked the idea of an off-site guestroom. It pretty much guaranteed no over-night guests.

On Halloween Day, Jake rolled up his plans earlier than usual. Teresa had planned an early dinner so Luis could have supper before going trick-or-treating and eating his fill of candy.

It wasn't quite dark yet by the time Luis convinced his mother it was time to go trick or treating. The little boy understood the concept, Jake had explained it to him, and couldn't wait to go get his own pile of candy, something he loved but was rarely allowed to have.

The four of them set out, Luis in his pirate costume, complete now with black boots and a patch over one eye, pulling Jake down the sidewalk while Teresa and Wilma followed with cameras to celebrate Luis' first Halloween.

They hit house after house, Luis marching up and ringing the bell or knocking and then jumping back to get into his best pirate pose. After a quick glance in the kid's bag, Jake knew Luis was taking in the kind of loot that he had always wished for as a kid on Halloween.

Halfway around the block, Teresa called it quits. She was concerned about the amount of candy the boy was accumulating, and eating, and the effects it would have on his teeth and his ability to sleep.

Jake didn't think sleeping was going to be a problem for Luis. He was already running out of gas, probably from spending the last two days vanquishing all those imaginary villains.

When his mother announced that it was time to go home, Luis looked in his bag, his face serious as he examined its contents and then looked up at Jake with a smile. "I think this is enough for my first time, don't you, Jake?" he asked with a note of pride in his voice.

"I think this is a very admirable haul," Jake agreed. "Did you have fun being a pirate?"

"Yes, I took out a lot of bad guys with my sword. But we should go home now, getting rid of bad guys is a lot of work."

"Yes, it is," Jake quietly agreed as he picked up the boy and put him on his shoulders for the rest of the walk home.

While Teresa was giving Luis a bath and getting him ready for bed, Wilma asked Jake for a moment alone to talk. They had just walked off the back porch heading for the tiki hut when Steve walked through the back gate.

"You weren't down at the Salty Dog so I figured I'd find you here," Steve said as he approached the tiki hut. "Buenos noches, Señora Santiago," Steve said with a nod her way.

"Buenos noches, Estaben," she said, nodding in return and using the Spanish version of his name.

"What are you doing here?" Jake asked.

"The *Lucky Lady* went in for some routine maintenance and they found a problem with one of the steering cables. They had to order a new one and until it comes in and gets installed, the twins and I have a few days off, so we came home."

"So how's the new job working out?" Jake asked, handing his friend a beer after Steve settled into the chair next to Wilma.

"I love it," Steve said with a smile. "Piloting that

monster around is so much fun. But it's nice to have some time off to hang out with old friends. How about you, how are things on the home front?"

"Everything is great here …" Jake began.

"But it is Mexico we're worried about," Wilma interjected, laying a hand on Steve's arm and looking into his face.

"What's going on in Mexico, Señora Santiago?" Steve asked.

"Please, call me Wilma," she said, laying her other hand on his arm as well.

Steve looked at Jake and Jake explained what they'd learned about Miguel returning to Playa and his concern for Teresa's parents and property.

"But that is not all," Wilma added looking at Jake.

"Why? Has something happened?" Jake asked.

"That's what I wanted to talk to you about," she said, "but I didn't want to frighten Teresa or Luis and you have been very busy the last two days," she said with a faint note of admonishment.

"What are you talking about?" Jake asked.

"Are you sure you…uh…?" she asked with a nod at Steve.

"He can hear whatever you have to say," Jake responded impatiently. "Just tell us."

"Okay," she said, removing her hands from Steve's arm and sitting forward in her chair. "Before I called and said I was coming for a visit, I got a phone call from José Luis. He said that Miguel had come by the resort to talk and apologized for kidnapping Teresa and threatening to take Luis."

"That's good, isn't it?"

"Let me finish. José Luis said they were in the office and he and Miguel talked for about fifteen minutes and everything was fine until the end. Then Miguel asked where Teresa was and when José Luis refused to tell him, he got nasty and slammed the guest book on the counter.

"You see, José Luis didn't realize it, but the whole time they were talking, Miguel had been looking through the guest register and had found your name and address."

"Oh, no," Jake said with a shake of his head. He knew what was coming next.

"Oh, yes," Wilma said. "Miguel said he was going to pay a visit to Jake Arnold in Port Salerno, Florida and would bring Teresa and Luis back even if he had to kill you."

CHAPTER 45

"Damn. We should have taken him out when we had the chance," Steve said, shaking his head.

"You had a chance to kill Miguel and you didn't do it?" Wilma asked, cutting her eyes sharply at Jake.

"No, we didn't," Jake cut in. "Miguel left Tulum before we went in to get Teresa, and when he returned he had the Mexican Army with him. Sticking around to take him out would've been suicide."

"Yeah, but we knew he was trouble long before then. If we'd been proactive, none of this would've happened," Steve said.

"No. We'd probably be rotting in some Mexican prison. And if by some stretch of the imagination we had managed to take Miguel out without getting caught then Teresa and I wouldn't be married and I wouldn't be sitting here with my long lost mother-in-law and my wife and son just inside."

"Is that why you don't want to kill him?" Wilma asked. "Because you want Teresa to stay here? José Luis said you just wanted to take her away. Was he right?"

"No," Jake replied adamantly. "I told Teresa I would stay with her in Mexico. We only came here because it wasn't safe for her and Luis there."

"And now she may not be safe here," Steve added. "Why not just take care of Miguel before he causes any more problems? You know as well as I do that sometimes the only way to fix things is to stop the bad guy."

"That's an interesting idea," Wilma agreed, squeezing Steve's arm and looking at him with a smile.

"We just have to make sure it can't be traced back to you. If Miguel should happen to die in an accident or…."

"No, Steve," Jake interrupted. "I can't take the chance that Miguel's men or the cartel will retaliate. Who knows what they might do?"

"What are you going to do if he shows up here?" Steve asked.

"I'll just have to cross that bridge when I come to it. Look Steve, you know me. I'm a live and let live kinda guy. I won't be a party to murder, but I can tell you this…the only way Miguel is getting Teresa or Luis is over my dead body," Jake said with steely determination.

"I'm just saying…" Steve began but was interrupted by Teresa calling to Jake out the back door.

"Just leave it alone, Steve. Excuse me for a minute. I have to go say goodnight to Luis," he said rising.

After Jake had gone in the house, Steve looked down at Wilma's hand on his arm and then back into her eyes. Looking into her eyes was like looking into a mirror. Their eyes were the same icy shade of blue and had the same steely sense of determination behind them.

"I like this idea you have of an accident for Miguel," she said, averting her gaze while moving her hand to loop it through his arm and sliding her chair a little closer. "Did you have something particular in mind?"

Steve caught her gaze again when she looked back up. He held it for a moment but didn't say anything.

"I was just thinking that since you and I both want the same thing…" she said slowly, letting her words trail off.

"And what would that be, exactly?" Steve asked.

"Why, we want my daughter and my grandson to be safe and happy. And Jake too, of course. Don't you agree?"

"Of course. Is that all you want?"

"Well…."

"Are you hitting on me, Señora Santiago?" Steve interrupted with a sly smile.

"Of course not!" she exploded with a trace of her Latin temper as she snatched her hands from Steve's arm. "I want Miguel out of the picture. He refuses to take a paternity test so there's no way to prove he isn't Luis' father. As long as he is running around loose, Teresa and Luis cannot come home. And now they are not safe here. He needs to go and that's all there is to it."

"I agree, Wilma, but you heard what Jake said. He told me to leave it alone."

"You don't have to tell him," she said, rising out of her chair. "Let him think the earth aligned and the Maya did it or that it was fate, or hell, maybe it was his fairy godmother," she said, waving her arms around in obvious exasperation. She stopped and turned to face him. "It just needs to get done," she said quietly, all trace of emotion gone.

Steve was quiet for a few moments as he looked at her. "I'll think about it," he said.

Wilma nodded, pulled a card out of her pocket and handed it to him. After he put it in his pocket, she returned to her seat.

Jake came out of the house a moment later and looked at Steve and then Wilma before sitting down. He knew they'd been talking about something and whatever it was; it looked like it was time to change the subject.

"So, how's your love life?" Jake asked "Have you met any single ladies that spark your interest?"

"Well, there is this one, Michelle. We've been seeing quite a bit of each other. As a matter of fact, I'm heading back to Savannah tonight after I leave here."

"What happened to hanging out with old friends?" Jake asked. He was always happy to see his friends, but after Wilma told them about Miguel's threat to pay them a visit, he'd been more than happy his friends were back in town. He'd been relieved. Now Steve was talking about leaving.

"I'm doing that right now, in case you haven't noticed," Steve said. "I just wanted you to know that I might be out of town for a few days. Is that a problem?"

"No, I guess not. Petey and Paul will still be here, right?"

"Yes, and Hank is here. That's who you really need to

call. Let the cops handle Miguel."

"I called Hank while I was inside. He's going to put a man on the docks starting tomorrow night. Someone has been stealing equipment off some of the boats down there lately so he's using that as an excuse to post a man to watch the house each night."

"So, there you go. Hank's got your back at night and Petey and Paul will spend most of their days five minutes from here at the Salty Dog. You'll be fine and I'll be back in a few days."

"If you wanted to see this girl, why didn't you just stay there?" Jake asked.

"Petey and Paul wanted to come home to check on their mom and I had the only truck. Plus I wanted to check in with you and Teresa."

"Sounds like a lot of unnecessary driving, if you ask me," Jake said with a shake of his head.

"You might not think so if you saw Michelle," Steve said with a grin.

"If you both will excuse me," Wilma said, rising. "I think I'll go in now to tell Teresa goodbye. I'm returning to Mexico in the morning and I still need to get back to the hotel and pack."

"Good night, Wilma," Jake and Steve said together.

She pushed her chair in, started to walk away, and then stopped. "Jake, I am taking you at your word and trusting you to keep my daughter and grandson safe. But if anything happens to either one of them, it had better *be* over your dead body," she warned.

CHAPTER 46

It was the first Friday night in November, but as she looked at the clock on the dash of her vehicle, she realized that it was now technically Saturday morning. Luckily the weather was cooperating with balmy temperatures and a nice breeze. With all the cologne she'd applied, she couldn't imagine sitting in a closed up space if it had been rainy or cold.

Every few minutes she looked down at the cell phone on the seat beside her. Because her windows were down, she'd put it on vibrate with the ringer muted. She couldn't take the chance someone would hear it but she didn't want to miss her cue either.

When it finally came a half hour later, she rolled up the windows and got out. She was dressed in a very short, very tight and very revealing black cocktail dress with elbow length silk evening gloves. She took a moment to adjust her dress and make sure her hair was secure in the knot at the back of her head, and then grabbed a large shoulder bag before locking the vehicle.

As fast as she could go in the heels she was wearing, she hurried around the corner and through the narrow alley to get in place. As soon as she approached her destination, she stopped and leaned up against the wall.

When he staggered through the door a few moments later, she grabbed his arm.

"Hola, Señor, would you like some company tonight?"

"Si, Señorita," he said looking her up and down, "I always like the company of beautiful women, and you are very beautiful. But it is too late to be working. Why don't you come home with me so we can get to know each other better?"

"We could just go to your car. Where is it?" she asked.

"My house is just around the corner. We will be more

comfortable there," he said with a leer.

She let him lead her around the corner and halfway down the street, passing a lawyer's office and a few other businesses that were closed for the night before stopping at a tall ornate door set into the concrete wall that bordered the sidewalk.

While her new friend tried to get his key in the door lock, she looked up and down both sides of the street, relieved to see that none of the buildings in the vicinity were more than one story tall.

After watching him fumble for a few more moments, she took the key from him and unlocked the door. She handed him back his keys and pulled him inside, quickly closing the heavy door behind them.

"Do you live here alone?" she asked as they walked through a small but nicely maintained courtyard to the front door.

"Yes, why? Were you perhaps interested in having a friend or two join us?" he asked with another leer. "Does that cost more?"

"Well..."

"It doesn't matter. My friends are busy tonight. You will just have to make do with me," he said as he pulled her into an embrace and started kissing her.

She pushed him away. "Wait until we get inside," she admonished.

As soon as they were inside, he flicked on the lights and grabbed her arm with one hand and slammed the door behind him with the other.

She broke his hold on her arm and walked through the small foyer and into the living room, looking into all the corners as she went. It was a small, but very nice, colonial home.

"My bedroom is in here," he said pointing to a room on the front of the house.

"Oh, sure," she said as she took a quick peek into the kitchen. "This is a nice place you have."

"This is just a vacation home, you should see my home in Veracruz," he boasted.

"You must work very hard if you can afford two homes," she said. "Maybe you would like a nice backrub to get things started."

"How about a full body rub?" he asked quietly as he nuzzled her neck and earlobe.

She pulled him into the bedroom, and pushed him down onto the bed. "Take off your clothes and lie on your stomach. I will go freshen up and be right back."

In the bathroom she removed her shoes and clothes down to her bra, panties and evening gloves. She reached into her bag and pulled out a towel, a pair of rubber gloves and the knife she'd brought with her for the occasion. She folded the towel into quarters, concealing the rubber gloves and knife in the folds.

She walked out of the bathroom carrying the towel. He had done as she'd asked, and was lying face down on the bed, naked, the sheet barely covering his ass.

She got up on the bed and sat astride him, placing the towel next to her leg.

"Ahhh, that feels good," he said as she wiggled her ass on his.

She started massaging his back with her still-gloved hands. "You are very tense."

"I have a very stressful job," he said, his voice groggy from the late hour and all the tequila he'd consumed.

"I am here to take all that away," she bent over and whispered in his ear.

"How will you do that?" he asked, beginning to fade into sleep.

"Be very still and I will show you," she said. She flicked the towel open with one hand and quickly put on the rubber gloves. Then she unfolded the towel and laid it across his back, smoothing out the wrinkles.

She picked up the knife and leaned over so she could see his face. "You might feel a little pain, but it will soon pass," she whispered with a smile. Then with all the force she could muster, she drove the knife through the towel and into his back where she thought his heart should have been had he actually had one.

She watched his eyes fly open and then his mouth as he tried to scream, but no sound came out. "You chose the wrong woman to fuck with, you slimy pendejo," she whispered in his ear.

His legs jerked like he was trying to get up, but her weight on his ass kept him down. With her hand still on the knife in his back she watched his eyes until she was sure he was dead. Then she removed the knife, wrapped it up in the towel along with the rubber gloves and then bundled the towel in the sheet she'd been sitting on.

She would've loved to have just gotten dressed and run the hell out of there, but knew she had to stay calm and make sure she didn't leave any of her DNA where it could be found. She doubted anyone one would bother to look too hard into the death of a piece of shit like Miguel, but you never knew.

Going back into the bathroom, she put the bundle and the clothes and heels she'd been wearing into a plastic garbage bag she'd brought, and then pulled a pair of jeans, a hoodie and a pair of tennis shoes out of her bag and quickly dressed. Then she wrapped the garbage bag tightly around itself and pushed it to the bottom of her shoulder bag. Taking a last look around to make sure she hadn't missed anything, she grabbed her bag.

Back in the bedroom, she found his pants and quickly located his wallet. She opened it and rifled through the pictures and cards to make sure there was nothing that could implicate her or anyone she knew. Then she removed the wad of cash, dropped it into her shoulder bag and threw the empty wallet onto the bed beside Miguel's naked body.

After giving the bedroom a final check, she took one last look at the man she'd killed. She hadn't expected to feel bad about what she'd done, and truth be told, she didn't. Men like Miguel didn't deserve to live.

Hitching her bag on her shoulder, she turned and left the house, locking the front door behind her with a gloved hand. She moved quietly across the courtyard to the street door and gently eased it open far enough to peek out. She scanned the area to make sure no one was out and about and then slipped through the opening, pulling the door shut as silently as possible.

Out on the street, she removed the gloves and added them to her shoulder bag as she walked rapidly down the deserted street, being careful to stay in the shadows.

Moments later, she turned the corner and disappeared into a dark alley.

CHAPTER 47

After learning of Miguel's threat to pay him a visit, Jake's senses had been on high alert. For the first few days he never left the house, suspending his crabbing and forgoing a paycheck to protect his wife and son.

Realizing something wasn't quite right, Teresa, of course, had asked what was going on. Not wanting to scare her, but needing her to be alert and watchful, he told her the truth.

She was frightened, he could see it in her eyes, but she was stoic, agreeing not to go anywhere alone and even offering to go crabbing with him and Luis so he could keep the markets supplied.

Jake thanked her but declined her offer. He knew she didn't really want to go crabbing. It wasn't the crabs or the smell that bothered her, it was the boredom. Between Jake and Luis there was nothing for her to do except sit in the bow and stay out of the way and he knew she'd rather be doing her own thing at home or working on the books at the Salty Dog. And to be honest, he didn't want to leave her at home alone.

When Steve returned from his trip to Savannah, he convinced Jake to go back to crabbing by offering to stay with Teresa while Jake and Luis worked his traps and went to the market. But that lasted only a few days and then Steve got a call telling him the repairs to the *Lucky Lady* were complete. He and the twins returned to Savannah to run another charter and Jake stopped crabbing again.

Jake understood. His friends had jobs and needed their paychecks. They couldn't just sit around here waiting for something that might never happen and he didn't expect them to. He would have been more comfortable with the situation knowing they were there to watch his back, but ultimately the responsibility for his family was his and his alone.

Two days later, Hank had come by and told Jake he was sorry but he was going to have to reassign his man on the dock. He was getting complaints from his department about the amount of manpower he was using to try to catch petty thieves.

That evening, after Luis was in bed, Jake went to the attic and took a short barreled shotgun and a .38 caliber handgun from his grandfather's gun safe. The shotgun had belonged to his great-grandfather Wade. He'd kept it behind the bar until he died. The .38 had belonged to his grandfather Wes, and he'd carried it in a holster at the back of his waist until he was killed in a car accident.

Jake had fired the shotgun a few times on hunting trips, but he'd never fired the .38. It was a gun for personal protection and up until Miguel came along, Jake had never felt the need to use it.

But that was then and this was now, he thought as he cleaned and loaded both guns.

He went back downstairs. Teresa looked at him with raised eyebrows but didn't say anything. When they went to bed a little later, Jake put the revolver on a high shelf in the pantry and lay the shotgun on the floor beside the bed for easy access.

When he heard Casey come in at three a.m., he got up, grabbed the shotgun off the floor and went to talk to him.

"Whoa, don't shoot," Casey said when he pulled his head out of the refrigerator and turned to see Jake holding the shotgun. "Just making a little snack here."

"Don't worry, I won't shoot you, but I do want to talk," Jake replied.

"What's up, Jake?" Casey asked as he unloaded the ingredients for a sandwich from the fridge.

Casey hadn't been around much since discovering the waitress at The Depot, a breakfast and lunch place a block south of the Salty Dog, so Jake filled him in on recent events. "Hank had to pull his guy off the dock, so I've taken over the job as night watchman," he said, indicating the shotgun.

"I can see that. How can I help?"

"I can cover the nights, but I need some help with the days," he said as he laid the shotgun on the counter.

"Sure, whatever you need, Jake," Casey said as he began smearing mayo on a couple pieces of bread.

Jake went to the pantry and brought back the revolver and set it on the counter. "In the morning I'm going to take this to the Salty Dog and leave it on the shelf behind the bar," he said. "Teresa is getting antsy cooped up here, so I'm going to let her work on the Dog's books in the mornings while Luis and I go crabbing. She'll be alone there until you go in but she'll be locked in."

"So what's the pistol for?" Casey asked before taking a huge bite of his sandwich.

"It's for you. If I'm not back to pick her up before you open for business, I want you to shoot anyone who tries to get into the office."

Casey's eyes bugged out and he started choking. Jake moved to him quickly and slapped him on the back a couple of times to dislodge the food. "Sorry about that, kid."

"It's okay," Casey croaked as he finally managed to swallow. "I just had a flash of what happened the last time there was a gun in the bar."

"I don't like this anymore than you do and I will make a point to be there to pick her up before you open, but she needs to get out of the house and get her mind on something besides Miguel and I need to get some work done."

"Then I'm your man. But Jake, are you sure about the 'anybody' part?"

"Anybody you don't know," Jake amended.

* * *

With Casey's help, Jake continued to make sure neither

Teresa nor Luis was ever vulnerable. He kept the shotgun by his side at night, locking it away each morning before the little boy awoke. The three of them spent all of their time together, most of it at home except for a few hours three times a week when he took Luis crabbing and Teresa worked on the books at the Salty Dog.

Teresa liked being able to get out of the house, so on the mornings when he and Luis went crabbing, they walked her to the Salty Dog before they left. Instead of using the sidewalk, they went out the back gate, and used a utility easement between property lines to cut through the neighborhood and minimize their exposure to any passing cars.

Once there, she locked herself in, promising Jake she wouldn't unlock the door for anyone, and wouldn't leave the office after Casey opened for business. Jake didn't particularly like leaving her alone, but the Salty Dog was built like a fortress and much more secure than his house.

It had been two weeks now and they had yet to see any sign of Miguel. Jake's nerves were shot and he was a little sleep deprived, but he'd managed to complete his house plans.

Wednesday was not a crabbing day so after they finished breakfast Teresa sat down at the kitchen island with some work she'd brought home from the bar. Casey had taken Luis across the street to the docks to fish for a little while and Jake sat on the porch swing with a cup of coffee where he could keep an eye on them.

He heard Teresa's cell phone ring and got up and moved closer to the open window so he could listen.

"Papa, what is it?" she said, concern in her voice. Jake knew it was unusual for the old man to be calling this early, he and Teresa usually talked late in the evening.

She listened for a moment and then switched to Spanish, speaking so fast Jake couldn't understand her. Except when she said 'Miguel'. While Teresa and her father talked, Jake wondered what Miguel had done now.

After she hung up, she came outside and sat on the swing. "Miguel is dead," she said quietly.

"Are you sure?" Jake asked, sitting down beside her.

"Yes. Papa said Elena came by early this morning and told him."

"What happened?" Jake asked as a big wave of relief washed over him. Now they could go back to living a normal life.

"Papa didn't have any details; he said he was uncomfortable asking a dead man's sister how he died, but he'd find out and tell me when I got there."

"So, this is a good thing, right?" he asked, confused by the sadness he could see in her eyes.

"It is good that we can go home now, but I don't think it is ever good to see an old friend destroy his life and die," she said quietly.

Jake took her in his arms. "I think your old friend died a long time ago," he said, remembering Elena's words about her brother.

He held her a few moments while she grieved for a childhood friend, and then held her back away from him. "So," he said smiling, "when do you want to go home?"

"But what about your plans for the house? And what about your mother's plans for Thanksgiving?" she asked.

"If we're not living here, then there's no reason to build the addition. Honey, if you want to go home, I'll take you home. I actually miss our life there. And we can always call mom and ask her to meet us there for Thanksgiving. I think she'd like to meet your family."

"Oh, Jake that would be wonderful," she said, "but Thanksgiving is an American holiday and we don't usually celebrate it in Mexico. Perhaps this year we can make an exception. I will call my mother but I am sure she will agree."

"Do you think that place next to Las Palmas is still for sale?" he asked, looking at the bookcase where the information on his settlement from Shamrock Salvage was still stuck between two books.

"I think so, but it's probably very expensive. Why?"

"I'm thinking maybe it's time to buy it and expand Las Palmas." He'd been thinking about the settlement a lot lately and had decided to use it to make a better life for his family as Teresa had once suggested.

"It does have twelve apartments and a pool. It would be a nice addition," she agreed. "But it will be very expensive. Do you have that kind of money?" she asked.

"I'm not sure, let me check," he said walking over to the bookcase in the living room and taking out a manila envelope.

He broke the seal and took out a single page that contained information on a bank account in the Cayman Islands. Finding the amount contained in the account, Jake felt a moment of shock, then folded it up and returned it to the envelope.

Patrick had only been half right when he'd guessed a million dollars.

Looking into his beautiful wife's deep brown eyes, he smiled. "We've got that kind of money," he said.

CHAPTER 48

Wilma had gladly agreed to host an American Thanksgiving Day at her ranch, so Jake coordinated the holiday flight plans so that he, Teresa and Luis would arrive in Cancun a few minutes before his mom's flight from New Orleans was due to arrive. By the time they'd exited the plane and walked over to the gate her plane had been assigned, she was waiting for them.

After going through customs and immigration, Jake rented a car and the four of them began the drive out to Wilma's ranch. Wilma had given Teresa directions to the ranch which was southwest of Merida, and after leaving the toll road, Jake noticed how much greener everything seemed to be. There were even a few hills that Teresa said were caused by the land rippling after an enormous meteor hit the Yucatan thousands of years ago.

By three o'clock they had turned off the main road onto a dirt drive lined with Golden Rain trees on either side. The drive was long and the car threw up a cloud of limestone dust behind them, but on either side of the road green pastures were divided into sections by whitewashed board fences. Several beautiful horses were in the pasture alongside the road and followed the car as far as they could go before reaching another fence.

Jake followed the dirt drive for a half mile or so until it became a cobblestone drive. A short distance farther, he came to an enormous set of ornate black wrought iron gates flanked by an overgrown hedge of bougainvillea that ran fifty yards on either side. The thorny bushes were currently in full bloom with burgundy, purple, salmon and white blooms that lit up the countryside like a box of spilled crayons.

The gates looked to weigh about a thousand pounds each and with fence on both sides there was nowhere else to go but backwards, so he pulled up to the gate and stopped.

After the dust cloud dissipated, he put his window down and looked for the usual security post with keypad and call button, but didn't see one. He turned to ask Teresa if she had any suggestions and suddenly the gates creaked loudly and began to slowly open. As he waited for them to finish, he noticed the video cameras mounted inside the hedge.

Whoever was on the other end of the cameras had opened the gates, so figuring he must be in the right place, Jake drove through them. A quarter-mile farther, the cobblestone drive ended in a loop in front of a large two-story adobe building with a red tile roof and a matching three car detached garage off to the side. Next to the garage was an old VW Bug that had once been light blue but was now in desperate need of body work and a paint job.

Jake parked in the drive and before they were all out of the car, Wilma and José Luis came out of the hacienda to greet them.

"Happy Thanksgiving, Papa," Teresa said as she hugged her father.

"Happy Thanksgiving to you, mi hija. We have so much to be thankful for," he said returning her hug.

"Yes," she agreed. "I am thankful we can all be together again."

"And I am thankful that slime, Miguel, is dead," the old man added.

"Papa! You should not speak ill of the dead."

"I'm sorry, I will take back the slime comment, but I am still glad he's dead."

After Jake introduced his mother to everyone, Wilma grabbed Claire's arm and led them up the front walk and through a set of ornately carved ten-foot double doors into the hacienda's foyer. The foyer was the size of a small living room, its floors tiled in a sedate but colorful

Mexican pattern. A huge crystal chandelier hung from the center of its two-story ceiling and a beautifully carved large round table holding a massive floral arrangement sat directly underneath it.

There was a small seating area on one side of the room and what looked to be an actual sixteenth or seventeenth century suit of armor and the biggest grandfather clock Jake had ever seen on the other. As Jake looked around at the antique furnishings and old paintings on the walls, he felt like he was in a museum.

The sound of water running drew his eye to the open courtyard at the end of the foyer and the twelve-foot tall double-bowled fountain that sat in the center of it, a steady stream of water bubbling up and spilling over the sides of the upper bowl. Lush palms and colorful flowering shrubs decorated the courtyard in a design that provided ample room for a patio table and chairs.

Jake had never been in an actual Mexican hacienda and found the architectural style interesting. It was a lot like a square box with a hole in the middle of it. Surrounding the courtyard was a gallery, a ten-foot wide covered walkway that separated the courtyard from the rooms surrounding it.

As they walked down the gallery, Wilma pointed out the different rooms and Jake noticed that only a bedroom, a bathroom and an office actually had four whole walls and a door. The kitchen, dining room and great room were separated from the gallery by a series of arches that held up the heavy tile roof. It was a very open air concept; Jake just hoped the bugs weren't too bad and the temperatures too warm to sleep.

Wilma turned to Jake. "Don't worry, there are four more bedrooms upstairs and they all have air conditioning," she said as if she had read his mind.

They continued down the gallery to the great room, which, as its name suggested was huge. Here the museum feeling was gone and the furnishings were more contemporary, antique style giving way to creature comforts.

On one end of the spacious room a couple of cozy seating areas flanked a large adobe fireplace. Between them was an oval coffee table with a glass top that held a two-foot tall bronze Remington statue. One the other end of the room, a compact but complete bar shared the wall with a set of French doors that led to an office.

The entire back of the room was floor to ceiling glass doors that, when opened like they were now, brought in the outdoors through three eight-foot wide openings. Beyond the open doors a few wide steps led down to a pool and patio area surrounded by lush landscaping,

While Señor Garcia fixed drinks for everyone at the wet bar, Wilma excused herself to go to the kitchen to check on the turkey.

Jake walked over and stood in one of the openings. As his gaze wandered over the backyard's colorful trees and shrubs and past them to the acres and acres of green pastures and the crisp white fences, he had to admit he was surprised at the magnitude and beauty of the place. Wilma hadn't been kidding about being wealthy.

After a few minutes of conversation, Jake excused himself and headed in the direction Wilma had gone, hoping to catch her alone.

"What do you think of my hacienda, Jake?" she asked as he stepped into a kitchen that looked like something out of a gourmet's dream. She had her back to him and never turned around as she stood over the open oven door and basted the bird.

"How did you know it was me?" Jake asked as he took another step into the room and noticed Wilma wasn't alone. There were two other women in the kitchen, one washing dishes at the sink and the other mixing up something in a bowl near the refrigerator.

"I thought you would come looking for information," she replied, pushing the pan back into the oven and closing the door before turning to face him. "That is why you followed me to the kitchen, is it not?"

"Well, yes, as a matter of fact, I would like some information."

"Then follow me and I will tell you what I can," she said as she headed past him and into a small butler's pantry sandwiched between the kitchen and dining room.

Jake followed her through the pantry and into the long dining room with its table for twelve before stepping back out onto the gallery and into an office at the back of the house next to the staircase.

"I've made some improvements to the place since my father's death. The kitchen's been updated, of course, and the pool was added. I also added the garage out front and moved and rebuilt the horse barn and paddock," she said as she moved to shut the door behind him.

"You've got a really nice spread here," Jake replied honestly, "but it's a lot greener than I expected. How does that happen?" he asked.

"We have a couple of cenotes on the property and have permits for several wells that we use to irrigate the pastures and farm land," she explained. "We grow all our own fruits and vegetables and raise chickens and pigs for eggs and meat. What we don't use, we sell."

"Sounds like a pretty efficient operation."

"It is. I hope you will bring Teresa and Luis here often. Teresa was born here and I want the three of you to feel like this is your home."

"Thank you," he said glancing around the masculine room with its hunter green walls and wainscoting stained so dark it almost looked black. Old landscapes in heavy gilt frames adorned the walls while floor to ceiling bookcases lined the wall behind a massive antique desk that faced two sets of French doors that opened to the back yard.

Another pair of French doors located in the nook behind the stairs allowed access into the great room, but were closed now. Jake walked behind the desk to read some of the titles on the shelves.

He was mildly surprised to note that her library was one you might find in a vets office, full of reference books on everything from chickens to horses, including a large collection of veterinary medical volumes. Wilma was turning out to be full of surprises.

"Except for adding some books, this is the only room I haven't changed," she said. "It looks exactly as it did when my father was alive. Now what can I help you with?"

Jake turned away from the bookshelves to face her. "What can you tell me about Miguel's death?"

CHAPTER 49

Wilma dropped her eyes down to her hands which were clasped in front of her. She seemed to study them a moment while she thought about Jake's question.

Then, with an almost imperceptible straightening of her spine, she returned her gaze to his. "He was killed in his home in Merida about three weeks ago."

"Three weeks ago," Jake repeated, searching for that time frame in his memory. That was right after he'd learned of Miguel's threat to pay him a visit. Unfortunately, he realized with a sinking feeling in the pit of his stomach, it was also about the same time Steve had decided to take that odd trip out of town.

Jake wasn't sorry Miguel was dead. In fact, he was happy that particular obstacle had been removed from his family's life, but he didn't want to believe his friend had anything to do with it. But another part of him said the cartel man's death coming on the heels of Steve's offer to eliminate him was too much of a coincidence to actually be one.

"Yes. The police think he left El Diablo where he'd been drinking all night and picked up a hooker who robbed and then killed him."

"Really?" Jake asked with a feeling of relief. If a woman had killed Miguel, then Steve couldn't have. "Have the police arrested her?"

"Not that I'm aware of. I heard through the grapevine he was found naked in bed with his empty wallet beside him," she said.

"Is this grapevine named Angela?" Jake asked.

"Why would you ask that?"

"Why not? You said she was a friend of yours and she was a bartender at El Diablo."

"She moved to Spain."

"When did that happen?"

"About three weeks ago," Wilma said with the barest hint of a smile. "She came into some money and since she'd always wanted to move to Spain, she did. Why? Do you think Angela killed Miguel?"

"I don't know. It just seems like quite a coincidence that the bartender at Miguel's favorite cantina came into some money about the same time Miguel was killed."

"And a lucky one for us," she said looking him in the eye. "Miguel was nothing more than a pimple on the ass of humanity and he got what he deserved. He thought he could take what didn't belong to him and didn't care what he had to do or who he had to kill to get it."

Jake heard the venom in her voice and the look of disgust on her face when she talked about Miguel. He couldn't blame her for that, he felt the same way, but he didn't believe in coincidences, at least not ones like this.

It was then Jake remembered Wilma's predictions concerning Miguel's karma. She'd been very convinced that Teresa's kidnapper wouldn't live a long and happy life. Had Miguel really been robbed and killed by a hooker, or had karma somehow had a helping hand?

Could Wilma have somehow been karma's helper? The timing of the bartender at Miguel's favorite cantina suddenly coming into some money and leaving the country at the same time Miguel was killed was too much to believe.

Had Angela killed Miguel for some reason and Wilma given her the money to flee? From the looks of her ranch, she could certainly afford to send an old friend out of the country where she couldn't be questioned. But why would Angela kill Miguel? Jake didn't know the woman, had never even met her, but she and Wilma were close friends and Wilma had been talking about getting rid of Miguel ever since he'd met her.

Had Wilma paid Angela to kill Miguel?

Then again, with her fiery Latin temper, Wilma could

have killed him herself with Angela as her accomplice. Wilma hadn't known what Miguel looked like, she'd never met him, but Angela did and seemed to know plenty about his comings and goings as well. How else would Wilma have been able to find him?

"Is there something you want to ask me, Jake?" Wilma asked calmly, still holding his gaze.

Her question mirrored his thoughts and caught him off guard. While he tried to decide how to answer her, he shifted his gaze from her icy blue eyes back to the bookshelves. It was uncanny the way she could read him.

Wilma walked over and laid her hand on his arm. "Are you looking for someone to thank or someone to blame?" she asked softly.

The way she phrased the question made him think. "I really don't know," he admitted, looking down at an older version of the woman who had captured his heart, "but I'm curious."

"Miguel is dead, and that is all we need to know. More information will not bring more value to your life, Jake. Let it go and concentrate on making my beautiful daughter and handsome grandson happy. Now that Miguel is no longer a problem, you will be bringing them home like you promised José Luis, right?"

He knew she was right. Knowing who killed Miguel would add no value to his life, but that didn't mean he didn't wonder. "If that's what Teresa wants."

"I'm sure it will be," Wilma replied with a nod. "After you get settled you can start working on making me another grandchild. I am hoping for a girl. Now go and tell José Luis to report to the kitchen for carving in thirty minutes and then spend some time with Claire. I'm sure you didn't bring your mother down here to ignore her."

After Wilma dismissed him to return to the kitchen, Jake went back to the great room and, after relaying Wilma's message to José Luis, was immediately pulled into the conversation Teresa and his mom were having about buying the property next to Las Palmas. They were still talking forty-five minutes later when Wilma called them all to the dining room.

After everyone was settled with plates of food in front of them, Señor Garcia said a blessing, of sorts. He thanked God for the food and for reuniting his family, but also thanked Him for taking Miguel home to be with Him.

While they ate, Jake looked at his family seated around the table, some of them sharing the holiday together for the first time and some of them for the first time in twenty-six years. They were his life and he was thankful to be able to share it with them.

He let his gaze linger on Wilma who was seated next to José Luis at the other end of the table. She was a beautiful, wealthy woman with a thriving business and, according to José Luis, very well regarded in the area. No matter how hard he tried, he couldn't imagine her killing a member of a drug cartel.

She was barely over five feet and probably no more than a hundred and ten pounds. Even falling down drunk, a man Miguel's size could have swatted her away like a fly. To think that Wilma, with or without her yoga partner's help, could have murdered Miguel was just ridiculous, wasn't it?

And even if his mother-in-law was somehow complicit in a murder, did he really want to know?

CHAPTER 50

After the holiday, Jake, Teresa and Luis dropped Jake's mom off at the Cancun airport for her flight home and returned to Playa del Carmen. Jake moved in with Teresa and Luis and went back to supplying the cantina with fish. Often Señor Garcia or Luis would go with him.

Teresa's mother came to visit when she could get away from the ranch and once or twice a month Jake would rent a car and take Teresa, Luis and her father out to her ranch for a long weekend. Luis loved her horses and Wilma had already begun teaching him to ride.

Teresa was delighted to have her mother back in her life and in the lives of her son and father as well. She'd been overjoyed with her father's improved health and decided Wilma deserved the credit for it. Jake hadn't had the heart to tell her the old man had been faking all along.

They'd gone back to Wilma's ranch for Christmas. She'd had a party on Christmas Eve and had invited Casey and Jake's mom, and had even paid their airfare and sent a car to pick them up from the airport.

After the first of the year there had still been no hint of cartel retaliation for Miguel's murder, so Jake and Teresa made an offer on the property on the north side of Las Palmas. After a couple of months of inspections and negotiations, it was theirs.

It had three buildings built in the same adobe style and the same coconut grove in front of them, and also had an area with a small pool and sun deck that had been built in front of the center building. The pool was in good shape, and the three buildings, each containing four apartments each, were sound, but had been in desperate need of renovations.

By the time the ink was dry on the contract, Jake had plans drawn up and had been anxious to get started. That had been six months ago, and two of the buildings were almost finished and the third was coming along nicely.

Finishing the interior painting in the third building late one morning, he decided to call it a day. He still had a few more last minute touches, but today was his and Teresa's first wedding anniversary and he had promised to spend the afternoon and evening with her.

As he cleaned up his tools and put everything away, he thought about his new life in Mexico. He missed his friends, sure, but he was happier than he'd ever been. Teresa was his best friend and an incredible wife and Luis had captured his heart. Even Señor Garcia had come around. And Wilma was something else. As much as he liked her, and Jake did like her, she was not the kind of mother-in-law he would've ever expected.

A very successful business woman, she dressed and carried herself with a grace and dignity that made everyone turn to look when she walked into a room. Jake had seen her in action and knew she treated her employees kindly but firmly, expecting and getting her orders carried out to the letter.

Despite her petite stature, Wilma could be very intimidating, but alone with her family she was open and loving, telling stories of the crazy things she'd done growing up. Jake thought of her as more of an older sister rather than a mother-in-law.

He still didn't understand her attraction to Señor Garcia, it was hard to imagine José Luis and Wilma ever being married, but it looked to him like Teresa's parents were beginning to hit it off again. Jake stayed with Luis on the nights Teresa had to work and Wilma was in town. Teresa reported that her parents often danced together and lingered over drinks at a remote table in the cantina, their heads together as they talked.

Shutting the apartment door behind him, he headed across the property to the cantina. He hadn't gotten far when he saw his gorgeous wife waiting for him on their hammock. Six months pregnant and more beautiful than ever, she was lying on her back looking up through the coconut palms and had a beer in her hand.

"I knew there was a reason I married you," he said, as he kissed her on the cheek.

"Because I have beer?" she asked.

"No, because you can read my mind," he said, plucking the beer from her hand. He took a few sips then set the can in the sand before getting in the hammock with her. He lay on his side next to her, one hand propping up his head and the other on Teresa's rounded stomach. He lay there looking at her and couldn't believe how incredibly lucky he'd been in finding her.

"I am reading your mind again," she said and smiled. "What is it you want to tell me?"

"What makes you think I have something to tell you?" he asked.

"The way you are staring at me makes you look like the cat that ate the canary."

"Well, there is something I want you to see."

"Okay, show me."

He helped her up and led her through the coconut grove to the closest of the three new buildings. Opening a door on the ground floor, Jake led her inside and watched her face as she looked around.

Because it was the closest to her original property and more or less in the center of the combined properties, Jake had converted the four apartments the building had once housed into one two-story home.

The ground floor held a nice sized kitchen and living room as well as a small office and bathroom. At the end of the living room, Jake had built a staircase up to the second floor and converted the space into three bedrooms and two baths.

"Happy Anniversary, Teresa."

"Oh, Jake, it's beautiful," she said, putting her arms around her husband and holding him close.

He turned her head up and kissed her, drawing it out until he felt his unborn child kick. Pulling his head back, he laughed. Life was good, he thought, as he felt their baby kick again.

"Now I have a surprise for you," she said as they walked back outside.

"What is it?" he asked.

"I rented the new apartments."

"Already? Teresa, they still need a little more work before they're ready for guests."

"I don't think these guests will mind," she said looking toward a group of people walking in from the parking lot.

Jake looked at the group closely and was surprised to see Steve, Hank, Petey and Paul following his mother and Casey down the sidewalk, José Luis and Wilma right behind them.

"Did you do this?" he asked.

"Yes, I called and invited them to help us celebrate. I hope you don't mind."

"This is perfect," he said to his wife, before giving her another kiss.

With hugs and handshakes all around after the new group joined them, Steve looked at Jake. "You've been busy," he said, with a wave of his hand.

"Yeah, it's coming together," Jake said proudly.

"I didn't mean the property. I was talking about Teresa," Steve said, indicating her protruding abdomen. "Looks like your dream came true after all," he admitted.

"Yeah, the whole Miguel problem was a nightmare, but it's over and life is good. How did you guys get here?" Jake asked.

"We had some down time, so we all chipped in for fuel for the trip and came down in the *Lucky Lady*," Steve replied. "We anchored right out there," he said pointing to the yacht Jake could see in the distance, "and Henry ferried us in. Now that we've taken the Boys Club international, we need to add him to the roster."

"And Casey too," Jake added. "Where are Patrick and Vanessa?"

"They wanted to come, but had to go to Ireland to visit Patrick's sick mother. They said to wish you Happy Anniversary for them and suggested we take you and Teresa on an anniversary spin down to Tulum."

"That sounds great. Can we take everybody?"

"The more the merrier," said Steve, pulling Jake away from the crowd. "So what's the scoop on Miguel getting popped? We really haven't had a chance to talk since all that happened."

"It's not something I wanted to discuss on the phone," Jake replied.

"I don't blame you. So what happened to the cocky bastard?"

"The police think he was robbed and killed by a hooker."

"A hooker, huh?"

"Yeah. You wouldn't know anything about that, would you?"

"What? You think I did it?"

"Well, it happened a couple of days after Wilma told us Miguel was planning to pay me a visit and you were pretty vocal about wanting to take him out," Jake replied, "but no, I don't think you did it."

"You told me to stay out of it and I did, Jake," Steve said. "And you should do the same thing. You know what they say, 'don't look a gift horse in the mouth'."

"Is that what you think I'm doing?"

"Isn't it? He was the only thing stopping you and Teresa from making the life here together that you wanted. Well, he's out of the picture now. I know you didn't kill him, and neither did I, so we've got nothing to worry about. Maybe you should just thank your fairy godmother and let it go."

"I wish it was that easy."

"It is, Jake. Now, excuse me. I see Benito and Henry

have arrived. We need to round everyone up and get them out to the yacht if we're going to make it down to Tulum and back by dinner."

As he stood there watching his friend's retreating back, Jake wondered about Steve's 'fairy godmother' comment.

CHAPTER 51

Under a cerulean sky dotted with little puffs of white clouds here and there and a nice easterly breeze, Henry shuttled them all out to where the *Lucky Lady* lay at anchor to board the yacht for the trip to Tulum.

Steve, with Hank at his side, piloted the yacht through the sapphire blue waters while Benito, Henry and Paul trolled for fish. Claire, Teresa and her parents were in the salon with Luis while Jake and Petey sat on the back deck drinking a beer.

Jake watched the wake made by the yacht's powerful engines, almost mesmerized by the uniformity of the churning water. He thought about Teresa and Luis and how lucky he was to have them. He thought of the new baby that would arrive soon. He'd never been around babies much, but he was excited to be having another child. He'd missed the baby part with Luis, but he wouldn't miss it this time.

He thought about his friends and family. None of them were perfect, but that didn't matter. He imagined they'd all violated some law at some time or another in their lives. He knew he certainly had. Even without the stunt they'd pulled to rescue Teresa, he'd done things that were legally wrong, but, in his eyes, morally right. And Steve and Hank and the twins had been right there with him each time.

As for Benito and Henry, Jake knew they weren't on exactly high moral ground either. They ran a high stakes poker game from time to time at Henry's house. But they had both done whatever he'd asked of them, watched his back, and expected nothing in return.

José Luis had hired thugs to sabotage Jake's boat and break into his apartment to try to scare him off, but Jake could understand that. The old man was only trying to protect his family.

Even his mother, he bet, was guilty of breaking some law, even if it was just a teenage stunt like toilet papering someone's yard.

And yes, even his lovely Teresa was guilty of assault. Jake had watched her bean Miguel with that wine bottle, trying to protect her family.

And as for Wilma, he would bet his last dollar that she knew more about Miguel's death than she was telling. But even if she did, she too, was only protecting her family. And like Steve said, sometimes the only way to fix things was to stop the bad guy.

Well, the bad guy had been vanquished and Steve and Wilma were right. Knowing who killed Miguel would add no value to his life and he shouldn't look a gift horse in the mouth. Maybe he had a fairy godmother, maybe he didn't, but these people were his family now and just as they had protected him, he would do whatever it took to protect them.

He would ask no more questions.

He shook his head to clear it and a smile lit his face as he looked around him at the clear blue water that surrounded them, the sandy beaches and rocky outcroppings beyond. The sheer beauty of the area was incredible and he was lucky to be able to call it his second home.

They made it to the ruins in good time and spent the remainder of the day, fishing, swimming and enjoying each other's company.

* * *

Dinner was in the cantina that night and the place was packed. Tia Carmen and Tio Carlos joined them for the celebration as well as numerous other relatives and, as usual, Teresa shared the evening with anyone else who cared to join them.

They ate a typical Mexican meal of tacos, tamales and enchiladas, along with the requisite beans and rice while a

Mexican band played softly. When everyone had eaten their fill and the dishes were cleared Steve stood up.

"Excuse me everyone," he said. A hush settled over the cantina as all eyes turned to face Steve. "I'd like to take a minute to wish my best friend Jake and his lovely wife Teresa a Happy Anniversary. My friends and I wondered if he'd ever find the woman of his dreams and we are convinced that he has. She's beautiful and smart and way too good for him and he's lucky to have her.

"He's also lucky to be able to re-live his childhood. Being outdoors, fishing every day, playing in the clear blue water, all the things a boy dreams of doing.

"I talked to Teresa today and she told me she'd always wanted to have a little hotel and cantina and share it with her friends and family. Looking around, we can see that she's accomplished her dream.

"So, Jake and Teresa," he said, holding up his drink, "here's to the two of you living out your dreams together. And may you continue to enjoy the happiness you share today for the rest of your lives."

"To livin' the dream," the room chorused as they clinked their glasses together.

Jake was happier than he'd ever thought possible. He looked around the room at his family. They might not all be related by blood, but it's not the blood you share, it's the life you share that makes a family.

Taking his beautiful wife's hand, he led her out under the twinkling stars and onto the soft white sand and while the band played softly, they danced.

ACKNOWLEDGEMENTS

Writing a book is not entirely a one person job. It takes a crew of dedicated people to actually produce the finished product.

With that in mind, I'd like to thank the individuals who gave me their time and attention. Danny and Donna, Tom, Mary, JoAnne, Butch and Dru. Your help has been invaluable.

And to my husband Dave, my researcher, photographer, IT man and my publisher, I couldn't have done this without you.

ABOUT THE AUTHOR

MJ Watson enjoys traveling, gardening and is an avid reader of contemporary and historical novels. A fourth generation native of the Treasure Coast, she resides there today.

Thank you for reading ***Livin' the Dream,*** the second book in the Jake Arnold series. If you enjoyed it, please take a moment to visit amazon.com and write a review.

Look for more of Jake's adventures in the next book currently in progress.
For information on release dates for print and electronic versions, you can email the author at
mjwatson2016@gmail.com

Made in the USA
Columbia, SC
12 June 2017